MAYLUNA

a novel

KELLEY McNEIL

LAKE UNION
PUBLISHING

Text copyright © 2024 by Kelley McNeil
All rights reserved.

Published by Lake Union Publishing, Seattle

www.apub.com

Amazon, the Amazon logo, and Lake Union Publishing are trademarks of Amazon.com, Inc., or its affiliates.

ISBN-13: 9781662516115 (paperback)
ISBN-13: 9781662516108 (digital)

Cover design by James Iacobelli
Cover image: © AleksandarNakic / Getty

Printed in the United States of America

To those who have loved and lost.
And those who have found themselves, along the way.

PROLOGUE

Evie

He often said that time travel was more accessible to us than we realize, and that music is one of the ways we do it. He's right, I think. After all, few things have the ability to transport us so completely and powerfully as the sound of the perfect, meaningful song. The music of our lifetime is woven into the fabric of our existence, our own personal soundtrack behind our stories. Maybe it takes us to a memory, an echo of something that once was, or maybe to a place where we can live out an imagined dream.

The great philosophers and astronomers believed that music could be felt from the stars and planets, traveling through space and time, and that there was magic in the design of the cosmos, connecting us in ways we can only begin to imagine.

I wonder, after you hear our story, if you'll believe it too.

PART ONE

Above the cloud with its shadow is the star with its light.

—Pythagoras

1

CARTER

In the hills of Yorkshire Dales, my mother and my brother are strumming guitars, side by side on a colorful picnic blanket beneath a tree. His is a slightly smaller version, perfect for the hands of a growing boy, purchased at a secondhand store with money left over from groceries, saved in a biscuit tin. The cool autumn air hints at the coming change of season, and the sun hits my mother's shoulders in a way that forms a kind of golden glow around her. It's a hazy image, as early memories are, more of a moving snapshot than an actual memory. A feeling. Comforting. Perhaps borrowing from a later memory, I hear my mother's gentle voice humming along as she strums the strings with delicate fingers.

My brother, three years older, was a natural musician, people would say. "Born with a guitar in his hands and perfect pitch even when he cried," they'd joke. I did my best to keep up, and sometimes I nearly did. A little, anyway.

My mother played all sorts of music—folk tunes, mostly, or church songs sometimes. But my favorites growing up were when she'd strum her own version of popular songs that we might hear on the radio. We'd copy her, and it would make us feel just a tiny bit cooler. "Forever

Young" by Alphaville was a favorite, I think. I loved the sound of her voice above the finger-picked notes that sounded more like a music box than a rock ballad. She was a secondary-school teacher, my mother. She taught mathematics to twelve- and thirteen-year-olds who learned to find beauty and art in all those numbers, in a small school outside the town of Ravensdale in northern England. The scenes of my childhood are a combination of fern-covered hills, smoky mills beside tidy hamlets, and moorland that rolled into the distance to reach wide beaches beneath chalky coasts. Our town sat between the country hills and the sea, nearly equidistant. So we chose our weekend outings based on mood and weather.

We asked my mother once why she wasn't a musician instead of a schoolteacher, and she didn't answer. But sometimes she would get a faraway look in her eyes that made me wonder if she was seeing herself in another life, perhaps on a small stage in a village pub somewhere, where fireside pints in the evening gave way to stage lights bouncing off long, straight brown hair, parted down the center. She'd met my father when she was just seventeen, became pregnant shortly after, and was married by nineteen. My father took a job at the local railroad company and worked up the ranks to management until the line closed down. Then he just took work wherever he could get it. Money was tight. Tensions and tempers were tighter. But on days like the one I'm visiting in my memories now, beneath the tree with just my mother and brother, we could relax. The music was our escape, something the three of us shared together like a private little club.

For the last hour, I've been telling this story and others like it to a journalist named Michael, seated in front of me on a long white leather bench, on a private plane high in the sky above the clouds, the evening dipping below the horizon. A cameraman sits alongside him, occasionally filming as I speak. It's a sparse setup (the film crew, not the plane), but that's what I like about it. Nothing fancy. Just how we'd originally intended it to be years ago.

"So would you say that you got your talent from your mother, then?" Michael asks.

"Probably. But my brother was the one with all the talent. I just made do."

"I'd say you made do pretty well."

"I could come up with the music in my head, but I wasn't always able to do what I wanted with it. But he could play any instrument you put in his hands, and I knew I would never be that good. I sort of figured out a way to make it work. I would tune the guitar differently, so that the few chords I knew could turn into a lot more depending on the tuning. It created a certain kind of sound that worked. I played the piano without learning to read music."

"Who came up with the name Spurn Head as that first band name?" He laughs a bit, the name sounding more than a little ridiculous at this point.

Nearby, Tommy chuckles out loud and groans. The sound of Tommy's laugh is one that could bring light to any weary soul. Not that mine is weary lately. But his optimistic nature certainly saved me in the past a few times.

"That was Jacob," I say, sharing an amused glance with Tommy that softens at the end. It's the first time I've said my brother's name out loud in a long time, and the word feels slow and smooth on my lips. Names are spells. "Man, that was such a terrible band name," I add, mostly to myself.

"It was you." Tommy points at me and laughs again. "Jacob said *you* came up with it one night."

"I did not."

"I think maybe you did. Sorry to say."

"It was him," I say clearly, putting the subject to rest. "It was Jacob."

"If you say so," Tommy mumbles.

"Well, anyway, it didn't stick, thankfully."

"Doesn't quite have the same ring to it as Mayluna," Michael says with a smile.

"Definitely not." But it was nice still, the name carrying me back to a different time, with sea salt and wild skies. "There is this remote bit on the Yorkshire coast, a tidal island where our mum took us a few times, called Spurn Head. It feels a bit like the end of the earth, once you get there. There was a legend that people there had seen what appeared to be a star twinkling through the dark side of the crescent moon on some nights." The first time I heard the story as a young boy, it fascinated me. It seemed magical.

"'Moonstar,'" he says, naming a song from our first EP, the hit that got us our record deal a lifetime ago. I nod.

"My mum used to dream of having a little cottage nearby with a view of the sea."

"Did she ever get it?"

"She did, as a matter of fact. It was one of the first things I bought her." I wanted to buy her the moon and the stars and a palace. But she just wanted that little cottage with a garden where she could grow old peacefully, with an eye toward the sea and plenty of constellations. I think of her there, imagining an old guitar hanging on a wall, mostly collecting dust these days.

A flash of lightning hits the cabin, illuminating the rest of the seats that were dimmed in the front of the plane. In its momentary brightness, which seems to last seconds rather than milliseconds, I see Tommy's jaw clench tight and his knuckles grip the seat in such a minuscule way that you'd have to know him well in order to see it.

Shortly after we'd taken off from Mexico City, we'd hit some turbulence, and the pilot announced that there was weather up ahead but nothing to worry about. I caught Tommy's eye and nodded in reassurance. He laughed it off and gave me a mock salute to let me know that he was all right. He gets anxious. More so these days with a wife and small children at home. He's having a harder time leaving them, and he's never been a big fan of airplanes, especially the kind like we're on now. Small, private ones. Neither am I, if I'm being honest. When I'm up in a plane, I can almost feel gravity's fury at having been defeated, as if lying in wait, ready to bring it all back down to the earth where we belong. We named her Lucy in the Sky, our private plane, a plush living room in the clouds. We all celebrated the day we got her. "We're big-time now, mates," I remember Tommy saying. But in truth, we missed our old tour bus sometimes. Miss Penny Lane, we called her a lifetime ago.

"Not terribly creative in hindsight," I say to Michael after mentioning the old bus and the coordinating names. He has a studious look about him, a little rumpled and affable as he sits there with the passive intrigue that I recognize as a common trait in rock journalists. When I finally agreed to the series of interviews that have been taking place, I wasn't sure who was more surprised—him or me. We seem too young for a retrospective. Are we really that old? Not really, I was told, but people want to know our story. See behind the curtain. And it felt cathartic. Like a new beginning with old shadows left behind. We decided together that it was time. It would be a benchmark before we began the path that headed toward becoming aging rock stars. (A frightening prospect.)

Michael laughs a little. "Eh, as band names and airplanes go, it could be worse. You could've painted a half-naked woman on the side of the plane."

I smile. Something I've been doing more of in recent days. Levity returning to my body. "It can always be worse."

The sky outside dims to a deeper navy, made darker by the imposing clouds sliding across its inky surface.

"So that's more of the backstory," I say, shrugging. We're discussing the start of the band and the album that launched it all. Michael already knows a lot of the public details, but this interview will be a new perspective, one that will cover a bit more of the history and rise of our little group of friends that had gone from playing in tiny rooms at university to all of this. Even now, it's still hard to believe sometimes that we're on our way to a sold-out stadium show in Rio. Then on to Costa Rica, where we'll finish out the last two shows of what's been a long world tour. We're ready for a break. I lean back into the cushions of the bench and stretch my legs out in the expanse between us.

"So that album, it was all a story about a girl," Michael says, shaking his head and smiling. A computer sits beside him, and I glance at the red lights of the recording display ticking the milliseconds of my life.

"Aren't they always?"

"I suppose so. But this was the story about a girl who inspired one of the biggest albums of all time. Launched a band into superstardom. That's a hell of a story, Mr. Wills."

"You really do have a hard time calling me Carter, don't you?"

"To be fair, you of all people don't really have the best reputation of playing well in the sandbox with the media and journalists. Our last encounter was a little"—he pauses—"dicey, I think would be a good word. So let's just say, I feel it's wise to proceed with caution." He gives me a wry look.

"Fair enough."

"When we last met, you refused to speak much about that album. Refused to answer most of the questions in general, if I recall. I had a hell of a time piecing it together and almost lost my ass on that one." He's referring to an article that came out in *Rolling Stone* earlier this year, meant to promote the tour. Promotions have never really been my thing.

"Sorry about that."

"It's fine. But now that we've brought it up, it leads me to ask how you feel about the fact that people say you're *enigmatic*, when they're being kind. But others use words like *dark* and more than a little *broken*. Are you really? Or is it just another story? Part of the mystique."

"You don't mince words, do you?"

"Would you rather I did?"

"No. I like that about you. It's part of why you're here. Besides the fact that you came highly recommended by someone I trust."

"Really?" He looks surprised and intrigued. "I didn't realize we had anyone in common. Who was it?"

I ignore this and return to his earlier question from a few moments ago about my troubled persona. So many rumors. "I'm just a guy. Just like you. Just like that guy." I point to a flight attendant fixing a tray of items at the rear of the cabin.

"Something tells me you're nothing like that guy," he says.

"You never know. People are rarely what they seem, right? Maybe he's thinking about how when we land, he's going to quit this job and convince his wife to start over somewhere green and quiet, where they can plan a life together in the country, raising five kids. Maybe his mind is swirling right now with images of what it'll be like to walk in and tell her his plan and is worried that she won't agree."

"A story about a girl."

"Like I said, isn't it always? In some manner or another, anyway."

"Is it always like this in your head?" he asks. "The stories?"

I return my attention to him. "I guess. Isn't it like that for everyone?" But I already know what he'll say. I was never able to quiet the stories or the music—the places I go to in my mind. No matter how hard I tried.

"No, I doubt that."

The rest of the guys have started dozing off, and I speak quietly, not wanting to keep them up. "You're giving me too much credit. They're just stories. I see it in my head. Sometimes it's a whole lifetime. Sometimes it's just an hour of a life. Only difference with me is that I strum it on a guitar, sing it, whatever. Bring it from here"—I reach up into the air above me—"down to here."

"So I shouldn't be surprised if there's a song on your next album about a guy who's going to quit his job as a flight attendant?"

"Doesn't sound terribly sexy, does it?" I say. "I better skip that one." I know for a fact that our flight attendant is named Isaac and has no aspirations of living in the country, and he wants to open a techno club in Rio at some point. He told me as we were chatting recently.

Michael laughs and takes a drink from the ginger ale he's been sipping. "It's been said that the *Sigma Five* album is like a full narrative, start to finish, when the songs are pieced together a certain way. Based on what you've been telling me, it sounds like that may be accurate."

"Right."

"And you've never spoken a word about it. The inspiration behind it, the recording process, none of it. You've barely told anyone anything about your life, really. Why now?"

We've reached an inevitable point, and I breathe in, closing my eyes for a minute. I never expected to be telling this story. Not that it's all that interesting or unique, anyway. A great love. A broken heart. A story like mine is one that is repeated in all walks of life, in every decade and century. Still, it's mine.

"Because you asked."

He gives me a look. "Lots of people have asked."

"Yes, but you asked at just the right time."

"And what time is that?"

"I suppose you could say that I've finally found a sense of peace. There were reasons why I chose to keep things quiet."

"What reasons?"

He waits, but I don't answer.

"Okay, back to the album," he continues after a beat. He seems afraid that I'm going to change my mind at any moment and wants to keep the momentum going. "The title? *Sigma Five.* There's always been a bit of lore behind it. What's the significance there?"

"It had a dual meaning, really." I meet eyes with Tommy for a beat and consider my words. "The word *Sigma* is pretty extraordinary. It appears all over math, science, philosophy, astronomy, going back centuries. For example, Sigma Sagittarii is one of the brightest stars in the constellation Sagittarius. And the lowercase symbol is used when trying to work out the theories of galaxies and the supermassive black holes that draw everything toward them. The uppercase symbol we used for the album denotes the action of summation, the combining of things to make a whole. There's poetry in all of that."

"And the Roman numeral five?"

I pause as a smile pulls at me. "We'll just call that a creative choice for now."

He shakes his head in amused exasperation. "Okay. So. When did you first start writing it? Was it when you first met her?"

"Earlier than that. I think I started writing songs about her before I ever knew she existed. Somehow, I knew she was out there. And it was as if the music led me to her. When I found her, it all came together. I just knew. There was something about her from the very beginning. She wanted nothing to do with me, of course. Clever girl. But . . . eventually I won her over. For a time, anyway."

"But not forever."

"Forever is relative." My thoughts flash to the events of the past weeks and then to a place further back. "One of the songs on the album came from the first night we spent together. The guys and I were on our first big tour and had a few days off. We had been staying at a beach house, and I remember sitting out on the dune in the middle of the night and thinking, *My whole life is going to change because of this woman.* Here we were, these two people who had been walking along in life, on two different continents, neither of us knowing the other existed and yet somehow knowing all along. In totally different worlds. And then in a moment, our paths cross and nothing is ever the same."

Two points of light, finally meeting.

"And that's just the way it is sometimes. But I just kept thinking, *My god, I don't want to mess up this girl's life. I would do anything for her.* When it came time to start putting tracks on the album, it fell into place. The idea of what it would be like for a girl to fall in love with a guy whose life was kind of a crazy, cursed place. These two damaged people making each other whole."

"Does your life feel cursed?"

"It did at one time, but not as much as it used to. I mean, we've been incredibly fortunate when you look at all of this. Had experiences that many people would dream of." I gesture around me to the opulent setting in which we find ourselves. "Obviously, I'm grateful for that. But it hasn't been easy either. Happiness can be an elusive thing and certainly isn't always linked to success."

He nods. "And so, going back again, the band had its own history before the success came. But when it came time to make that album, it sounds like it was a whole new beginning. And she was part of it," Michael clarifies.

"Exactly."

"Whatever happened to her?" He pauses. "Where is she now?"

"I imagine she's at home with her family."

"Ah." He gives me a sympathetic look and waits a moment. "So . . . what was her name?"

"Which one?" Tommy chimes in with a chuckle. "She had a few."

I smile, recalling the slight origins of humor in the question, combined with years of secrets and memories. The letters and sounds forming on my brain the way they have millions of times before. There was a time when I could barely whisper her name in my head for fear of what it might cost me. But now, it's different. And I find the letters, two little syllables that encapsulated a lifetime, taking shape.

2

EVIE

"Mom?"

I hear my daughter's voice calling me from the distance and pull the light throw around my shoulders a tad bit higher. I close my eyes and inhale the crisp air, savoring its combination of sweetness and wood-smoke. There was a time when I didn't like autumn, when it was my least favorite season.

I was a summer girl in my earlier years. Loved the feel of loose cotton and sun-kissed cheeks and bare feet. Warmth was fleeting in eastern Pennsylvania and never seemed to last as long as it should. When autumn would come, I saw it as the unhappy reminder of the end of summer's warmth and the beginning of dreary, gray cold, never quite understanding why people liked it so much. Leaves changing from fresh green to shades of dull orange and dead brown held no interest to me, and I dreaded the uncomfortable itch of wool on my softened summer skin.

But that was a long time ago and a different version of myself.

If, somewhere in the grand universe of life, one could put a divider through the timeline that stretched from birth to death, I thought that mine might be labeled "Part 1—Before I Liked Autumn" and "Part

2—After I Liked Autumn." Since that time, many years ago, autumn has become my favorite season, and like so many, I love the scents and sights and emotions that the season brings.

"There you are." Lainey's footsteps offer a pleasant crunch as she walks toward me and stands a few feet away. "It's getting chilly out here. The sun's going down." She looks to the trees, filling the space between us with comments about the weather.

"The fresh air feels good," I tell her. I look at my daughter, who stands with her hands on her hips staring out into the woods that border the backyard of our Pennsylvania house. At the edge of the trees are dots of grass where the green is a different shade, marking the spot where, at one time, a wooden swing set lived, complete with a slide and a little playhouse. I can see the younger versions of my two now-grown children, swinging with glee, trying to touch the tips of their toes to the leaves on the tree. I can hear the sounds of their crystal voices giggling as we run around the yard and our dog barks and leaps nearby.

"Want to join me?" I pat the bench beside me.

Lainey looks down, and for a moment, I think she might sit, but she doesn't.

We used to cuddle under a blanket and watch the stars together on that bench, just as I did once upon a time in a different place with my own mother. *Look, there's Orion. See?*

"We're going to order some Chinese food. How's that sound?" she asks. But before I can reply, she quickly adds with the underpinnings of exasperation, "I know there's still plenty of food in the house, but I'm not sure we can possibly eat any more lasagna. Rick offered to run out and pick it up. Why is it that people think lasagna and funerals go so well together?"

I laugh a little and nod agreeably. "Sure. Sounds good." I see the slightest hint of surprise on my daughter's face and feel a quiet sense of satisfaction. *I can still pleasantly surprise you sometimes, I guess. Even if it is about something as meaningless as take-out food.*

"Okay. Good. What would you like?" Lainey doesn't bother rattling off the menu of what they'd be ordering for themselves. I'm not a big fan of American Chinese food, and to me, it's either beef with broccoli or chicken and vegetables, and I know she believes this is the extent of my adventures in exotic foods. I don't like that she sees me this way—as a kind of sheltered woman with a small life in a small town. It isn't her fault. I'd think the same about me if I were her.

Sometimes I imagine telling her the stories. The ones she deserves to hear. About my life. I wonder, at times, how things might have been different had she been raised with a different impression of me, instead of the version she got.

"Anything's fine, honey. I'm not that hungry."

Lainey turns, taking a step. "Are you coming in or . . ." She trails off. She's fussing over me a bit, worried and taking care of me. In truth, it's her I'm worried about.

"I'll be in in a few minutes."

She nods, and I watch her return to the house, her footsteps quieting. Alone again, I trace my fingers along the bench, feeling the rough, graying wood slats. At one time, it was shiny and brown, the lacquer as bright and smooth as the side of a boat. Steve and I purchased the bench from a nursery in town, while out buying impatiens and marigolds a long time ago. I was nine months pregnant and in nesting mode. I would spend hours enjoying the peaceful spot, grateful for that bench as I cradled my newborn daughter and sang lullabies. A few years later, when Lucas was born, I would do the same again.

One of my favorite photos is a picture that Steve took of me in a peach-colored sleeveless dress, with both kids curled into my side on a spring day. One child on each side, their faces are turned upward to gaze at mine with the adoration and love that only a child can offer a mother. There's so much contentment in that photo, which sits on the piano now.

As if recalling it all along with me, the bench makes a loud creak where it slopes in the center, splintered and tired from the years it's been sitting in this very spot.

Funerals are like this, I figure, the impetus to countless voyages down memory lane and all the regrets and joys that come with them. Even when expected, they jolt us out of our daily routine, causing us to question anything and everything.

I should probably get rid of the bench before it breaks one day. But despite its cracks, it had represented the initiation of stability into my life for the first time, many years ago, and I can't seem to part with it.

"I heard you were out here. Are you hiding?"

I turn and see my best friend, Kate, as she walks toward me, clearly having just left the gym—or at least dressing the part. "They've sent the troops out, eh? I didn't hear you pull up," I reply.

"I think they're worried about you. It's a good thing. At least they give a damn. My kids would probably leave me out here to rot." She drops down onto the seat next to me.

"They would not." Kate's grown children practically live at her house.

We sit in comfortable silence, breathing in the cool air. "How are you holding up, kiddo?" she asks after a moment.

"I'm fine. Really. I don't know why they're hovering. We're not *that* old yet, are we?"

"We're not *old* at all."

"They've started treating me like I'm ancient."

"You do kind of act like it," she says, giving me a playful nudge. I can't entirely disagree.

"I passed Lainey on my way out," Kate continues. "I hear they're leaving the day after tomorrow." She looks over at me with a knowing, sympathetic smile.

"I miss her," I say quietly. "Even when she's sitting right next to me, I miss her." I think of the way we were when she was a baby. A toddler.

I would sit for hours and hours just playing and coloring and watching her discover the world around her. I was completely enamored, and she was never farther than a few inches from me, it seemed. "But she has her own life now. I know that. And Lucas, he's close by. So that's nice."

"But?"

"We used to be so close. Now we just talk about take-out food," I say with a shrug. "I guess this is just the way it is with grown-up kids, I suppose."

"Hmm, sometimes maybe, sure. But in this case? You could make it better, I think."

I turn. "What do you mean?"

Kate pats my hand. "You know exactly what I mean." She pauses. "Secrets. They're a subtle invisible line, like a wall you've built all around you, sweetie, for years now, keeping everyone just a little bit apart."

I nod, looking away.

"Maybe it's finally time they don't anymore," she adds.

I knew how she felt about this. We discussed it over the years. Kate, my childhood best friend who knows where all the proverbial dead bodies in my life are buried. She has never approved of my decision to keep a part of my life secret from my children but has supported me anyway, as best friends do.

"I haven't been able to get it off my mind. The thought of telling them," I find myself saying.

"I figured as much."

"But I promised," I say, shaking my head. "And I . . . I just can't. And I don't know how I'd even start." My emotions have been close to the surface over the past few days, and my eyes well.

"But Steve's gone now," she says gently. "And he did say 'someday.'"

"It's not the right time."

"It might be exactly the right time."

I ponder this for a while. "It'll just make things worse."

She shakes her head. "You don't know that. What if it makes things *better*?" She squeezes my hand. "For all of you."

With the sun now beneath the horizon, the air turns from crisp to cold and starts to bite. The first star appears on the horizon, and I look up at it, as if for answers.

"Come on. Let's go in. We're getting takeout. I'll even give you my fortune cookie," I say eventually.

She gives me a look and is about to continue but quiets. The conversation is over.

I raise the cardigan higher on my neck, my hair tucked inside as I walk up the gentle slope toward the house to the deck, where a barbecue grill sits with a cover. As I place my hand on the door, I turn to look back at the yard once more and smile. My husband had loved this yard.

3

EVIE

From the end of the upstairs hall the following day, I hear the kids talking behind the cracked door, sunlight casting a narrow beam into the dim hallway. The room has served different purposes over the years. At one time, it was a playroom full of LEGOs and G.I. Joes, dinosaurs with tutus and dress-up clothes. I once strung alphabet letters on pretty ribbons and hung them below a mosaic tree painted on the wall. It had been a monumental effort to keep the room in any semblance of order, but when the kids grew older and the toys began making their way to yard sales and garbage bins, I longed for the days of cleaning crayon marks from the walls and Play-Doh from the rug, wishing they were little again.

These days it serves as a den/office, with boxes of mementos and outdated technology cords filling the deep recesses of the closet. A jar of smooth white stones sits on a shelf. A guitar from Lucas's college years gathers dust in the corner alongside a record player, and racks of albums I once collected sit beside a small sofa.

Along with the regular family photos, the walls are decorated with framed images representing my own private memories on display. Ancient astronomy prints, a photo of the spiraling Tulip Stairs, artful geometric designs, that sort of thing. My family assumes this is just a decorating quirk. They don't know the meaning behind them, of course. Then again, maybe Steve did. Each time I added a new one over the years, he would get quiet for a bit but let it go. The only clues to my inner world. Reminders of what once was or might have been. I wonder now what it was like for him to live in a house haunted by someone else's ghosts.

I set down the laundry I'm holding as I hear my kids talking inside the room.

"What are you guys up to, anyway? What is all this stuff?" Lainey's husband, Rick, asks between forkfuls of food.

I crane my neck and catch sight of where Lainey sits near her brother amid a pile of things from the recesses of the open closet doors, its contents spilling into the room.

"I was looking for a sweatshirt." She gestures at the faded, oversize Penn State sweatshirt she's wearing. "One of Dad's from college." I hear the sad smile in her voice. "I guess we started going through the boxes and got sucked in."

"Lainey, look at this."

"Stuffy!" She jumps up, taking the stuffed pink dragon from her brother's hands.

I smile.

"Stuffy?" Rick asks.

"That's why he blew fire, because his nose was so stuffy! Stuffy the Dragon," she replies.

"I see. Very cute."

I know I shouldn't eavesdrop, and I don't mean to, but as I stand quietly outside the door, I can't help it. It makes me smile to hear them in their natural adult state, freely talking, and I don't want to interrupt. Through the crack in the door, I see them, both perched side by side on the floor, my two grown children. And in my mind's eye, I imagine them in the same positions playing as children in front of the same closet, once filled with toys. Somewhere in the loop of time, I wonder if they were sitting with figurines or a pile of crayons.

"Look! The Fun Night Can!" Lucas says then, eliciting another smile from me as the memories flash through my mind like a movie, recalling the contents inside. "We had fun with this. I wonder if the scraps of paper are still in it." I hear him ruffling through them. "Make-your-own-sundae night. It was always my favorite. What was yours?"

"I don't remember," Lainey says dismissively.

He scoffs. "Yes, you do. C'mon."

She ignores him, moving on.

I'd come up with the idea at some point, and we'd done it every Friday night for more than a year when they were little. That's more than fifty-two times. But that's the way it was with kids sometimes. They don't remember all the fun times their parents spend on the floor being silly or running around a yard pretending to be a pirate. They remember our failures more. I read somewhere once that a parent needs to create five positive experiences to make up for one single bad one in their child's life. Seems a cruel trick on parenting—the chips stacked against us from the start.

"Hey, guys, look how cool these are." Lucas has evidently abandoned the Fun Night Can and continued deeper into the closet. "These old magazines and CDs."

"Where were those?" Lainey asks.

"In a box with a bunch of Mom's old things."

I stiffen, my heart rate picking up a bit.

"Don't go through that stuff. It's Mom's."

"They're magazines, Lainey. Not diaries. Chill," Lucas says. "This is so cool. 'The Otherworldly Masterpiece of Mayluna.'" He's reading from an old music magazine, and I close my eyes and take a breath.

"This was from when they were first starting out, before they became huge. I bet we could get something decent on eBay for this," Rick says. My son-in-law, ever the practical one.

"No way. We're not selling these." Lucas sounds aghast. "I had no idea we had them." Despite it all, I smile at his interest. It's funny that he's the one who ended up liking this sort of thing, even though Lainey had been the musical one as a child.

"Hey, look at this photo," Rick says a moment later.

"Which one?"

"This one. This girl kind of reminds me of you, Lainey." He holds it out to her. "Doesn't she?"

"You can't even see her face," she says, dismissing it with a glance.

"You can see her nose and her chin. I don't know . . . there's just something about her posture."

I know what they're looking at, and I peer in just a bit, tempted to interject, my breath shallow.

"Huh. I see what you mean," Lucas says, and I see him alongside Rick, both standing by the desk, inspecting a page from a magazine.

There's a long silence. "See!" Lucas exclaims, watching Lainey's expression a moment later. "Something weird about it, right?"

"Yeah. There is, sort of. It's . . ." Lainey's voice has grown quiet after having another look for herself. I can see her profile a bit through the door. "It is kind of beautiful, isn't it?" She looks more closely at it, and my heart thumps hard against my chest. "Weird."

"What is?" Lucas asks.

"Nothing, it's just . . ."

"Mom has a bracelet like that." He completes her thought.

"It must've been a trend at the time," Lainey says. I look down and twist the silver bracelet on my small wrist, as familiar to me as my own skin. "It was her mom's. I used to beg her to let me wear it, and she never would."

"How old was she when her mom died?" Rick asks.

"Around eight or so, I think. She doesn't like to talk about her childhood much."

I peek in, and the three are huddled together by the window, crowding around the magazine with their backs to me.

"You don't actually think . . . ," Lucas starts, looking at his sister.

Lainey chuckles, abandoning the others and walking away to pick up another box. "Her idea of a big night out is going to the movies. And I've literally never seen her go to a concert. She's in bed by ten p.m. Her . . . in *that* world?" She points at the magazine. "Hardly."

My shoulders wilt and I take a step back.

"Look at this room," Lainey continues. "Books about Paris museums and Indian cooking. A print of London from what . . . like, a college school trip or something? They never went anywhere. She never even left this town. Just sat here and thought about it all."

I swallow the lump that's begun to form in my throat.

"Why do you have to be so hard on her?" Lucas asks.

She sighs. "I'm not. I . . ."

There's a shuffle, and suddenly the door opens as she walks out of the room, just as I'm reaching out to place my hand on the doorknob. "Mom!" When she sees the look in my eyes, heat fills her cheeks as realization dawns that I might have overheard her talking. "Hi. I . . . I thought you were out. We didn't hear you come in."

I look over her shoulder to where Rick and Lucas glance at each other and then busy themselves with the items in their hands.

"I was having a cup of tea with Ingrid down the street. She tried to give us more food, but I declined, you'll be happy to hear." I muster a little laugh—my instinct to soothe my daughter naturally taking precedence over my own hurt feelings.

"That's good. We were just . . ."

"You found it. I'm so glad." I look down at the sweatshirt she's wearing and smile. "Your dad would want you to have it."

"We were just going through some old things in the closet." She gestures sheepishly to the mess in the room. "Don't worry—we'll clean it up."

"It's fine, sweetie. I can get it later."

"I didn't know you had these, Mom. They're cool." Lucas shows me the small collection of magazines he's holding. Another box, tied with twine, sits unassumingly in the corner, unopened. "Where'd they come from?"

I open my mouth to speak, but as I look at their faces, all that comes out before I turn to leave the room is: "Dinner in a bit. Come on down whenever you'd like."

And so it goes.

4

EVIE

It's been a restless night, and I toss and turn until well after midnight, wishing sleep would come. Just as it's pulling me into its sweet respite, I hear the faint sound of music. For a moment, I think it's coming from another room, or perhaps the beginnings of a dream, until I realize it's coming from a place that's somewhere in the ethereal in-between, hovering in the room with me as it has before. It comes less often these days, and it instantly warms me.

"I'm trying to do what's best, and I don't know what to do," I whisper aloud, as if an answer might come, wishing he were beside me. And then . . .

It's time, love.

The words come to me from inside my mind, in my own voice and yet . . . not. Tears fill my eyes. I imagine him there, still with me.

Everything is going to be okay.

I'm right here. I'm right beside you.

5

EVIE

A while later, having abandoned plans for sleep, I'm back in the den, pondering my thoughts and the whispers of ghosts when I hear Lainey's door open and she appears in the doorway. Still wearing her father's sweatshirt along with pajama pants, she pulls the sleeves down over her hands. Her hair is topped in a messy bun, tousled from the pillow.

"Mom? What are you still doing up? Everything all right?" She squints in the dim light.

"I couldn't sleep, I guess. What about you?"

She shakes her head. I think she's going to leave and return to bed, but to my pleasant surprise, instead she joins me, curling up on the sofa with her legs beneath her.

"Sorry we forgot to clean up. We'll get it tomorrow." She leans down and collects a few of the things into a small pile next to her feet.

"Oh, don't worry about it." I'm holding Stuffy on my lap. "Sometimes it's good to get things out and have a look."

She smiles, taking the stuffed animal into pale, delicate hands that are younger versions of mine, but she seems preoccupied. I know she's busy with work, and her dad's funeral has come at a difficult time. Not that they ever come at a good time, of course. But after a six-month illness, Steve dying came as no surprise, with a gradual mourning that had started weeks before we all had our final goodbye.

"I feel like we've barely had a chance to talk since you've been home. How are things? How's work?" I ask, and she tells me it's fine. Good. Busy.

She works as an associate film producer, funny enough. It makes me happy that her creative mind found its home in a career that she loves. One that I once wished for, as well, albeit briefly. When she announced she would be going into that business, she'd given me a sheepish and proud smile. Maybe I got some things right.

"Everything okay with Rick?" I venture to ask.

She glances over at me. "I guess."

I know they're struggling. I can feel her restless unhappiness and hope that she'll tell me what it is, though I know she won't. At least not until she's ready. I allow the silence to continue, giving her space to speak if she'd like.

She pulls at Stuffy's frayed ear. "It's not him, it's . . ." She grows quiet. "He's a lot like you. And Dad. He'd be content, I don't know, eating lasagna at home for three days, I guess. He's so set and settled. But I'm still trying to figure out who I am and can't seem to do it. Sometimes I feel like . . . like my life should be different in some way. Bigger. Wider. Or . . . something. I don't know, just different." She looks so sad as she says this.

It's the most she's spoken to me about a subject of any depth in a long time, and my heart swells and breaks a little at the same time. I want to tell her that I understand. I want to tell her . . .

"I know you must think that sounds crazy. Forget it. I'm fine," she adds a moment later and moves to stand. "'Night, Mom."

"No, wait, sweetie," I say. "I was just thinking that it doesn't sound crazy at all." Her intuition is shouting to her that something is off, and I can't deny her this. "I understand more than you think."

"Really?"

"Really."

If only you'd known me in a different time. A different place, I want to say.

"But you made it work, right? You and Dad. You were happy here in your life? In this house?" she asks, sitting again. "Mostly?"

It's a complicated question.

"We were." I nod. "Or . . . we did our best, anyway."

Children don't know who their parents are, really. Don't know the secrets and dreams that lie deep within their hearts. They know the faces of the parents who raised them, but not the struggles and demons and things that make their hearts sing. My kids know my mannerisms. Where I keep my reading glasses. They know how I like my coffee and that I'm afraid of heights and that inconsiderate people drive me crazy. They know the familiar scent of my perfume, left over at the end of the day when I used to read them bedtime stories, and what I usually have in the grocery cart. The markings of a human life that are known by the ones with whom we share our time. Something about this brings me comfort. But it's a little sad, to not really be known by the ones we've loved. They know only half of my story.

I made a promise to Steve years ago not to tell our kids the secrets we'd kept. And to be fair, I also have my own reasons for keeping them locked away. But as I look at my daughter's face, I know that Kate's right. She needs the real story. The truth. Even if it means that I might lose her.

It's okay. It's time. It'll be okay.

I feel his voice with me again. Maybe it's my imagination; maybe it's not. I don't ask anymore.

I'm right here with you, love.

Thinking she's changing the subject, Lainey picks up the magazine that she and the boys were looking at earlier and holds it out to me.

There are signs everywhere, Ev, he used to tell me. *You just have to pay attention.*

She points. "We were kind of laughing earlier because the girl in this photo has a bracelet like yours." I glance at my wrist where the silver bangle normally sits. "She even reminds me of you." She picks up another. "See? Here it is again. It does kind of have a haunting look to it." She seems a bit captivated by the image.

"It's been a long time since I've seen this photo," I tell her after a long moment. It's a dark, grainy image—a scene of a band in a recording studio dotted with candles. Two people are in profile at the front, while the rest of the band is in the background. A young woman with long dark-brown hair hanging in thick layers down her back is wearing torn jeans and black boots. An oversize sweater hangs slightly off one delicate shoulder. From her seat on a stool, she's gazing upward in profile as the lead singer looks down at her while singing into a microphone, their fingers entwined and their faces just inches apart, as if about to kiss. Shot by famed music and celebrity photographer Derek d'Orsay, the photo was taken from behind, with the couple largely silhouetted by the lights of the studio and the woman's profile in shadow. The "mystery girl in the studio," they called her.

The photo had become somewhat famous over the years—appearing in coffee-table books on music photography and such things. There was an intimacy and romance to it that captured the imagination of the world. It was one of the most iconic photographs from the 1990s, and even now, thirty years later, among famed celebrity photos.

The photographer never revealed the name of the girl in the photo, despite its significance.

"Did you collect these? Music magazines?" Lainey seems amused. "Doesn't really seem very like you."

"Just these few, really," I reply quietly.

"Big Mayluna fan in secret?" she jokes, referencing the band in the photos.

Lainey sees then, the look on my face. "Mom?"

"What are you guys doing?" Lucas has appeared, and my son-in-law behind him, both shuffling toward us in sweatpants and T-shirts, faces puffy from sleep.

"It's nice having you all here sleeping under the same roof," I say, mostly to myself, smiling. "I think the last time was that Christmas when you were still in school." It occurs to me to wonder when I might get an opportunity like this again. And then I've decided.

I take a deep breath, releasing it slowly.

"You okay, Mom?" Lainey asks again.

I return my gaze to the image of the couple. "That's his sweater she's wearing," I say eventually. "The girl in the photo."

"You think?" Lainey asks.

"I *know*."

"But—"

Then, in one small gesture that takes all my courage, I point to a spot on the photo and wait. Lainey peers closer at it, and her eyes widen. Realization dawns as she sees the small birthmark on the girl's wrist, and the matching one on mine, alongside the bracelet she recognizes. Then Lucas takes it from her hand.

"It *is* you?" he asks, and I nod, my heart racing.

Lainey's mouth drops, trying to reconcile the young woman in the photo with the mother beside her. I can see that she doesn't believe it, though why would she? "You knew Carter Wills?"

"Yes. I did. And besides you and the people in this recording studio that day, barely anyone ever knew it was me in this picture. But yes. I much more than knew him. All of them." My voice cracks. "They were like my family. Once upon a time." I run a fingertip over the members of the band in the studio so long ago. Unassuming young musicians at the start of their career. I feel like I was just in that room with them on that night with candles burning alongside the music, wondering how time could go by so quickly.

"Okay, that seems kind of impossible, I won't lie," Lucas says, and I smile at the little boy I can still see in the handsome husband and father my son has grown up to be. "Carter Wills," he says again, clearly impressed and excited by this new development.

"Why didn't you ever tell us?" Lainey asks. The million-dollar question.

"It's a long story. There were a lot of reasons. But mostly, I made a promise to your dad while he was alive. And I kept it."

"But why would Dad care?" They look at each other, confused.

I'm trembling, and I close my eyes again briefly.

I'm right here. You're not alone.

I flip to the cover. *Inside the Mind of Carter Wills: Tales from the dark side and a look at rock's most mysterious god,* it reads. I take a deep breath at the sight of him, tracing the image, where an intricate Fibonacci-spiral tattoo fell in delicate lines across his lean back.

"I remember so clearly the day I bought this one." It was a whole new beginning. "Years later. I had stopped at the grocery store with you after school, Lainey." I think of googly-eyed dinosaurs on construction paper and two little kids who had a mom who played with them in the backyard.

Before everything changed.

Lainey reaches out and picks up yet another clipping of an article from an older magazine. It's a bit tattered, paper-clipped in two sections and dotted with a smiley face. Alongside is a scattering of stars and clouds doodled in black pen. *Stargazing with Mayluna,* the title says. *By: Cameron Leigh.*

"Carter doodled that." I smile widely, tears pricking my eyes. Something about the sight of her holding it in her hand makes my insides come alive. *Okay, you're right. It's time.* I want to say it out loud, though of course I don't. They would never fully understand that part of the story, I suspect. The connection.

"Who's Cameron Leigh?" Lainey asks, noting the heart drawn next to the name.

"I am."

She and Lucas look at each other and then back at me. "You're not making any sense. I don't understand," Lainey says.

"I know," I say with a wan smile. "But you will."

If, as I said, my life was bookmarked into two sections—"Before and After I Liked Autumn"—I suppose there would be one more part. There was summer, and I was twenty-five years old. I remember that the air was heavy with the perfumed scent of mulch and pine and the faintest hint of salty air drifting from a few miles away.

There is geometry in the humming of the strings, there is music in the spacing of the spheres.

—Pythagoras

6

EVIE

1998

The heat rose from the patio beneath a cloudless morning sky while I sat sipping a cup of tea on a trellised stone patio—my tiny apartment's prize selling point. It had been another long, sleepless night but a pleasant morning in my little apartment. I enjoyed the perfect Friday weather, closing my eyes to savor the late-morning sun on my face well before the years when sunscreen would become a daily thing.

My mother had loved warm weather, and I could still see her in my mind's eye, with baby-oiled skin on a plastic lounge chair in the back-yard, sipping iced tea and smiling as Rod Stewart played on a nearby radio. I inherited my love of summer from her, I guessed.

I hadn't ever planned to live on Long Island. More like Manhattan. The East Village. Los Angeles or London, maybe, if I was thinking big. These were the kinds of places a kid dreamed of when they grew up in a small town. I'd had NYU and their offer of a rare full scholarship to thank for bringing me out of small-town life and into the city originally. A search for affordable housing a few years later and an ad in the paper eventually led me down the Long Island Expressway in a beat-up white

Volkswagen Cabriolet convertible. After that, I'd stayed for the reasons so many do—the combination of suburbs, farm stands, and the sea in a place still near enough to the best city in the world to make it worth the trouble and expense.

And also, I liked it because no one knew me and I could reinvent myself. A new state, a new life, filled with the youthful optimism and feeling of endless possibilities laid out before me, free of my past. I had nothing tying me down—not even a goldfish or a potted plant—so I could go wherever my job or life took me.

Sometimes it bothered me when I thought about it, usually in the long hours after midnight when darkness descended and my heart pounded in my chest—that I could be one of those people who died in their apartment and no one found them for days. Dreary, I know. But thoughts like that were chased away by the morning light and, with it, the last remnants of fear scurrying away to the dark corners where they belonged.

Years later, I would learn about anxiety and panic attacks and post-trauma and all the myriad tools to cope with them. But this was a different time—the late '90s—and the mental health awareness movement was still a few years away. So my coping mechanisms were few. One of which was the appearance of light and the sun. The world was less scary after dawn.

Mild caffeine from my tea had hit my bloodstream, clearing the cobwebs. And it was going to be a pleasant, sunny day. I could just feel it—the magic sparkle that tickled my skin when something good was hovering in the universe, waiting to descend.

Late nights and I were old friends, and I'd been born a naturally nocturnal animal, which was handy in a career like mine where late hours turned into early morning. My mom used to call me her baby owl, so I supposed it went back that far.

After she was gone, I needed to be on guard throughout the night, when chaos could threaten at any moment with my father bursting through the front door of our trailer in any state of mind. Or worse, not coming in at all, so I'd have to stand sentinel all on my own, curled into the corner of my pink bed, clutching a unicorn for safety.

He wasn't a bad man, my father; he just wasn't a good man. Rough, unreliable, with a propensity for alcohol, selfishness, and a general distaste for anything related to parenting. But not a bad man. Which I suppose is me being generous. But forgiveness happens in time.

I don't remember when it was that I began writing and telling stories, but the first record I have of it appeared in a small off-white diary with a Precious Moments character on the front and a tiny lock that didn't need a key. I still had it, tucked away in the small box of keepsakes I'd allowed myself to bring with me when I left home. I'd write about my day, write about my mom, write about who liked who in third grade or what I wished for at Christmas. I'd write about my father showing up with a three-dollar gas-station knockoff Barbie the day after my birthday, smelling of cigarette smoke, and my mother asking him to leave. I'd write about the world around me.

The last entry in that first diary, written in blue pen with stubby letters, was simply the date, November 25, 1980, and the words: "My mom died today." After that, the writing ended for a while. But in my teens, I picked up the pen again, started filling up notebooks, and it turned into a way of self-soothing. It took on a kind of therapy, along with the one blessed thing I could thank my father for—his collection of albums and an obsession with rock 'n' roll.

Music, words, and films. Put those three loves together, and that was pretty much me.

I haven't talked about my parents in many years, and to do so feels strange. Like opening one of those old diaries and reading aloud. I probably should have been more open about it, but it was a time of my life with so many shadows that it was better to leave them alone.

Anyway, after years of pushing my way into the largely masculine music industry of the early '90s, paying my dues at countless clubs on countless late nights, I found myself as one of those rare music writers who had made it far enough to count it as a real career (sort of) alongside my real passion, which was music filmmaking. MTV was still everything in the '90s, and even more so, band documentaries were all the rage. My goal was to direct my own film one day—a behind-the-scenes documentary about a band or an artist. The calamitous spectacle of the Stones' *Gimme Shelter. Leonard Cohen: Bird on a Wire. Ziggy Stardust and the Spiders from Mars.* The grittiness of *The Decline of Western Civilization.* Even *U2: Rattle and Hum,* before I developed a more discerning eye. These were my bibles. I know that today I just work on small local stories, and I don't talk much about my old career, but back then, it was music only. And I was pretty good at it, I'll admit.

Which is all just to explain how I found myself in the spring of 1998 getting ready to head out for an interview with a British alternative rock band for a story I'd pitched to *Spin* magazine, which was a huge deal at the time.

The band I'd be covering on this particular evening was, as I'm sure you've guessed, Mayluna. They were the opening act, and I'd gotten the assignment only because a more senior writer had declined to stoop to the level of it, opting instead to cover the main act. To give her some credit, Mayluna was the more interesting story, and I'm sure she knew it. I was pretty sure she declined simply because she was afraid to fail, and I'm glad for small miracles. They had already gained a reputation for being press-shy and difficult to pin down. When I'd pitched it, I'd gotten the feeling that the editor had chuckled at the idea of sending me, knowing the enigmatic nature of the group. I imagined him saying, *Eh, why not. Let's see what happens.* But I did have a knack for those sorts of stories.

Profile pieces were my skill. I had developed an uncanny ability to slide into the shadows and into the trusted inner sanctum of bands on tour, grabbing snippets of conversations and quotes in vans, buses, dressing rooms, backstage at music festivals, recording studios, and smoky hotel rooms where the magic often started and ended simultaneously. Standing in the corner, observing, taking notes, recording when I could. Barely noticed. I didn't even use my real name, opting for a pen name instead.

From the time I was little, I'd been the most invisible, forgettable girl on the planet. Easily left. Easily forgotten. Another thing I'd learned from my father, besides good taste in music, I suppose. But I'd taken those traits and learned to make them work for me. Made a whole damn career out of it. Sometimes you have to do that—take the thing about you that makes you the saddest and learn to spin it into a superpower.

7

CARTER

"The thing was, she was unforgettable." I've ignored Michael's question about her name and gone off in a different direction. "I think that's what drew people toward her and what made her good at her job. That, and she had a quality about her that made people want to be around her from the moment you met her. There was a peacefulness to her, with these dark-blue eyes you could get lost in—it was almost as if she shape-shifted into her environments and the people around her to the point that it felt natural. Just observing quietly until you couldn't help but want to be near her energy." A chameleon, quietly perched nearby, seemingly invisible, until you looked closer and realized the miraculous and shimmering display of nature taking place.

8

Evie

And really, I had nothing to lose by trying for the long-shot interview with Mayluna and the elusive Carter Wills. More importantly, I was genuinely intrigued. The Evolution was the main act, so you'd think that would be the big story. But when doing stories about bands who have been a success for a number of years, it could be difficult to find new things to say unless they changed direction or you managed to find a new angle.

So Mayluna was interesting to me, you see. The secret formula seemed to be that they masterfully combined the edginess of moody, alternative rock guitar with a little more emotional depth, stirring melodies and endlessly tortured lyrics penned by their stylishly brooding and somewhat mysterious lead singer.

I thought of this as their new song began to play on the radio while I got ready for work. It was a sleeper hit from an EP released a few months earlier. Their first album was forthcoming, and I'd been sent an advance copy of another unreleased single and could immediately see what the buzz was about. There was something different about them—a complete departure from the current mood of American rock—with lush, textured melodies that wrapped around your ears and made you unsure whether you wanted to cry in your bedroom or feel elated with joy.

But America didn't always embrace these bands, and I was looking forward to seeing for myself if their music would translate well to a new audience and to meeting the personalities behind the songs.

I had more confidence back then. And I remember having a complete certainty that somehow, the stars would align in my favor to make it happen despite the odds. I'm not sure where I got that or where it went in my later years. But back then, I was kind of a force.

I lived sparsely then—owned exactly three pairs of shoes: faded white slip-on sneakers, perfectly worn-in black Doc Martens, and a pair of brown sandals. I chose the boots and a pair of denim shorts—there's a photo of me in this outfit somewhere—tossed a canvas messenger bag over my shoulder, located my sunglasses, and switched off the stereo. Just as I was leaving, I reached back in the door and grabbed my lanyard off the doorknob. The all-access passes from dozens of past shows, marking the passage of time, rattled together as I threw it around my neck and headed to work.

The most pivotal days of a person's life often start out just like any other. You wake up, brush your teeth, and go about your usual routines, having no idea that by the time you go to bed that night, your entire path will have changed. When I looked back on my life, I would always think of that day as the exact pinpoint of when my world stopped, imperceptibly shifted on its axis, and started turning again at a new angle. But of course, I didn't know that yet.

I wonder, did I always think about things this way? Or was it his influence on me? He loved talking about things like this. The mysterious intersections of timing and fate.

9

CARTER

"Fame wasn't coming naturally to us, mostly because it happened so quickly. For years, we had just been a group of boys playing to small venues for fun. A few of us were at university, planning sensible careers and such. I was studying the philosophy of mathematics and astronomy, nearly obsessively. If music was the heart of me, part of my soul, then the study of the cosmos was my mind. I would have been content enough on either route, I suppose."

"But then?" Michael asks.

"But then we did a small gig in Camden Town, just a few songs really, and there happened to be someone important in the room. That's how it happens so often for bands, you know. Right place, right time, right person—all aligning perfectly in sync, as if orchestrated by a greater hand. In the span of a few weeks, we had signed a record deal, were on the radio, and launched onto stages as the opening act for bands we'd looked up to as heroes. It was disorienting. We had broken up for a while and just gotten back together with new songs and a new name. And it happened so fast. The EP, then Paramour Records, then the tour. In most cases, bands expand outward, soaking up the rays of the sun and reflecting them in every direction. But us, we were the opposite, and fame made us want to draw inward, contract, and hide from it all. Obviously, this created a promotions problem. Still, the tide continued carrying us into bigger waters, and before you knew it, we were in America, opening for The Evolution—a band we'd grown up listening to."

"But they were one of our more cautionary tales, mind you—inspiring as much as warning us," Tommy adds.

"In what way?" Michael asks.

"I guess we didn't want to end up a mess," he replies.

"Speak for yourself." Alex has opened his eyes, crossing his hands over his hips while offering a snigger that crinkles his eyes a little.

"When I was a kid," I say, "I used to look at Jim Morrison and Jimi Hendrix and great bands that had crumbled and think, *They seem like such a wreck. All those drugs and the sheer decadence. I don't want to end up like that.*"

"And I'd look at the same pictures and think, *Yeah, but that's what made the music turn out to be so legendary*," Alex says, completing the circle of thought.

"Ah, that does explain a lot." Michael is absorbing this. "Quite a split there."

"Angels and demons." Tommy reaches over to pour a beer and leans back into his seat. "There needs to be both in life. Without one, the other gets uninteresting pretty damn fast."

"We had already been through a lot, and we weren't even all that famous yet. So I worried about what it would cost us. Maybe that's why we were hesitant. I also just didn't much trust the press in any way. But like I said, she was different. She could get the story behind the music, not just the artifice the band wanted people to see, so it made people talk to her when they wouldn't otherwise."

Michael doesn't hide his surprise. "Are you saying she was a journalist?"

I nod, and he absorbs this information, the irony of it.

"But we hoped to get to a point where the music would stand on its own, and that someone in some town, listening to our album in their bedroom, would hear it and not give a damn who said what about us."

There was a time when music was something simpler—a soundtrack playing alongside life—songs on the radio, advertisements and jingles, the strums of my mother and brother, I continue telling Michael. But then, maybe around the age of twelve or thirteen, that all changed for me, like a recessed gene becoming activated. It became part of my inner world, impressing itself upon my DNA and weaving into my soul, whispering at all hours of the night like ghosts in a hall. I began spending every penny I could spare in the Crossroads Records, the nearest store to carry the kind of albums I craved. Splitting them with Jacob. Using what I heard to teach myself to play, to become the sound, to absorb the feelings *between* the notes. This was my relationship to the music. But then, in a relatively short span of time, an intersection had formed when it crossed over into a path seemingly paved with opportunity— my private world put on display in front of thousands of people. I had a nearly obsessive desire to keep it close to me back then, I think partly out of fear that if I spoke of it too much, it would be lost. It's been years now, of course, so I've learned to balance it all a little more. But back then, I tried to avoid talking about our experience or the music. Until that day, really.

"We were playing our first show at Jones Beach, which, even to a few boys from Britain, was absolutely iconic," I continue. I know we're presently on our way to play a sold-out stadium of 70,000 people, but I still remember the 15,000-seat Jones Beach experience as a momentous accomplishment. Which it was at the time. "In terms of American venues, it was up there with the Hollywood Bowl and Madison Square Garden and Red Rocks, even if we were just the opener. But as visually impressive as it can be, with all that water and concrete and sky, the backstage area is a claustrophobic corridor of humid sensory overload, and there was a heat wave that day. Have you been there?"

Michael nods. "Sure. A number of times. And I know what you mean."

"There's this spot outside one of the back doors, where you end up on a narrow strip of walkway that sort of hangs just over the water. It's on the back of the building, out of view." I draw the curvature of the building with the tip of my finger on the armrest beside me. "There's a nice breeze and something resembling a bit of quiet, along with the sound of seagulls. So that's where I was for most of that day. A few years later, I found out about the hidden tunnel beneath the water that connects the front of house to backstage. But even I'm not that dismal."

"He does this. Whatever venue we're in, you can count on him to go hide in a nook far away. It is literally the most annoying thing ever when it's time for sound check," Tommy explains to Michael. "Especially because he never has his phone on him."

"I'm not hiding exactly. But otherwise, he's not wrong," I say.

"It's often the very top row of a stadium these days. Nobody going to find you up there. Except me, of course. But I know where to look."

"Remind me to get more creative with my locations," I joke to Tommy before continuing. "That day, I heard Ian from The Evolution finishing up sound check and knew we'd be up soon, so I went inside. I simply walked through a door, and that was it."

Everything changed.

"When I first saw her, I—"

"You mean when *I* first saw her," Alex corrects me. His eyes have closed again, a napping panther. I smile at the long-running joke between us. He's right. Out of all of us, he saw her first.

"Freddie had something to do with it all too," Tommy adds, and I nod in agreement and continue.

"At first, I didn't know what she did for a living or why she was there at the time. But it wouldn't have mattered. I would have told her anything that day, I think."

10

Evie

It was an interesting time for live music, with tours departing from the dark interiors of indoor arenas in favor of giant outdoor venues inspired by the summer festival stages of Europe. I traveled all over the northeast for assignments, but this one was right in my backyard, at Jones Beach Amphitheater. Right on the bay in Wantagh on the South Shore of Long Island, it featured some of the best concerts of the summer. At early June, it was poised to be one of the busiest touring seasons ever.

After supplying my name and credentials, I was given the green light to pass through the backstage lots, packed with a sea of noisy production trucks and shiny tour buses. As the late-day heat rose from the cement, I swept my hair up off my back to let the breeze hit my shoulders.

Jones Beach was set up with a central stage surrounded by water, with stadium seating where fans could revel in the music, enjoying the show beneath the moon rising over the bay. The seats were still quiet, and I'd always thought there was something peaceful about being completely alone in a vast space meant to hold thousands of people.

Walking up the steps to the right of the stage pops you into a different world. The energy of the stage buzzed with the sounds of the tour's production crew as they rigged lighting and finished building sets. I'd look up and see a man dangling on a thin wire three stories or so above the stage, while casually eating a sandwich, and shudder as I thought of my own fear of heights. Another member of the crew sat at the drum kit, tapping the snare repeatedly in the familiar slow, monotonous rhythm I was accustomed to hearing as they tested the sound.

These details are all so remarkably clear in my mind, I think, because my brain later registered it as a day to remember. One that I would replay over and over on late nights in distant years. It's odd hearing them all out loud now, free.

I made my way along the curved cement corridor, past equipment and rows of guitars and piles of coiled cable to the production office just behind the stage. As I turned to enter, I passed a man sitting on a black road case outside the office, awash in surly silence and angst with his head leaning against the wall, hands linked and resting on his hip. His eyes followed me from behind a shadow of dark hair. I nodded a hello, which he ignored as he slid off the case and slinked away, disappearing through a door. I'd done my research ahead of time, so of course I recognized him—the talented lead guitarist, responsible for the hallmark tones of their unique sound. I've often found it funny that it was Alex I met before any of the rest of them (a fact that he reminded me of many years later). He was never one to exactly roll out the welcome wagon for anyone.

A white sheet of paper with the words PRODUCTION—MAYLUNA was taped to the white cement wall, and inside the open doorway, I found a bear of a man, their tour manager, sitting at a cramped table, typing with thick fingers on a big laptop. One of those early models that looked like a heavy black brick.

"Fred? I'm Cameron Leigh; I'm doing the piece with *Spin*." He took my hand briefly when I extended it but otherwise kept his gaze on his computer. The fluorescent light above our heads flickered in the dark space. I relaxed a hip, settling in for a wait. Finally deciding to grace me with his attention after shuffling some papers, Fred looked at me, disinterested at first, before clearly sizing me up. I watched his eyes start at my legs, then pause for a fraction of a second at the scant bit of skin showing above the low waistline of my shorts and then continue upward. He didn't mean anything by it, but I'd grown accustomed to this greeting in a profession that was so completely dominated by men, and I inwardly rolled my eyes.

"Writer, eh? What'd you say your name was again?" He had the kind of thick Welsh accent that was nearly indecipherable for an American girl who had never been abroad.

"Cameron Leigh. *Spin* magazine. I'm here to do the feature."

He grunted in response, returning to his paperwork, and just as he did, I felt a breeze behind me and turned.

"Hello, Miss Vivien from *Spin* magazine, at your service." Tommy Rollins was this lanky guy who sauntered past me and leaned against the wall—tall (they all were, really), with long bones and sharp shoulders and shoulder-length dirty-blond hair. With an easy grin and glassy eyes, he reminded me of Shaggy from the old *Scooby-Doo* cartoon. I caught the familiar scent of something distinctly herbal and expected a haze of smoke to roll in behind him.

"Vivien," he repeated. "You know—like Vivien Leigh?"

I stared at him, confused.

"You said your name was Cameron Leigh. Like *Vivien* Leigh. The actress? Get it?"

I offered a chuckle at his goofy humor, just to be polite. "Ah. Gotcha. Nice to meet you. Tom, right?" I held out my hand to Mayluna's drummer.

"Indeed, I am. Though really, it's Tommy, not Tom." He bowed in the style of a proper gentleman, pretending to remove an invisible top hat with a flourish. "Pleasure."

"Do you have some time to talk?" I asked.

"The day is young and the sun is still high in the sky," he sang out in a melodious tune.

"Okay, great, but . . ."

Before I had a chance to react to his colorful introduction, he spun around, humming a tune, and left the room as quickly as he'd entered, while I was left staring after him. "Great," I murmured to myself with a sigh.

Despite the fact that Tommy was always the friendliest and warmest one of the group—perpetual rays of sunshine around him—he was just as much of a closed book as the rest of the bunch.

I turned back toward Fred, beginning to see that the day was going to be more of a challenge than I'd hoped.

"So, Miss Leigh, whaddaya need? Anything else?" He reminded me of a grumbling bear. Road guys weren't known for their winning personalities—in a constant state of busyness handling ticket requests, routing, travel . . . pretty much everything. But I'd asked around ahead of time, and fortunately, his reputation as being a decent guy held true. By the end of our brief conversation, I found myself nearly liking him.

"Would the guys rather talk before the show? After?" I asked.

He chuckled. "Whenever you can catch them."

Not entirely helpful.

"Well, could you tell me where I can find Carter?" Without something from the lead singer, the whole thing was going to go as poorly as it had for everyone who had tried before me. Outside of official PR photos and performance shots, most members of the press had never managed to see his face offstage, let alone talk to him.

"He's around somewhere, I s'pose." He ended this with a thick cough just as his phone rang.

He tossed a black Local All Access pass across the desk. The satin material—emblazoned with the tour's artwork and the date in black Sharpie. It would be one of the last few I would collect. "Make yourself at home. Good luck, kiddo."

The sparse nature of such exchanges, coupled with a complete lack of direction or information, wasn't a new thing. Nonetheless, he no doubt appreciated that I wasn't complaining and seemed unfazed by the experience, while I appreciated that he wasn't a complete asshole.

"Thanks. I'll catch up with you later if there's anything else. And could you please remind them that I'm here?"

"You got it," he replied. And then, just as I was leaving, he called out, "Hey."

I turned back toward him, and he looked at his watch.

"Try catering. Maybe make yourself a cup of tea." He winked as he lit a cigarette.

I smiled and nodded. Years later, he would tell me that he remembered that exchange. He dealt with faceless people coming in and out of his office on a daily basis, but Fred was much more perceptive than people gave him credit for. His off-putting gruffness was his exterior, but he was always watching, and still waters run deep. It's what made him so good at his job and kept him going for all those years with a temperamental young band heading for the stratosphere. He said there was something about me that day, though he couldn't put his finger on it. Other writers, reviewers, photographers, et cetera, would come and go, but he wondered if I might be one of the rare few to get through. A hunch, he'd called it.

I had been backstage at the same venue doing work with a local film crew just a week earlier, interviewing one of the bands on the side stage at Lollapalooza, and a number of other times before that, so I knew my way around. Indoor space backstage was somewhat limited, but just a few doors down from the production office sat a catering room with tables and assorted drinks and coffee. It wasn't normal for me to make myself at home like that, but I sensed Fred's hint. While brewing a cup of tea, I dug through my bag to find a pen so I could start taking notes on the brief interaction with Tommy, as well as my impression of the guitarist, Alex, whom I'd caught sight of again, like a dark shadow, haunting the corridors. As I turned, I tripped slightly, causing the boiling hot tea to slosh out of the cup and onto my wrist, and then dropped my open bag.

After muttering a series of curse words, I looked around for the contents that had spilled from my bag, including my pen, along with the batteries from a tape recorder that had scattered along with it.

I'd thought I was alone, so when a man behind me chuckled, it startled me. "Is there something I can help you find?" he asked.

Frustrated, I barely glanced his way. "No, I'm good, thanks," I mumbled, more to myself than to him. I peered beneath the banquet table where bowls of snacks and FIJI water bottles were neatly lined up next to the coffee and tea service. "I just dropped something."

"Is this what you're looking for?"

I spun around and saw him reach down to pick up a battery and a pen. When he stood to face me, I just barely concealed a double take.

"Oh. Uh, yeah. Thanks." I recovered and then gathered the rest of my things. Walking over to where he stood, I found myself face-to-face with Carter Wills, the elusive lead singer of Mayluna. He had the most hypnotic pair of piercing hazel eyes. They're what struck me first.

"I think you just saved my day, sort of." I was vaguely aware of his hand brushing mine as I took the items from him.

"Sort of?"

I scanned the floor, coming up empty. "I'm still missing one battery." Without it, I would either have to source out a new one (unlikely) or go strictly off my written notes. Not ideal, but I could work with it.

"Ah. I see. I'm afraid I can't help with that." His voice was quiet and surprisingly gentle for the lead singer of a rock band. I could see why he had been getting so much interest in the press in recent months. Even I had to admit that there was something about him that immediately drew one's attention. He definitely had the whole mysterious, brooding thing going on.

I held his gaze for a moment longer than absolutely necessary, then went back to retrieve my bag and the cup of tea, giving myself the opportunity to collect my thoughts. When I turned around, he was still standing there looking at me under hooded eyes, one hand in his pocket, with a curious smile on his lips. He was tall and slim, if not perhaps a tad too thin, but it suited him. People often said he was six foot four, but it was more like six foot three in reality; he just had a stature that gave the impression of being above most people. Which I guess was somewhat symbolic.

"I'm Cameron Leigh, with *Spin*. I'm here to do the profile piece. Do you have some time?" I gestured to the table.

He sighed, dropping his chin to his chest, disappointment evident. "Sorry. Maybe later." He turned and walked back toward the doorway. "You should put some ice on that, by the way." He nodded to where my hand was still red from the tea.

"Just a few minutes?"

"Have a good day, Cameron." He lifted up a hand to wave as he walked away.

He was just about to disappear through the door.

"I saw it once, too, you know. A star," I called.

He hesitated.

"In the moon," I continued.

He looked back, and I could tell I had gotten his attention. "Is that so."

"In a crescent moon once when I was little. It didn't make sense. There aren't stars between the moon and Earth, so it shouldn't have been there. My mom said it was probably just a trick of the eye or something. But still, it was a star. Twinkling through the dark half of the moon. Like it was translucent."

He cocked his head, watching me closely.

"That's what it's about, isn't it? 'Moonstar'?" I continued. It was their poetic single, climbing the charts with its liquid, driving melody.

A song that would eventually go on to become one of the biggest songs of all time, covered by countless other musicians across genres and regarded as one of music's greatest, once it made its way into history. But at that point, it was still new and making its way onto radio station playlists.

"What makes you say that?" he asked.

"Am I right?"

"You . . . aren't wrong."

I smiled. "Just ten minutes. Please?"

He seemed to be considering it, and I held my breath.

11

CARTER

The distance between two stars is generally so vast that it's incredibly rare for them to collide. When they do, it's because they share a mysterious gravitational bond that draws them toward one another, across millions of miles, in the most unlikely of ways.

The two stars orbit around one another until they eventually merge to form a supernova, luminous in its grandeur, each star forever changed in composition by the other, so powerful that the supernova can be detected as far as 130 million light-years away, shuddering through space-time.

It was a bit like that.

12

EVIE

A moment later, he strode over to the table where I stood. He had on a pair of well-worn jeans, resting on sharp hips, and standard-issue black military boots that were part of a look that was his usual outfit. It was by no stretch an original style, but he wore it so well that it could've been all his. If the weather was chilly, he'd wear a fitted, long-sleeve white thermal or maybe a black hooded sweatshirt. In winter, it was dark, woolen fisherman's sweaters. No fuss. Nearly every photo I had of him from that time period included some variation of that combination.

Running down the length of his entire right arm was an intricate pattern of geometric circles and lines in varying shades of black and gray ink, so flawlessly woven into his overall look that I could hardly imagine him without it. But despite his good looks, he often made a person pause before approaching him. It was a persona that followed him throughout the years.

He picked up a cloth napkin and gathered a fistful of ice, twisting it into the napkin, then brought it over to where I stood and gestured to the table beside us. Triumphant, I took a seat, and then, to my surprise, watched him take my hand and place the ice pack on it.

"Okay," he said. "But if this goes badly, then I know I can deny it, because you can't write with that hand, and I know you don't have batteries in that recorder."

"Well, how do you know I'm not left-handed?"

"Are you?"

"No."

"Okay then."

I couldn't help but laugh. "You must have had some very bad experiences in the past with interviews. You really hate this, don't you?"

"It's not my favorite thing, to be sure. I think we're our publicist's worst nightmare," he told me.

"Why do you hate it so much? Surely you must like talking about the music, if not yourself."

"I don't, actually. Like it, that is. And I don't have faith in the interpretation of my words. You spend all this time building an album that you're proud of, and then a ten-minute interview goes wrong and ruins it all. Suddenly the music and the band take the back burner, and all anyone cares about is how the lead singer said something stupid one time, and it all goes to hell. Just because I wasn't in the mood to talk or had a shit night's sleep or was focused on the show, or maybe I just didn't like the question. I've seen it happen too many times."

"Did you have a good night's sleep last night? Or should I be ready for you to say something awful that I can quote?"

He laughed, raking a hand through his dark hair—short and tousled. He had a two-day beard and looked like a person who often saw the early hours of dawn. "I rarely sleep through the night. And as for the rest, I guess we'll see."

"But surely you must know it's kind of part of the job, isn't it? Talking about the music?"

"Sure, I could talk about the music, but it's not about that, is it? Like right now, you're pretending we're having a conversation when in reality, you're dissecting everything I'm saying, distilling it into sound bites. People like you love to act as though they're your best friend and love to say they like the music. But then people who don't like the music make us sound like idiots. So there's this mixture of gratitude and panic when it comes to the press covering what we do."

I didn't take offense. He wasn't wrong. "People like me, eh? Journalists?"

"Reviewers."

"I'm not a reviewer. I'm here to learn about the story behind the music."

"Oh, you're reviewing. And you know it." He held my gaze for a moment as the corner of his mouth turned upward just slightly.

Heat flared in my stomach, and I suspected this guy knew the effect he had on people, when it suited him. All the girls he must leave swooning in his wake on a daily basis.

I gave him a look. "Ahem. Don't worry—it's just a conversation between two people."

He laughed then, the spell breaking. "I always worry. It's like my superpower."

I thought of the others who had been in my place, trying to interview him. It was as if one minute he was searching for an escape, afraid to speak, and the next, you could tell there was so much for him to say.

"Sorry, this probably isn't helping. Complaining about being interviewed during an interview. Very meta," he said finally. "It's just that it feels a little ridiculous. All these questions, over and over, with a false sense of intimacy, when in truth there's another journalist waiting outside the door. And another. And another. It's just . . . not who we are. But we have to do it, the promotions, and then if there's *too* much of it, it's embarrassing and everyone gets sick of us. We can't win."

"You're not very comfortable with fame, are you?" I found this endearing, though I didn't add that out loud.

"Well, again, I wouldn't say it's my favorite part, but I'm doing my best. It certainly beats the alternative—playing in dismal clubs to an audience of three and a drunk guy who wandered in off the streets. The thing is, our lives are pretty great. It would be much worse to be doing all of this and be completely ignored, so I won't complain. But even saying that makes me sound bad. We have to be grateful, but not too grateful, otherwise it comes off as arrogant. See what I mean?"

"So you'll just avoid."

It was his turn to smile.

"If I can. How's the hand?" He looked at where he'd placed the bag of ice as I sat awkwardly pinned down to the table with one hand.

"Getting better, thanks." I brought the subject back around. "Success often causes a person to get a narrower view of the world, building walls and creating a kind of learned distrust of those from the outside. Would you say this has happened to you?" I asked, finding my stride.

"Has the world become narrower? I'd say it's the opposite, actually. It's become grander and wider and more colorful. I've come across some real asses along the way, so I tend to be cautious, as I've mentioned, but my being quiet and reserved is more due to predisposition and life than it is the result of being in this band. If I ever get to a point when I let the bad side of this job affect who I am as a person, then I'll find a new job."

I narrowed my eyes at him. "You don't seem quiet."

"Believe me. I am." He gave me a look. "Usually."

As he briefly brought up the past, I wanted to ask him about Jacob, the fifth member of the band, his brother who died in 1996. But instinct told me to tread very carefully. Had I asked, I suspect our story would have ended that day with him immediately walking off. It wasn't a subject he readily discussed.

"Your star is shining pretty brightly right now. Are you worried it'll burn out?" I asked instead.

"I don't think anything could really stop us at this point. Not in a way that matters. Even if we lost our record deal and the album tanked and everything went to hell, we'd carry on like we always have, playing and being the best of mates and enjoying the music we create together. If anyone ruins it, it'll be us, because we decide to or because we screw it up. There won't be anyone to blame but ourselves."

"I see what you mean now."

"About what?"

"I could easily take that first sentence on its own as the pull quote and leave out the rest of the statement if I wanted to make you sound like an arrogant jerk. But I won't."

"And why is that?" He gave me a sidelong look.

"Because the rest of it is what's going to make this band special." The bunker-like brotherhood among the four of them that was already apparent.

"Hmm, maybe we should be paying you to be our publicist instead. Give us press tips. How to not mess everything up."

He stood then, and I thought the interview was over. I was often left midconversation by someone I was talking to once they got bored. But to my pleasant surprise, he went to make himself a cup of tea with honey. Something I eventually learned he did every day before a show, without fail. Later in the day, he would add scotch. While he made the tea, I jotted down a few notes with my stinging hand.

"Was that true?" he asked as it brewed and he leaned against a wall. He crossed his arms, and as he did, the bottom of his white T-shirt pulled up slightly, revealing the top of a circular gray tattoo that disappeared down the curve of his hip beneath the waist of his jeans. "The story about the moon when you were little. Or did you just make that up to get my attention?"

I remembered the night I'd sat on the beach with my mom when we saw the crescent moon. We had very little money when I was little, but we'd taken one vacation together in May during the offseason. A priceless trip to a modest little cottage on the shore, lent to her by a friend she worked with, where we listened to music on the drive east and snuggled under a blanket on the beach beneath the stars for one week that I treasured like the greatest of jewels in a box of memories. She'd pointed out constellations and told me that was where she would go when she was old and gone. All I had to do when I missed her after that was look up. The real reason I ended up on Long Island, I supposed. Like maybe the ghost of that week still lived somewhere in the past.

"It was true," I replied simply.

Maybe it was also one of the reasons their hit song had caught my attention in a way that made me pitch the story harder than I had any in recent history. It was that golden moment of personal connection that I craved in music.

"When you're writing, do you have a sense of when you've created something really special? Did you know it when you were recording 'Moonstar'?" I asked.

"Do you like it, then?" His eyes glowed, and for a moment, I saw a boy wanting approval.

I nodded.

"It came to me very quickly, around four o'clock in the morning on a particularly low and dark night. I'd say that it has to do with something from childhood, but it would make the guys a bit nauseous to know I'd admitted that." He looked as though he instantly regretted saying it and looked away.

I was still slightly caught off guard by the similarity between our history with the moon, and I wanted to ask more but didn't. "Four a.m. huh? So you're a night owl." I saw then, the hint of sleepiness in his eyes that I could see being described as bedroom eyes in the right light. Or maybe just melancholy.

"Always have been."

"And in the rare moments when you do sleep, do you ever dream about what's next for Mayluna?"

"Do you always talk like this?" He joined me again at the table, wrapping both hands around the cup of tea. A group of braided leather bracelets rested on his wrist.

"Like what?"

"Like you're playing the character of an interviewer for a magazine."

I smiled. "Are you always like *this*? A rock star?"

"I'm not a rock star." Not even the beginnings of a smile there.

Oh, he most definitely was. Put him in a room with ten other men dressed in exactly the same clothes and you'd still be able to pick him out in an instant as the one most likely to be the lead singer of a famous band.

"Well?" I said, pushing the question.

"I just am who I am. And I do my job."

"There you go. Same with me," I said.

He laughed then, a rich, warm sound that went to my toes.

"So? Do you?" I asked again. "Dream of what's next?"

"I do dream, but hopefully none of it comes true," he said, growing more serious. "I have more nightmares than dreams." As a shadow crossed his face, I believed this entirely.

He took a sip from his tea and then let the silence settle, regarding me closely. "So what about you, Cameron Leigh? What do you dream about at night?"

I shook my head. "I'm not the one being interviewed."

He raised a brow. "I thought you said it was just a conversation."

"It is. But I'm on the clock."

"And I'm not?"

We were in a standoff, and I resisted laughing, but just barely. I sighed. "Well, right now, today, my dream is to get an interview with a band that hates to do interviews and hopefully write something that isn't terrible so that I can get the chance to do more interviews with more bands and write even more words and do more films and somehow eke out enough of a living to not worry so much about paying my rent and hope that somewhere along the way, someone will think that the stories I tell matter."

Light hit his eyes, and a moment later, I got the first real smile, just for me, and somewhere in the universe, time stopped.

"So we're the same, then," he said. "You just answered all the questions."

"What do you mean?"

"Everything you just said. That's us. That's our band. And our future, all in one sentence. To keep the dream alive and make a living at it and hope that somewhere along the way, someone will think that the music we made mattered."

"I like that."

He nodded, shifting the ice back onto my wrist. "You mentioned 'films' before. What's that about?"

I shrugged. "Just something I'm working on."

He narrowed his eyes with that look of his. "And . . ."

"Don't get me wrong, I love what I'm doing here, and I'm lucky to be able to do it. But filmmaking is the bigger goal."

"Really? That's very cool, actually. What kind?"

"A music documentary eventually. Music. Words. Films. They've always kind of gone together in my mind." I made a camera shape out of my hands and peered through them at him with one eye. Then waved it off. "We'll see."

"You don't like writing?" he asked.

"I do like this part. I like telling someone's story. But I like doing that with a camera even more. So . . . hopefully one day. It's a dream, I guess."

"Dreams are good. Don't lose sight of them. The best ones seem to come through in the most unexpected ways, don't you think?"

"I'll keep that in mind."

"Any projects you've worked on?" he asked.

I told him about the work I'd done over the years. A couple of music videos. Producing some local things. Nothing groundbreaking, but still, work I was proud of. My last project had been a thirty-minute piece I had directed with an indie label for a New York band called Green Witch to promote their debut album.

I realized I had been talking as much as he had. "I hate to break it to you, but this interview seems to have turned into a legitimate conversation. You're going to have to live with that, you know." I leaned over and whispered, "The fact that you actually had a genuine conversation with the enemy."

He smiled warmly. "Well, to my surprise, it has been a pleasure. I'll never admit it, though." He looked over my shoulder then as a bass guitar began strumming from the stage. "But on that note, so to speak, I'm afraid I'll have to be off."

At one point in the years that followed, he told me how much he'd wished that I'd had the batteries in that tape recorder. To have recorded that first interaction on a sunny afternoon on a day in June. But what he didn't know at the time was that while he'd been gathering ice, I'd spotted the missing battery under the table and popped it into the recorder—its light having cracked and broken in the fall, giving nothing away that might spook him. I wasn't proud of it; it was exactly the kind of smarmy thing he worried about with journalists. But all was forgiven when I eventually wrapped the little microcassette in gift wrap and sheepishly presented it to him as a surprise years later. The beginning of a story that mattered, frozen in time.

"Think the others will talk to me?" I asked as we both stood.

He chuckled. "Doubtful. But I'll put in a good word for you. You might have better luck after our set. Maybe."

"Right. Okay then. Well, thank you."

He bowed slightly.

"No, really. I mean it. Thank you so much."

"You're very welcome." He disappeared around a corner, and after a moment, I did the same, heading in the opposite direction, still reeling from the fact that he'd talked to me as much as he had. I was already formulating words in my head and was on my way to find a place to scratch down notes before they disappeared into the ether. But I hadn't gotten far when I heard him call after me.

"Hey, wait." I turned to see him walking toward me. "It's my turn to ask for a favor," he said.

"Don't worry. I won't say anything to make you look bad."

"It's not that. Something else. We've got some time off coming up in a few days, sticking around New York before we jump back on the tour. What do you like to do around here?"

"Here? Well, I mean, it *is* New York. It's like the world's biggest all-you-can-eat buffet of things to do." I bit my lip to stifle a laugh. I found it humorous that a somewhat famous rock star was asking me, of all people, for entertainment tips.

"What?" he asked, apparently taking notice of my reaction to his question. "What did I say?"

"Sorry. Nothing. It's just . . . I'm probably not the best person to ask."

"Why not?"

"I don't really get out much, so I'm not sure where I'd even suggest. But you can ask Gary, the production manager here. He can give you some ideas of what tours coming through here like to do."

"You don't get out much? What—you don't follow bands to all kinds of amazing places for all kinds of debauchery and fun?" He gave me a look that clearly showed he was joking.

"Hardly. Well . . . sometimes." I laid a hand aside my face and whispered, "But I just watch."

"Of course. The image of propriety, no doubt."

"I hear there's a gardening expo at the convention center going on this week. Maybe try that?" I joked.

"Ah, now you're talking," he said a beat later, rewarding the humor with a laugh.

Reminiscent of a smitten schoolboy on a playground, he tucked his hands into his pockets and gazed down at his boots, the barest smile still lingering on his lips. He cocked his head to one side and regarded me for a moment. "Okay, in all seriousness, I don't want to know what everyone else coming through this place likes to do. I'd like to know what it is that you like to do. That is, when you're not rushing back to your notepad to avoid talking to riffraff like myself."

I smiled, considering my answer. "I drive to my favorite beach. Cupsogue. It's about an hour drive from here and tends to be more secluded and quieter than the other beaches. I take a good book, enjoy a slow drive with some good music, and spend a day being lazy on the beach. That's about it. Nothing terribly exciting."

"Okay then. I'll keep it in mind. Thank you. Also, just to make it formal—by the way, I'm Carter." He extended his hand, and I laughed.

"I kind of sussed that part out. But it's nice to meet you, officially, Carter."

"This is the part where you take my hand and introduce yourself, officially, in return." The moment I did so, I felt it all the way down to my feet just as we both looked curiously at our entwined hands. I know people say things like that happen, electricity and such, but it was honestly exactly that way.

"Cameron Leigh," I told him, suddenly hating the way the name sounded on my lips.

"Hmm."

"What?" I asked.

He narrowed his eyes. "You don't look like a Cameron."

"No?"

"No. But it was still nice to meet you." He paused, pointing a thumb over his shoulder. "Well, I have to get back. Some radio promotion thing we have to do before sound check." He shook his head, and I could tell he wasn't happy about it.

I hesitated for just a moment, then: "Can I offer some other advice? Not about the beach."

"Sure," he said.

"Most bands starting out in this business are greedy for press. Not all, of course. But a lot. They'll shun the attention but crave it at their core and do anything to keep it. When there's too much of it, they get annoyed at the tedium. But when there's not enough, they're crying for it. The promotional machine tumbles them into shiny, smooth stones. They lose some part of whatever made them interesting to begin with. If you're genuinely the opposite of all that, if you really do hate it, then maybe you should use it to your advantage."

"How do you mean?"

"Make it work for you. Be the antithesis of it. Let that be part of your story. The antidote to all the mindless repetition of media interviews and the hamster wheel that keeps you on it. You can't completely avoid it. So do a few interviews. Do a few promotions. But on your own terms. Choose who you let in, but keep a little of the mystery behind the curtain for yourselves. Choose your own narrative. Reinvent the model. The wisest aren't usually the ones who talk the most, wouldn't you agree?"

He pondered this. "I like that. Okay. Thank you."

"You're welcome. Just an idea." I'd later learn that this little impromptu bit of advice, just a few words really, had made an impact when he shared it with the others. Ripple effects.

He'd been having a difficult time that day, I learned later, sticking to himself and in one of the dark places in his mind that he often went to, like many songwriters. He could be like that, which probably isn't surprising if you've ever read his lyrics. He told me I'd quieted the demons. As if his nervous system required a missing element, and he'd found it in my presence that day. He had a similar effect on me. Maybe that was part of what drew us to one another so quickly.

"And now I really should let you go," I told him. The front gates would be opening shortly.

"And you have an important article to deal with," he replied, "and some truly awful bandmates to hunt down. Terrible bunch." I wondered if I would be able to translate his understated humor to the written page and suspected not quite. "So I'll see you later. Be careful with that tea," he added.

I watched him walk away. "Have a good show. And a nice time off, whatever you decide to do," I called. He turned to glance over his shoulder at me, twice—just before disappearing through another door as I stood there staring at the empty space. Then, like a bubble popping, the moment passed.

A few minutes after he'd gone, I took a seat amid a sea of empty chairs, beneath puffy white clouds on the horizon and the descending sun still bright. On the other side of the sky sat the hazy white moon high above, visible in the day. I began to formulate my initial words, scratching a pen across a lined notebook. Oddly, I remembered wondering if sometime later that day, he might end up doing the same— scratching a few thoughts on paper about a girl he met once.

13

EVIE

Over the years, I could recall only one other time when I'd been asked what Carter was like "in real life." It was during a conversation with Kate in the kitchen one rainy afternoon when I finally told her about him a decade later. Otherwise, I've said nothing. So it feels odd to be describing him like this. His mannerisms. The interactions of that day. I want so much to capture his personality, but at the same time it's not enough, trying to encapsulate an entire human being with mere words. Trying to describe the moment you first meet someone. He was so young at that time. We both were. Very different, in some ways, from how we ended up. But it was such a sweet time, and I marvel at it still.

You might have noticed the attention I've placed on this first day. It's because all stories have a beginning that define them, and ours was no different. And you have to understand that I had spent nearly an entire life without a family. The day I'm telling you about is the day that I found the first family I'd ever really known, other than the mother who left me because of a drunk driver and the father who left me because . . . well, just because he didn't bother to stay most of the time. So these things matter, you see. To me. These little details about the people who, for a time, became my whole world.

My work was a solitary experience, mostly freelance, and aside from the musicians I spoke with, few knew my face and even fewer knew my (real) name. I wondered sometimes if this was the reason why my thoughts tended to crystallize in the moment when I was interviewing someone or observing from the side of a stage, the rest of the world fading away. I wasn't part of the party; I was a witness to it.

While deep in conversation on an assignment for *Creem* magazine, I once had the lead singer of Soggy Feather ask me if I was a witch because of the way he felt eerily compelled to spill all of his secrets to me. (His words, not mine.) To this day, I still don't know if he meant it as an insult or a compliment. Probably a mix of both.

Still, while the life suited me fine, the time alone could stretch endlessly in the vacuum of existence that defined my midtwenties. Had defined my entire life, really. Always alone, even in a room full of people. Sometimes I wondered if I should at least get a cat. I'd always wanted a cat.

I also didn't have a lot of friends at the time, mostly due to the nature of my work, I suppose, and a natural predisposition to introversion. I had my two best friends from high school, of course, just your dad and Kate, but they were in the periphery of my world at the time, connecting only every few months, if that. And I had a small cast of characters who inhabited the enclaved world of the music business— tour managers and roadies who became familiar faces along the way. Other writers. Production people. That sort of thing. But nothing of any real depth.

But I did have Derek. One of my favorite people of all time. We had initially met in a visual studies workshop at Tisch and then later formed a kind of kinship when we were both covering a dicey show at the Limelight one night. I hadn't been sitting long, scribbling notes from my meeting with Carter, when Derek created a long shadow as he loped over and plopped down beside me. "Hey, stranger," he said with an easy grin. "Long time no see."

Derek d'Orsay—yes, by the way, *that* Derek d'Orsay, the award-winning photographer—existed in either a state of relaxed ease or intense focus. He ran a hand through his mop of dark dreadlocks and attempted unsuccessfully to tuck them behind his ears. Wearing a Massive Attack T-shirt, he looked more like a college dropout than an accomplished photographer as he placed his bag alongside mine.

Derek was just a stringer photographer at the time, a freelancer working for the trades like me, and we both worked the East Coast circuit, climbing the ladder to the big leagues at a similar pace. We were satellites, revolving around the bands that defined our career. He was talented and slowly making a good name for himself—and he was the closest to what I would call a good friend in the business, alike in that our lives completely revolved around work. He was often a welcome greeting to the day, and I still miss him sometimes.

"Hey, yourself!" I said. "I didn't know you'd be here tonight."

"Yep, I'm here with you know who."

I groaned. "I heard she was coming to cover The Evolution. Is she here yet?"

"I don't think so. We were in Jersey last night for Warped Tour, and I think she was out especially late in hopes of finding a good time, or whatever it is she's looking for."

"Ew." I shook the image out of my head. "She still thinks it's 1972, doesn't she? She's determined to relive her Hyatt House dreams."

"Truth," he said, lighting a cigarette. It's absurd how many people still smoked back then. I think he quit a few years later, but I'm not sure.

"And funny how she never seems to act like this at shows like, oh, I don't know, Lilith Fair?" I said.

"Has she ever heard of boundaries? Makes us look bad, you know?" He stretched backward, putting his hands behind his head. "But hey, if she's toast, maybe you'll get more of her stories and live the good life."

"Yeah, well, here's hoping." I raised my paper teacup, now luke-warm, in a mock toast.

"Hey, that piece you wrote last week for the *Voice* was amazing, by the way. Really good stuff," he told me.

"Thanks."

"But you should have stuck around—you missed a good time." He dug his hand into a bag of cashews, popping a handful into his mouth.

"Did I?" I'd been to enough requisite hotel after-parties with bands and their entourages to last me awhile.

He nodded in agreement, inhaling deeply and blowing out the smoke above us. "You here for Mayluna, I assume?" he asked.

I nodded.

"I'll get some good shots for you."

"You're the best. And most definitely appreciated. Thank you."

"No prob."

A moment later, the thumping beats of a sugary pop song, humorously incongruous to Derek's personality, started pumping through his headphones as he leaned back and closed his eyes.

That night was the first time Derek photographed Mayluna, and the start of what became a longtime professional relationship between them in both photography and video work. Funny how that day impacted his life so much, as well. Must have been something in the air.

There's a coffee-table book of Derek's work now, called *D'ORSAY 25*. It includes a few photos taken that evening, alongside images from the next two and a half decades of his photography, covering major celebrities and events. *Vanity Fair*, *Vogue*, *Rolling Stone* . . . His work made it onto the cover of all of them. He went on to receive three Grammy nominations for music videos he was a part of, including two for Mayluna, and he repeatedly made it onto lists like "Most Influential Black Photographers" and "Top 10 Greatest Music Photographers," alongside his heroes like Annie Leibovitz and Danny Clinch. You can see why we got along. Similar dreams can do that. I was glad when his came true.

~

Just before the show began that evening, I'd been standing backstage with Derek and the writer we'd been discussing, named Sylvia, glowering as usual and sucking the air out of the space. The music business was not for the faint of heart. It sniffed out weakness and ate nice people for breakfast. And yet, despite my tendency toward actual human kindness, it was the place where I felt like I belonged. Mostly because I knew that I was good at it. And the writers stuck together, often having each other's backs. Sylvia was an exception and universally disliked, partly because when it came to famous people and their entourages, one must always maintain the appearance of cool nonchalance and disinterest. She routinely broke this rule, constantly name-dropping about her days partying with this band or that. Never a good idea, considering the chances were very good that someone in the room had an even better story but also possessed the aplomb to keep it to themselves. And she also tended to spend a bit more time than necessary hanging around the tour buses and artists' dressing rooms, all the while laughing a little too loudly and batting her eyes. It was a cautionary tale, I suppose, and may be why I was hesitant when Carter and I first met.

But she was also to be avoided because she had a habit of poaching stories from junior writers. Case in point:

"So you're here to get a profile on Mayluna?" She brushed her inky bangs from her face and dug through the depths of her bag for a lighter. "Good luck with that. What's your name again?"

"Cameron," I told her for the umpteenth time. She always pretended to forget.

"I saw them last week. Mayluna," she told me.

"And?"

"They're good." She gave me a sideways glance. "Really good. Prepare for the unusual."

Damn, that was an annoyingly good line.

"You get anywhere with them yet?" She peered around the corner, toward the stage, as the energy began to build.

"A little." I knew enough to keep my cards close.

"Miss Vivien in the house." Just then, I turned to see Tommy strolling down the hall toward me, holding drumsticks, giving me a lazy grin. He was followed closely by Alex and their bass guitarist, Darren Andrews, preparing to take the stage.

Sylvia looked from Tommy, then to me, apparently noticing the familiarity of the exchange with curiosity.

"Vivien?" she asked. "But didn't you just say—"

I waved it off. "It's just a joke."

She narrowed her eyes, and then we stood in silence as the roar of anticipation from the crowd beyond climbed and the house lights dimmed. Just then, I felt the weight of another person suddenly pressed against my hip and shoulder. I knew it was him the millisecond before I looked. I turned to my left to see Carter, leaning against the wall beside me, our hips touching, and I couldn't help the slight smile that appeared.

"Hi there," he said. He'd changed his shirt, and it smelled of fresh laundry and something distinctly him. Of aged whiskey and powdery summer nights and earth. "Are you having a productive day so far?" He was nearly whispering, with mock politeness playing in his voice. It gave the impression of two people engaged in an intimate secret.

I replied in kind. "Yes, I am. Thank you for asking. And you?"

"Better than usual."

"I'm glad to hear it." The crowd beyond roared again as the stage lights swirled.

"How's the hand?"

"Better, thanks."

"So who was it—Virginia Woolf or Sylvia Plath?" He took a drink from a water bottle and twisted the cap back, setting it beside him on a road case, then folded his arms and leaned against the wall, like he had nothing better to do.

"Pardon?"

"The book you last took to the beach. I'm guessing . . . Woolf."

Who is this guy? "Neither, actually."

"Really?" He cocked his head. "I'm usually right about these things."

"Well, you're not." Not technically, anyway. "Don't you have someplace to be?" I gestured toward the stage.

"Okay. Fine. Don't tell me, then."

"If you must know, it was Graham Greene."

"Interesting. Nice taste."

"I'm so glad you approve."

"I'm an Austen fan myself." His tone was familiar and warm, like we had known each other for years, not hours, but playfully formal.

I laughed. "You are not."

Sylvia cleared her throat. I'd somewhat forgotten she was there until I felt her stare boring into the side of my face.

"Sorry, uh, this is . . ." I gestured to Sylvia.

"Well. I've gotta go. Stuff to do, you know?" he said, ignoring the introduction as if she didn't exist, then walking backward toward the stage, eyes locked on mine.

I made a show of glancing at my watch and raised a brow at him. "I imagine you have someplace important to be, yes?"

Sylvia quickly followed. "Carter? Hi, I'm Sylvia from—"

"No." He didn't even look at her when he said it. Dismissed her without so much as a glance. Eyes wide, Derek stifled a laugh with his fist as Sylvia was left cold, with her mouth hanging half-open. He really was a publicist's nightmare. Sylvia was one of the top reviewers in New York, not someone you wanted to offend.

"And we have massive partying to do at the gardening expo," he called over his shoulder, joking. I couldn't help but laugh at his teasing, even if it was at my expense. He slid a monitor over his ear and disappeared onto the side of the stage.

"What an arrogant asshole," Sylvia said, recovering.

I stood a little taller that night.

"Um." Derek leaned in, clearly amused. "What exactly was that?"

"I bumped into him in catering earlier." I shrugged and looked away as if it were nothing, while attempting to suppress a smile.

He gave me a look. "Uh-huh."

"Really. I bumped into him and got my story. Nice guy."

He raised an eyebrow, and Sylvia audibly scoffed. I could feel the heat of her glare as clearly as I could feel the heat of where he had pressed up against me.

"Okay, well, on that fascinating note, I'm heading down." Derek nodded toward the area at the front of the stage where local photographers had lined up.

I'd always loved the energy in the air as the show was just starting, standing at the base of the stage and looking out at the thousands of people while music resonated in my bones. Like the crackling air that precedes a thunderstorm. Moments later, from the press pit at the front of the stage, amid a sea of thousands, I watched the crowd as the sounds of Alex's guitar intro began playing through the massive speakers that towered two stories above me. Mayluna would come to be known best for their nighttime shows—they weren't a band that shone as well during the day. And while their production was minimal as an opening band that night, it hinted at the enormous productions that would one day be their future. Everything was cast in ghostly black and white, creating deep shadows, while a large screen behind displayed mesmerizing geometric shapes spinning slowly, the whole effect creating a kind of trancelike setting.

As the slow burn of the music played, Carter appeared, somehow completely transformed from the man I'd just interacted with. He walked out onto the stage, his features lit only from above, and took his position at the microphone, head down at first, his face in shadow as he began to sing. I understood immediately why he had been called "haunted." And while previously brought to reverent silence, when he eventually looked up, the crowd went wild. Despite being the opener, I could already see they would become stars.

Beside me, Derek followed every movement, capturing it on film in a distinctive style that would come to be well known as the years went on.

Carter sauntered deliberately and dramatically over the stage, pouring the music out to the crowd now clamoring at his feet. When he looked over and spotted me standing there, the corners of his mouth turned up ever so slightly, and he strolled over. He stopped just short of where I stood and stared down at me as he sang the lyrics to one of the biggest songs of the summer. After a moment, he was gone, and when he winked goodbye, time stopped just a little.

We often joked about that wink. No matter the prodding I gave him, he always maintained resolute innocence, refusing to admit that he had known the effect it would have on me. "You probably pulled that wink thing a dozen times before, at every show," I'd say, teasing him. "Make that one special girl in the audience's knees buckle. It's a good trick." He would shake his head and laugh. Insisted otherwise. Insisted that he barely made it through that performance, wanting to jump off the stage and disappear with me.

What he saw in me that night, I'll never know.

~

Later, I stood to the side of the stage as a group of about twenty promotional winners from a radio station huddled in anticipation, waiting to be escorted into a meet and greet with The Evolution. As I quietly watched from the corner, they glanced at the Local All Access pass that dangled around my neck with an expression I'd come to recognize. The look that asked, *How on earth did you get this job?*

Yes, I wanted to respond, *it is quite glamourous. Raymond Tompkins actually threw up on my favorite boots last month. And I was in the room when a doctor shoved an IV line of some sort of cocktail into Glenn Brixton's arm to prepare the seventy-two-year-old to strut his stuff onstage. "Just tuning the instrument, darlin'," he'd said when he spotted me watching. Fabulous stuff, really. What can I say, living the dream. Great job? Yes. Always wonderful? No.*

As Mayluna filed past from the stage and Carter noticed me once again, he slowed, sweat glistening on his face from the heat and the performance.

"Are you following me?" he asked, glancing at me with a playful expression. Nearby, a teenage girl, one of the winners from the radio station promotion, looked from him to me and then back to him again, eyes wide.

"Following you? Something like that. I guess I must find you irresistible. Seems to be catching," I quipped before instantly regretting it. I might as well have slapped a name tag on my chest with the name SYLVIA written on it.

Someone pushed a ticket stub and a Sharpie toward him, and he paused, signing it quickly as he bit his cheek with a smile. He looked up at me sideways, beneath hooded eyes, held my gaze intently for a few moments, and then:

"I think I know exactly what you mean." His eyes flickered, and then he was gone. Disappearing behind a black door.

By that point in my career, I'd met dozens of musicians, big and small. Men and women who made a living being irresistible to an audience, while I always remained passively immune. And yet this one, on this night, was the only one to make time freeze.

Twenty minutes later, they had left the building.

I figured he was gone for good and that would be that.

June 1998

By Cameron Leigh

STARGAZING WITH MAYLUNA

(DRAFT)

WATCH THE MIDNIGHT SKY closely and you just might see Mayluna shining like a comet that's only getting brighter the closer it gets to us here on Earth.

It's been nearly five years since four schoolboys from northern England reunited from the days of their youth and decided to see what would happen if they gave this music thing a real shot. Fresh off the release of their first album and finding themselves equally fresh off the proverbial boat in the midst of an American tour as the opener for The Evolution, Mayluna isn't an easy band to reach, and to do so feels a lot like chasing the stars that dot their sky.

"When I was a kid, I used to wonder what it would be like to be on that big stage. But I didn't see it for myself. I always saw myself kind of behind the scenes or something." Carter Wills is leaning over a cup of decidedly un-rock-'n'-roll Earl Grey tea that he's selected from the catering table backstage before the show at Jones Beach. Later, he'll add a dash of honey and a heavy helping of Macallan Classic. He wears a haunted look and gives the impression of someone who sees more moon than sun. A simple white T-shirt contrasts sharply with the dark geometric ink along his arms. Seeming to regret speaking, and with something resembling a smile, he immediately adds, "God, that sounds like such a load of BS now, all things considered, but it's true."

There's a self-effacing nature to him that borders on the kind of self-loathing, musical-genius dichotomy that has been the hallmark of more than one lead singer in rock 'n' roll's famed halls.

Moments earlier, I'd spilled my own cup of tea on my hand, and the lead singer and guitarist with the dark, enigmatic reputation was disarmingly thoughtful in a way that illustrates how he turns pain into honey in the lyrics he pens. But make no mistake, he can also cut someone with a look.

Having played the indie circuit first in York and then in Manchester, Mayluna went from scraping by on a 4 p.m. set played to friends at seedy North London dives to a side-stage Glastonbury performance that sent shock waves throughout the music industry, with reviewers running the gamut. With a London sound that's been compared to a mix of Radiohead and U2, they've been called everything from the less favorable "rock's sensitive little brother" to, more impressively, "The Rolling Stones of Gen X."

Neither seems to be true, as they appear to be paving their own new trail. And as a wave of near-euphoria greets the band when they take the stage, the audience—at least those in the know—seems simultaneously mesmerized by the music and by Wills's performance, which elicits moments of hushed anticipation followed by roars of enthusiasm from the fans who have shown up for them. Transfixed by the spinning sixteenth-century geometric designs and Wills's magician-like persona, the majority of the audience may have come to see The Evolution, but by the end, it's Mayluna who casts the spell.

When I mention this to him later in the night, Wills seems amused, a kind of reluctant laugh that causes the corners of his eyes to crinkle, somewhat incongruous to the performer onstage. I tell him that the night's show was sold out and that there had been 15,000 people in the crowd. "They weren't here for us," he clarifies. Then adds, "Well, maybe a few, but who knows."

Despite his twenty-six years, there's a weariness to him already that I suspect may have as much to do with his nocturnal nature (he claims he rarely sleeps and has more nightmares than dreams) as it does with the past two and a half decades of life that have come with their own set of challenges. Wills started out on piano with the band; his brother, Jacob, was the original lead singer, prior to his sudden death in the year before the band signed their first record deal with Paramour Records.

Noel Gallagher and Michael Stipe, among others, have been known to check out Mayluna's gigs. "I remember," Wills continues, "just after we'd played at Shepherd's Bush—looking out into this group of press, with people I'd admired watching from the side of the stage, and thinking, *Oh, shit, I've gotten myself into some trouble here. It wasn't supposed to be like this.*" He says this with a resigned shake of the head, insinuating that it was supposed to be his brother in the lead.

I tell him that outside the backstage gate, there are enough fans screaming for Mayluna (and Wills, in particular) that it's difficult to know just who is headlining this tour—Mayluna or The Evolution—and he winces. "Trust me, it's The Evolution. We're just grateful they've invited us to tag along."

This is not a person who is eager for fame. It's the music that matters, which he admits sounds like a nauseating cliché but somehow registers as authentic. He doesn't seem concerned or even aware of the rock-star persona that so many others take time to craft and agonize over, mostly because he would never describe himself as a star, though it's clear that's exactly what he is—or, at least, has the potential to be. "You can't think of yourself that way, otherwise you become equally obsessed with everyone who says you're not one."

He has enough noise in his head; he doesn't need the opinions of the entire world in there too.

The story of their origins seems to change each time they're asked, but it generally goes that Mayluna was formed when Tom Rollins strolled by the row house where the Wills brothers lived in a hamlet outside of York, somewhere around four in the morning, and heard music.

"I had recently moved to town and was pretty much still just a kid, but when I heard what was going on behind that door, I wanted to be a part of it," Rollins, who prefers to go by Tommy, says. After a series of changes and a couple of years off, they reunited with another friend from adolescence, guitarist Alex Winters, whose frequent presence at the Heavenly Sunday Social club nights made famous by the Chemical Brothers, seems perplexing at first and yet somehow not. They joined forces with bassist Darren Andrews, who was studying art in London at the time. "The neighbors hated us," Wills jokes again, talking of their early rehearsal days in a cramped flat in Camden Town.

With a distinctive sound that's a little melancholy yet oddly catching, Mayluna has come about as a distinctive contradiction to the testosterone-fueled alternative rock and grunge scene in the US, with equal doses of poison and poetry. Wills does all of the preliminary writing, though credit is given equally to all four.

But with their success has come some backlash. There have been rumors surrounding addictions; the death of the aforementioned original lead singer, Jacob Wills; tempers; and the reclusive nature of Carter Wills—all chipping away at the empire that four British boys—and a growing legion of fans—are still building.

Within minutes of coming offstage, the band is mobbed by a small group outside the back gate near the entrance to their bus. Wills, keeping his head down, leaves the minimal interactions—just the barest wave—to Rollins, the affable drummer with a long stride and an easy smile, while Winters and Andrews are nowhere to be seen, and I begin to see why Wills wonders if they're going to be able to handle this newfound fame.

The bunker-mentality friendship among them is evident, and perhaps that's part of the reason why things are going well. Winters, frequently perched on a road case in the dark shadows of the hallways amid a cloud of smoke, watches like a protective gargoyle throughout the day, wary of outsiders.

Wills rolls the tip of his finger in lazy circles around the top rim of his cup of tea as I ask if he's worried that the band's brightly burning star might burn out. He's not. Because as confident as he is in their trajectory, he knows it could just as easily disappear—something he seems to have accepted as equally possible.

"If anyone ruins it in a way that matters, it'll be us. There won't be anyone to blame but ourselves. But we really are just getting started, so who knows what could happen. We could be forgotten tomorrow. But even if we lost our record deal and the next album tanked and everything went to hell, we'd carry on playing and being the best of mates and enjoying the music we create together. We've gone through so much worse than that, that's for sure."

Onstage, Wills is a combination of seductively minimal and cocksure swagger that follows him offstage in the same kind of way a tiger gives you the sideways glance just before he struts back into his lair. He could eat you for breakfast but would rather be a gentleman. It's a delicate balance of light and dark. At least for now, light seems to be winning. Case in point, he asks about my hand again, reminding me to keep the ice on it.

Offstage, they all separately use words that are similar when asked about their success—"odd," "surreal," "madness," as if they're still acclimating to the bewildering odyssey they've been on since their first single, "Moonstar," caught the attention of a local radio station and got them signed to their record deal while Wills and Rollins were still at university studying math and philosophy, and engineering, respectively. Ladies and gentlemen, these aren't your average rock stars.

Their debut self-titled EP, *Mayluna*, has been hovering around the top of the British charts all year and has begun blowing up college radio and alternative charts in the US, but when asked about his prediction for the band's future, Wills takes it all in stride, with a gentle tone above tough, worn boots.

"To keep the dream alive and make a living at it, and hope that somewhere along the way, someone will think that the music we made mattered."

Are they enjoying success at all? Or do they find the growing fame claustrophobic?

"It's easier for the rest of us," says Rollins, lounging across a black leather sofa with long, sapling limbs in the band's dressing room. He tosses a mop of blond hair from his eyes and when not talking, seems to be in his own kind of spacey wonderland of ease, while maintaining a close eye on the others. The laconic Andrews passes by, offering a mere nod in agreement, as Rollins continues. "I do what I do and can walk off the stage and down the street and nobody knows who I am. The pressure is all on Carter, or at least, it will be, and we know it. When we made the EP, an indie little affair, no one was watching. Now everyone is, and it's a very different energy."

They're taking regular breaks on the tour while writing their first album. Pressures are high for it to be a massive success, and they're well aware of what's at stake. To be fair, while the stars may be aligning in their favor amid their apparent insouciance when it comes to success, they're not about to take anything for granted.

"Five years ago, I was just a kid from a small village outside of York, with the limited experiences of my little world," reflects Wills. "I don't mean that in a bad way. But it was small. The colors are brighter and fuller now, and the world has become a very, very big place. There will always be good and bad in that. We're learning to enjoy it, or at least to take it as it comes. But it'll take time; nothing is a guarantee."

He takes an infinite pause before looking up. "And sometimes you just have to trust that the universe will surprise you. Usually when you least expect it."

14

EVIE

Sometimes I wonder about that little feature assignment that catapulted me into a new galaxy. Originally just six hundred words. Started out as a long shot. Assigned by a magazine editor who I later learned considered it to likely be an empty pursuit with an uncooperative, nothing band. A standard review that could've been assigned to anyone.

Instead, a few days later, when I turned it in alongside Derek's photos as a bold 1,500 words—the first substantial interview with Carter Wills to ever go on record—things started to change in more ways than one. A pebble dropping into the water, the rings continuing outward. Words that turned into a story that turned into a film assignment that turned into a lifetime.

The elusive musician, and every word he'd spoken, had spun in my head like a spider's web in sparkling patterns over every surface of my world. While he eventually said something similar about me. Amazingly.

It was an unusual time—between that first day of meeting and the ones that would eventually follow. In those hours, those days afterward, I frequently found myself brushing a finger over the soft pink burn from the tea on my hand, watching it fade, just as his existence had from that night, until it disappeared entirely. I was left imagining the exact spot where he'd held the ice. He had that way about him with me—his gentle nature contrasting with the harsh edges of his more public self. People didn't know that side of him. Well, a few did maybe.

When I travel back there in my mind now, I see it as a kind of black empty space, peaceful and quiet, where points of possibility shimmered in waiting. The beautiful unknown, he called it.

As Carter tells it, everything we'd talked about, and the advice I'd given him about the press, had stuck with him, helped the band see that their reticence about the press could be an attribute instead of a flaw. He said that it eased a bit of the pressure.

Just after the story came out, I got a call from Paramour Records. It turned out that at the same time as our interview, an idea had been percolating within the record label, unbeknownst to me. A video they were considering. It just so happened that it coincided with the conversation I had with Carter. Synchronicity at its best. The next thing I knew, I was being asked if I'd be interested in filming a kind of mini-documentary, a promotional piece to generate buzz for the upcoming album. Meant to cover the band's experience on their first American tour and the production of the album—a behind-the-scenes look at the demanding balancing act of promoting, performing, and writing while becoming the new biggest thing in rock music.

It was one of those pinch-me kind of moments, and I remember looking at the phone in my hand and wondering if they had called the right person. When I said as much, they said that the band surprised them by revisiting the idea with their publicist and, in the process, one of them (Carter, most likely) had floated my name. I remember asking why they wouldn't be hiring someone with more experience. A bigger name, perhaps. But apparently that was part of the appeal—a fresh, new approach by a promising new talent, they'd said. Just like them. A perfect artistic match. Still, I wondered, and knew better than anyone not to look forward to something until it actually happened.

But sure enough, it was true. Before I knew it, they were sending information. That's how these opportunities happen sometimes. A coincidence of timing. Carter would disagree with that, of course, and I can't help but smile now as I think about it. "There are no coincidences, Ev," he would say. "You put the idea out into the universe, and if it's in your potential to match, it'll happen. It's a grand orchestration."

The band had a break for a few days, and they wanted me to spend some time with them first to get a feel for things. The details would be forthcoming, but I was tasked with sketching out a few concept ideas while I was there, after which I would send them to the label.

When I'd left the venue the night after that first show, heading home on my own, my life could have easily continued just the same as it had before—with me going to work, coming home to a quiet apartment, one day after the next, a routine that went on into the years. And that was what I'd expected. Because it was safe not to imagine something better—the best way to avoid disappointment.

So I suppose I'd never let myself imagine I would see him again. Not in a meaningful way, at least.

But that's the funny thing about the universe—it has such wondrous possibilities for us, far beyond anything we could imagine for our own lives. Even yours, Lainey. Even when it seems like life is going to be a series of predictable days. All we have to do is open our eyes and believe in them: the possibilities.

Expect the unexpected and that's where you'll find the magic.

That's what he liked to tell me.

And it's what he would tell you.

15

Evie

Just like I always have, I'd often be restless throughout the night back then, giving up on sleep, kept company by the hooting owls in the maple trees outside my door. When the sun rose, sometimes I'd just stay up and work, and other times I'd crawl back into bed. On the morning he called, around ten, I'd just picked my head up off the pillow and started a shower, ignoring the phone. When it rang again a few minutes later, I reluctantly picked up.

"Hello?" I answered.

"So I met this girl who gave me the brilliant idea to go to the beach." His voice was unmistakable, and I snapped awake as my stomach leaped and I laughed.

"Uh, yes, I think I remember something about that. You're the guy I met the other day out food shopping, right?"

"Exactly. I love that I'm so memorable."

"How did you get my number?"

"I'm the resourceful type." Carter paused a beat, then admitted, "I asked Fred to get it from the label."

"I see. So the beach . . . taking my advice, huh?"

"Yes. About several things. Bit of a muse, aren't you?" He paused for a moment. I imagined a smile on his face. "What are you doing at the moment?"

I looked at my reflection, wide-eyed in the steam of the mirror, wondering: *Why exactly is Carter Wills on my phone?*

"Working," I lied.

"Is that water running?"

I rolled my eyes, clutching a towel around me with my free hand, and left the bathroom.

"Uh, could you hold on for just a moment?"

"Okay, but don't take too long." He sounded amused. "There's good sunshine being wasted."

I set the phone down, staring at it in disbelief for a moment, before turning off the shower and throwing on a T-shirt. The last thing I needed was to be on the phone with him while stark naked.

I took a breath, then picked it back up. "Sorry about that. You were saying . . ."

"And I hear from the label that you'll be spending some time with us, it seems. The watchful eye covering the inside scoop on a young band's rise to obscurity."

I smiled, narrowing my eyes then. "Did you have something to do with all this?"

"I didn't . . . *not* . . . have something to do with it."

I paused, waiting for him to elaborate before he eventually let out a breath. "Look, truth is they've been trying to get us to agree to doing something like this for a while. But the idea was truly horrible. I'd rather stick a fork in my eye than have some strange person in the room with a camera, judging everything about us, but—"

"Wonderful. This should go beautifully."

"But," he continued, "something about you made me think it could work. And then I saw what you wrote in the story . . . and even though I still sounded like complete shit, at least it was real, so I know I can trust you. Also, I *may* have watched your Green Witch film and passed it along."

"You've seen it?"

"Just a peek."

"And?"

"You're very good."

I smiled widely.

"And we thought maybe we'd give it a try. The promo film. We told them we'd agree to it if they left us alone and didn't make us do any more press for a while. The antipromotion tour."

"Oh, I'm sure they just loved that."

"But back to other important things. You forgot to give me directions to the beach, so I thought maybe you could be my tour guide and we'd drive out there together. Today. You know, like a traveling companion."

"I thought you all were going to be in the city—aren't we meeting at your hotel tomorrow and then the label?"

"So then let's just hang out a day early. For fun. Off the clock."

"Drive to the beach with you guys? On the bus?" I laughed, realizing that I was, by that point, so disoriented by the unexpected strangeness of this entire conversation that I needed to shake my head clear.

"Well, not exactly. Just me. I need some time alone for sanity." He paused a beat. "Or, not strictly alone, but you know what I mean."

"I don't typically spend a day at the beach with people I barely know."

"Isn't that the whole idea behind all of this? To get to know me? Or . . . us? More precisely."

My face had begun to hurt; I was smiling so hard, but I tried to keep him from hearing it in my voice. "Professionally. Not to just hang out at the beach. And I have some prep work to do."

"But—"

"And for all I know, you could be a crazy person planning to kidnap me," I joked.

"Right. I see your point. And for all I know, I could have fallen prey to your diabolical plan to lure me to some remote beach location, where you would pull out all my secrets."

"Hmm. Remote beach location? Suddenly this isn't sounding so bad."

I dropped my head in my hand, cringing. I tended to lack a filter when I was flustered, and it had just slipped out. Fortunately, I was rewarded with a warm laugh from his end of the line.

"So does that mean you'll go, then?"

I was about to start the biggest project of my life alongside a band I was genuinely fascinated by. I couldn't afford to screw it up by getting tangled in something personal. We were dancing dangerously close to crossing a line that I couldn't afford to cross, and I think we both knew it.

"Are you still there?" he asked.

"Sorry, yes, I'm here."

"What do you think?"

I pinched my eyes closed. "You know, I'd love to. Believe me. But . . . I feel like I should probably not."

"I was afraid you might say that." I could hear the disappointment in his voice.

"It was nice of you to call, though. And honestly, I'm really grateful that you guys are giving it a chance. Giving *me* a chance. And I hope you have a really great drive and a nice afternoon. It's beautiful outside. And I'll see you all in a day or so."

He sighed dramatically. "Okay. Well then, I guess I'll see you when *your* people coordinate all the details with *our* people. Formally."

"Right."

"Right." There was a long pause, in which normal circumstances would warrant a goodbye. But these weren't normal circumstances.

"So are you guys already in the city?" I asked eventually, mostly to fill the space.

"Actually, no."

"No?"

"Well, *they* are. I'm still at JFK. Figured it was a waste of time to head in an opposite direction, since I'd be going to the beach with you."

I picked up a pen, making deep, scarring doodles in a notepad. Stars and such. "Bit presumptuous, don't you think?"

"I already know you want to come."

"Do you, now?"

"I do. So just do it! It's only an afternoon. Beach. Food. Water. You said yourself you never do anything fun. And I'm guessing you're kind of a planner, huh?"

I smiled. "Sad but true."

"There's a lot to be said for spontaneity. You never know what can happen. Right?"

He made a good argument. I looked around at the walls of my apartment, suddenly appearing a bit devoid of life. "You know, you're very convincing."

"Is it working?"

"Do you always get what you want?" I asked.

"No. I don't." There was an earnestness to this. "But I'm hoping maybe I will today."

I didn't say anything for a bit.

"Are you still there?" he asked.

"Okay. I'm in."

"Wonderful. I'll pick you up in thirty minutes."

"Wait! I don't even have anything ready for the beach. I'm going to need a little more time than that."

"What's to get ready? We're not going to a ball. You don't have to wear a gown."

I started tossing a few things in a small bag. "You won't be wearing a tuxedo?"

"First of all, I will never, in my life, wear a tuxedo."

"Never? Bet you do."

"Never," he reiterated. "And second . . ." We were both laughing then. The thought of him in a tuxedo at the beach, beyond ridiculous. "I'll see you in forty-five minutes. But that's all you get."

Of course, he did end up wearing a tuxedo in his life. On many occasions. Award shows, black-tie events, etcetera. Unfortunately, I wasn't there to say, *Told you so*. When I think of him wearing one, I always think of a night years later, standing in our living room. He was on TV wearing a tuxedo. His arm around Iliana Billings. A rumor that he was getting married. My chest constricting a little and the two of you playing with your dad nearby while I pretended everything was fine. Eventually, my night went on. There were a lot of times like that.

16

EVIE

There are some decisions you make in life that you know at the time may be questionable. I was still concerned about the boundaries thing at that point, and it weighed heavily on me during those early times and particularly on that day at the beach. I was sensitive about it and afraid of how it might look. When you choose to ignore your intellect and follow that inner voice, it takes a little effort to quiet the chatter of the cynic inside you, judging your every move. It's an act of consciously choosing to trust that maybe life has some bit of playfulness hidden around the corner. So you take the chance and quiet the voice in your head and think with your heart instead. It's important to do this sometimes. Because otherwise, it's impossible to move forward. To live. Otherwise, we might as well just give up. An impetuous decision, perhaps, but the best one I ever made.

Carter showed up in my driveway in a black Jeep Wrangler that day, looking at me from behind dark sunglasses, saying hello with the kind of smile that is full of oceans of meaning. Like our seeing one another again was an inevitability.

We talked about work—both his and mine. "Getting to make your way doing something you love. It's a rare gift, isn't it?" he said.

I told him about the stacks of *Rolling Stone* and *Creem* magazines—old ones, new ones—at home when I was growing up. Even a few *Melody Makers* when I could find one. I'd read those incredible profiles that had been done in the '70s on Zeppelin and the Stones and the Who, and I loved seeing into that world. We talked about the upcoming project a little, discussing other films. Things like *Hype!* and *The Last Waltz*. I'd just seen what Dave Markey had done with Sonic Youth and the festival tour in Europe and at my recommendation, he said he'd watch it.

"I saved up money to buy a used VHS camcorder and spent most of my weekends going to shows in town. And that pretty much sums up the social life of my teen years," I told him.

He laughed and shook his head. "You and Tommy will get along famously."

"Really?"

He looked over at me. "Yeah. You'll see."

A moment later, he asked, "Did you grow up here? New York?"

"No, I'm from a small town north of Philadelphia. I moved here after school."

"No boyfriend waiting at the end of the day, then?" He darted a glance my way, and I couldn't help but smile.

"Okay, I can see we're going to have to get this out of the way," he said when I didn't answer. "I have an idea."

"Yes?"

"How about for today, we're just . . . two friends."

"Friends?" I raised my eyebrows.

"Okay . . . two very normal people hanging out, heading to the beach, chatting about life. No band. No story. No film. No interviewer and interviewee. Just us. Carter and Cameron. Deal?"

"Sounds messy." I didn't like messy.

"It doesn't have to be. Our professions don't define who we are."

I worked very hard at keeping things tidy and structured. It was how I maintained peace in my life. Maybe I tried too hard sometimes.

I thought about it and finally replied, "You're right."

"Good. That's settled."

"But . . . one thing?" I added.

"Yes?"

"My name's not really Cameron. It's Evie."

He burst into a laugh. "Ha! I knew you didn't look like a Cameron! Evie . . . short for Evelyn?"

I nodded.

"Evie," he said again, softly. I liked the sound of him saying it. It was so rare that I heard my name those days. Even Derek called me "Cam."

"That's very pretty. I like it. Suits you much more. Why don't you use it?"

I told him that an androgynous name had been helpful in pitching stories, which it was at the time. There were other reasons I preferred anonymity, but I kept those to myself. The only people in my professional world who knew my true name were the payroll personnel, and they couldn't care less if my name was Minnie Mouse. Evelyn Waters was one person. Cameron Leigh was another.

"An alter ego. Very intriguing." He smiled.

"And also . . . no," I said finally. "No boyfriend."

"Good to know." He gave me a sideways look, and the corners of his mouth turned up just slightly. "Surprising, though."

He fumbled with the radio a bit before the sounds of the Psychedelic Furs' "The Ghost in You" began playing.

"I love this song," I told him.

"Oh, well, now I know it's meant to be," he replied, and I glowed inside.

As he drove down the coastal road, he started to sing along, his voice melting into the wind. A song about newspapers lying and loss and times gone by, how falling for someone would be so complicated in the world of public life, and of stars and of love . . . love.

Now that I think about it, it's funny, that song on that day. Little prescient messages from the universe.

17

EVIE

We didn't feel like strangers, but rather like we'd found someone who had been missing for a lifetime and then suddenly there they were. Puzzle pieces sliding into place, my nervous system both stirring and calming in the most remarkable way in his unusual presence.

On our way to the beach that day, we drove at a lazy speed, as if we had all the time in the world, which I suppose we did back then. A beach hut that came alive with live music at night was quiet as we picked up lunch after navigating down Dune Road, past views of stunning houses and the bay and eventually to my favorite spot—by the inlet on the westernmost point of Cupsogue Beach. On one side was the Atlantic Ocean, with waves and a few kids playing in the low surf. To the right were the waters of the bay.

Do you remember that thin tapestry I never let you borrow? You thought it was because it was some '90s relic that used to hang on my dorm room walls. But that wasn't it. It was because I forever associated it with that day and couldn't bear the thought of anything happening to it. We lay side by side on that tapestry, our skin turning golden.

"Thank you for being here," he told me. He reached over and spun a turquoise beaded anklet above my bare foot. "This is nice."

There was an unspoken intimacy in that gesture. The electricity coursing through my veins, originating from the point where his hand had touched my ankle. "The day or the anklet?" I asked.

He smiled. "Both."

We had a conversation at one point, about bands on the road and the lifestyle that comes with it. "We're not all the cliché, I promise," he reassured me. Then he waffled a bit. "Well, I mean, we're not *always* like that, anyway."

"You don't have a girl in every town who you randomly call on Tuesday mornings to go to the beach with you?" I joked.

He laughed. "Not so far." I remember how thoughtful he looked when he turned more serious and continued. "It would be easy to fall into that kind of life. Except that it's not really me. Never has been, I guess. I don't like to waste my time and energy that way." He watched me for a moment. "Is that why you said no at first? Is that what you were worried about?"

"No, not really. It wasn't that. It's the rest of it. My job mostly."

And the fact that I promised myself I would never get involved with a musician.

"Okay, good. Well, at least that part is settled. Because this"—he gestured in a small circle between us with his finger—"is definitely not typical for me. At all." He narrowed his eyes, smiling. "Okay? Okay then," he repeated, settling the issue.

"But just so you know . . . ," I added. "This *is* typical for me. The norm," I teased.

"Is that right?" He smiled at the joke.

"Absolutely, I block off every Tuesday. Multiple days, really. Whoever played in town that weekend, I end up at the beach with them, half-naked in a bikini. It's just what I do. The invitations abound. I have to choose the cutest guy. Usually the lead singer, but not always. You'll do." I shrugged and winked at him.

"Oh, I see! Good to know where I stand!" He laughed gamely at my obvious joke and then stood. "All right, you. Come on, let's go." He took my hand and tugged me to my feet, taking us to the water.

"I should warn you, this isn't the kind of water to swim in," I told him. "The currents are unpredictable near the inlet. I usually just cool off in the shallow parts."

He pulled me along into the water. "Come on. I'll keep you safe."

It was as if someone had given him a manual—a playbook of things to say. He had an uncanny way of making comments that felt like a vitamin I hadn't realized I'd been deficient in. Nourishing.

"The sea where I grew up is pretty rough. Very different kind of water—and freezing cold all the time—but still, beautiful," he told me. "I don't go in much."

I gestured into the distance, where a few surfers sat waiting. "No surfing for you?" The suggestion seemed to amuse him, and he shook his head. "What?" I asked.

"I've sorta got a thing about sharks." I think it might have been the only thing I'd ever heard him say he was afraid of, and I still think he was mostly joking. He was fearless, which, to me, was dazzling.

Something about the way he said it made me giggle, and I pretended to write it down. "Oh, that's definitely going on the record. Sharks."

He cocked his head. "Oh, really? Now who's the one who should be nervous? Hmm?"

"Don't worry. I'll keep you safe." I echoed his earlier comment. The warmth that spread through me as I said it was reflected equally in the way his eyes softened. After a beat, I added, "Well, I'll keep your words safe, anyway. I don't know what I can do about the rest of it."

"Is that all? Just my words?"

"Mm-hmm."

He was standing just inches away from me, the water glistening on his skin. His gaze left my eyes and moved down, landing on my mouth. I thought he might kiss me then, but just like that, he was gone, making me laugh as he dove under, picked me up, and brought us splashing into the water.

That was a perfect day. A warm, sandy blanket; piping plovers darting this way and that; the salty water; and watching the sun cross the sky. When the sun started to dip, he reached into his bag and pulled out an extra shirt. Soft, worn chambray, a bit tattered at the cuffs. "You're getting cold," he told me, wrapping it around my shoulders.

I walked back down to the water's edge one last time in an attempt to hold on to the fleeting day. As the cool water danced around my feet, I felt his warmth behind me. He took my hand in his and slowly turned me around to face him, brushing the windblown hair away from my face and adjusting the collar on the shirt. He met my eyes for a long moment and took a step closer.

"We can't do this," I whispered, the words taking every bit of strength.

"Why." He said it like a challenge.

"You know why. Carter, I've worked . . . so hard to get here. You have no idea how hard. And I can't mess it up. I can't get involved like this. It's too confusing."

"Evie, I care about this project. I promise I will do whatever I can to make sure it goes well. For all of us."

I looked away, but he turned my head back to face him. "Okay?"

When I nodded, a smile began to form on his face. "Just consider yourself warned."

"Warned, eh?"

"I think there's a whole lot more going on here than just the film. But we can pretend a little longer if you'd like."

I rolled my eyes and laughed, exasperated. "This is ridiculous. I can't objectively do a profile piece on a band when I'm sleeping with the lead singer!"

The moment it came out of my mouth, my cheeks flushed crimson, and he cocked his head as devilish amusement danced into his eyes.

"Ohhh, now who's being presumptuous?" He laughed, clearly enjoying the moment.

"Oh, stop it. You know what I mean." I walked away so he couldn't see me laugh.

"Fine. But I'll have you know that I had only the utmost gentle-manly intentions with you," he called.

I spun around and gave him a look, picking up my bag.

He put his hands up. "Truly. You won't get a single bit of impropriety from this moment on. Strictly business."

I put my hands on my hips stubbornly. "Ugh. I'm writing about the sharks."

"Try it." His eyes danced, turning dark.

I swallowed, melting. After recovering, I sighed. "All right, c'mon. It's getting late and we have a drive ahead of us," I said, changing the subject.

"You're not coming to the house?"

I stopped. "What house?"

"Oh, right, so about that."

That's when he told me that instead of spending time with them in the city to discuss the film, as had been the original plan over the next few days, the band had rented a beach house—just up the road, in fact. A change in the itinerary he'd conveniently neglected to mention.

"You are supposed to be living alongside us, after all," he said. "So . . ."

"Alongside. Not *with*. Big distinction. I have a meeting with the label in a few days, and in the meantime, I have work to do, and I think we're supposed to be coming up with some ideas. Seeing . . . I don't know . . . what the chemistry is like."

He raised a brow. "Oh, really? And how would you say the chemistry is going so far?"

He was incorrigible.

"Don't worry, it's a very big house," he added a moment later.

"How do you know? You haven't even seen it."

"Okay, you win. But let's at least have dinner somewhere. I know you're hungry."

I narrowed my eyes. "What are you up to?"

"Just trust me."

Trusting him was never a problem for me, for the record. Not really, anyway. It was trusting myself that often needed some work.

18

CARTER

We had rented this beach house where we were supposed to be working on new songs for a few days, but really, we just needed a break. Our record label was on us hard about promoting the new album, and we'd been uncooperative, unsurprisingly. We were exhausted. We were just kids, really, in our midtwenties, and so turned around from going from one town to the next, we barely knew up from down. I had been completely stalled, creatively, and couldn't take being in some generic hotel room. Something about that beach house turned out to be perfect. An energy about it. It reminded us of the ocean back home as kids, being near to the sea, and gave us space to breathe and just exist for a bit, having fun.

She never knew this part, but the label had been planning to send out another writer to go on the road with us at first. The original idea was for it to be a series of interviews that would take place throughout multiple cities on the tour and in the studio as we were writing, all filmed. Obviously, this was pretty much our worst nightmare.

This horrid woman, Sylvia I think was her name, was one of the top music writers at the time, and she had been at the show at Jones Beach. My guess is that maybe she caught wind of it and nabbed the idea, though I'm not sure. Anyway, we refused, but the label wouldn't hear a word of it. They'd begun making threats of dropping us if we didn't start cooperating and doing more to promote the album. Of course, they would've never in a million years dropped us, not with things going the way they were. But we didn't know that at the time. Our manager, John, told us we needed to do it. That we would have to agree to let one of the writers come out and spend time with us—we had no idea what that meant. What were they going to write about— what we ate for breakfast? We didn't understand how the whole thing worked. Finally, we agreed to potentially move forward, but we told them they had to look into another writer. John had managed to get an early copy of the story she had turned in, and when I told him about her film background, it caught his attention. She could write, film, and direct. There was some back-and-forth, I guess. I don't know the details. But finally, everyone agreed. Mostly, anyway.

She asked me later if it was me. If I'd arranged it all just as an excuse to be with her. I think she needed to know that she had gotten the project on her own merit and not because of something I had done. I told her the truth and that we'd agreed to let her—and only her—do the film. But that didn't really answer her question, did it?

"So was it all orchestrated by you? An excuse to be with her?" Michael asks.

"No. But I certainly made it work to my advantage, which makes me sound a bit manipulative, though I don't mean it that way. I was just a guy who had met the girl he was meant to be with, and as sometimes happens, things began to align for us. Divine opportunities and connections. When they insisted on the film, I saw my chance. But it only worked because she was so good at what she did. We trusted her."

She was concerned about objectivity at first. She knew that her reputation was on the line and that to get involved with any one of us could have damaged her credibility. I completely respected this. It was hard enough for women at the time to get into that sort of filmmaking. And to have people say she got it for reasons other than her skills would have been insulting, to say the least. So I was fully aware of her reservations.

But it was more than that. There was this delicate sort of fragility about her beneath all of her strength, and something inside me felt protective of her. People have always said that I'm guarded, but if the walls around me were ten feet tall, hers were ten feet thick.

That day at the beach, I gave her the space she needed to feel safe and in control of things. I sensed she needed this. I was careful about encouraging her to spend time with us at the house. She was originally going to just be there for dinner and then come back the next day. I think she was planning to stay at a local hotel, or maybe we were going to drive back. I can't remember now. But once she was there, it just felt natural. I'm sure she thought my idea about her being with us there was all some play at seduction on my part at first, but our goals were more aligned than she realized.

You see, the film was nearly entirely a go, and Tommy and I felt confident that she was the right person for it, maybe because we'd had a little more interaction with her at the show. Knew her tastes and sensibilities and felt she'd fit in well. But the others—especially Alex— weren't on board at all. And from the earliest beginning, all decisions had to be unanimous, so if he didn't agree, that would be it.

I knew that if we all met in some cold and sterile conference room at the record label, with her walking in completely professional, note-books and recorders and such, Alex would never in a million years go for it. He wouldn't have trusted her. It was Tommy's idea to have her spend time at the beach house instead. (I don't think she ever knew that.) To see if the fit would evolve more organically. I was completely on board, for obvious reasons.

They didn't make it easy on her at first, though.

"You were such a colossal asshole to her," Tommy tells Alex, who has been sitting quietly with his eyes closed as we talk.

"I truly was." Alex laughs somewhat regretfully, and I shake my head, recalling the way it unfolded.

"You have to give her credit, though; she held her own," I remind them.

"That she did," Tommy agrees.

Of course, she got the green light to move forward with the film. But I didn't realize how complicated it would become, how intertwined. To be fair, it wasn't convenient that we were falling for each other. But we were an inevitability.

And I suppose that's the theme here. From the moment I met her, it was too late to go back. She became part of us, from the moment she walked into our lives.

"I think we all fell a little bit in love with her, in one way or another," Tommy muses.

I glance over at Alex, and our eyes lock for a millisecond before he looks away.

"Some more than others, of course," Tommy adds after clearing his throat. "She was the yin to our yang. This calming presence in those early days. We were always a family, but then she became the fifth member of that family. For a while, anyway," he adds with a doleful smile.

"So she was around for the tour and for the year you were making the *Sigma Five* album, but what happened? I mean, there is no evidence of her in your career or personal life. No sign of her anywhere."

Even Alex has to laugh a bit at that, and I see the corners of his mouth turn upward beneath closed eyes.

"What?" Michael asks, noticing the apparent humor we found in his comment.

Alex replies. "You're not looking close enough."

19

EVIE

I absolutely loved that beach house the moment I saw it. We both did. Carter always said it was a little bit magical. Maybe it was. I had been so reluctant to go at first, not because I didn't want to, but I suppose I was just trying to be responsible. But Carter was right, of course. We were an inevitability. Eventually, we'd put all my concerns to bed, so to speak, simply by deciding on secrecy for a while, and inertia carried us forward after that.

I still remember the song that was playing when we walked in the front door—greeted by the cheery and unexpected sounds of Stevie Wonder's "Superstition." The bright foyer spanned the full height of the house and was flanked by a staircase winding upward to the second floor on one side and by a cozy den on the other. The living room had a view of the bay through floor-to-ceiling windows, with a canvas of stunning water, only made bluer by the slanting angle of the setting sun. On the far side of the open floor plan, the kitchen was occupied solely by Tommy, with his blond hair pulled into a ponytail, a one-man party amid a buffet of food preparation, dancing unabashedly to the music.

"Dinner 'somewhere,' huh?" I said, giving Carter a look.

"Tommy happens to be a great cook, believe it or not."

I cocked my head and laughed. "Oh, I see. Nicely played. The house it is, I guess."

"Miss Vivien! We meet again!" Tommy stretched his arms out widely in welcome.

Carter gave me a quizzical look, amused. "Vivien? How many names do you have?" he whispered.

"I see our ego-obsessed lead singer took the liberty of once again hogging all the press for himself. Typical," Tommy joked.

Carter flashed him a wry look. "What can I say, I want all the media to be about me."

I laughed, enjoying a brotherly kind of affection between the two of them that put me instantly at ease. "Nice to see you again, Tommy. I hear you all are trying to take a mental break from people like me. So I'll try not to get in the way too much."

"Nonsense." He waved me off. "Welcome to the party, Miss Leigh. It's good to see you . . . and maybe this one will finally shut up about you now that you're here." He grinned, winking at me. "It's been nonstop."

I raised an eyebrow at Carter as I sat at the breakfast bar. "Is that so?"

He shook his head and took a sip from a beer while offering one to me, as well. "Don't listen to a word he says."

Tommy was one of the most warmly charismatic people I'd ever met, with this infectious personality that was both lighthearted and sweet while full of depth. I think that's what made their music work so well—Carter's and Alex's darkness balanced out by the others' light.

He returned to the pile of jumbo shrimp that he was cleaning, tails and shells on every surface of the granite countertop. "I hope you two are hungry. We've got enough food to feed an army." The scent of Old Bay Seasoning filled the room from a steaming pot. "How about some margaritas? Cameron?"

Carter gave me another pointed look, teasing. "Oh, so we're just supposed to reveal ourselves to you, but you get to keep all your secrets. Is that how this works? *Cameron?*"

"What?" Tommy asked, noticing the exchange.

"Fine." I explained the name thing to Tommy then. "Now do you want my middle name too? Or is that enough?"

Carter smirked. "We'll get there."

"You are so annoying."

"Some might say charming."

"No one would say that," Tommy interjected, and tossed a kitchen towel over his shoulder. A minute later, he was singing again, this time the lyrics from "American Pie," rhyming my name with Chevy and levee and *Evvvvie*.

I laughed. "Do you always do that? With people's names? Associations and rhymes."

"Habit, I guess. Never forget a name, though. It's like a vault up here." He tapped his head. "Anyway, Evie, Cameron, whatever your name is, my dear, I present to you the world's best margarita. My secret recipe." I took a sip just as someone turned the corner.

"I believe you know Darren, yes?" Carter said, placing a hand on the man's shoulder. "What do you do around here, exactly?"

"I'm pretty sure I'm your nanny," he joked in reply.

"Nice to see you again, Darren," I said. The band's bass player was quiet and seemed perpetually lost in another world, peaceful in the way that a shadow always lingers nearby to a tree, providing shade in contrast to the blazing light. He warmly shook my hand, offering his welcome.

~

Alex, however, was a different story. His personality so perfectly matched his appearance, tall and thin with chiseled features and eyes that were so dark, they were nearly black, pushing everyone outward.

At one point on that first day, we all sat in the living room, furnished in British Colonial dark wood, indigos and pale blues, centered by a large sectional ivory linen sofa. French doors were opened out to a wide deck ending in a wooden dock that jutted out onto the dunes. I took the seat that was the farthest from Alex, who sat sprawled on one side. In the middle, Carter leaned back with one foot over his knee, absently twirling a finger over the rim of a beer bottle with his head resting on the back of the sofa.

"So how's this going to work?" Alex finally said, speaking to me for the first time. "Are you just going to what, record us for the next three days? Because that's not awkward or anything. Are you working right *now*?" he asked icily.

"Do I look like I'm working?" I gestured to the salt on my legs and the obvious beach attire.

"Just asking." Alex could be such a brat.

"It's just dinner," I assured him. "And no. Not yet."

"Just dinner? Is that so?" He looked at Carter. "And here I thought . . ."

"For fuck's sake, Alex. Can we just, I don't know . . . exist? Relax? Have dinner? Stop giving everyone a hard time," Carter snapped.

"Yes, but the whole point is to see if we can all work together. Live together, even. Is it not?" Alex replied. "So tell us, Evie, is it? What's it going to be like, on a night like tonight, only . . . later. When you *are* working."

"My job is to be a fly on the wall. To document it all. To tell your story," I replied simply. "You'll barely know I'm there."

"And you'll have a camera—what, the whole time?"

"Sometimes I'll have a camera. Sometimes I'll have an audio recorder. Sometimes I'll just be writing."

"Writing?"

"They want a story to accompany the release of the film, so I'll be writing at the same time."

"Great. Starting when?" He leaned forward and narrowed his eyes. "Are you writing right now, for instance? Observing?"

"I'm always writing. Occupational hazard. And we're supposed to be putting some ideas together, after all. To take it to the label and see what they think. But you guys decided to go to the beach instead. So here I am."

"Okay, well then, let's just start. Shall we? Give it a go. Just for fun. Do you have a tape recorder in your bag right now?" He looked at the canvas bag that sat at my feet. I always had those things. Just a habit. Which I suppose he'd guessed. Alex had a talent for reading people quickly. I nodded.

"Perfect. Get it out. Let's do an interview right now. Just to get a feel for it."

I reached in and took it out, setting it flat on the table between us, and pressed the red "Record" button as the miniature cassette tape begin to swirl. Carter and Alex looked down at it, and Fred did the same as he joined us on the sofa.

"Okay, so let's get started, then," I said. "Something easy? Alex, tell me about the first concert you ever went to."

He looked at me pointedly for a moment before he sat up, reached a long arm across the table, picked up my beloved tape recorder, and, with a perfectly slow arc, threw it out the open doors, where it crashed onto the deck, scattering pieces in every direction. I swear it was cursed, that thing.

The corners of his mouth turned up as he looked at me, crossing his arms. "Okay, now that that's settled . . . first concert, you asked?"

Carter shook his head and sighed into his hand.

And that was how my first conversation with Alex Winters began. Charming, wasn't he?

I'm thinking about those first days with Alex now, and all I can do is smile, with my heart filling my entire chest. But back then? All I could think about was what a complete asshole move that had been. At that point, I nearly walked out. But I took a deep breath and reminded myself—I hadn't gotten this far by letting men like Alex Winters bully me into skulking away into a corner. It was a standoff. And I needed to win.

"Great, okay then," I said with some degree of sarcasm. "Everyone feeling more comfortable?" I met eyes with Alex and didn't so much as blink.

He smirked. "Much."

"Are you done now?" Carter asked. "Can we move on? Or are you going to throw another temper tantrum?"

"Hey, look, I just figure, if we're buddies and all, hanging out at the beach all day together—nice tan by the way," he said, giving Carter a look and Carter flipped him off, "then why would we need to record anything? Right?" He looked at me. "We'll just see how it goes."

I leaned over and extended a hand to Alex. "Sounds like a plan."

He looked up with dark eyes and reached over, shaking it in return with a strong hand. "In that case, pleasure to meet you, Evie."

"I really think you should consider a new line of work," Carter joked to me.

"Oh, is that so? So you want me to leave, then? Okay." I pretended to stand, and he reached out and tugged me back down by the back pocket of my shorts as both Alex and Fred took notice of the exchange, the inherent intimacy of the gesture.

Fred started chuckling as he took a loud sip from his margarita, which was a drink that was a humorous contrast to the burly man. "I've got to give you credit, kid. You don't flinch much, do you?" He leaned over and clinked my glass, and the tension in the room began to evaporate.

I let out a breath and dug into my bag for effect. "So, Alex, how do you feel about . . . pens?"

There was a moment of silence, and then I got a rare gem—something almost resembling a laugh—from Alex. "Good god, do you ever just have a conversation? Somebody get this girl another drink!"

Carter gave me an amused look. "See, it's not just me."

"Okay, fine! Fine," I said, laughing, putting my hands up and tossing the pen. "You all win." I leaned back into the comfortable sofa and took a long drink. "No talk of work until tomorrow."

"What on earth made you want to get into this business?" Fred asked. "Dealing with a terrible lot like us all the time."

I told him I'd been hooked on it from an early age, from the music I'd listened to growing up and the first time I'd been to a concert (a friend's parents had taken me). We'd had seats on the side, in a position where I could catch glimpses of the work going on behind the stage, and I'd been fascinated by the process. I told him about the assignments at local clubs I'd managed to snag while still in high school.

"I bet you got a nasty dose of reality," Fred said. "Sweet girl like you. Mummy and Daddy were probably worried sick. Giving you money for emergencies and dropping you off at the front door, worried sick."

I thought of the trailer where I grew up and the way I'd hustled for bus money to get into the city for the first assignment I ever worked, stealing two dollars from my father's wallet while he slept off a drunken stupor on a broken couch. Trudging through ice in black boots, the one coat I owned barely keeping me warm on a frigid night. I'd missed the last bus home and slept on the bench in the train station. When I finally got in the next morning, my father was on the sofa smoking a cigarette and watching television. He didn't even look up. Just asked me to make him breakfast. "Yeah. Exactly. Worried sick."

A look passed over Carter's face that told me he'd seen something more behind those words.

"You know, I like this girl," Fred said. "She's got it right. She's like us. Behind-the-scenes people. Not your pampered pansy asses." He pointed the top of his beer bottle toward Carter and Alex. "We're where all the brains are," he said, "not to mention the good looks." He rubbed his substantial belly for effect.

Carter was about to say something when Alex interjected. "Who was it?" he asked, looking at me.

"Who was what?"

"*Your* first concert. The one your friend's parents took you to that you loved so much."

"Well, considering I've been talking for the last five minutes, and you're the one who is supposed to be getting interviewed, I'd much prefer it if you would answer that question instead."

"You first."

Oh man. I knew it was going to hurt, but I looked at him squarely and exhaled. "Neil Diamond."

"Nice!" Carter cheered.

Alex gave me a wry look. "You're kidding me, right? Neil Diamond?" He looked at Carter. "Did you put her up to this?"

Carter shook his head. "Neil Diamond's the best, and everyone knows it. It's universal. Get with the program."

Fred chuckled, nodding in agreement and starting to hum a tune.

"Whatever." Alex grimaced. "But if I ever catch you even looking at a sequin shirt, I'll shove you off the stage."

"Okay, so can we get back to talking about you guys now? Alex . . . I'll ask again, for the third time—what was your first concert?"

"I'm not telling." He winked and strutted off, leaving me exasperated.

Carter looked up at me and feigned an amused wince. "Sorry. He'll cooperate . . . eventually. Maybe." Then added, "Probably not."

He stood then and followed Alex, but on the way, he stopped, leaned down, and whispered into my ear, "It was Queen."

I looked up at him, our faces inches apart, and he reached down again, his voice warm in my ear. "He was twelve, and his dad took him. Says it changed his life."

Heat filled me. "Good to know."

As he walked away, he called backward, "We'll buy you a new recorder."

Up until that point in my life, I had used work as a sort of coping mechanism so that I wouldn't have to experience life. Whether it was schoolwork when I was young or journalism as an adult, immersing myself in work made me feel safe and secure. It was a place where I belonged. But that group of men managed to slowly chisel away at those hardened edges, showing me a little more each day, how to find joy in life. To relax and be at peace. They showed me what fun looked like and how to be in the moment without worry, just a little bit better.

20

EVIE

Snapshots bounce around my head of the group of us laughing and drinking around that giant table, enjoying the feast that Tommy had created while music played in the background. An eclectic mix ranging from Led Zeppelin to Prince to Primal Scream and Duran Duran. The moon was high while the guys carried on as the waters lolled in the bay.

One time in New York, I was invited to the penthouse to do a feature interview for *Creem* magazine. The guy—a timeless rock singer—invited me to sit down at his table, where a spread of food had been prepared for both of us. This wasn't common, but it wasn't unique either—this kind of warm welcome, especially from the professionals who knew the value of entertaining the press. He poured wine for me and answered my questions with a friendly face. It was going beautifully. I was midbite when he looked up and said: "Okay, thank you, please leave now," dismissing me in an instant. Anyone else would have been startled. But it hadn't fazed me. I'd lived like that since childhood. There one moment, forgotten the next. So I suppose I waited for that moment to arrive at the beach with them, the moment I would be asked to leave, and yet somehow, it never did. Something about that night soothed a part of my loneliness that often ate away at the inside of me. Maybe he sensed it. Maybe that's why Carter did it. Invited me to stay.

"As long as Alex doesn't smother me with a pillow in my sleep," I joked.

"Who, me?" Alex strolled past, evidently having been made aware of the situation. "Nothing to be afraid of. It'll be a slumber party." He rolled his eyes.

I returned to the back deck, and before I knew it, Tommy handed me another drink.

The air was warm and thick with the humidity of the salt water lazily drifting around the dock that jutted out into the bay. Someone had brought out a radio. I drifted in and out of the conversation with the guys, losing myself in a hazy bliss that was a heady combination of a warm ocean night, cold beer, pleasant and somewhat surreal company, and a sky filled with stars, inviting me to keep my eyes turned upward. Sometime past the witching hour, as sleep began to seduce me, I found myself sitting with my head on Carter's shoulder, the two of us curled together as if it were the most natural thing in the world for us to do. As he talked, the vibration soothing against my ear, he lazily played with the delicate silver bangle on my wrist—an heirloom piece that once belonged to my mother. He loved that bracelet, and it became a habit of his to fidget with it. As the conversation quieted, one by one the rest of the guys started heading inside until eventually we were sitting alone.

"I left a girl at home," he told me. "She'd love it here."

I stiffened slightly and looked up at him, raising an eyebrow.

He chuckled, stroking his thumb across the top of my hand. "Mandy. My dog."

I exhaled. "Ah. Very sweet. What kind?"

"A retriever. She stays with my mom when I'm on the road. I miss her like crazy. She loves water." He cocked his head. "What about you?"

"I've always wanted a cat." I still do.

He laughed. "No, I meant do you get home to see your family much?"

I didn't say anything at first. "I don't have any family."

"No one?"

"Not really."

His brow furrowed, and he watched me closely, waiting for me to elaborate.

"My mom died when I was little," I said eventually.

"And your dad?"

I looked away. "Not really in the picture."

"Brothers and sisters? Grandparents? Nobody?"

"Nope."

He seemed to be absorbing this. "Do you get back much at all, then? To your hometown?"

I told him about your dad and Kate. Our friendship. "I don't think they quite get my job. I think they're secretly still hoping I'll change my mind and come home and live a quiet suburban life alongside them. They're like family."

"Marry a nice, steady guy. All of your kids playing together," he said.

"Exactly."

"Think you'll stay here on Long Island?"

"I doubt it. I think eventually my job's going to take me into the city. Or maybe LA. But we'll see." I waved my hand in the air.

"London, definitely. I think that's what you meant," he whispered, and I smiled.

As we talked that night, I think we both sensed that there was far more at stake than just the fate of a film I was supposed to be making. Far more at stake than my career. Or his, as I would learn later. None of that would matter in the end. We were these two damaged people coming together, with scars and wounds that ran deep. We had reason to stay apart. But it was inevitable.

There are few things in life more powerful than inertia.

We talked more about his time in London, the various stages of the band as they came together, his first torturous gig as the front man—three songs at a pub in Camden. He loved school. He'd studied the philosophy of mathematics at university. Not many people know this about him, surprisingly. He loved it as much as music. Astronomy as well.

He gazed up to the night sky that night. "'There is geometry in the humming of the strings; there is music in the spacing of the spheres.' Pythagoras said that." And then a moment later, "It's all related, you know. Numbers. Music. Philosophy. The sky." He pointed upward. I shook my head in wonder, and he looked over and smiled. "I told you I'm not exactly who you think I am. I'll convince you eventually." I got the sense that people rarely truly saw him, and for some reason, it was important to him that I did.

"I'm already convinced."

"Charmed yet?"

I smiled and shook my head. "Nope."

"Good. You shouldn't be."

As I looked at him, I realized that it was his eyes that had disarmed me from the beginning—so full of pain and hope and a deep heart that was filled with kindness and romance and belief in things far beyond this world. When he turned them toward me, time stopped.

"Evie, what are we doing here? What is this?" He spoke softly.

I took a deep breath and released it. When I didn't say anything, he continued. "I know it's complicated. But . . ."

"But there are lines we probably shouldn't cross, at least until after the film."

"They're already crossed. And you know it." He was right, of course. "Okay, I have a boundary for you, then," he said after a moment.

"Oh yeah?"

"One minute." His eyes flashed.

"One minute?" I asked.

"Yes. One minute. For one minute, forget everything else but here and now. This moment."

A smile danced on my lips. "And then what?"

"Then the minute is up. And we say good night."

I nodded slowly. "One minute."

He took my face in his hands, leaned down, and kissed me then.

"One minute," he murmured against my mouth like a safe word. "One . . ." He kissed me again, and I arched up into him, and he held me tighter. Then he dragged his lips to my neck, where I could feel his breath heavy, warm on my skin.

"My god, the way you kiss . . . ," I whispered, gripping the warm skin beneath his shirt.

He smiled against my lips. "We are good at it, aren't we?" After the seconds flew by at the speed of light, he stood back.

"That was the shortest minute in history," he said, eyes dazzled. "I need hours . . . days, years with you."

I was lit up inside, on fire. "We did a good job. Barely." I straightened my shirt and backed away from him. "That could've gotten away from us."

"Oh, you think, do you?" He reached over and took my hand.

The word *boundary* became kind of a thing for us after that. A double-entendre sort of thing. We had a lot of fun with it. I'll leave it at that.

"You're getting tired. Come on. Let's get you settled in upstairs. Ready for bed?"

"Mm-hmm."

He inhaled. "Oh god, if you look at me like that . . ." And he pulled me toward him again.

"One minute." I held a hand against his chest playfully. "Right?"

"Right. Yes. Okay then. In we go."

He led me inside, past bedrooms of pillowy white linens and mahogany woods with breezy curtains over windows that overlooked all of the beach and the bay. Duffel bags and guitar cases and boots were strewn about three floors all the way up to a rooftop deck, dotted with terra cotta pots bursting with bright-pink geraniums and a view that looked out over the water.

"Good night," he whispered into my ear that night before he disappeared, leaving me alone with my thoughts in a room all my own.

"Good night," I said to myself.

I hadn't brought a single thing with me. I slept in one of Carter's T-shirts, which I'd found neatly folded sitting at the foot of the bed. The moonlight shone through an octagonal window beneath a pitched roof in an all-white room that would live in my thoughts for years to come. In the distance, I heard the sounds of a guitar carried in on the breeze through the curtains. Just as I drifted into the most peaceful sleep, I heard him playing a familiar melody. It was a lullaby of sorts that I had heard in my dreams since I was a child, comforting me in the dark of night. I remember thinking how odd it was that he knew it.

21

EVIE

I didn't go back home again the next day. Or the one after that.

It was an initiation of sorts that took place that weekend. They didn't let anyone in easily, this band of brothers. Even Fred had been with them since the early days, as much a friend as a road manager by that point. It was new territory for them, and I hadn't realized how rare it really was to have an outsider be a part of their story. But moments were strung together over time, one by one, until I looked back at some point in the days, weeks, months that followed and realized I had become part of the fabric. Woven in delicate moments until one day it ripped wide open. But those first days at the beginning are bathed in a kind of golden glow, all of us together.

It was a cozy, picturesque little beach town, and it's funny to think of the commotion they would've caused stepping out as a group like that years later. But this was all still just the beginning, and most people didn't recognize their faces yet. Except for the accents, they could've been any group of wayward friends—a bit rough around the edges but boyishly so.

Carter and I strolled in and out of shops that lined the quaint streets. I remember him buying a handmade leather-bound notebook.

I bought an uncharacteristic sundress. I still have it. I've never been able to let go of it. I also have his notebook, amazingly enough, where lines of lyrics are scrawled in his swirl of thoughts, upside down, right side up, along with the many deeply scratched-over words he decided he didn't like.

We'd been walking past a playground one evening, and when I close my eyes, I can hear the sounds of it. Squeals of delight filling the air, mothers calling after their children, the high-pitched whine of a screeching swing. A ball bounced out onto the sidewalk, and Carter tossed it back gamely to a little boy with a tiny voice. The boy caught it clumsily in his outstretched arms, and his face lit up with glee.

"Ah, perfect catch!" Carter exclaimed.

He would have been a good father.

He took my hand in his again, and we continued walking. I couldn't help but smile at him.

"You're good with kids," I told him.

"You think?"

"Yeah. I do."

He looked off into the distance. "Maybe. Other people's, I suppose. I don't think I'll ever want kids of my own."

"Really? Why?" This surprised me a bit, a bold statement appearing from nowhere.

"I don't have the personality for it. And I sure as hell don't have the lifestyle for it. I think I'm too selfish for parenthood." He laughed a bit, looking over at me. "I don't mean that in a self-deprecating way; it's just that I think you need to be willing to give so much of yourself and your time to raise children right. My mind doesn't work that way. I'm in my own head too much. I get lost in my writing and in my music, and I like to live on my own terms. When I do something, I like to do it well, you know? I wouldn't want to be the kind of dad who leaves a kid at home. I've chosen my path. If you don't want to give it your all and be great at it, then don't do it." An edge had creeped into his voice.

"Totally agree."

"Really?"

I shrugged. "Some people just shouldn't have kids, but they do."

"I think I'm one of them—the ones who shouldn't."

"I'm not so sure about that," I said, pointing a thumb backward toward the playground and smiling. "But I like that you're honest enough with yourself to know what you want."

As we walked, I began to learn more about the skinny boy and the rough father who had raised him. The gentle mother and the brother with the tortured soul who once inhabited the daily world of the man I was falling for. He didn't mind being out on the road.

"I think I miss the memory of them more than the actuality," he said. "The way things used to be. My mum, I miss. But our family fell apart at some point. After my dad lost his job, we didn't see much of him sometimes, which was a good thing. He's around now, and he mellowed a bit, I guess, after . . ."

"After what?" I asked.

"After Jacob."

"Your brother."

He nodded and looked away, and I reached over and held his hand. He never liked to talk much about Jacob.

"We don't get on very well, though. My dad and me. Probably best I'm on the road."

A bit of time passed as we walked. "I know a little about that kind of dad."

"Ah. I'm sorry." He brushed his thumb against my hand.

I shrugged in agreement. "Me too."

I should have known then—that we were completing each other in all the most dangerous ways. Trying to heal old, deep wounds in a shared sadness of the past together with the hopeful belief that we would somehow fix each other. Two puzzle pieces, matched together from lifetimes before.

I remember sitting across from Carter's father, years ago, and wondering how it was possible that he had been responsible for someone like Carter. I can see him sitting across from me at a pub in York, talking in mumbled tones, his mannerisms so very unlike Carter. He wore deep, etched lines in his face above layers of wools and a quilted vest, and I had to strain to understand him through his gruff accent. He had a habit of looking down at his raw, weathered hands while he spoke, as if beneath the layers, perhaps he shamefully remembered the dark presence he had been in his family's life. He was worn and tough as leather, but having mellowed with age, he noticeably drank nothing stronger than one single pint of beer in the afternoon we spent together. "So this music thing is working out for you, then," he had said. He paused, looking up only briefly with a frown. "I guess it's all right as long as it pays the bills." Mayluna had just been nominated for a Grammy Award, and it still was the closest he might come to praise for his son. Carter's mother sat beside her husband—a timid, graceful woman as quiet and reserved and gentle as the soft rain that fell outside the pub's window. Her eyes lit up with pure sunlight every time Carter spoke.

I'd never felt so protective of Carter as I did that day, my heart breaking a little at the sadness in his eyes. His desire to be enough.

"But I like the idea of growing into an old, quiet man, secure in his solitary life, fading off into the sunset with someone to love," Carter said as we continued our walk.

"I like that," I told him. "It's sweet."

"But who knows? You never know how life will turn out."

22

EVIE

We began formulating ideas for the film. In the back of my mind, I reminded myself of the stories I'd read in my youth, of journalists on the road with the bands, telling of nights that bled into days into cities and towns in a haze. Photos in hotel rooms alongside the likes of Mick Jagger and Jimmy Page and Grace Slick. Those journalists managed to produce some of the most incredible stories on bands that had ever been created. Maybe I could, too, I hoped.

Throughout the weekend, I watched, scratching down words that came to me from scenes with each of them.

> Mayluna could hardly have chosen a less rock 'n' roll kind of place than a house that sits on an otherwise peaceful bay in a town that was almost the Hamptons but not quite. "There goes the neighborhood," Tom Rollins jokes. The drummer has blue eyes that crinkle at the corners when he laughs.
>
> "Then again, we were always causing a bit of a ruckus in the neighborhood, I think. Could've been worse,

though. We could be Oasis. We haven't managed to completely destroy a hotel room." He offers a mischievous look and adds, "Yet." The peace and natural beauty of the bay sit in contrast to the nature of the house's occupants, who often stay up until dawn while on a short break from their tour with The Evolution. "When I was a kid," he begins, while reclining on a wooden chair along the bay while flourishing a joint in one hand as he talks about his days growing up outside of York, England . . .

There was always music playing, with each of them having distinct tastes, like the world's best jukebox. One night, Carter and I had escaped to our little bubble outside, and Elton John's "Tiny Dancer" began to play. It wasn't as popular back then, that song. It had been decades since Elton John had landed it on the charts, but in the late '90s, it had faded a bit.

"I love this song," I told him, thinking of the cassette tape my mom used to play.

"Do you?" He took my hand, wrapping his other arm around my waist, a slow dance. His voice was warm in my ear as he sang of sheets of linen and a girl who married a music man. I think of him every time I hear that song.

Tommy approached, holding a small home-video camera, and my eyes went wide. He leaned down, one eye hidden. "Say hi, Evie!"

"Hey, why does he get to film this weekend and I can't?" I exclaimed.

Alex gave me a look. "Do we really need to answer that?"

"Don't mind him," Carter said, pushing the camera out of our faces. "He's obsessed with the thing. He saved up for it when he was sixteen and has been lurking around with it ever since. Convinced we'll want to play it back when we're all ancient. He has old videos of us playing to huge crowds of, like, fifteen or sixteen people. I told you that you two would get along." He shook his head, laughing at his younger self. "So humiliating."

I stopped short. "Wait a minute." I looked at all of them, eyes wide. "Are you telling me you have video footage going all the way back to the beginning?"

"Yeah. I mean, it's shit, but yeah. I guess we do," Carter answered.

"And you're just telling me about this now?" If I were the type of girl to jump up and down when excited, that's exactly what I would have been doing.

"Well, we try to ignore him," Carter joked, shoving Tommy.

"Hey, you'll be glad someday!" Tommy added and then skipped off. I shook my head, ecstatic.

"That's it!" I said, mostly to myself. I could see all the frames coming into my mind. The combination of Tommy's old VHS footage and the new tour footage that I would get out on the road was going to be the perfect story. "Don't you see?"

"What is?" Carter asked.

"This is the movie we're going to make." And suddenly it all started falling into place as I looked around, imagining how beautifully it would all connect.

"I could kiss you, Tommy!" I called out.

"Pretty sure you're taken, darling," he called back, and Carter pulled me closer, smiling at the exchange.

I'm telling you these stories—these seemingly silly and frivolous snapshots of time strung together like pearls—not because individually they're anything remarkable, but rather because I want you to see who I was back then. Who *we* were. You've known me as this somewhat quiet mother, going about life with a gaze often settled into the middle distance as I washed up the dinner dishes or arranged playdates. But I had this entirely different world I once inhabited. And so did they. Before they became such giants, they were just boys, really, with heads filled with dreams.

Late that night, I opened the french doors to let the warm breeze in, dancing through the curtains that draped from the bedposts. Hearing a familiar melody once again, I looked out the window to where Carter sat on one of the lounge chairs on the deck, wearing a gray T-shirt and loose pants with bare feet crossed at his ankles, an acoustic guitar in his hands as he began writing what would become one of the biggest albums of all time. In his moonlit profile, he had a peaceful, wistful look on his face.

He felt familiar and new and like someone I'd known in every lifetime, if I believed in such things. When he was gone, I felt like I couldn't breathe. And when he was with me, I felt completely alive. It was too much. I know that now, of course. It's dangerous to love like that. To spend years wishing more than anything that you could go back to a night, standing barefoot with a guitar calling you like a siren song.

But before I knew it, I took a step. And then another.

When I reached him, he didn't say a word, just laid down his guitar, looked up, took my hand, and led us quietly through the darkened halls, up to the third floor and into the moonlight pouring into my room.

"I can't stop kissing you," I murmured, barely able to breathe.

He took my face in his hands and whispered, "Then don't."

He eased his shirt over his head in a swift move and returned to kissing me, his mouth pressing into mine in perfect rhythm with the motion of our bodies against each other. I slid my hands down the taut muscles of his back, feeling the curve of his waist and hips. He picked me up and set me down on the deep, luxurious bed and then suddenly, the quiet restraint we'd been showing was replaced by frenetic urgency. Hands were everywhere at once, clutching, gripping. His fingers tangled in my hair, pulling me deeper into his kiss.

The full moon filled the entire room with such bright light, it was almost like dawn. Or maybe it actually was dawn. In the hours that followed, I'd lost track of time and everything else. Later, we were lying in bed, limbs tangled together, and he said something to me:

"I've been waiting for you for a long time. My whole life, maybe."

When someone says something like that to you, it can be dizzying. He was always so sure of us. So certain. I wanted so much to be that way with him, too, but it just wasn't the way I was wired. When you spend most of your life hearing that you don't matter or that you're a burden, it's nearly impossible for your nervous system to accept anything but that message. Yet somehow, he began to heal those parts.

I didn't tell him this story at the time, but in the weeks before I met him, I'd started having strange dreams. Each night, I saw a man standing in front of me, holding me against his shoulder as he whispered four words in my ear—"I'm on the way." It was a message to have faith. To not lose hope in lovability. I could never see his face but could sense his very essence, as real as if he had been standing there. In the morning when I woke, I would swear I could still feel the fabric of his shirt beneath my fingertips and sense the scent of his skin. I didn't think it was anything at the time—merely dreams. But in the days after I met Carter, I couldn't deny the uncanny feeling of having met him before and the overwhelming sense of familiarity. I told him this story a long time later, and he gave me that knowing half smile he would give. Because after all, this was how his mind worked. He believed in these things without question. In his mind, we had always known of the other's existence.

To this day, I can still feel the words of both of those phrases on my neck, the feel of his skin against mine.

I'm on my way.

I've been waiting for you for a long time.

23

EVIE

I'd never liked tattoos—the blurry-edge versions of ones that had been inked at budget spots in suburban strip malls. But his were exceptionally well done, with an artist's precision.

He opened his eyes and flashed me a groggy smile before burying his face into his pillow and laughing. He peeked at me with one impish eye. "Good morning, you." He pulled me closer.

I brushed a finger over the meticulous swirls, shapes I recognized from math textbooks and posters artfully entwined with vines. "Tell me about this one."

"Fibonacci." He lifted his head onto his hand, blinking away sleep. "Sacred geometry. The golden spiral. It's a reminder that there are precise energy patterns—everything in life and consciousness is connected if we pay attention."

I continued tracing my way around his waist. A circle with intertwining circles and triangles and dots, the black ink contrasting with the white sheets. "And this?"

"*Musica universalis.* The music of the spheres."

"What does it mean?"

He rubbed his face and ran a hand through his hair, still waking up. He began tracing a similar circle, drawing across my bare stomach with his fingertip as he talked in sleepy tones.

"Centuries ago, Pythagoras and Kepler developed theories that there's a mathematical correspondence between the resonance of music notes and the exact configuration of our solar system. The belief that the motion of the planets creates a type of music and harmony that we can't hear with our ears but can feel or sense on a subconscious or intuitive level. Some believe it's a type of grand spiritual language. The universe speaking to our soul. We just have to listen."

"That's beautiful."

"Yeah?" He leaned over and kissed me. "Which one? The meaning or the tattoo?"

I smiled. "Both."

I dragged my fingers down the length of his left arm and to a series of interlaced circles. "This one?"

He laughed. "I used to doodle those in my notebooks, daydreaming about being a musician while I was supposed to be paying attention in school. Drew it in pen all over everything. Drove my teachers crazy, and I used to get in trouble for it. Seemed appropriate to make it permanent."

The thought of the kid in school, so clearly intelligent and yet getting scolded for daydreaming about his future, made me smile.

I brushed across the top of his stomach, where a sun centered a wide span of two wings, and raised a questioning eyebrow at him as he explained: "I love the angles of light in different places in the world at different times of the year."

"This one's my favorite, I think." I continued to run my fingers over the lines around the sun and the wings. I felt a quake in his stomach muscles, and he sucked in a breath through his teeth. "Yeah? Why's that?" He pulled me closer.

"The sun has a bit of a healing effect on me as well. I don't think I ever outgrew being afraid of the dark. I love the first light of day. It's comforting. Most of the time, I don't fall asleep until it's nearly dawn." As soon as the words left my mouth, I smiled. "What is it about you? I never tell people things like that."

"I like knowing things about you that no one else knows."

I leaned back into my pillow and curled into him, pulling the thick duvet up around us as my eyes began to close again.

"I can hear the ocean from here," I murmured a moment later. The doors had remained open throughout the night, and the room was full of fresh sea air.

"I know. It freaks me out," he replied with his face buried in my hair.

"What does?"

"The sound of the ocean. It freaks me out. I know most people love it. And I get it; it's nice. But I don't know why people think it's relaxing. It's such a big sound. It reminds me how tiny we are, how fragile."

"Agreed. I'm not a fan of deep water in general. I feel like it could just swallow me up. I think I might find more peace among the trees."

"Ahh, well, now you're speaking my language."

"Am I?"

"There's beauty in the ocean, but there's magic in the forest."

No wonder he was a songwriter, I thought at the time, charmed. That line, born that morning, ended up in a song from the *Sigma Five* album. Over time, it became one of those music quotes that ended up on coffee mugs and social media captions and such.

"We used to spend whole days in Yorkshire Dales, getting lost among the leaves," he told me. "It has a mystical quality about it. My mum grew up in a town near there and knew all the best places. She would take us there, and my brother and I would play at the bottom of Janet's Floss, where they say there are faeries at play." He twirled his fingers in the air, his eyes lighting up playfully. "Could hear them

135

beneath the waterfall when the wind grew quiet. Sparkling in the corner of your eye above the mist that hovers around."

I laughed gently. "I have no idea what you're talking about or where Yorkshire Dales is, but it sounds wonderful."

His face grew soft. "It's my favorite place to be, the Dales. It's as if, when I'm there, the illusion of the world disappears and I feel closer to whatever it is that has created all of this. A big contrast to the working town we lived in outside York, that's for sure. All that green. And in the autumn, where it looks like the world has turned to every shade of gold."

"Sounds beautiful. But I'll admit, I'm not a fan of autumn. Everything gets cold and dreary and summer is over." I grimaced.

"What?" he exclaimed, leaning up again. "That's impossible! How can anyone not like autumn?"

"Told you I wasn't perfect."

"Hmm. I think I'm going to just have to convince you, that's all."

"That I'm perfect?" I joked.

"That you like autumn! I'll take you there. You'll see."

I bristled and looked away. "Don't say that."

"Don't say what?"

"That you'll take me there. Because I know it sounds good now, but the thing is, somewhere inside, I'll believe you. And then when it doesn't happen, it'll ruin this moment. Let's not do that, okay?" I closed my eyes again.

He inhaled deeply and watched me closely. "Evie." He turned my face toward his. "I'll take you there. And . . ." He dropped a kiss on my nose. "I'll make you love autumn."

"No, you won't."

"Challenge accepted."

I laughed outright then, despite myself. "Okay, well, we'll just have to see."

"I'll make it my life's mission," he said, planting a gentle kiss on my lips.

With his middle finger, he drew tiny circles around my shoulder and peeked over at the clock. "Speaking of sun."

I turned over to look, realizing with a shock that the day was nearly half over.

"I guess we should probably get up," I said. "I need to get you all together this afternoon to go over what I have in mind. I have a call in the morning with the label, and I need to—"

"I don't want to let you go yet," he interrupted, wrapping his arm around my waist.

"No?"

"No. I want to take you downstairs and make you breakfast. Spend the rest of the day on the beach—keeping you safe in the deep water, of course."

"Of course."

"Then spend another night in bed with you."

"So that's what you would do with me, huh?" I asked slyly.

"Well, no, not yet, actually." He pulled the covers over our heads, submerging us in thick, dim light. "First, I'd make love to you again," he said in a throaty voice, brushing across my neck. "And then I would take you downstairs and make you breakfast."

"I guess it can wait just a little bit longer."

We were like a drug to each other. Every time one of us started to get dressed, the other would pull us back into bed, or onto the chair, or down to the floor, and we would have continued all day, until eventually, we were interrupted by a loud knock at the door.

"Go away!" Carter yelled, making me laugh.

"Phone call," Tommy said in a singsong voice. "It's the label. Calling for some chick named Cameron. I could tell him we don't actually *know* a Cameron, of course. But . . ."

"No, wait! I'm coming!" I jumped out of the bed.

Carter groaned, rolling onto his stomach. I wrapped myself in a sheet and ran to the door, tripping on the way. When I opened the door, Tommy smirked. "Good morning, Princess."

I gave him a look. "Good morning."

"Not you. Him." He pointed into the room, sticking his head around the door. "Good morning, Princess! Or should I say, afternoon."

Carter promptly flipped him the middle finger.

"Can you just give me the phone?"

"And good morning to you, too, my dear," he said softly, covering the phone with his hand. "Do you want this?" He held the phone high above his head.

"Give it to me!" I demanded in a whisper.

"Are you sure?" he teased. "You're not busy? You seem busy."

I glared at him until finally he gave me the phone just as he pushed past me and proceeded to make himself comfortable, lounging annoyingly on the end of the bed.

"Hello?" I took the phone quickly, retreating back into the room. "This is Cameron."

Fred passed by the open door with a mocking hand covering his eyes, apparently finding humor in the whole scene.

Like I said, I'd never had much of a family. They were obnoxious, but it was my idea of heaven. To my relief, the label was actually thrilled to learn that I was staying with them at the house, taking it as a good sign, I guess. The meeting in the city wouldn't be necessary, but I still owed them a plan.

"I have to get some things together. Some initial ideas. We should all talk about it this afternoon." I pulled a T-shirt over my head and went to my notebook as Carter propped his head up on his hand. I took my notes back over to the bed, grabbing a pen.

"Let me read what you have," he said, holding out his hand.

"No."

"Why not?"

"That, my dear, would be *so* across the line." I clutched the notebook to my chest. "Boundaries, remember?"

"Oh, so everything we did to each other last night wasn't crossing a line, then?" he asked with a sultry smirk.

I gave him a look, exasperated. I was determined to not completely lose myself in the whole situation. It would be a delicate balance. One that would eventually cost me my career, of course. In hindsight, that was obvious. But at the time, we can tell ourselves anything and believe it.

24

Evie

"You know, this would be a whole lot easier if I wasn't leaving," he said on the last day at the beach house.

"This would be a whole lot easier if you weren't such a good kisser," I replied.

He smiled and continued.

They were going back on tour. I was going back home to gather the minimal gear we needed and plan the logistics. If all went well, I would join them two weeks later. By the way we'd acted that day, you'd have thought we'd be apart for two years, not two weeks.

"If you two are going to be like this the entire time, then the whole thing is off," Tommy joked, coming around the corner with Alex, Fred, and Darren behind him. "All right. Let's sit down and figure out what we're going to do with this little film once and for all, yeah?" he said.

"For the record, I've been trying to do that from the moment I got here," I replied.

"For the record, you made us sound like a bunch of little girls who play with unicorns in the *Spin* piece. All that stars and moon shit," Alex complained.

Carter grimaced. "I did come across a bit like a sap, didn't I?"

"Yeah. He's *such* a nice guy. All warm and sappy, this one," Darren chided.

"You *are* a nice guy," I said.

"Ha. Tell that to the kid whose nose he busted up in year six," Alex added.

I looked at Carter, having a hard time imagining this. "You broke a kid's nose?"

"And don't forget—"

Carter gave Alex a sharp look, putting an end to whatever insights Alex had planned.

I heard the story later. The kid had been making fun of Carter's father, and eleven-year-old Carter had hit him. He hadn't meant to break his nose when he hit him. But it wasn't long after that kids began realizing they needed to stay away from Carter Wills, just as they had Jacob. Teachers had a soft spot for them, though; the two boys were quiet and polite and studious and looked out for the other kids in school as much as themselves. But everyone knew . . . you didn't mess with the Wills boys.

I conceded. "Okay, fine. No more stars and moons."

Despite the hard time he'd been giving me, to my surprise, I learned later that Alex had been the one who loved what I'd done on the Green Witch video more than everyone else. He had gone back and read nearly every single story I'd ever written before even considering having me at the beach house that weekend. I don't think even Carter knew that. But Alex had told me later. He and I often sat together sketching out ideas during the filming over the months. He had a big hand in the way it took shape, and we had similar sensibilities. He just liked to give me a hard time because, well, because that was just the way he was.

He gave Carter a hard time too. Sometimes more than others. I'd overheard them arguing that morning behind the closed doors of the den. They'd thought I was in the shower.

"None of my business?" I'd heard the anger simmering in Alex's voice. "Are you kidding me right now? We had a deal. No complications. No distractions. And now you're going to start some relationship . . . with a girl who is actually making a film of us and works with the press? What the hell are you doing?"

In muffled tones, I heard them going back and forth, Carter assuring Alex that he could handle it.

"Fine, if you can have your little distractions, I guess I can handle mine, then, right?" Alex said.

"Alex. Don't."

"Shut up, Tommy. You know I'm right about this."

"What the hell did you say?" Carter sounded furious. "Your little *distractions*? Is that some kind of threat? I hardly think this is the same thing, and you know it."

"It's exactly the same thing. We all have our poisons, and this is yours. Mine may be chemical, but yours is in that messed-up place in your head, and we can't deal with you going off the damn deep end. When this ends badly, you'll cut her out of your life like she never happened, and we'll be the ones left having to dig you out of whatever dark hole you crawl into."

"Oh, I see, so you can run around with whomever you'd like, but I actually have something real and you want me to end it? I'm not doing it. And besides, you know as well as I do that she's perfect for this project."

"He's not wrong, Alex," Tommy added. "You saw what she did with Green Witch. It was perfect. And you've heard what she has in mind. If we have to do this damn thing, she's exactly the right person."

"Well, maybe he should have thought of that before he started f—"

"Don't." Carter cut him off sharply. "It's not your decision. The film, yes. But the rest of it is none of your goddamn business."

"Look," Alex said, his voice turning into a plea. "It's good to see you happy again. But not like this. Not right now. What happens when it's over? When we head home?" There was silence before he continued. "I honestly don't care if we do the film or not. But this is a bad idea and you know it. There's too much on the line. It's not just about you."

Carter's voice was low and steady. "Fine. You've made your point. If this goes badly, it's on me. Not on you. Okay?"

A few moments passed, bits of conversation I couldn't hear. "It's settled, then," Tommy said finally.

"But, Alex," Carter said a moment later, "let me be clear. If you ever treat her again like you did earlier this week, then we really will have a problem. Do you understand me?"

We all had our fears and demons. I'd almost left after that. Carter had found me putting my things in my bag, planning to leave early. He never knew the reason why. Of course, he'd convinced me to stay.

It feels like I was standing in that kitchen just last week, all six of us talking. I read somewhere once that when a brain experiences something new or outside the usual routine of life, that's when it creates a lasting memory. Simply repeating one day after the next is the enemy of a fulfilling life. It's the reason why months go by too quickly, or years, even, and it's like there's almost no memory of it—an overload of routine that the brain registers as unimportant. But a new experience is something special. A bookmark. A highlighted section in the pages of your life. It's the reason why you can remember the exact way your shoes felt on your first day of first grade or the exact light of the room when you had your first kiss but can't remember what you did last Tuesday.

But when we said goodbye that day, I think I was still worried that it might not happen. That it might be the end. That something would go wrong, or that the project would fall through, or that Carter would change his mind about us. Something. I imagined myself later in life; maybe I'd tell my kids about it one day, just like I'm doing now. *The week I spent with Mayluna,* I would say, and they would laugh at the idea of it. And maybe I would bump into the guys at other venues. Work-related events. Our paths crossing. Would Carter and I look at each other awkwardly? Would he avoid me? Or would we hug and remember the tryst with wistful sweetness? It would be a nice memory, I'd thought. A glimpse into a different world—one where I almost belonged among an unlikely crew of English men.

But good things do happen sometimes. Two weeks later, I was on the road.

25

EVIE

We'd all agreed on the vision: a combination of digital and analog that would tell the story of a band from the beginning of their careers and leading up to the release of their next album—which the label was expecting to be nothing less than a worldwide phenomenon that would catapult Mayluna into superstardom. The film and the album would be released simultaneously. No pressure on any of us, of course.

Maybe something like the themes in Alan Yentob's *Cracked Actor*, where David Bowie is captured in the throes of American culture on tour. Though with less sparkle and pizazz, obviously. Something understated that showed the band's reticence about stardom as opposed to the chasing of it. New footage would be filmed primarily in black and white. We would intersperse it with Tommy's grainy home movies that started from around the age of eighteen, with the band playing while sitting on mattresses on the floors of bedrooms or in the dormitory halls at university. In cramped tiled bathrooms where they liked the acoustics. But then we'd cut to live performances on tour with giant crowds. From small recorders and home setups to fully produced studio time as they worked on their next album.

I was a ball of elated energy when I stepped off a plane at Boston Logan International Airport on a morning in late June. I had a duffel bag of clothes and my gear. A Canon Skoopic would give us the right amount of natural grit we were looking for in the black-and-white footage. A new DAT recorder and microphone, courtesy of the record label. A Bolex for the color footage we'd intersperse throughout. It was going to be a low-budget kind of deal, which suited me just fine. I knew the guys would be guarded if the setup was too big, and I could be both in the shadows and in the midst of things equally with a setup like that. It helped that they were used to Tommy and his camera. In the meantime, we had decided to keep our relationship as quiet as possible, with only the closest in the enclave knowing about us, everyone agreeing that it would overshadow the entire project if word got out that Carter and I were involved. People on tour picked up on it, of course, but those on the road tend to stick to their own business.

I had planned to take a cab and meet Carter at the venue, but he surprised me outside the airport gate, standing about thirty feet away with one hand hooked in the pocket of his jeans and wearing a plain white T-shirt and dark sunglasses. I paused in surprise for just a moment before I ran to him and dropped my bags at his feet. I swear we did that thing they do in the movies where he lifted me up and I threw my legs around his waist amid the busy crowd around us. Things like that really do happen sometimes.

We arrived at the venue not long after. "Let's get you settled in on the bus." Carter took my bag, and I raised an eyebrow at him.

"Well, I'm pretty sure they have me on a crew bus."

He laughed, ignoring me, as if this were the most ludicrous thing he'd ever heard. "Yeah. Okay."

"Seriously," I said.

"Uh-huh." And that was the end of that. I don't recall spending a single night on that crew bus.

He gave me the royal tour, gesturing as I walked up the stairs toward the interior. "Evie, meet Miss Penny Lane, our bus, though it hurts her feelings when we call her that. Miss Penny Lane takes good care of us."

I'd seen my share of tour buses over the years, and this one certainly wasn't the plushest, but it was comfortable in the kind of way that happens when bands make the big graduation from their worn-out van. It was appreciated and loved—never taken for granted. The main living area featured dark faux-wood walls with a marble tile–like floor. A line of tiny built-in lights bordered the ceiling.

"So here we have the living room." He gestured like a docent. Two built-in, cushioned gray leather benches sat opposite each other, in view of a large TV that was set into a wall that separated the living area from the driver's seat. It was surprisingly clean. So much so that I couldn't help but wonder if they'd tidied up on my account. A kitchenette featured a small sink, microwave, and various boxes of junk food, bottles of water, two half-empty bottles of vodka, a bottle of Knob Creek bourbon, a mix of glassware and plastic cups, and a dining table. Carter poured a glass of amber liquid for both of us.

"It looks like the housekeeper has been here recently."

He winked in response, gesturing again. "And there, we have six large, well-appointed bedrooms." These were actually six cramped bunks, three stacked on both sides, each about the width of a twin-size bed, with a privacy curtain and a miniature TV screen in the distant corner of each.

I spotted a dog-eared copy of Kerouac's *On the Road* in the back of one of them. "Yours, I'm guessing?" I pointed to the middle one on the right.

He nodded.

I lingered for a minute, imagining him resting there. "Cozy."

A single bathroom wasn't much larger than one you'd find on an airplane, though outfitted with more dark wood and faux marble and a tiny shower stall. At the very back was another set of built-in sofas, with guitars and duffel bags throughout. We took a seat, and he pulled me into his lap, kissing me.

"You taste good," I said.

He smiled. "Do I?"

I nodded and kissed him again, tasting the sweet and smoky whiskey on his lips, along with the flavor of him. The aftertaste of both lingered deliciously. "So what do you think?" he asked.

"I like it. And I like it even better when I'm here in it with you instead of in another state across a phone line." He pulled me closer and I curled into him.

As I understand it, it took them years to finally give up that bus; they loved it so much. I think they were superstitious about it—like it was a good-luck charm of some kind. But eventually they did, of course. Graduated to something more luxurious, until eventually, it was replaced by a private jet in later years when the venues became much larger and the dates on the calendar were more spread out. But wherever it is now, I bet it could tell some good stories.

26

EVIE

The first pieces of footage we shot started with the guys as they goofed around in the dressing room working out any preshow jitters. From empty seats, I filmed sound check. Preshow, I'd perch among the road cases and capture them joining in a sort of pregame huddle.

Fred would often orient them to their location before the show with signs like REMEMBER, YOU ARE IN CHICAGO TONIGHT. One by one, they would each run up the ramp to the stage, while Carter hung back for a few moments longer. Bouncing from one foot to the other, he'd wink at me and flash an excited grin before disappearing through the stage door. I'd hear the crowd roar and I'd smile, catching gold on film. At night, we'd file out, the six of us with Fred in the lead, into hotel lobbies or onto the bus, traveling throughout the night. Cities began to blur from one to the next, and I was in a state of mind so foreign to me that I could barely remember a previous life.

We captured the press, asking the same questions over and over again, repeated in each city, to show the banality of the promotional machine—the way it stole just a little bit of the soul while at the same time bringing the music to the world. (We didn't realize that Radiohead was doing something similar at that time with *Meeting People Is Easy*, so maybe it wasn't that original, after all. That's a great documentary, but I could barely watch when it came out; it cut so close to the quick.) This was the vision we created for the film—these four boys becoming something greater than their individual parts while trying to hold on to the core of who they'd always been.

I learned about Jacob one night in those early days. Carter rarely spoke of his brother and always seemed to be running away from a past that felt like a dark shadow.

Alex and I had snagged a couple of beers, and the two of us were lounging on a picnic table at the edge of a backstage lot. Somehow the conversation turned to Jacob.

27

CARTER

"She must have kept her promise to you in her writing—barely a mention about your brother has appeared anywhere. And nothing about the problems with Alex or any of your personal struggles. Your history," Michael says.

"It's because I hadn't told her," I tell him. "Not until a little later, anyway. It was such a strange thing—wanting to share everything with someone for the first time in my life, but not being able to. I understood the conflict of interest she was dealing with. She did a great job, though. She was moving away from writing profile pieces in favor of the films she wanted to make, anyway, so it was fine. But truthfully, I couldn't wait for the whole project to be over and done with so we could get on without it hanging over her—the idea of us having to cross lines in working together. I think she worried at times that I didn't support her career—that everything became about me and my work. I probably should have done a better job at that."

"Bits of the story about your brother did end up coming out over the years, but nothing from you. Are you ready to talk about it now?" he asks.

Michael had seen his opportunity, and I respect him for taking it. But my mind is in a different place. I consider his question for a moment. "We just wanted to get on with our lives. But when you keep secrets while living in the public eye, people start to make things up just to color in the blanks. I regret that a bit."

"Nah, we did the right thing," Tommy says, chiming in then.

I look over at him. "You think?" I ask.

"You were still dealing with the loss. We all were. And Alex was . . . Well, we were just worried about him. We all still missed Jacob, and nothing about any of it felt right without him during those early years," Tommy says, and he's right.

"Jacob and I were inseparable growing up—or at least, as the kid brother, I used to like to think we were," I tell Michael. "I fairly worshipped him even though my mum used to tell us that we were as different as night and day. I was the quiet kid, and Jacob was the one who got all the attention, often for all the wrong reasons. He had a sort of street-smart intelligence that made him popular and feared at the same time. Once, a kid had tripped me on purpose while playing football on the field, and I turned up at home with my face all scratched up. The next day, the kid landed in the nurse's office, and Jacob ended up suspended.

"He would stay up late so he could look after my mum in case my dad showed up in one of his states and she needed help. My dad could get pretty scary. More bark than bite, really, but a bark can often be far worse sometimes, if you ask me. The worse it got at home, the angrier Jacob seemed to get. He had a temper. Funny it ended up being me with that reputation in the end; he would be so confused by that, wouldn't he?"

Tommy nods, looking to Michael. "Carter was the quiet kid who stuck to himself. But Jacob was the opposite. He was wild. Unpredictable. He had no fear. Kind of the town rough kid, you know? But deep down, he had a heart of gold and was totally protective of his family, especially when kids started getting mean about their home life. Their dad and such. Carter withdrew. But Jacob lashed out."

"We both shared a love of music, thanks to our mum," I continue. "When a few of us started playing in that shoddy little band in secondary school, Jacob was the lead singer. We were all Brit pop, rock, and teen angst, you know? Bit of a mess, but it was a hell of a lot of fun.

"For the first couple of years, we mostly played pubs around Yorkshire. Jacob and our original bass player, Deke, being a few years older, moved down to London eventually, and you grow up a little faster once you're there. Tommy and I were quieter, but Jacob and his friends—they were headed down a bad path. Even though we were all close, we were different in that way."

"He always had his head in a book. We used to call him the Professor, and he hated it," Tommy says with a laugh. "Carter, I mean. Not Jacob."

"I forgot about that," I say.

"Well, now it's on the record."

"Great. Eventually, Tommy and I headed down to London and were at university. Music was still a dream, though, and by then, Alex and Jacob had made some good contacts. But he and Jacob would take off after shows and turn up the next day all strung out. They started disappearing for days at a time. Blowing off practice."

I hated it. And I hated having to keep it all from my mum, who knew enough to be worried, but not nearly the full extent of how bad the drugs had become.

"We were at a place in Camden, supposed to be opening for a band we pretty much worshipped," I continue. "It was meant to be a huge break for us—but Jacob showed up too late and was completely a mess. We got into a massive fight." I remember at the time pretending it was all about the show, but the truth is, it was the first time I was ever truly scared for my brother. "We were this gang of brothers, and it was all falling apart. We blew the show, and it was a disaster. We broke up for a while. Decided to give up the whole thing. Focused on school."

"School always came easy for him," Tommy says, pointing a thumb my way. His arms are crossed, and his eyes are closed as he talks. It's getting late. "Used to drive me crazy. This guy could ace exams after being out all night."

"So you two weren't into the same scene as Jacob. The drugs?" Michael asks.

"No." I shake my head. "Drinking, well, that was more of a challenge. But I saw what had happened to Jacob, and I didn't want any part of the rest of it. He was barely around for a while."

"And Alex?" Michael asks.

"He'd taken off down the same path with Jacob," I say, and Alex shrugs in acknowledgment. His stint in rehab was public knowledge by now.

"They were both a mess." Tommy had grown quieter and opens his eyes. "It wasn't long after that when they found Jacob." His voice falters a bit at the end as he speaks.

"It was always said that he died in a fire?" Michael asks.

Neither Tommy nor I speak for a little while.

Like good memories, the bad ones are embedded just as surely. The night of the fire, I went out looking for Jacob and found him at some girl's shoddy place in Brixton. They were all strung out, and I tried to get Jacob to come with me. But he was totally out of it and wouldn't go. Finally, I stormed off, leaving Jacob there. Told him I was done with him. I should have tried harder. I should have done more. A few hours later, he overdosed, the place caught fire, and Jacob never made it out. Because of me. And Alex was the one to get them the drugs that night. He'd left just before I arrived, planning to return. He never got over the guilt.

But some stories are better left untold.

"Yeah," I say simply. "That's right. Electrical fire."

Tommy meets my eyes in mutual understanding. He nods his head just slightly, knowing the details of the wheels turning in my head.

"Jacob had some kind of demon that no one was going to change. No one could get through to him after some point. Not even you," Tommy says eventually, reading my mind. Always looking after me, even after all these years. But that's who we are.

The lights in the cabin have grown dimmer, and the plane hits a bit of turbulence, jostling us in our seats ever so slightly. The club soda I've been drinking sloshes a little, and Tommy shifts in his seat.

"I disappeared for a while after that," I say. "But when I came back—"

"Out of nowhere one day, this guy shows up at my door looking five years older, with a stack of the best music he's ever written. Beautiful stuff. He hands it to me and says, 'Let's do this.' Just like that. We got the other guys and convinced Carter to take over on vocals.

"Everything that happened with Jacob had scared Alex straight, and by some miracle and a lot of willpower, he showed up clean as a whistle," Tommy says. "For a while, anyway," he adds with a shrug. In response, Alex salutes.

"We made this pact. We'd seen the way other bands had self-destructed. So we told ourselves we'd walk the straight and narrow. Focus on the music. No distractions. Nothing. For Alex, that meant drugs. For me, that meant . . . well, anything that could throw me into a downward spiral. They'd never seen me in love, but they knew I could get a little . . ."

"Intense?" Tommy says, raising a brow.

"Devoted," I correct. "And I think they were worried that if things went poorly with her, it would break me." They weren't entirely wrong.

I never told Tommy the full story of what went on during those months when I disappeared after Jacob's death. Only Alex knows the full extent of it. That I barely survived the depression. I still don't know how I did. Or why the universe bothered with me. But Alex was the one to remind me that my mum had already lost one son. It was why he was so concerned when he saw me diving into something with my entire heart.

"How long did you keep the pact?" Michael asks.

I shrug. "Not long enough."

A minute passes while Michael is taking all of this in. "It's funny," Alex says a moment later.

"What?" I ask.

"Do you remember? I'm the one who ended up telling her everything about this back then."

"That's right. I'd forgotten about that. One of those early nights with her out on tour, right?"

"Who? Cameron?" Michael asks.

Tommy chuckles, and a smile crosses my lips. Michael looks to both of us questioningly.

"We're laughing because that's not her real name," I explain. "She had reasons to stay anonymous, so she used a pen name."

Realization dawns on Michael's face. "Ah, that explains a few things."

Alex looks off into the distance, pictures playing in his mind. "I told her over a couple of beers before a show. She'd overheard a conversation and knew we were worried about you. But she couldn't understand why. She needed to know."

"She did," I agree. "I probably should've thanked you for that."

He bows his head slightly in reply.

28

EVIE

"Carter never forgave himself for that night. Even though it wasn't his fault." Alex took a long draw from his beer. "The music and band have been what's kept him going—kept him from flipping out. So he's been dead focused on that and nothing else. Until you."

Understanding dawned on me. "You guys are afraid that if we mess things up, if he gets hurt, then he'll fall apart and disappear again. Or worse." It started to make more sense.

"Maybe. I feel bad saying it like that, but yeah . . . if things don't go well . . ." He tucked his hair behind his ear, trailing off. "Look, he's always been kind of a weird dude when it comes to girls, never much for the whole one-night-stand thing. All angsty, intense, sensitive song-writer dude. I don't get it." He laughed, shaking his head. "So then you come along and he's suddenly pouring everything he's got into you. It freaked us out. We're all just trying to hang on, trying not to mess up. This may be our only shot."

"I see."

"But I'm glad to see him happy. I thought we'd lost that part of him," he said more gently. Alex and I had come a long way after those initial days at the beach house. As time went on, we'd often find ourselves perched together in quiet little nooks around venues or up late on the bus, talking about life.

I watched the condensation drip down my bottle, letting the information settle in my mind. "Thanks for telling me." I laid my hand on his arm. "I'm so sorry you guys had to go through all that. I'm sorry about Jacob."

He shrugged. "Eh, you know. All part of life's crazy ride, right?"

"And what about you?" I asked, searching his face. "How are you in all this?"

He looked away to the distance, chewing on the inside of his cheek for a few moments. Then he let out a long breath, tapped my knee, and jumped up. "So. Anyway. I've got some guitar to play, right?" He cocked his head and gave me a sad smile, which I returned.

He strutted away, calling over his shoulder, "It's been a pleasure, my dear. Thanks for the party. Let's do it again sometime soon. Maybe without all the sad, sappy shit." With a bow, he ran off toward the stage.

I sat for a few more moments, digesting everything I'd heard, before hurrying to the stage. I got to the stage door just in time to catch Carter. I slid my arms around him and kissed him hard, bringing the conversations among some nearby stagehands to a halt.

He smiled, momentarily confused by my sudden outburst, then kissed me back.

"You know I'm in love with you, right?" he whispered in my ear.

"I know." I bloomed. "I love you too."

From that point on, we learned to balance everything—though I have no idea how we did it. But Carter wasn't the only one with a past.

29

EVIE

I wasn't with them every single night—not at first, anyway. I went back and forth a lot, so we were often apart for periods of time. We hated it, the constant goodbyes. But the reunions were wonderful.

He surprised me once.

He showed up at my apartment door unannounced, leaning against the doorjamb, all smoldering eyes and wicked grin, before scooping me up into his arms. As usual, he took my breath away. I stood speechless for a few moments, then threw my arms around him. He backed me up against the door, hard, with one hand behind my head to cushion the force and the other pulling me against him.

"You are killing me," he whispered.

"What are you doing here?"

"I couldn't stay away," he muttered against my mouth.

"But you have a show. You're supposed to be in Pittsburgh."

"Not for twenty-four hours."

"You're crazy, you know that?"

"So I've been told."

"I'm not complaining."

I quickly closed the door, and we stumbled over one another, unwilling to split apart.

"Welcome to my apartment," I said, barely removing my mouth from his.

"Nice place," he said, without looking, as his hands pulled the dress over my head.

We were like this. Addicted beyond reason. It's an extraordinary feeling when you have it, but it turns your whole world upside down in the most beautifully delicious and frightening ways. Still, I hope you've experienced it at least once in your life. Because it's worth it.

A while later, in a sleepy daze, he twirled his hands in my hair. "What are you doing here?" I whispered through a sleepy smile.

"I was halfway there and I hopped off the bus, wrangled a car, and took a turn."

"Seriously? You just drove a six-hour detour to get here?" I couldn't believe he'd done that, just to see me.

"I like driving. It's where I do my best thinking. I'll leave in the morning and get there in time. It'll be fine. Assuming I can stay here, that is."

I grinned from ear to ear.

"I'll take that as a yes."

I sat up, pulling my fingers through my thoroughly knotted and tousled hair in an attempt to smooth it. A moment later, he jumped up and walked to the bathroom, returning with my hairbrush in his hand. "Here, sit up." He propped himself up against the headboard and set me between his legs. He ran the brush through my hair in long, slow, soothing strokes.

"So this is where you live? Can I have a tour?" he asked.

I giggled. I could pretty much give him the royal tour of my studio apartment without ever leaving the bed. "Well, this is the bedroom." Wispy white curtains served as a wall to separate the wrought-iron bed from the rest of the living space. "I'm thinking of hanging my new

Mayluna posters here above my bed. What do you think?" I teased, pointing at an exposed brick wall.

"Uh, I'd rather just be here in person."

"And the living room." I gestured with a flourish toward the sitting area, which consisted of an ivory sofa with nail-head trim and an antique steam-trunk coffee table, upon which sat a stack of books and a small vase of wilted flowers.

He jumped out of bed, slipping on a few pieces of clothing along the way, and went to the table. "Ha, I knew it!" he said, holding up a well-loved, dog-eared copy of *The Bell Jar*.

"What? You did say the last book I read at the beach. So technically, you were not correct."

"Uh-huh. If you say so."

"Excuse me, we were in the middle of a grand household tour."

"Yes, carry on, please." He gestured grandly for me to lead him to the open kitchen that looked out into the living room.

"You already found the bathroom, and now we've arrived at the kitchen." I suddenly noticed the time. "Speaking of . . . Are you hungry? I don't think I have much here, some fruit and cheese. An avocado or two."

He smiled. "What is that again?" He pointed.

"An avocado?"

He laughed then. "That's hilarious. The way you say that. 'Avocado.'" He did a ridiculous attempt at an American accent.

I gave him a look. "Okay, is this the part where we start making fun of each other's accents?"

He pulled me closer, kissing me. "It's cute."

Every time I've said "avocado" since that day, I've thought of that moment, standing in my kitchen. Silly, I know. *Avocado*.

"Well, anyway, we can go out if you'd like."

He lifted me up onto the counter. "I like being in your space. And you couldn't get me to leave tonight for anything, including food."

We dined on the few items that we found in the kitchen—sandwiches, fruit, and a bottle of white wine I'd been saving for a bubble bath. And yes, a perfectly ripe avocado.

As night settled in, we left the lights off, lit a few candles, and curled up on the sofa, listening to the sound of the rain outside the open patio door. I wore a loose pair of cotton drawstring white pajama pants and a sheer pale-blue shirt that hung loose off my shoulder, and he wore just his jeans, the top button undone. I rested my head in his lap and closed my eyes while his fingers twirled in my hair. A few minutes later, I realized I'd dozed off. When I looked up, I saw that he'd been watching me, and I covered my face, laughing.

"I like watching you sleep. You look peaceful." His voice was tender.

"It's a rare thing, that's for sure. But you seem to have this effect on me. I've slept better lately than I have in years."

"I put you to sleep. Excellent. Just the effect I hope to have on women."

"No, no. That's not what I mean!" I said, laughing with him. "I just don't sleep well. I never have. Even when I was little. But with you, it's different. Like you said, peaceful." I nuzzled into him. "I curl up with you and drift right off. Seems you've cured my insomnia."

"Again with the compliments." He picked me up and carried me into the bed.

"I still can't believe you left the tour for the night. I would've seen you in a week, you know."

"Too long."

I let out a sigh. "But this isn't good; you know that, right? You should be there. You all have worked so hard for this. I know it'll be fine for a few months while we're doing this project, but then what? The last thing you need is some girl back in the States, holding you back from enjoying the ride of a lifetime."

"I want you in my life, Evie," he said after a moment. I looked away, knowing he meant it now but also knowing that it would be much harder once he was back in the momentum of his world.

"Look at me." He held my chin, forcing me to look him in the eyes. "I want you in my life," he repeated. "In all of this with me—wherever it leads. And if that means only seeing you when we can or between shows or whatever, fine. You'll come to see me; I'll come to see you. We'll make it work."

As the clock ticked on, I fought sleep, desperate to not waste a single minute with him, but I was losing the battle. Finally, he wrapped me in his arms and whispered in my ear, "Go to sleep. I'm here."

It was like a lullaby. There was something about him, about his presence, that soothed me. The dark was less dark with him by my side. I took a deep breath, inhaling his scent, absorbing it as I settled against him to sleep.

The next morning, he stood close by, watching me dress, looking at me like I was some kind of exotic creature that he was studying.

"You're beautiful, you know that?" he said to my reflection in the mirror.

No one ever said things like that to me. Or looked at me that way. Sometimes, even now, when I'm getting ready for the day, seeing myself in the mirror with tired eyes or putting on my makeup or turning this way and that in a mirror and judging myself harshly, I'll see him like a ghost behind me. "You're beautiful, you know that?"

It seemed like things were going wonderfully.

We were on our way back from getting coffee when it happened. When my two worlds collided right on cue, just as I was beginning to think happiness might have finally come my way. I remember I had been smiling. Until I wasn't.

Carter was still back at the car when I rounded the corner and saw the figure standing outside my apartment, and I stopped breathing.

"Hello, pumpkin."

30

EVIE

I know I haven't talked much about my parents over the years. I think there comes a point when it's best to leave things in the past rather than dwelling on them. A few thousand dollars' worth of solid therapy taught me that. Still, they come to me sometimes, especially at night. Sometimes I'll catch a hint of my mother's Shalimar perfume. I'll remember her silhouette in the orange glow of a nightlight and settle back in to sleep beneath warm, safe covers in a room decorated in gingham pink and yellow. Small flowers dotting white wallpaper.

It was early February when her car skidded across a spot of black ice on the way home from her hospital shift one wintry night somewhere after two in the morning. Funny thing about that night is that when I awoke the next morning to the confusing sound of my aunt Kitty's voice in the living room instead of the smell of Saturday-morning french toast, I could swear I remembered the scent of Shalimar and the good-night kiss just hours earlier, and I still had the faint hint of perfume on my pajamas to prove it. I remember my aunt dismissing it, telling me in her gravelly voice that it was impossible, because my mother had never made it home, of course. Just my imagination, she said. "Poor thing." But to this day, I'm sure it was real. It had been her last ghostly goodbye, I suppose.

My aunt Kitty wasn't the "kid type," she'd proclaimed as they scrambled to sort out what to do with me in the aftermath. "All the mothering genes went to Leigh Ann," she'd said, referring to my mom. I'd had a babysitter—a neighbor from next door—but she had her own family. I had no grandparents. No anyone, really. It had just been my mom and me in our little house. Until it was just me.

A week later, I was deposited on the front step of my father's place in a small trailer park on the edge of town, carrying all my belongings in a small red suitcase with Strawberry Shortcake on the outside. I'd met him only a few times early on and had nothing but uncertain memories of it. I begged and cried to go anywhere else, but even at eight years old, you're smart enough to know when to give up. I was given a small room in the back with wood paneling that was peeling in the top right corner beneath a yellow water stain on the ceiling. After throwing a bit of a tantrum, I'd managed to convince the adults, I don't remember who now, to allow me to bring one small box of my mother's things. Her cassette tapes, a bottle of her perfume, a silver bangle bracelet and a pair of earrings, along with one small framed painting of a daisy from our kitchen that I'd snatched at the last minute for some reason. Those sorts of things. I often wonder what happened to the rest of our stuff from our little house on Wellesley Street. Flea market, I suppose.

Someone had thought to bring my bedspread, which was placed on the mattress in the dark little room. I set the painting of the daisy on a bedside table and began what would become the rest of my childhood, if you could really call it that.

"Well, pumpkin? Aren't you going to say hello to your own dad?" my father said, now standing in front of my apartment door.

I felt the familiar feeling of weight, causing my shoulders to sag a little. "Hey, Dad," I said, mustering some sort of smile for a reason I'm not quite sure of. People-pleasing, I guess. It's always been a problem. Still hoping for some sort of approval from him.

He leaned against the door, holding a menthol cigarette that smelled like my old home. "I told the super that I was your dad, but he wouldn't let me in."

I'd have to remember to thank the super, Mr. Wallace, for that later.

He looked down at the two coffees I held in my hand. "You got company?"

I stammered a little. "I . . . What are you doing here?"

"What? I can't come and see my little girl?"

Carter rounded the corner then, and I looked up at him. "Okay, so I've got exactly 7.25 hours to . . . ," he started. I clenched my teeth, determined to keep the tears from forming. He stopped short when he saw me. "Everything okay here, Ev?" he asked.

My dad laughed then. "Evie? But here I thought it was *Cameron* now." He drew the word out long, mocking.

"Um . . . could you give me a minute, please?" I looked at Carter, feigning a smile, practically begging him to leave. I didn't want him to be a part of this.

"Aren't you going to introduce us? I brought you up better than that." My father dropped his cigarette on the sidewalk and crushed it with the sole of his boot.

I reached out to give the coffees to Carter, and he looked down at my trembling hand. "Can you just put these inside, please? I'll be there in a minute." I started to hand him my keys, but he remained firmly standing in place.

"Who is this, Ev?" Carter asked.

"I'm Evie's dad, Raymond, but you can call me Ray." He gave a jaunty smile. "Can't you see the resemblance? She got her good looks from me." When neither of us said anything, he continued. "Are you going to tell me your name, son?"

Carter narrowed his eyes, seeming to size up the situation. "I'm—"

"He's nobody, Dad," I said quickly, glancing at Carter, but just barely met his eyes. "Just a guy from work. You know what, actually?" I turned to Carter. "I know you're in a hurry. You can go, and I'll talk to you tomorrow."

Carter watched me carefully but didn't move. "Uh. Like hell."

"Ooh, fiery one you've got here, pumpkin. I like him." He winked at Carter.

I gave Carter a look, my eyes filling, begging him to leave. "I'm fine. Just wait inside. Please."

"You don't have to rush him off on my account," my father said. "Let's all go inside together and get to know each other. It's been a while." He pointed a thumb at me. "You know this one hasn't been home to see me in what . . . seven years? Isn't that right, Ev?"

"It's not really a good time, Dad."

"Now, Evie, don't be like that. I drove a long way to see you."

I sighed. "How did you know how to find me?" There was a reason why I used a pen name.

"Oh, come on, give me some credit. I figured you would still be in New York after college. And I heard bits and pieces and that you were trying to be some fancy journalist or something." He looked at Carter. "She used to write in these little notebooks for hours, this one. Always writing something with her head in the clouds." He rolled his eyes.

When neither of us said anything, he continued. "Anyway, word gets around. Cameron Leigh, huh? Pretty good, I've got to say. Using the combination of your mother's name that way."

"I know you didn't drive all the way out here just to see me."

He looked a little sheepish. "Well, I was in the Big Apple to meet up with some of the guys, and one of 'em has a cousin out this way, so I figured, might as well stop and visit my little girl. I looked up your new name and, sure enough, found your address, and here we are."

"What about work, Dad? They gave you time off?"

"Eh, not exactly. More like an extended leave of absence."

I sighed. "You got fired again."

"It's just temporary."

"I don't have any money, Dad."

His cheeks flushed, and he glanced at Carter. He leaned over toward me. "You're a working girl now, aren't you? I read a few of your stories. They're not bad. I bet they pay you pretty well. Even though there's no good music out there anymore. Shame." He raised his chin, putting his arm around me. "You know, she learned all about music from me. She used to steal my magazines. Sit around and listen to us practicing for a gig. I had to drag her everywhere we played." He laughed.

"You didn't take me anywhere, Dad. You just left me at home."

"Now, that's just not true. You loved coming to shows."

"I was nine. I had no business being in the back of dive bars after midnight."

"Eh." He waved a hand. "You loved watching us play."

I didn't love it. Sometimes I just couldn't take being at home all night alone anymore. It was a choice between two evils. Carter's eyes darted to mine, this new information processing heavily.

"After her mom died, I carted her around, taking care of her. Did you know that? I raised this one all by myself. Isn't that right, pumpkin? Just you and me." And he made sure I never forgot it. Even though he often forgot all about me for hours, sometimes more, at a time.

I nodded somberly. "Yeah. That's right, Dad."

"Family looks after family," he said pointedly.

Ten minutes earlier, I had been smiling and joyful and felt light as air. And then, just like that, it was like I woke up from a dream to find myself in the fourth grade again, trying to make myself invisible. So he wouldn't see me. So no one would see me.

"Just a bit to tide me over, pumpkin. I'll pay you back. I promise," he said in the saccharine-laced, gravelly tone I knew well.

"They don't pay me much, Dad. I just earn enough to get by." I could barely meet Carter's eyes, wanting the sidewalk to swallow me whole.

168

"Look, Evie, I'll tell you what, let's go out and talk. Get some lunch. Maybe get to know your new boyfriend here."

Carter stepped beside me and took my hand. "I don't think so. You heard her. She asked you to go."

My father puffed out his chest. "Look at you. Big man with your fancy accent. This is family business. Between my girl and me. You need to step aside."

"If she wants to talk to you, she'll call. But right now, you need to leave." Carter stepped forward, placing himself between my father and me. "Now."

"Temper, temper on this one!" My father was making a joke, but Carter had a full three inches in height over him, and I could tell he was unnerved. My father had always seemed to tower over me, but for the first time in my life, I realized that it had been an illusion, as he suddenly seemed to be smaller.

"What do you know, anyway?" He looked Carter up and down. "Not much, I'm guessing, by the looks of you."

Carter's jaw clenched. "Go."

"Now, step aside, son. Let's go get some lunch, Evie. Come on— we'll catch up."

My eyes were filled with tears, and I looked down, quiet. My father ruined everything. Nothing would be the same now that he knew where I was. He'd always want something.

"I can't today, Dad. Sorry. Maybe next time," I said quietly. I went to my bag and pulled out a few bills from my wallet, hoping it would be enough to get him to leave for a little while. "Here's a bit to help with gas. Maybe we'll catch up tomorrow. Okay?"

He looked at me, then back to Carter, who wasn't backing down, and then seeming to think better of it, gingerly stepped around him. He walked over to me, and I could smell the stale cigarette smoke on him that permeated every fabric of my childhood. Instinctively, I made myself smaller, hoping he would just leave. I reached out and gave him the cash.

"That's good of you, kiddo. I'll come back next time I'm around. There's a job in Jersey that'll pay me a few bucks. And we might get a gig while we're there. I'll come up here, take you out for something nice."

I nodded somberly. "Okay, Dad."

"Don't be a stranger, kiddo. I'll see you soon." He gave a sidelong look at Carter and then finally was on his way. Just as he was going, he turned. "Hey, you should know. I'm sober now. Two months." He seemed bashful and proud at the same time.

I smiled a little, hopeful that it would stick this time for his sake. "That's really wonderful, Dad." And I meant it. "Really."

His face softened, and he looked at me again. "You really do look good, kiddo."

"Thanks, Dad."

I stood where I was for a moment, sad and trembling, and watched him leave, while tears began to spill down my cheeks. I didn't look at Carter. I didn't want to look at anyone. I picked up the keys from where I'd dropped them, unlocked the door, and stepped inside. But when I looked up through the window, I saw Carter talking to my father by his truck. After a few words, he drove away.

I heard the door open and a moment later, Carter joined me where I sat on the sofa.

"What did you say to him?" I asked, still not able to fully meet his eyes.

He didn't answer at first. "I just made sure he wouldn't be coming back for a while."

"He'll always come back." He stole the light from whatever good I had in my life.

"Ev, you're going to have to tell me what that was all about."

"You have to get to Pittsburgh."

He pulled me close. "We have a little longer."

I'm eight years old and it's after ten o'clock at night and I have school in the morning. I'm already in bed but can't sleep when I hear my father walk in. I hear the tinny sound of the television coming from the living room—I leave it on for company—and a moment later, the sound of him kicking off his boots. At his stumbling arrival, there's the familiar pressure in my gut, coupled oddly with a sense of relief because at least I'm not alone in the trailer anymore. "Hey, Ev, you still up?" he calls. I want to be asleep, but I'm not, so with some reluctance, I get up. As I pad down the narrow hall, I notice just a split second too late a toy Barbie car I've left on the kitchen floor. He kicks it out of the way with a force that slams it into the wall, scattering it into pieces. I wince and then quickly run to it. "I'm sorry. I meant to pick it up, but I forgot. I'm sorry." I bend over to retrieve the broken pieces of the treasured toy that had been a gift from a friend's mom and try not to cry. Maybe I can fix it.

"I told you to keep your crap in your own room," he says. "I don't need kids' junk laying everywhere." I nod and make myself small against the wall, as I often do. Maybe if he doesn't see me, if I'm less trouble, he'll love me more.

I'd made a peanut butter and jelly sandwich earlier, packed and ready in the refrigerator for school lunch the next day, and I watch as he reaches in and opens it, gobbling it in three bites. The last of the bread. My stomach growls. He sways a bit, and I can smell the alcohol on him. "I'll go to the store tomorrow," he says then, as if realizing I'm still there.

"Okay," I say, though we both know he won't.

I've been telling Carter stories like these. I had been reluctant and quiet, but once I started talking, they just poured out. He had that effect on me. I told him about the way I'd learned to cook simple things from around the house when I was little—using the chair as a stool to boil water for macaroni and cheese. Learned to wash clothes and sheets in the bathtub when he didn't get to the Laundromat. Aside from the few rough patches like mine, I lived in a nice town, with a good school that was my favorite place to be. Teachers watched over me. Checked in on me from time to time with an encouraging word.

I met your dad and Kate in middle school. They became like family and lived in comfortable homes with good parents who always just happened to have leftovers around to give me. And then later, your dad and I started dating—winning Best Couple in the yearbook and all. With the help of his parents, both attorneys, I'd become legally emancipated at the age of sixteen so that I would be able to make arrangements for college and scholarships and financial aid without needing to depend on my father's signatures and all the necessary documents. I might as well have done it when I was eight, if anyone had let me.

I told Carter all of this. I told him a few good things too—like the time my dad surprised me with a Christmas tree and we decorated it with colored lights and icicles. And the Shirley Temples the bartenders would sometimes make me when he took me along to a bar for a gig and the way his friends' girlfriends would do my hair and make a fuss over me. I didn't tell him about the time when I was ten and my father somehow thought it was okay to go away for a week and leave me home alone and that while he was gone, a storm hit and the power went out in the middle of the night. I'd been afraid of the dark ever since and learned to fall asleep with the coming of the dawn. Or how I'd had to lie about where he was sometimes so no one would report him to Child Protective Services. And that eventually, when I was fourteen and old enough to get a job at the local Dairy Queen after school, how I began to support us both. He took almost every dollar I made. Though Carter had probably figured that part out on his own, I'd imagine.

"It makes more sense now," he said a little later, while gently sliding my bracelet up and down my arm as I sat leaning against him with my legs curled beneath me.

"What does?"

"Why you told me you swore you would never date a musician." He stared off into the distance. He used to do this thing where he sort of pursed his lips as a kind of punctuation to his thoughts. Funny how clearly I can still see him doing that.

"It was all he cared about. His band. It wasn't his full-time job—he worked for the town doing road work and plowing snow—but music was what he wanted to do. It was all he talked about. He was always bitter and used to blame me. Said he could've been big if it hadn't been for my mother getting pregnant and sticking him with me—if he'd only been able to get out on the road more. Stuff like that." He used to hang pictures of cities on the wall by the phone in the kitchen. All the places he said he'd take me when he made it big. Before I knew better, I would nod and smile in response because he looked happy in those moments, and I would imagine us having fun somewhere wonderful in the future. We never went anywhere, of course. But it was a nice thought for a while. Truth was, he wasn't a great musician to begin with, and the band was just average noise, but even after everything, I would never betray my father by saying such a thing out loud.

Carter listened patiently that day, as if he had nowhere else to be. We spent the rest of the morning and into the early afternoon talking. But I think that was when we started making choices that weren't always the best—our lives coming to revolve completely around the addiction we had to each other. We were in each other's veins. He nearly missed the show in Pittsburgh that night. He made it only in the nick of time.

Carter had his history. I had mine. And now we both knew each other's skeletons. That day was also the first time he heard me talk about your dad.

31

CARTER

Her father. He was a piece of work. I realized later that I should have never given him the money that day at her apartment. But I didn't see any other way at the time. I would be back on the road and she would be back at her apartment alone, and I couldn't stand the thought of him harassing her. I had no idea at the time what the background story was, but watching her that day—she just withered. This vibrant woman full of light, suddenly small and pale before my eyes. I think the most difficult part was the moment I watched her reach out and give him this sort of half hug as he left, and instantly I saw her as a child, hoping for whatever crumbs of affection and care she could get. Here he was being such an asshole, and her response was to hug him anyway. I don't think she even realized she was doing it. It was instinctual. Hopeful, despite it all. It killed me.

So I gave him a few hundred dollars. Lied and told him we were moving in together, leaving town, so she wouldn't be around anymore. He wouldn't be able to find her again. He was going to come back no matter what I did, I suppose. But maybe he wouldn't have paid so much attention to me. Maybe he would've forgotten my face. But people like that, opportunists, they don't forget things like that. Money. I knew from other stories that he wasn't always a terrible man. We tend to make out characters like that in life to be monsters, but that's not the case. There are gray areas, and he was no exception. He was just a selfish kind of guy who didn't know how to be a father and got lost.

She used to say he stole the light from her world. I just didn't realize how strongly she believed it. And eventually, she was right.

I heard he got sick some years later. But by that point, the damage had already been done and it was too late. Ripple effects going on for years.

In the dark cabin of the airplane, Michael has been working, taking notes on everything I've been telling him, while my thoughts drift to those early days. We're about halfway to Rio, and just about everyone but Tommy, Michael, and me are asleep.

Over the years, I couldn't remember what city I was in from one night to the next—Amsterdam or Berlin? I couldn't remember what I'd eaten for dinner the previous night or any number of trivial things from just the past week, and yet, despite every aggravating attempt to erase it, I can still remember the exact sound of the gravel outside her apartment as I drove away that day. It was like being separated from a part of myself, tearing me in two.

32

EVIE

People often ask each other, "What was the happiest time of your life?" For me, I think this was it. I had started a project that I was so proud of; it made my skin tingle with excitement. I had become a member of a family for the first time in my life. It felt like sleepaway camp with a bunch of brothers I never had, all set amid the sounds of music being created in large and small form. And I was loved by a man who had chosen me, just as much as I'd chosen him, someone who knew how to hold my love and keep it safe. We had such a long way to go and so much softness and so much darkness to come, but in those moments, I felt pure joy.

We ambled down roads, as cities and towns began to blur from one night to the next, weeks turning into months, and I remember it all now like a rush of swirling water, catching glimpses of shimmering moments as they pass by in my mind's eye.

I surprised him in return once, on his birthday. I showed up in Phoenix, unannounced, sitting in the front row and taking delight at the elated look in his eyes when he spotted me there. Backstage, to the dismay of a few girls who "knew someone" and stood huddled around the dressing room door, hoping, as always, for a piece of the band, Carter threw his arms around me the moment he left the stage. I gave him a vintage copy of Kepler's *Somnium* that night as a gift. It became one of his favorite possessions.

33

EVIE

By the time the American tour was over, Mayluna, and Carter in particular, seemed to be gaining more and more attention, each crowd getting larger as the months went on. Maybe that's why I felt like I wanted to keep our relationship quiet when I went back home to Pennsylvania for a few days that winter. I think somewhere deep down, I felt more secure keeping us in our own little private bubble for as long as I could.

I'd spent Christmas in a hotel room with Carter and the guys. Tommy went out at the last minute and dragged back what was quite possibly the ugliest tree I'd ever seen, trailing needles the whole way down the corridor until it was nearly bare. But it was so perfect. We all decorated it with ornaments we'd picked up from the local drugstore on Christmas Eve and had a festive dinner in a hotel restaurant strung with holiday lights. Even Alex was in cheerful spirits. I have an image of him wearing a black Smiths T-shirt, holding a Santa hat in one hand and a bottle of whiskey in the other, along with a rare, light smile. Tommy actually filled dollar-store stockings with candy and stapled them to the upholstery on the headboards of the beds after we all fell asleep. Christmas music was played. I think there are grainy photos of the scene somewhere. Maybe Tommy's wife still has them. More likely they got lost amid the mayhem of the time. I still have the bleary-eyed one of Alex and me, though. I love that photo.

Except for the years with my mom, that was the happiest Christmas of my entire life up until that point—surrounded by all of them and silly makeshift holiday decor, just a group of four displaced Brits and a formerly orphaned girl. Joyful in our youth.

They headed to London to start recording the album with a fancy new producer the label had brought in. Much different from the first EP, which they'd recorded in a small cottage studio in Oxford a year and a half earlier. I would join back up with them in January, but for a few days in between, I went back to my hometown in Pennsylvania. Kate had gotten engaged and wanted me to come back to talk celebrations and wedding planning. I think we really just missed each other, and it had been a long time. Though, honestly, the timing of that visit still to this day strikes me as so strange. I wonder, did the universe orchestrate it that way? With such intentionality? Or was it just a happenstance of calendar dates? Even Carter would probably wonder about that, no doubt.

You may be wondering about your dad at this point, and where it all comes together. Of course, if you're doing the math, you know that none of the plans that Carter and I were making turned out like we thought.

34

CARTER

We didn't get into London much when I was growing up. But every couple of years, my parents would pack us up for an overnight or two and we would board the train in York. Jacob and I would be buzzing with excitement for the three-hour journey, emerging into Paddington Station with wide eyes. When I was around twelve years old, I'd become sort of fascinated with outer space, as many kids tend to be around that age. But I tended to be obsessive about things. When I locked on to a subject, it was all I wanted to talk about. Funny it's just occurred to me now that my interest in all things space came about right around the same time as my first guitar.

We were on one of those rare trips into London, and my mother suggested we visit the Royal Observatory, which meant very little to me at the time, mainly because I think she'd wanted to keep it a bit of a surprise. All I really knew was that it was a museum, which sounded fairly boring. We took the Thames Clipper that day from the city, traveling past Canary Wharf and into Greenwich. Jacob and I complained about the rare heat wave that had descended upon the city as our parents dragged us through the streets and up the endlessly steep path through Greenwich Park that I thought might never end. But when we arrived at the top of the hill, I shaded my eyes with my hand and stared at the strange dome towering over me, rising above all of London and the Thames. My mother leaned down with sparkling eyes and smiled, pointing upward as she explained. "It's the home of the largest refracting telescope in the UK, you see. Here in this building, hundreds of years ago, some of the finest philosophers and scientists in the world learned to plot the planets and stars." At fifteen, Jacob was fidgety and bored, but I was completely enchanted, walking through the Flamsteed House where astronomers had once lived and worked, gazing out of windows through newly invented lenses, making discoveries about not only space but time. There's a photo of me straddling the Prime Meridian beneath leafy trees with a wide, lopsided grin, and another beside the twenty-four-hour Shepherd Gate Clock.

"This explains a lot," Michael says with a chuckle, listening to me tell this story. "The cover for the *Mysterium* album . . ."

I nod. "The Tulip Stairs in Greenwich."

I took her there once, eager to share the spaces of this world that made me tick and knowing she would love it in the same way that I did. After the Observatory, we'd walked down the wintry hill to the Queen's House, and I watched her smile at the magnificence of its classical design. Sneaking away from the crowd at just the right moment, we lay at the bottom of the Tulip Stairs, holding hands as we gazed upward through the geometric black-and-white swirl of stairs that looked like they might go on forever, a golden spiral leading up to a glass window resembling an all-knowing eye.

"After the tour, we all headed back to the UK to finish writing and recording the *Sigma Five* album," I say, returning my attention to Michael and picking up on his earlier questions.

"Did she come with you?" he asks.

I nod. "For a while, yeah. By then, she'd pretty much stopped taking all other assignments and was with us all the time. She wanted to devote her full attention to the film, and it was tough to coordinate other assignments while on the road. She planned to just pick up where she'd left off eventually. But I don't think she ever did." I look away then. She told me she didn't regret the way her career had gone, but I can't help but wonder if she did sometimes.

"Why not? She had had a successful career before working with you. Why not after?"

I hesitate before answering simply. It isn't my answer to give. "Life, I guess." He doesn't push this, and so I return to the subject we've been discussing. "Then there was talk of sending us back out on the road at the end of March for our first headlining dates. She had turned in some initial footage of the documentary, and the label decided to extend it, which meant that she would be on the road with us in Europe. Believe me when I say, we were on top of the world. It was such an amazing time for all of us," I tell Michael.

"Those were good times," Tommy adds with a small smile as we think about the making of the *Sigma Five* album. The light before the dark.

35

EVIE

On my first night back in Pennsylvania, I went straight to Kate's. We had plans to meet some other old friends, including your dad. We'd tried to stay in touch every few weeks, but it was a weird time for communication. Emails were still mostly for work. Not everyone had mobile phones. It was an easy time to get disconnected. Nonetheless, despite the time and distance, Kate and I were always able to pick up easily without skipping a beat. Our senior year, she'd been voted both Best Smile and the less traditional Most Likely to Get Caught . . . , which made her fairly perfect in my eyes.

"AHH! You're home! I missed you!" She nearly knocked me backward outside her front door, and I returned her hug with equal celebration as we dragged my luggage inside. Her apartment was part of a larger brownstone in a trendy neighborhood just outside of Philly. Always dressed well, she wore her long blonde hair pinned in a delicate clip to one side, and it hung poker straight down a stylish gray A-line coat. "Hey, pretty girl! I missed you too!" I exclaimed, shivering. "But, man, I've been out west for a while and have not missed this weather."

"I feel like we haven't talked in ages," she said, half pouting.

"I know; I'm sorry. Me too!"

"All right, lots to catch up on. But let's get you settled in later. First we go out!"

"Yes! Where are we headed? And where's Jim?" Our breath was gray in the frigid winter air as we quickly retreated to the warmth of her car.

"He's coming with Steve. A little reunion! Everyone is in town, Ev!"

"You're kidding. Steve's in town this year?"

"Yep, he just moved back, actually. Got a job at a fancy firm downtown. I thought you guys were still in touch sometimes?"

"Not as much, lately. We haven't seen each other since that party a couple of New Years ago." I looked over and saw her grinning at me with a know-it-all expression on her face. "What?" I asked.

"Oh, please, don't pretend you're not excited to see him."

"Of course I'm excited to see him; he's Steve."

"That's not what I mean, and you know it."

"We haven't dated since high school. There is absolutely nothing between us."

"You're still the love of his life, you know," she said.

"Me and about twenty other girls. And whatever, that is so not true. We outgrew each other years ago."

"Whatever you say. But anyway, he'll be there tonight, so we'll see-ee," she said in a singsong voice.

"You do remember I have a boyfriend, right?" My heart warmed at the thought of Carter. Everyone I'd ever dated before him, and every other man on the planet, paled in comparison, instantly forgotten.

"Oh, right. Your imaginary boyfriend and all that. What's his name again? Connor?" She looked around. "And where is Mr. Mysterious exactly?"

"I did not make him up. He just travels a lot." I'd mentioned Carter only briefly to Kate during our few conversations. I'd refrained from telling her more about him because as much as I loved her, she was like a pipeline to the hometown gossip pool, and given the circumstances, I'd grown protective of my privacy in the matter. But I was looking forward to finally telling her the whole story. Maybe when we had some quality alone time at the end of the night, I thought.

Out of the corner of my eye, I caught Kate rolling her eyes. "He's a musician, and he travels a lot? Oh, that sounds just fabulous. Such a catch, Ev." Her voice dripped sarcasm.

Though Kate and I were similar in many ways, she was as grounded in her thoughts and dreams as most everyone in our hometown—good job, good family, good house, solid 401(k)—that was the dream. I couldn't always relate.

We arrived at our destination in Old City. At night, the neighborhood sprang to life with an eclectic crowd carousing the cobblestone streets as they hopped from bar to bar. That night, our friends had taken over a tufted velvet sofa and a mix of upholstered chairs and tables at a favorite bar, strewn with pitchers of pale beer and plastic cups beneath strands of colored lights. We greeted one another, a group of nine or so, exchanging hugs and kisses that could only be achieved so warmly by having been practiced since grade school. I was immediately handed a beer and was about to take a sip when a pair of arms wrapped around my waist from behind.

"Hey, stranger." I spun around and smiled widely at the sight of your dad. His blond hair, which he'd worn long and tucked behind his ears most of our teen years, was now stylishly cut short. And the blue of his eyes was brought out by a black wool sweater over a chambray collared shirt that had replaced the ubiquitous flannels of our earlier youth. He smiled his toothpaste-commercial smile at me and opened his arms.

"Steve!" I returned his hug eagerly, buoyed by the sight of one of my favorite people in the world.

From the time we were kids, your dad had a politician's ability to make and collect friends, and I'd never met a single person who didn't like him. Since the age of eleven, girls had been smitten by him, and boys wanted to be his friend. All the while, he was one of the most humble and kind people I knew and had an openness that drew people

KELLEY McNEIL

in naturally. Few people could elicit as instantaneous of a smile from me as he could. He held me at arm's length and looked me up and down.

"Damn, girl. Whatever you're doing agrees with you."

"Thanks, you're looking pretty good yourself, sir."

He mock bowed in appreciation.

"So I hear you're back in town for good this time?" I had to yell into his ear to compete with the music.

"Yeah. I just got hired at a firm here in town. My parents are thrilled. And it's good to be back."

"Congrats! Glad to hear things are going well."

"What about you? You've fallen off the planet! No one ever hears from you. Off in the world doing whatever it is you do, hanging out at rock concerts or whatever. Our little free spirit."

"Ugh! What is it about my job that's so hard to understand?"

"It's not. I'm just giving you a hard time." He winked at me.

"Uh-huh. But yeah. It's been kind of a crazy year."

Just then, Kate pushed him out of the way, teasing, "Oh no, not you already! Don't you go monopolizing her time; I just got her back!"

"Uh-oh, here's trouble." He laughed, embracing her. Steve and Kate had the habit of behaving a lot like brother and sister, with a combination of affection and annoyance. "Okay. In honor of our little reunion here, shots all around," Steve announced, earning a loud cheer from our group, which now took up nearly the entire back of the bar.

We have these two pictures in an album somewhere side by side: one photo is from seventh grade, at our first boy-girl party, Kate on one side, me on the other, and Steve in the middle; the second one is an identical pose in our twenties, taken on that night in Old City in front of chalk-graffiti brick walls beside a pinball machine. The three musketeers.

Steve was staying with Jim at an apartment nearby, and it was decided that we'd all crash there for the night, thus eliminating the need to drive home later. So the drinks flowed. As we all talked and laughed, Steve, Kate, and I stayed in close proximity to each other. Some things never change.

186

"What?" Steve asked at one point, noticing my expression as I looked at him.

I laughed. "Nothing. Just reminiscing."

He slid his chair closer to mine so that we could talk more easily. Steve's whole personality could be seen in the warmth of his eyes, and I saw a familiar glint there. "I've missed you. We should keep in touch more," he said.

"Yeah. I know. It's hard, though, isn't it? Careers and all. Life takes over."

"And you're never back in town, I hear?" he said.

"Less and less these days. My work keeps me busy. And it's just better this way. I won't be back again for a while," I said. "I try to avoid it."

"I understand. Have you seen him yet? Your dad?"

I shook my head. "I just got here a few hours ago."

"When's the last time you saw him?"

"It's been a few years. But he showed up at my apartment unexpectedly a while back."

"How did he find you?"

I shrugged. "It's just a pen name. Not the witness protection program. I'm sure it wasn't that hard."

He took a deep breath and let it out slowly. "I'm sorry. I'm sure that wasn't easy."

"It was okay. Just the same old thing. He needed some money."

"Shocking."

"But otherwise he was fine. He just took me by surprise. I think he may be getting sober."

Steve knew the history better than anyone. I'd spent more nights than I could count over the years sleeping at his parents' house. Between his family and Kate's, I'd always had a place to go when I was growing up. And despite the differences in our background—him living in one of the biggest houses in town, while I struggled in a trailer on the edges of town—Steve's parents never once judged my humble and difficult life. They welcomed me with open arms.

He attempted an encouraging smile. "That's great. I hope it sticks this time."

"Me too." I hadn't decided if I'd go see my father yet. Part of me wanted to, but the other didn't. I changed the subject. "But otherwise, work is really taking off! I've been working on a film with a band, and everything feels like it's fitting into place in life, finally."

"What? You and this rock-'n'-roll stuff. Aren't you the cool one." He said it with a good-natured nudge.

"Yeah, yeah. I know. But you sound like a grandpa."

"You're an easy target. But honestly, good for you." His eyes softened. "I mean it. I'm glad you're happy and enjoying your work. I always knew you'd go places and leave us all in the dust," he added with a touch of uncharacteristic melancholy.

A waitress came up to him, asking if he'd like anything else. "Ev? Want anything? Another drink?"

"Yeah, that'd be great, thanks."

"Could we get two waters and . . ." He eyed the empty pitchers at the table. "Two more pitchers, please?" She nodded and hovered around him a little closer than necessary before reluctantly disappearing back into the crowd.

"Still making the girls swoon, I see?"

"Eh, whatever," he said, blowing it off. "Speaking of romance, our girl over there tells me you have some new boyfriend, plays in a band or something?" He pointed his drink toward Kate. I smiled widely and felt my cheeks warm. "So I guess that means I can't persuade you to go to dinner with me before you leave?"

Always the flirt, I thought, smiling. "I'm leaving the day after tomorrow. But thank you."

He took a drink and nodded, considering me sideways. "Hmm. Well, good for him. And you. I hope he's taking good care of our girl."

"He is. Thanks. We're happy." I took a long drink and leaned over, nearly having to shout in his ear over the loud music. "And what about you? Seeing anyone?"

"Sometimes!" he said, laughing. "Maybe I'll even find someone my parents like as much as they liked you!"

"Impossible!"

"Probably right." He smiled gamely. "But maybe someday down the road." He looked at me closely. "Are you and this guy that serious?"

I nodded. "Yes. Very. In fact, we're planning to move in together. I'm moving to London." I put a finger up to my lips. "Shh. I haven't told Kate yet."

He suddenly looked surprised and then seemed to swallow a look of disappointment before brushing it off. "Whoa, look at you! All swoony and making grown-up plans! Well, he's a lucky guy."

"Thanks, Steve."

"Wow. London. Okay then." He met my eyes and gave me a long look. "Wherever you go, you know I'll always be here for you. No matter what. Right?"

"Back at you."

"Okay then." He stood and kissed the top of my head. "All right. Who's up for pool?" he announced, raising his arms in the air, effectively ending the conversation and gearing up for more fun. He always had so much life in him. It's hard to believe he's gone.

"Still sexy as hell, isn't he?" Kate said, taking his empty seat. "Hmm. A hot, successful guy who treats girls well. Tell me again why you two haven't ended up together yet?" she asked, feigning confusion.

I shook my head. "No way. He and I are so different. It would've never worked, and we all know it," I replied. "And besides, if you like him so much, why didn't you ever date him?" I joked.

"Ew, no, that would be . . . just no. But I will thank him for introducing me to a certain gentleman." She raised her beer. "Like that super-cute roommate of his who I get to marry! I'm getting married!"

"You're getting married!"

I hugged her again, and just as she eyed Jim across the room with a grin, the jukebox blared into action, and I instantly recognized the intro to a Mayluna song. "Ooh, I love this song!" Kate exclaimed.

"Hey, Kate! About this song? So, I have something to tell you."

"Be right back, Ev!" Kate shouted over the din of the crowd and the blaring music.

Suddenly missing Carter like crazy, I quickly escaped to the bathroom, where a line of girls with glassy eyes waited. I pulled out my phone and dialed the number.

"Hey!"

Carter laughed at the sound of my overly chipper voice. "Oh no, you're drunk, love!"

"Am not. Well, maybe just a little, but I'm fine. And I miss you like crazy!"

"Where are you? I can barely hear you."

"At a bar downtown with some friends from school. A little mini-reunion. Here, listen . . ." I held the phone up so he could hear his song playing.

"Ah, I see. Made you miss me, huh?" he said, groaning.

"Absolutely! And what are you guys up to?"

"We're headed out to some club. Alex's idea. I have no idea where."

"Two more days until I get to see you!"

"Two more days!" he replied. "And then forever."

A girl bumped into me, moving me forward in the line. "I'd better go. I love you."

"You too, love. And please be safe tonight, okay? Be careful getting home."

"Don't worry, I think we're all crashing at Steve's. You be safe, as well, okay?"

I heard the pause on the other end of the line. "Hold on, you're staying at Steve's? As in, high school boyfriend Steve?"

I smiled. "As in, ancient history, nothing for you to worry about Steve."

He grew quiet. "Ah. I see."

"It's no big deal. I promise." I hoped he could hear how true it was.

"All right, well . . . you'd better be dreaming of me while you're sleeping, in three layers of clothing, in Steve's house tonight."

"I always dream of you."

We said our goodbyes, and I rejoined my friends just as the Mayluna song ended. I don't remember much from the rest of that night, if I'm being honest. There was a lot of alcohol, and it was hours before we finally ended up back at Jim and Steve's place after the bars closed. But at some point, I called him again, and a woman answered his phone, full of innuendo. "Carter's phone, I'm sorry he's busy right now." I don't remember the details, only that I'd nearly thrown up when I'd heard her voice. There had been some sort of scuffle for the phone, and when Carter got on the line, trying to explain, "It's not what it sounds like," I'd hung up on him midsentence. The next day, I would learn more about that night and that of course I'd had absolutely nothing to worry about. It truly had been an unfortunate mess of bad timing—my call coming in just as Alex had been making a bad choice with one of his new fans. She'd snagged Carter's phone when I'd called. But at the time, from three thousand miles away, it hadn't sounded that way. The night went hazy after that.

The next morning, the shrill jingling of my phone pierced through my head. The side of my face was stuck to the leather of the sofa I'd slept on at Jim and Steve's place.

"Shut it the hell off. It won't stop ringing," I heard Kate whine from elsewhere in the room. I opened my eyes, and the floor spun. I had no idea where my phone was, but after a few minutes, it rang again, earning another chorus of moans.

Steve picked up my phone then, answering it. "Whoever you are, please, for the love of God, stop calling." He'd been sleeping nearby and sounded groggy. "Dude, chill out," he said into the phone. "She's right here." He struggled to reach the phone up to my face.

My head pounded as I dragged the phone to my ear. "Hello?" I croaked, trying to suppress a wave of nausea.

"Evie, where the hell have you been? I've been calling you for hours." The sound of Carter's voice brought back the misery that had gotten me here.

"Hmm. Have you?" I couldn't muster even a little sympathy, thinking of the woman who had seductively answered his phone.

"Evie, we have to talk. But first, you sound awful. Where are you? And who the hell answered your phone?"

"Always sooo protective. And funny question, I could ask you the same thing."

"Nobody. Which should be obvious. Are you planning to hang up on me again?" I could hear the anger in his voice.

"I don't know." I sighed.

"Can we please talk about this? What the hell is going on?"

"She was *right* there. She had *your* phone. I don't like this. I miss you."

"You think I'm not wishing you were here too?" he snapped. "What the hell happened? Was that supposed to be some kind of payback, having some guy answer *your* phone while you sound like you're about to throw up a bottle of tequila? Because that was really shit, Evie."

"I don't know. Maybe. It was just Steve, by the way."

Silence. "You slept in his room?"

"It's not like that."

"Really?" His voice was icy.

"No. And by the way, it's no picnic for me watching women throwing themselves at you every night."

"I realize that. But it's not exactly easy for me either. Trusting. We're even in this, you know."

I closed my eyes. "I know. I'm sorry." I genuinely was.

"I love you, Ev. And this is going to get easier. We'll get to be in one place. Together."

"Okay. I love you too."

"Listen, I'm so sorry, but I have to run. Do me a favor—drink some water, eat something, and take an aspirin. I'll see you in a couple of days, okay?"

The conversation was over, but the sting remained for both of us. Drinking lost its appeal for me after that night; I won't lie.

But he was right—it was supposed to get better. It did for a little while.

36

Evie

I'm not sure why I've never told you about the time I spent in England. I know you're aware that I've been there. I think I said something about a college trip or some such because it was easier than telling you the truth about it, which I couldn't do. But I never told you about the rest of it. Or about the plans I'd had to move there. I was afraid it would raise too many questions, I suppose.

And also, it was difficult for me to think of it. Just the thought of London would bring up images of us walking on rainy, dark wintertime streets, holding hands in the drizzling rain that reflected the streetlights. Touches of snow that would melt on the cobblestones below, both of us in dark hats and dark boots and dark coats and light hearts.

In London, we piled into the cramped flat in Camden Town where Tommy and Carter were roommates, with empty fireplaces and candles on the mantels, lyrics and art posters taped on the white walls. We'd sit around big tables at Indian restaurants, and then we'd endure my sorry attempts at cooking *kitchari*. We went to pubs near the Lock where the guys were welcomed back with open arms like old family, having once played on tiny black stages to small crowds for little more than beer money before hitting it big. At night, we'd go to Alex's favorite clubs, the tightly knit group of us creating an energy that people seemed drawn to watch. Those were wild nights, I won't lie, all blending together forming the most fun of my life.

Of course, they would all have much nicer places to live in one day than that old flat on Harmood Street, but I think they held on to it for a while, if only for sentimental reasons. I like that they did that. Later, Carter's place in particular was stunning, with works of art through-out. Though Tommy's country house near the Devon coast was pretty incredible as well.

But I'm getting ahead of myself.

We also were in the north back then. The label had rented them a residential recording studio that was situated in the picturesque hills outside of York, converted out of a seventeenth-century estate and barn, near to the Dales. With some of the most impressive recording gear in the UK, six bedrooms, and a full mixing and editing suite on-site, it had all the comforts of home without any distractions. A welcome escape from the world for the impressive list of musicians who had recorded there.

Carter spent long days writing and recording and long nights in the studio. But we had quiet moments as well, sometimes watching the rare snowfall outside the windows onto the pastures beyond. I worried, as I so often did, that my presence was a distraction and that perhaps I should leave them to it. I said as much one day.

He set aside the book he had been reading in bed and looked over at me. "You're serious right now, aren't you?"

"I just don't want to hold you guys up."

He paused, a smile playing on his lips. "Hold us up?" He rolled onto his side, propping his head on his fist. "Ev, I'm writing better now than ever before. And it has a lot to do with you."

I looked up at him. "Really?"

He touched his fingers to his lips, a gesture he often did when he was forming a thought and choosing his words with care. Every time he did it, it made me want to reach over and kiss him. "When I write now, it's like you're always sitting close by, even when you're not around. I picture you listening. I write every note and lyric as if you're the only person who's going to hear it, and it doesn't matter if anyone else in the world likes it as long as you do."

"But, Carter, you wrote some amazing things before we even met."

"Thanks, and . . . I guess. But still, it's true. It's like you're this source of life and creative energy that was missing in my writing before, as if it has blood flowing through it now. Whether it's directly about us or not, every song feels like it's for you. But what's even more amazing is that before I met you, I used to go crazy because I couldn't shut the music off when I wanted to. Once I met you, I found this sense of peace. The whole world, even the music, could disappear for a while when you were around. And then when I'm ready to write, I can turn it back on and it's better than ever. It's the best of both worlds. Balanced. So if it were up to me, you'd never leave my side." He reached over and kissed me. "But then again, you already knew that part."

It was the most beautiful compliment I'd ever received.

"Thank you," I whispered, kissing him back.

"Okay. So now that that's settled, speaking of the tour, what's the plan for the next month or so?"

"I'll get the last bit of footage we need while you're in the studio, and then I have to head back to New York at the end of the month for a few weeks to start editing and finish packing my apartment."

"Do you think you could squeeze in a couple of days to come to LA?"

"Why? What do you have in mind?"

"We have this thing we have to do. And . . . I'm going to need a date."

"Yeah? What kind of thing?"

"The Grammys."

I remember my eyes going wide. It was their first nomination of what would become many over the years, and they had gotten word of it while I'd been asleep the night before. "Moonstar" had been nominated for Best Song, and they had been invited to perform.

"So you'll come, then?"

I smiled. "I wouldn't miss it."

He looked at me, tucking a strand of hair behind my ear. "Ev, look—I know that things are all getting kind of crazy—the album, the new tour, all of this—and they're only about to get crazier. I know that your life is affected too."

"It's fine. Really. I'm happy." And I was. But I'd begun to realize that it was true what I'd heard—my life was becoming completely defined by his, and I'd been feeling a quiet uneasiness.

Once, when we were out on tour, the wife of the lead singer of The Evolution had come to visit. Monet Garett wasn't someone you easily forgot, and I always remembered the kind way she'd spoken to me. "Be careful," she told me. "It's wonderful now, believe me, I know. But later, when you're at home with kids and the man you love is off in the world, you may just wish you'd made different choices. No matter how much it breaks your heart to think it." Watching her and her husband, Sam, they were completely enamored with one another. Still, the conversation had stuck with me.

"I promise you. We're always going to come first, okay?" he told me.

"Promise?"

"First. You and me."

Like I said, we had a bit of trouble keeping our word sometimes. But we did the best we could.

~

The day before I was scheduled to fly back to New York, I joined them in the studio, where they were recording the first songs for the new album, which was still untitled at the time but would become *Sigma Five*. I loved watching them work, whether they were writing or recording.

Carter would often play them the first draft of the song on the piano. Gradually, the others would join in, arranging their own parts, tweaking lyrics or notes, until the end result was a distinctly Mayluna sound that could be achieved only by a group of musicians working perfectly together to create magic. It was otherworldly, as if some greater source energy was shining down on them and through them, and they were merely the instruments and scribes.

Sometimes I filmed. Other times I sat curled up on a black leather couch in the dimly lit room with the producer and engineer, the scent of whiskey and the occasional cigarette filling the air. When the label suggested a photographer be brought in, I recommended Derek. I trusted him and knew that he would be the perfect fit. It began his lifelong friendship with the band.

We were all there one day, and it was nearly midnight when it came time for Carter to start laying down the lead vocal track to a new song that I hadn't yet heard in completed form. He'd been somewhat secretive about it—working on it while I was away or asleep. Before he started recording that day, he went outside on his own for a bit. I remember it was a clear night, with a few rare stars peeking through the crisp winter sky. When he came back in, he took me by the hand to follow him.

"Come on, I want you here in the booth for this, next to me," he said.

Tommy, who was usually the joker of the group, grew serious as Alex started the intro. It had a haunting quality and an ever-building crescendo that captivated me instantly. A few measures in, I recognized it as the song that Carter had been fiddling with our first night at the beach house. That strange melody that felt so inexplicably familiar to me from another time. It sounded like the feelings of falling in love—intense, passionate, sweetly lulling, and dark and safe—all at the same time. When Carter sang the lyrics he'd written to accompany it, a stillness came over me as I listened.

An ancient road down we'll go
You and I
The moon that to the water led
A dance along the razor's edge
With tangled hands in secret lands
You and I

The music sounded like us. With the microphone in hand, Carter watched me, reflecting the darkly sultry feel of the song, eyes locked on mine. He leaned down, singing just inches from my face, and my eyes warmed with tears. He repeated the final words with the perfect simplicity of just Alex's guitar behind him.

There was at once
an appearance of light
Above the cloud with its shadow
beyond the pale of night
You and I

As you know, that song, titled "An Appearance of Light," would become their breakthrough hit the following year—the one that propelled them into stardom. It soared up the charts, reaching number one in multiple countries, helped by heavy radio rotation and a near-constant buzz. It earned widespread critical acclaim, including another Grammy Award for Best Rock Song and a Brit Award for Best British Single. The *Sigma Five* album was nominated for Best Album, while yet another song on the album was nominated for Best Performance.

The lyrics "Tangled hands in secret lands, you and I" became the anthem of hip lovers and defined a particular time of life for a lot of people of that generation. Over the years, it was featured in TV shows and films and has been covered by dozens of other artists. It often tops the lists of best songs of all time.

But then, on that night, it was just a moody alternative-rock song. A pure love song. And as it concluded, Carter leaned down and kissed me in a way that I'd never been kissed. No one else in the room existed.

"Ahem, guys?" The producer's voice sounded over the speaker in the ceiling. "Uh . . . guys?"

We ignored him.

We finally ended our embrace when a loud cacophony of sounds erupted around us: guitars screeching, drums banging, and a chorus of amused laughter. Carter stood and looked down at me, and I looked up at him.

Behind us, Derek d'Orsay held a camera. Sent in to do a few promotional shots that day, he captured the two of us in silhouette, my hair hanging long down my back, and the details of my face hidden by Carter's hand as it lay gently on my cheek. A photo, captured in the grainy light of a candlelit studio, that would become one of the most iconic images in music history. Knowing the delicate nature of the relationship, Derek never revealed my name. The mystery girl in the studio.

But now you know the story behind it.

37

EVIE

Sometimes we make plans for our lives and can see it all mapped out so clearly that we forget we're not actually fully in charge of how everything goes. That something beyond us—the universe, God—has a different idea. Carter used to believe that we were brought to Earth to fulfill a contract we made ahead of time—that we choose our parents, good and bad; we choose our experiences, pleasant and challenging; and we do it all for the betterment of our soul. It was his way of dealing with things when they were difficult—believing it served some greater purpose—and it was how he stayed grateful for the good things.

During those weeks, I walked on air, barely able to contain my smiles, looking forward to everything we had planned. My career was blossoming. I was about to move to a different country—far away from the crappy little bedroom with the stained ceilings I'd grown up in. I had the love of a new, chosen family. And of course, above all, Carter. I felt unstoppable, as if I had a magnet attracting my wildest hopes and dreams.

But you never quite see what's around the corner.

I want you to know that this next part will be hard for you to hear. Sometimes I think I made huge mistakes—and I'm sure that's true. But other times, like on Christmas mornings and family vacations and quiet family movie nights on the sofa, I would feel like everything was exactly as it should have been. That maybe I did some things right.

I suppose both are true.

I hope, by the end of this, you'll feel the same.

38

EVIE

I returned to New York a few weeks into February, using the time to go through new footage while also packing and preparing to leave. But I found it nearly impossible to concentrate and couldn't seem to shake the exhaustion that had followed me from London. And then I started getting sick. In pajamas, I sleepwalked through packing boxes, organizing things into tidy piles marked MOVE, DONATE, TOSS. In the end, I decided I wanted a fresh start and pared it all down to a single suitcase and a few mementos and nothing else. Funny I became kind of a pack rat later in life, maybe as a way to feel more secure, like an antidote to the scarcity of my childhood. But at the time, it felt like burgeoning freedom.

It's never convenient or fun being sick, of course. But I can tell you that there was never a day in my life when I was more frustrated about being sick than I was the day of Mayluna's first Grammy performance. I'd been so excited to go. Excited to finally appear on Carter's arm. Thinking of Kate calling that night and hearing her squeal something like, *Why didn't you tell me?!* But that's not what happened.

I'd thought I had the stomach flu at first, barely able to keep anything down. After breaking the news to Carter that I couldn't make the trip to LA, I ended up watching the televised show while wrapped in covers on my couch. Afterward, they called me, all of them yelling into the phone excitedly, and I could barely make out anything they said over the din of the after-party in the background.

The Monday morning after the Grammys, I felt worse than ever, and after a week of feeling terrible, I dragged myself to the doctor.

This is how I found out about you.

"Well, the good news is, I can tell you that you don't have a stomach bug," the doctor told me. He was an older, grandfatherly type with salt-and-pepper hair and glasses. I'd been waiting in the room for the last twenty minutes and had nearly fallen asleep sitting up.

"I don't?"

"Nope. What you have is a baby."

I didn't say anything. Just stared at him.

"Miss Waters, you're pregnant." He'd said it in the matter-of-fact way that doctors do, with a hint of a chuckle.

I let this sink in.

"You'll want to make an appointment with your OB/GYN, of course." The doctor and nurse continued talking, explaining everything one needs to hear upon learning that they're going to have a baby. "In the meantime, though, I think we need to get you some fluids right away. It sounds like you've been feeling pretty crummy?" he continued.

"Yes," I mumbled, still in disbelief. Apparently, I'd gotten pregnant right after Christmas. As he talked, the nurse wheeled in the IV and a bag of fluids.

"You're extremely dehydrated, and your electrolytes are low. Have you been eating?"

"Quick pinch, honey." The nurse smiled, and I winced as she inserted the needle into my arm.

"I try, but everything comes up. Even water," I told them.

"Hyperemesis gravidarum," they called it. I had never heard of it, and to me, it sounded like a type of amoeba or something.

"It's a condition that causes severe nausea, vomiting, dehydration, and weight loss during pregnancy. Basically, the opposite of what we want when growing a baby. We don't see it very often—less than around three percent of patients—but we do see it on occasion," the doctor told me. "You'll want to be cautious. It can be hard to get enough fluids and nutrition when you can't keep anything down, so they'll watch you pretty carefully in these early weeks. But as long as you take good care of yourself, you and the baby will be just fine."

"What about travel?"

"Normally I'd say no problem, but for now, in your case . . ."

I hadn't grown up with women around me. I knew absolutely nothing about pregnancy. Sure, I knew morning sickness was a thing. Who didn't know that? But this? This was nothing like what I'd seen on TV—with pregnant women tossing their cookies in the morning and laughing a moment later while returning to their desks at work or going for a jog. I remembered years later, when Kate Middleton was pregnant with Prince George, it finally made it to the mainstream news when she ended up in the ER on several occasions. It began to get the awareness it needed among women. But back then? There was still a kind of stigma that women needed to be strong and get through it with a smile and a patronizing look from elders who made them feel small and weak for complaining. But it was no joke. I read once that Charlotte Brontë is believed to have died, along with her unborn baby, due to complications from it. Fortunately, I didn't know that story at the time.

The nurse patted my hand and smiled. "You'll figure out how to manage. Small meals. Try to keep crackers in your stomach. You can try Popsicles for fluids. Sometimes mamas in your condition and with your delicate frame need to come into the ER for an IV if it gets too bad. But I promise, it'll be worth it in the end when you see those ten little fingers and ten little toes." She patted my hand. "Do you have someone at home to help you out?"

The moment she asked, everything sort of went blurry, time pausing. *Do you have someone at home to help you . . .* An old wound I thought was healed suddenly opened deep inside me. *Do you have someone at home to help you . . .*

No. I did not.

I think some part of me still believed that somehow we could still go on like we thought. That all the plans Carter and I were making for a life together would still happen. But as the news began to settle in, I watched those plans begin to unravel in far-reaching threads. While at the same time, I felt this quiet and unfamiliar sense of unexpected joy begin to rise from a place I didn't know existed inside me. So please know, my sweet girl, that though you weren't what I had planned, from that very moment, the instant I learned of your existence, you were loved.

39

EVIE

It's odd how clearly I remember that Grammy performance, watching it on the television, just like any regular person from the sofa of my apartment, completely outside of their world. Tommy playing his heart out in a driving rhythm on the drums; Alex's hair tucked behind his ears, bent over the guitar; and Carter gripping a microphone with a dark intensity backed up with a production of screens and lighting, while music royalty sat mesmerized in the rows at the front. They became stars that day. I see it as this sort of slow build to a beautiful explosion, making Carter's world open up, a mass expansion of matter and energy heading out into the universe, unlimited, while at the same exact point, mine began telescoping inward. I watch it like a film in my mind, every time the song is played on the radio, every time it's played anywhere throughout the years—that song, that moment in music-industry history, marking a new trajectory of my life. The moment he entered the world of celebrities and stars, and I fell back to Earth, a mere mortal.

Afterward, while I sat at home pale-faced in week-old pajamas, the guys were in a public relations frenzy. I had so much I needed to talk to Carter about, but no matter how hard we tried, we couldn't seem to connect. At any other time, I would have been okay—confident that he was just busy. That we would talk soon. But I was completely alone and had the weight of the world on me, and what originally started as nervous thoughts soon turned into the terrifying realization that I might be losing him. I would drag myself to bed, leaving messages for him in the evening, but when I woke up, I'd see he hadn't ever called back—even though he knew that I wasn't feeling well and that something important was on my mind. *It's okay,* I would rationalize. *He's in the middle of a crazy day. We'll talk soon.* I would tell myself these things.

A sense of dread grew inside me as reality began to set in. I grew more anxious and practiced conversations with him endlessly in my head. Still, the conversations didn't come.

It was the longest we'd ever been apart. Despite everything I'd been through in my childhood, all those dark nights spent alone by a nightlight, those few weeks in my apartment were the loneliest I'd ever felt in my entire life.

He'd touch base here and there, little bits and quick updates or *Good morning, love.* But getting him on the phone for an actual conversation that lasted more than a few minutes was next to impossible. I left a desperate voice mail for him one night, choking back tears. "Carter, please call me. It's important." I waited for hours. But he didn't call.

Just three weeks earlier, he'd told me we would always come first. But then I couldn't even get him to call me back. One by one, cracks began to form in the foundation we'd so lovingly built.

He told me later that there had been no cracks at all. That throughout this time, his love had remained completely steadfast and, remarkably, his commitment to us had only been growing deeper. But I didn't know that at the time. All I believed was what I had always believed on some level—that I would, of course, eventually lose him. And we have to be careful about these things, because often what we most believe will actually manage to come true. It was too far outside of my experiences at that point in my life to believe that I might possibly be someone worth holding on to, especially considering everything that had developed. And I saw everything through that lens.

Finally, he called one night, waking me out of a deep sleep. "Hey, baby! I miss you!" I could hear the bourbon in his voice and music in the background.

"Hey," I said softly.

"Got your message. I'm so sorry I'm just getting back to you now. What's up?"

"Um, I just, I . . ." My voice broke.

I heard Tommy laugh in the background, and Carter laughed in response to some unheard joke. I twisted the edge of my sheet in my hand, trying to not break further into tears.

"Hey, hey, Ev, what's wrong?" The party in the background—the party that I was not a part of—raged on. I took a deep breath, collecting myself.

"I'm . . . I'm just half-asleep, I guess. It's after three a.m. here," I reminded him.

"Oh, man, I didn't even think about it." I heard the guys call him again in the background, telling him to hurry up and that they were leaving. He told them he'd be there in a minute. I wilted.

"Where are you off to?" I asked, trying to keep the peace.

"I'm coming!" he called out. Then, "The Viper Room," he told me.

"What?" I sat up. "No! Carter, Alex can't go to the Viper Room." The drug-soaked hangout of the Hollywood and music elite had developed a reputation of being cursed, thanks to the number of tragedies that had taken place within its walls.

"It'll be okay; we'll keep an eye." He shuffled the phone and called out, "She's worried about you, Alex."

"Then tell her to get her ass out here already," I heard Alex reply.

Again, a commotion and then silence. "All right, they're not waiting. I have to go. Sleep well, love. I'll call you tomorrow. We're fine. All of us. Don't worry."

I paused. "Yeah. Okay."

A quick exchange of "Love you," "Love you too," and I hung up, in tears again. The call had only made me feel worse.

The next afternoon, he phoned me again. "Hi, Ev. Look, I only have a few minutes, but I wanted to call to say I'm sorry about last night and to see if you're okay."

I sank. "You only have a few minutes?" Again.

"Yeah, sorry. I have to run out. But I wanted to call you first."

"Carter, have you even noticed that we've barely spoken in weeks? And that every single time you call, you're either in the middle of something or about to run out? It would be really nice if you would try maybe calling when you're not busy?"

"Ev, look, I'm sorry. We've just been—"

"Busy. Yeah. I got that. But it's funny, because you don't seem too busy to stay up partying all night," I snapped, immediately regretting it. I had no right to be angry with him.

"Wow. That's not fair. What's going on, Ev? You're never like this."

He was right. I sighed, frustrated with myself. Frustrated with him. "I'm just . . . I don't understand. Where the hell have you been, Carter?"

"Everywhere! Rehearsals for the tour, promotional bullshit, studio time, whatever we can do. Listen, Ev, I'm sorry. I am. But I'll see you in a couple of days in New York, and I promise, we'll talk then. And after that, we'll have all the time in the world together. Right?"

Of course, he didn't know the half of it. I stayed silent.

"Listen, I'm so sorry I have to say this. But I really do have to go. I promise I'll call you later. I miss you."

"Wait, how's Alex?"

He paused. "He's okay. But . . . you were right. We had to get him out of there last night. But he's okay. All's well."

I took a breath. We finished the conversation, and a moment later, he hung up. I accepted the fact that I would just have to wait to talk to him in person, which, really, would probably be better, anyway. In the meantime, I glanced at the suitcase and the empty rooms around me, completely uncertain about my future.

40

EVIE

I finally arrived in the city on a blustery day with winter holding a tight grasp on spring's arrival. When the cab got closer to the hotel, the driver grumbled about the traffic. It would be better to get dropped off a little farther away. As I approached the hotel on foot, I realized with a shock what the commotion was all about. There was a crowd of people outside the hotel, spilling into the streets a bit, hoping to get a glimpse of the band. *My* band, as it had come to feel like. *My* family. Carter had told me that the response after the Grammys was explosive, but I had been so wrapped up in everything I was dealing with that I hadn't realized the degree to which he was referring. I fought through the crowd to get to the front door. I saw a girl holding up a sign that said I LOVE YOU, CARTER. Normally, I would have laughed, but my sense of humor had grown elusive, and it scraped my nerves. I approached a bellman and told him I was a guest of the hotel, then went to the receptionist.

"Hi. I'm meeting my boyfriend here. He left an envelope with the key."

"No problem, ma'am. What's your name?"

"Evelyn Waters." I leaned my head wearily on my hand, looking forward to lying down before Carter got back. I was woozy, and the trip had taken nearly every last drop of my energy. I'd left a few boxes in storage with the landlord and lugged the remains of my life in a heavy, hopeful suitcase that I trailed behind me.

The receptionist looked around the desk but came up empty-handed. "I'm sorry, ma'am, but there's no envelope for you here."

"Are you sure? When I spoke with him this morning, he said it would be here."

"I can check again. What's the guest's name?"

"Carter Wills," I replied distractedly.

Her face went from friendly to pinched in a millisecond, and then I understood the situation I was in. The new reality of things.

"Right. Well, if you're Carter Wills's girlfriend, then I'm sure he'll be running right along any minute to fetch you. In the meantime, you'll have to wait outside with all the others. I'm afraid the hotel lobby is strictly for guests. Unless you'd like me to call security to escort you out, that is." The receptionist smirked at me, and I wanted to strangle her with her tacky silk scarf.

I started to say something back, but before the words could come out, I spun on my heels and ran to the lobby bathroom. When I exited, she glared at me. Drained of energy, I left the lobby and, rather than walk another block to the nearest coffee shop, I took a place sitting on the sidewalk at the back of the crowd, leaning my head against the wall, as icy rain started to drizzle. I was too tired to walk anywhere else.

They had been due any minute, but I didn't know how long I'd been sitting there waiting, and it felt like forever. Finally, two large black SUVs pulled up to the curb in front of the hotel, and I pushed my way through to the front of the growing crowd in a fit of frustration and annoyance. Several security guards I didn't recognize jumped out of the first car, and then Fred climbed out, followed by Darren, then Carter and the rest of them. If one more girl had screamed "Carter" in my ear in a high-pitched shrill, I would have lost it.

He didn't see me in the crowd, and he didn't hear me when I called out. I pushed my way farther through, lunging toward him, but was roughly shoved back by a burly and sweating member of the paparazzi holding an enormous camera. The frustration of the day was too much, and I pushed him, trying to get through, while he shoved me back.

"Get the hell off her!" Alex shouted, pushing past a security guard while trying to pull me through, cradling me against his chest. There was a scuffle, two men, Alex lost his grip on me, and before I knew it, I heard a shriek from some girls as Carter's fist came out of nowhere and pounded into the side of a photographer's head. I went down with the guy as he lost his balance and tumbled. Just before I hit the ground, Carter's arms scooped me up, and he carried me through the doors of the hotel.

Stunned and dazed by the scene, I burrowed against his shoulders, my hands instinctively wrapping protectively around my stomach as I thought of the way a knee had knocked the wind out of me in the chaos. In an instant, I thought of the fragile life inside me and was flooded with the most intense feelings of love and protection I'd ever experienced. As we walked to the elevators, I heard Carter yelling, "Freddie! What the hell was she doing out there with all those people? What kind of guy shoves a girl like that?" I had never seen him so furious. "I want him gone. *GONE*, Fred! And that idiot in security. Who the hell was he, anyway?"

As we waited for the elevator, Carter continued to hold me. "I'm so sorry. I'm so sorry."

Just before the elevator doors closed, I saw the snooty receptionist look at me, slack-jawed.

Carter placed me on the bed in his room and sat down next to me. "Are you okay?" He brushed his lips on mine. We hadn't seen each other in weeks, and it was not the reunion that either of us had had in mind.

"I'm fine," I said, my voice breaking. He dabbed a cold cloth where a bruise was forming on my eye from where an elbow had slammed into my face. "Better now that you're here."

"I'm so sorry. I thought someone had left a key for you."

I shrugged, hurt that he hadn't taken the time to do it himself. "I just want to lie down for a little while." I set my hand on his face. "Just a few minutes. I didn't sleep well, that's all," I told him, seeing the way he looked at me. "It's just a scratch. I'm fine."

He kissed me lightly. "I'll be outside. Take your time."

I was asleep in an instant, and when I awoke, it was dark. Carter sat beside me, and the smell of food wafted in from the penthouse living room, making my stomach feel both nauseated and hungry at the same time. I took a sip from a glass of water he'd placed on the table.

"I ordered some food, love. Are you hungry? You slept all afternoon."

"Did I really?" I said, a little embarrassed and disoriented. I sat up and leaned into his arms.

"Hey, are you okay?" he asked, stroking my hair.

I wrapped my arms around him and snuggled close, listening to his heartbeat. "I just really missed you."

He chuckled. "Quite the sexy romantics, aren't we? Fistfights and naps."

I leaned against the leather headboard, and he crawled across me onto the bed, lying beside me. I laced my fingers through his, a habit that had grown from lazy Sunday mornings in hotel beds.

He sighed heavily. "Can you believe all of this? That crowd?"

"It was definitely a surprise."

"It's been like this lately, but I had no idea it would be this wild." He turned to his stomach and propped his chin on his hand, looking up at me with eyes as wide as a young boy's. "It feels like overnight, everything just . . . changed."

"Tell me about it," I whispered.

"It's good, though, I suppose, right?" He looked as though he were weighing the truth of this statement. "Do you ever feel like your life is so perfect that you're afraid to breathe? Like at any moment, something will shift and cause the whole stack of cards to tumble. First the tour and then the Grammys. And you and I are going to be traveling to all of these amazing places, running all over the world. Together." He paused and sighed. "Is it okay to be this happy? To actually be this excited about the future? I feel like I'm going to jinx it."

I watched him talk. He was bubbling, lit from inside. I swallowed hard against the lump forming in my throat as I shook my head and smiled. "It's really wonderful to see you this happy."

"I just . . . I have this feeling like the other shoe is going to drop. Like at any moment, someone's going to say, *Surprise*, and it's all going to disappear."

His eyes searched mine, wanting me to share his happiness.

I tried my best to mirror his expression, hoping my face didn't reveal the storm inside me and the guilt that had settled in my chest.

He looked at me closely for the first time since I'd arrived, a line forming across his forehead. I knew I looked terrible. I was pale and gaunt, and I knew it. And I also knew he'd never say anything about it. "Are you sure you're okay?"

I didn't answer.

He raised his eyebrows and cocked his head, prodding gently.

I inhaled a breath and opened my mouth to speak, holding in a thousand words. "I just missed you, that's all." I exhaled, pushing it all down again. Funny thing, I often go back to that exact moment in my memories, wondering why I hesitated. I still don't fully understand it. Instincts, maybe. Fear? Love? I'm not sure.

He narrowed his eyes. "I . . . missed you too." He brushed my lips with his. "But why do I get the distinct feeling that there's something else?"

Once again, we were interrupted by a hard knock on the door. "We'll be out in a few," Carter called.

"I'm so sorry; we have this thing tonight, and I have to jump in the shower. You still want to come, right?" They were doing a late-night talk show, and I'd planned to tag along.

"If you don't mind, I think I'll skip it tonight."

Disappointment crossed his face. "Are you sure? I can't stand leaving you already."

"I'm okay. Really. Have fun."

"All right. But while I'm gone, will you do something for me, please?" He jumped up and started shedding his clothes.

"What's that?"

"Eat something! You're beautiful"—he kissed me, heading for the bathroom, naked—"but it's been hours and you need to eat!"

After draining the glass of water, I pulled one of his sweatshirts over me and zipped it up as I padded into the living room, finding Alex on the sofa, all limbs and angles, feet propped up on a coffee table. I curled up beside him and reached over to kiss him on the cheek. "There he is, my hero." I rested my head on his shoulder. "Thanks for your help, mister."

He draped his arm over my leg and in turn rested his head against mine. "You look like shit, Ev."

"Thank you, I'm touched. And it's nice to see you too," I joked.

"Want to tell me what's going on with you?" he asked.

My eyes welled, my defenses failing. "No. Not really," I whispered.

"Okay. Have it your way."

"What about you?" I asked. "You doing okay?"

He took a breath. "Yeah. I mean—every time I look in the mirror, I have to remind myself that all of this is exactly what we've always wanted. But it's good."

I looked up at him and the deep darkness inside his eyes.

"I think you're doing a pretty good job, all things considered."

He leaned into me with a faint smile. "Thanks, Ev."

"I'm ordering some food. Can I get you anything while I'm at it?"

He exhaled a weary laugh. "An ounce of high-quality Peruvian marching powder would be great."

I smiled and gave him a look as I reached for the phone. "Right. So . . . tea, then?"

"Perfect."

I patted him on the leg, and he placed his hand on mine before looking up, both of us watching Carter walk across the room, light as air.

I would recall that quiet moment with Alex for years. The comfort and warmth between us, both in our own struggles, trying to manage. Alex let almost nobody into his world, and yet over time, he had let me in. I never took that for granted. I was proud of him for how well he'd been doing. I should have told him that night.

Later, I sat on the sofa, nibbling at some fruit while I watched the guys on the late-night talk show. The host chatted easily with Carter.

"So I hear there's quite a commotion over you guys downstairs. Panties flying everywhere," he joked, handing Carter a pair of cherry-red lace panties. I rolled my eyes. "So, Mr. Wills, speaking of panties on the stage, is there a girlfriend in your life?" he asked. The audience screamed in enthusiasm. Carter grinned that adorable, boyish smile that I loved.

"Yeah. In fact, there is. She's pretty amazing."

"Anything else you'd like to add?"

"Nah. We're trying to stay in our own little bubble. Keeping it as private as we can. Trying to steer clear of the whole public roller coaster, you know? No complications. Enjoying life. I'll just leave it at that," he said with a smile.

"Smart man, Mr. Wills," the host replied.

"No complications," I said out loud to myself, repeating his words as I looked down at my stomach and let out a long breath.

"So you're fresh off the Grammys. What's coming up next?"

Good question.

Would it always be like this? I began to wonder while sitting alone in that hotel room. I set my hand on my stomach again, on this tiny life depending on me. This little person who would spend their childhood looking out the window, wishing for a traditional family that they might never get. Questioning if they'd truly been wanted or had been a burden on the lives of their parents. Just like me. I wasn't sure what was harder—growing up so much of the time alone or knowing that once upon a time, I had been loved by a parent who was gone. I wondered if it would have been better to have not known what I was missing.

41

EVIE

I don't remember why I went downstairs to the lobby before everyone else that morning. You'd think I would, but I don't.

"Move it, you two. The car's downstairs. We've gotta be outta here in twenty minutes." I'd startled awake a bit earlier to the sound of Fred's booming voice and blinked at the light pouring into the room as he pounded on the door a second time. Carter had pulled the covers over both of us in defiance.

"Hey, sleeping beauty, we have to get up, I'm afraid. You were already asleep by the time we got back last night, and I didn't want to wake you."

"What time is it?"

"Time to go, I'm afraid."

I looked at Carter, confused. "I thought we weren't leaving until this afternoon?"

"Pretty sure it's nearly there."

I groaned, curling into his chest.

"I could stay in bed with you for hours." He kissed me, pulling me closer to him. "But sadly, duty calls. Come on, you." He kissed me once more, then jumped up, heading out of the room before I could respond.

I sat up for a moment, trying to get my bearings, and then, with some amount of determination, managed to shower and dress.

When he returned, he found me sitting on the edge of the bed.

I looked up at him. "I don't think I can do this," I said quietly, as much to myself as to him.

"What?" he asked.

"Any of it."

But he didn't understand my meaning, chuckling and giving me a gentle peck on the lips and telling me I'd be fine. He'd thought at the time that I was just complaining about being sleepy. I'd never been much of a morning person, after all. He'd gone to get me coffee.

It was an unusual confluence of events that morning in March, several things all coming together and meeting in the unassuming lobby of that New York hotel.

First, he was unusually distracted that weekend, totally out of character and overwhelmed with the schedule and the new flurry of fame that had suddenly descended on his once-quiet life.

Second, I'd become unraveled by the anxiety and the weight of the prospect of bringing a child into the world—feeling completely alone and afraid of being a part of Carter's life and simultaneously afraid of losing him. I was terrified to tell him about the baby and everything it would mean. Terrified of what it could do to him. No matter how hard I tried, it just wouldn't come out. I had told myself it would be better to wait until we were back in London. I'm not proud of any of this, and I wish I could have been stronger, but sometimes old wounds break us into the lowest version of ourselves.

But then there was the third and final blow: my father.

I'd been getting tea, I think, maybe. Or ginger ale. I don't know. But I remember the burgundy lobby walls spinning a bit and my head feeling foggy. I had barely been able to keep down any of the food I'd eaten the day before, and I was shaky. The trip had taken its toll on me, and I could tell that I was getting dehydrated again. I wasn't used to things being so hectic with the band.

That's when I saw him talking to the receptionist. My father. I thought it was my imagination at first until he turned his face and saw me. I was going to ask him why he was there, but I realized I already knew, and my shoulders fell.

"Surprise!" he said, stretching his arms wide. Despite everything, I leaned in and gave the slightest hug, and as I did, I saw him look over my shoulder. "Where's your other half?"

I hesitated. "Not sure what you mean, Dad."

He leaned back and gave me a wry look. "You know, it's funny. There I was last night watching *Letterman*, and I see this guy come on and think, *Man, he looks familiar.* And then, pow! It hits me! That's Evie's guy! So I hopped on a train this morning and came up here to see my girl." He looked excited. "Hey! You should've told me your new man was a big rock star."

"It's not like that, Dad."

"Sure sounded like it! And here you are!"

"I'm just here for work, that's all." I was weary and a little unsteady on my feet.

He watched me close, taking my arm. "Hey, you doin' all right? You don't look so good, kiddo."

I swallowed, about to reply, but in an instant, darted down a side hall to the nearby bathroom and threw up the toast and coffee I'd had, bursting into tears as I did so. I'll never forget the way I looked in the mirror that day. I barely recognized myself. I washed my face, and when I walked out, my father was standing outside the bathroom.

"Everything all right?"

"I'm fine. Just a stomach bug."

"Stomach bug, eh?" He gave me a long look and then laughed a bit, as if waving the thought away. Still, he watched me closely.

He scratched his chin. "If I didn't know better, I'd say . . . Eh, never mind."

"You'd say what?" I don't know why I asked. I think sometimes when you're in your weakest and frailest state, it's instinctual to long for the comfort of a parent . . . even a bad one.

He looked at me sideways. "You're not knocked up, are you? You look a lot like your mom did when she was pregnant with you." His face softened uncharacteristically as a memory seemed to pass through his mind. "Boy, was she sick."

If I'd had just another moment to process it, or maybe if he hadn't mentioned my mother, whom I was so desperately missing and needing, I would have been able to distract him. But my eyes filled with tears. And despite it all, he was still my father, and he must have seen something in my face.

His eyes grew wide. "I'll be damned; I'm right. Aren't I?"

He took my silence as confirmation and shook his head as he let out a big sigh.

"Well, where is he?" He looked over my shoulder for Carter.

"Don't start, Dad. You don't understand anything about this."

He narrowed his eyes. "Hey, I saw in the paper what he did to that reporter. Is that son of a bitch the one who gave you that bruise?" He touched the bruise on my face that had bloomed after the scuffle outside the hotel. "I knew it. I knew he was a loose cannon. I'm gonna give him a piece of my mind."

"What? No! He would never hurt me."

"Ah, so you are with him, then."

"No." I sighed. "Dad, please, can you just stop? You have no idea what you're talking about. Things are complicated enough for me right now. They're waiting for me. I need you to go. Now. Please."

He looked offended, and I couldn't tell if it was sincere or not. "I can't leave my baby girl here, pregnant."

"Since when do you care?"

"Oh, don't be dramatic. You sound just like your mother." My heart tugged at the mention of her again. And the resentment from deep down inside bubbled up in full force.

"Funny how you suddenly seem to care when I'm in the middle of all this. See an opportunity, huh, Dad? Well, there isn't one. It's just work."

"Looks like you've been doing a whole lot more than working." He looked pointedly at my stomach. "You always hung out with the fancy kids at school, trying to fit in. But I always knew you'd end up in some situation like this. Figures he'd leave you high and dry. I imagine that's what's going on, right? Not too happy with the situation? Sure ruined my shot when it happened to me. But hey, I did my part. And you can't let him get away with this."

No matter where I'd gone or what I'd accomplished, my father still thought of me as the kid who would amount to nothing. The kid whose very existence he blamed for ruining his dreams. I closed my eyes, begging. "Please just go back home. I'll call you tomorrow. I promise." I didn't tell him I'd be gone by then.

He put up his hands. "All right, all right. I'm going. But I'll be calling you, okay?"

"Fine."

"Take good care of yourself, peanut. Your mom had a real hard time. Was terrible sick. Just take it easy, okay?"

I think part of me thought he might actually be concerned. Maybe he was a little bit. I don't know. "Okay. Thanks, Dad."

I waited until I was sure he was gone before going back upstairs, still unnerved by everything he had said.

A short while later, there was a flurry of activity out in the living room before we paraded back down through the lobby en masse, while Carter kept a tight grip on my hand. As we approached the front doors, I saw the wild group of fans outside the lobby doors, screaming the names of the band, and I recoiled, dizzy.

Will it always be like this? I remember wondering again.

I'm sure it all happened in just a few seconds, but in my mind, it feels like everything went in slow motion. Carter moved quickly, eyes forward, holding me close.

And in that instant, I realized the truth: I couldn't let it happen. I couldn't be the person who brought it all crashing down for him.

He would do anything for me.

But I couldn't be the other shoe dropping.

I'd always known I would lose him. I'd been preparing for it all along, I supposed. I just never imagined it would be this way.

Maybe it was the mess of my father being there reminding me of who I was. Maybe it was the excitement I'd heard in Carter's voice. Or knowing how big they were all going to be. Whatever it was, I knew in that moment what I had to do. How this whole thing would have to go. All along, I'd been worried about how Carter would react to everything, when in reality, he would never have to know at all. It seemed selfish to fight for him. I could let him go in peace. I braced myself for the moment that would break me in two, and before I knew it, I stopped.

"You okay?" Carter turned around and looked at me. Fred hovered nearby. "Ev?"

I dropped his hand. "Carter. I can't do this. I'm sorry."

He cocked his head and smiled a little. "It's okay; just hold my hand tight. We'll jump right into the car." He reached out. I saw Alex stop and turn around, watching. I avoided his eyes.

"No, that's not what I mean. You don't understand. I can't go with you." I stepped back.

He froze and then turned to face me. "What are you talking about?"

I looked over Carter's shoulder. "Fred, tell the guys to get my bags and leave them here, please."

Just get through this, Evie. Let him go.

"I've been trying to talk to you since I got here. But I . . ." Just then, a cramp sent a shock of pain through me, along with a flash of fear. I swallowed hard to cover it.

His eyes narrowed, watching me closely. "Evie, I don't know what's going on. But let's just go, and we'll talk about it on the plane. Is that okay?"

"I haven't seen you in weeks, Carter, and I've had to beg you for every precious second I got you on the phone. You knew I needed to talk to you. Was it too much to ask for five minutes of your time?" I hissed, barely recognizing my own voice. I needed him to believe me, because otherwise he would fight for me. And I couldn't let him do that. He looked wounded and surprised by my outburst. But how could he be surprised when, after all, everything I'd said was true? I'd felt like I'd been the last person on his list of priorities for weeks.

"Is this what you've been trying to tell me?" he asked gently. "Evie, please . . . look. You're right. I'm so sorry." He glanced again out the door, while Fred watched on.

"This is what's best for you, but not for me. Not right now." I pushed on. "Just go on the tour. You'll be great. I'll stay here. I . . . I just need some time. To do my own thing." I felt like I was tearing my own heart out.

A fresh look of surprise and hurt crossed his face. "Time to do your own thing? Where is this coming from? I thought this was what you wanted as well?"

I shook my head. "I thought it was. But it's not. I'm sorry."

"I know this has been a miserable couple of weeks," he pleaded, "but I promise it'll get better."

I stood my ground, willing my feet in place. To breathe slowly.

"So just like that," he said. "Here. In this bloody lobby. You're doing this?"

He reached out one last time just as the doors opened and a mass of people swarmed. In one smooth motion, a bodyguard moved Carter along into the throng. He looked back at me, the moment frozen, as I stepped away, letting him continue on without me. Fans filled the void between us, and he disappeared behind them.

Fred looked over at me, met my eyes, and held them tight before getting into the passenger seat. A moment later, I saw Alex open the car door, searching until he locked eyes with me, where I stood on the steps above the crowd. His look of concern turned to frost.

A sob emerged from me for just a moment before I clamped it down.

From elsewhere in the lobby, my father appeared, walking toward me. "What are you doing? Where are they . . ."

"They're going back to the UK," I told him. I stared at the car as it was pulling away. Willing myself not to run after it.

"But what about . . ." He looked at my stomach, then launched forward. "Hey! You can't just leave like—"

"Stop!" I said, grabbing his arm. "I told you, Dad. It's not like that. And you don't understand. Just go."

He pushed past. "But—"

I said it quickly. It just came out. "It's not Carter's baby."

He stopped short and turned around, confused. "What? But then who the hell . . ."

"It's Steve's."

His head dropped backward as he groaned. "Steve Hutchinson? Aw, Evie, you've got to be kidding me. You mean to tell me that you had a rich, famous rock star in the palm of your hand, and you threw it all away for some varsity-letterman pretty boy? From high school?"

I remember going completely numb. Speaking flatly as I told him, "I was home during the holidays, and we spent some time together. He doesn't know yet. I've been waiting to tell him; I just needed to figure out a few things first."

What I'd needed was to figure out a way to say goodbye to Carter. I just hadn't wanted to admit it to myself.

He groaned again in frustration. "People always said you were sooo bright." He sneered. "The Hutchinsons, of all people." He spat the word out. He detested your dad's family. Resented them not only for the way they'd helped me but for everything they represented. "Well, that just figures." He sighed. "And what about your job?"

"This was my last day working with the record label, and they're all heading back. I think they're bringing someone in with more experience to finish the rest of the job."

Of all things, this, of course, he didn't question.

Just then, a cramp gripped my stomach without warning, followed by terror.

It's okay, I told myself, numbing just as I'd done as a child.

It'll all be fine.

But would it?

The truth was, I had no idea where I was going to go. Or what I was going to do next. I was only beginning to see the ramifications of what I'd done.

"Ev? You okay, peanut? You don't look . . ."

Everything went blurry, and an hour later, I was in a hospital bed with an IV hooked to my arm, staring blankly out the window, my father sitting beside me as he called your dad.

PART TWO

*I too play with symbols . . . but I play in such a way that
I do not forget that I am playing. For nothing is proved
by symbols . . . unless by sure reasons it can be demon-
strated that they are not merely symbolic but are descrip-
tions of the ways in which the two things are connected
and of the causes of this connection.*

—Johannes Kepler

42

CARTER

When I was a boy, my mother would sometimes take us to a particular spot in the eastern Dales where the meadows were high and wide and the towns were far, allowing the night sky to show a blanket of a thousand stars, free from the light pollution of nearby cities. We would take blankets and food and a lantern and stay out well past midnight into the darkest hours of night on a kind of mini camping adventure that was pretty much the best thing ever for a boy of that age.

On one such night in May, just before my ninth birthday, Jacob and I sat together on a blanket, just the two of us, and saw something unusual. It was a remarkably clear night, and as we looked up at the crescent moon, we saw what appeared to be a star that sat in *front* of the moon. Not a shooting star or a meteor, but a singular star, twinkling and stable. Both of us were startled by the inexplicable strangeness of it, and I remember the frisson of excitement that coursed through me at having witnessed something unexplainable by science.

Unbeknownst to me, on that very same night, across the ocean on a beach not far from the one where we eventually fell in love, a seven-year-old girl would see the exact same phenomenon while sitting with her own mother. We were some of the many who apparently saw it throughout the world that evening, though I never met anyone else, and really, it wasn't something easily shared. A similar event had been documented by the Royal Observatory two centuries earlier, but the event that took place in 1980 was never officially recognized by astronomers.

That same night as a boy, as I lay awake thinking of it, I remember a particular series of notes and a melody coming into my mind, the beginnings of my first song, just as I was falling asleep. I saw the motion of it, the spaces between the notes and the story they were trying to tell, a lullaby of sorts. I hummed it aloud into the dark, allowing it to unfold from the mysterious place where such things come from.

Years later, I would turn that night into the name of a band and then eventually the melody into a song, while sitting on the dock of a bay, falling in love with that same girl. She was always so captivated by the way that song had sounded familiar. "I swear I used to hear it in my dreams from the time I was little," she would say in wonderment. The magic of that starry crescent-moon night in May, long ago, somehow linking us across space and time in a way we could never explain.

We had been planning to move to London together that day she left me in New York. Our whole life in front of us. What she never knew, though, was that that spot in the eastern Dales, beneath a waxing moon, was the place where I had been planning to ask her to marry me that spring.

Sometimes the paths of stars don't cross, after all. After that, I stopped looking up at the sky for a long time. We released the album later that year, with the song that was once captured on a nighttime breeze and sent across an ocean, "An Appearance of Light," as the final track.

43

EVIE

If I'm being honest, it never occurred to me that I wouldn't see him again or that—while standing in some nondescript lobby in New York on a shitty March day—it would be the end of us forever. How much time would be thrown away between us and wasted. It never occurred to me how permanent it would be, and it wasn't my intention. I knew he deserved a better explanation than the one I had given him. Over and over on an endless loop, I would reimagine words I might have chosen better or other ways that it could have turned out. But days went by, then weeks and years, and eventually more than a decade would pass before I saw his face again.

You'll remember a lot of what happened in those years that followed, of course. You were there, after all. But there are some details from the early days, when your dad and I were first starting out, that I need to tell you about. I'll get to that in a minute. But first, you need to understand that eventually I did find happiness. I want you to know that. Because I don't want you to think that all the wonderful things you remember from your childhood were in any way artificial. I loved being your mom, and the years when I got to be at home with you, watching you grow, taking care of you, were some of the favorite times of my entire life. So what I'm about to explain shouldn't take away from a single moment of that, okay? I loved your dad and he loved me. Very much. And the years when you were little were the happiest times of our marriage.

Having said that, you know that we had our problems. I felt like I disappointed him everywhere I turned. And I think he felt the same way toward me. That's why we separated for a time. Somewhere along the way, we fell apart, as can happen. Ghosts from our past—or mine, really—began to surface, and no matter how hard I tried to make them go away, they wouldn't. Because I never really healed from what had happened early on—not in my childhood, not in my time with Carter, none of it. I'd simply forced it down into a deep, dark place within me and willed it to stay there, hidden behind perfect photos and coordinated outfits and front porches decorated for fall, all the things I'd never had growing up. I had never told anyone the full story about Carter. Your dad knew some, of course, but not all of it. He didn't want to. Not until later. So I was able to keep it all locked away where it belonged during those early years.

But when you keep the darkness hidden like that, it always makes its way to the surface eventually. Always. It needs to be dealt with. Otherwise, it steals the light.

~

Do you see it now? The album title? My name. Or at least, his version of it. Hidden in plain sight for all the world to see. He told me once that it had been a message to me, calling my name, shouting it out into the universe in both title and music.

I had been walking quickly past one of Philly's last record stores when I saw it for the first time—a large window display covered in Mayluna promotional posters—and I stopped short. The solid black artwork design, the name of the album in white, lined up for display, repeated in various formats, large and small throughout the entire window, the album's title, *Sigma Five*, consisting simply of two characters. The Greek letter sigma and the Roman numeral five.

Upon seeing it, my knees had nearly buckled while standing in the rain. On that album, I heard the music and the songs I'd watched them create during late nights on the bus and in that studio in England. After that album was released, they were everywhere, and I couldn't escape him. I'd watched the world fall in love with him while I quietly tended to my life and to a broken heart that seemed unwilling to mend. So I buried it all in a box in the back of my closet, along with every trace of my life with them—photos, mementos, notes—and promised to never go back to that time in my life again.

Until one day at the end of summer, more than a decade later, when letting go had suddenly become harder than ever. I don't know why or what it was about that time that made me suddenly feel a nearly obsessive pull back to him. It was as if some unseen force kept drawing me back, refusing the past to free me of its clutches, and then instead of whispering to me as it had for so many years, it had begun shouting with urgency.

There is this one night, I can still remember with such clarity. I'm not sure why, exactly. But memories are funny that way. It was as if somewhere inside me, I sensed that change was coming and my brain marked the passage of it. The smell of the grass. The sound of Roxy barking as she played alongside both of you. The magical way the sunlight caught the glitter. I'm sure I'm remembering it like something out of a picture-perfect movie—far better than it actually was. But that's okay. I don't mind. I'll keep it—my golden memory of motherhood.

44

EVIE

2009
Age 36

"Okay, everybody, votes in?" I joined my two children on the floor and gave the coffee can a shake. It was decorated with a colorful assortment of stickers, marker drawings, and a tattered wrap of white construction paper.

"Wait! I'm not done yet!" Lainey knitted her brows together in serious contemplation, purple marker poised in her small hand. I couldn't help but smile as I watched the gears turn in her head, the coral rays of evening sunlight filtering onto the side of her face from the living room windows. Nearly a full minute later, she folded the tiny slip of paper into a tidy square and dropped it with satisfaction into the can.

"What about you, monkey, is your vote in?" I asked as Lucas plopped down with a clumsy thud next to me, crisscrossing his legs.

"Yep! I picked bike ride."

"You're not supposed to tell!" Lainey chided.

He shrugged, pulling a goofy face. There were few things a five-year-old loved more than aggravating a bossy big sister.

My life was a series of moments like this, tied together with gossamer threads. It wasn't the big things, like weddings and vacations and milestones, but rather the simple moments that I loved, hidden in the unremarkable, mundane evenings of daily life. I'd made my choices—done what I thought was best for everyone. I'd crafted the quiet life behind the white picket fence far from the shiny lights and secrets that lingered in boxes tied with aging ribbons. I had chased the ghosts of the past away and kept them at bay. Or so I told myself.

Steve and I had started the Friday-evening ritual of Family Fun Night just over a year earlier, and by some miracle, it had stuck, despite all the changes that had occurred in the midst of a recent separation. The can was full of slips of white paper, accumulated votes of weeks past, marking the passage of time and the emerging interests of growing children.

"Okay, mine's in too!" I had made a show of thinking hard, then dropped my own vote into the can. "And look out! It's a good one tonight!"

"Let me guess, board game?" Lainey asked with a smart, silly grin. Moms can be so predictable, after all.

"Ooh, I hope it's make-your-own-sundae bar," Lucas added. "I love when we do that."

"Hmm, I guess you'll just have to wait and see, won't you?" I tickled Lucas in the ribs. "Okay, Lainey Bear, I think it's your turn to pick this week." I gave the can a ceremonial shake and held it out. With relished authority, she reached her hand inside and made a big deal of blindly selecting the evening's activity. She unfolded the paper and jumped up with glee, making her long chestnut ponytail bob with excitement. "Peter Pan!" She'd gotten lucky and chosen her own vote. "Let's do it in the backyard!"

"I'm Peter!" Lucas shouted after her and took off running.

"Fine, I'm Tinker Bell and, Mommy, you're—"

"Wendy. I know." I laughed and stood, summoning the last reserves of energy from the day. I was always Wendy when we played this game of pretend, acting out the scenes from the beloved tale. Kids can be predictable sometimes too.

Summer had ended in Eastern Pennsylvania, but the evening still held the last drops of golden sunshine and green trees. We spent the next forty-five minutes running around the backyard in character. Sugar for pixie dust, a green tutu, and a plastic sword. Arms flapping in pretend flight, and our boxer, Roxy, chasing and being chased, loping on long legs as she unknowingly played the role of the dreaded crocodile with a toothy grin. Similar sounds were heard from swing sets and patios over the fences of neighboring yards and beyond. The evening chatter of picturesque suburban life.

As the sun dipped and the air began turning cool, I glanced at my watch. "Okay, guys, just a few more minutes till we have to go in. It's almost—"

"Dad!" Both children took off running past me, and I turned to see Steve coming around the side of the house. "We're playing Peter Pan!" Lainey added. "Wanna play?"

"Aaarrr! Ahoy, that makes me . . ." Steve threw his arms around our two children and scooped them up, one on each side. "The dreaded Captain Hook!" He swung them around, kissing the tops of their heads before turning toward me.

"Hey there," he said. "I'm sorry I'm a little early. My last meeting rescheduled. Hope it's okay. I rang the doorbell but—"

"Yes, it's broken." We both chuckled. "Again." The thing had been a perpetual thorn, even before he'd left. It was one of those little tasks that always ended up at the bottom of the list.

"Do you want me to fix it this weekend for good, finally? I don't mind."

"Thanks, it's okay. I've got someone coming to look at it."

He continued to hold the kids at his sides as they squirmed in fits of giggles. The top buttons of his blue oxford dress shirt were undone. His tie had likely been strewn aside in the car on the way over, and there were now flecks of glitter from Lainey's tutu on his sleeve. One minute the sharp and tidy businessman, and the next, the image of the perfect father—that was Steve. Blond Kennedy looks and the face of a man who had perhaps at one time spent sunny dawns on the river with his rowing crew in college but who'd gotten pleasantly soft with age. It could be annoying—his perfection. A lot to live up to.

"The kids aren't quite ready yet. I have to finish packing their bags," I said, wishing I'd had the chance to change into a nicer shirt.

"I can wait. It's no trouble." As we stood somewhat awkwardly, the kids flitted around us like fireflies.

"Okay, I'll just run in." I started up the wooden steps of the deck he'd once stained almond brown and turned. "It'll take me a little while; come on in. Can I get you anything?"

"I'm good, thanks." He gave me a warm smile—the same one that had first struck me smitten in the sixth grade—then returned his attention to the kids as I went inside.

The aftermath of a separation, the time between sharing a life together and signing names on a divorce decree, is a fuzzy, gray area with blurry lines. There hadn't been animosity between us, no screaming fights or thrown dishes. No red flags to say, *Danger. Trouble ahead.* Just the slow fade of what once had been love and affection, disappearing into the mist like a shadowy ship from a cold-climate harbor. It was there, and then it was gone. Or maybe it had never been there in the first place. Eventually, he decided he needed a fresh start, and I decided it would feel less lonely to be alone than to pretend to be happy when we weren't. It was mutual, really. No bad guys. We even got along so well that we'd come to these conclusions at just about the same time, which was almost funny but not. We'd been figuring it all out and navigating the new order of life.

I started the well-choreographed routine of packing bags. It was Steve's weekend with the kids, and by that point, I'd finally gotten the process down to a science, including the endless search for Stuffy the Dragon and the pangs of guilt. A short while later, I deposited the bags at the front door and returned to the living room to find Lucas dozing on the sofa, curled into a nest among the oversize taupe cushions. Steve sat perched on the edge of the sofa with the TV remote in one hand and a glass of water in the other. He glanced toward Lucas. "He was tuckered out, so I brought him in. He just crashed."

"Where's Lainey?" I asked.

"I told her she could run next door for a few minutes and see the Rileys' new turtle." As he tuned to the finance report on the television, I glanced at the room. The day's toys were still on the floor, and I collected a plastic cup of apple juice from the end table, depositing it in the dishwasher. I noticed a line of red crayon had somehow appeared on the leg of my jeans. Steve flipped the channel back to an entertainment news show and set the remote down, turning to me. "Hey, it's really great that you're trying to keep up with the whole Family Fun Night thing."

"Thanks. Trying, anyway. They still love it."

We both paused, not knowing what to say next; then he looked up at me sideways and smiled a little sadly. "It was really nice joining in again for a few minutes."

I continued tidying the room, placing a few DVDs back in the drawer, the activity filling the silence that followed. "Just a heads-up, Lucas has been making me read four books a night . . . including *Tootle the Train*," I said with a weary half smile.

"Ouch. That's a long one." He feigned a comical wince.

"And watch out for Lainey's loose tooth. I think—"

"We'll be fine."

"I know. It's just—"

"Evie."

I bristled at the familiar tone of voice but nodded, letting it go. It wasn't easy for either of us; I knew that. And we both seemed to be engaged in the constant, unspoken competitive sport of Who's Got It More Together. I often felt like I was losing.

"So, any plans this weekend?" he asked, changing the subject after a few moments had passed.

"Nothing much. Kate and I might have lunch, but I think I'm going to catch up on work mostly."

"How's work going? Still adjusting?"

"It's good. Thanks. I got a new story this week."

"Hey, that's great! I told you they'd be beating down your door."

I don't know about beating down my door, but things had been going okay. In my twenties, my career had been everything. But after that fell apart, I didn't know quite what to do. Steve's career had completely taken off, whereas mine had died a slow death. In the process, I'd discovered that the only thing I loved more than my career was being a mom. It was okay. Truly. I'd felt grateful to be able to stay at home with my kids. But the lines between Evie the woman and Evie the mom were pretty much gone.

When the kids got a little older and things started to go downhill with Steve, I'd slowly started working from home, pitching stories and taking freelance jobs, writing about pretty much anything I could get paid to write about (except music, that is—strictly no music). It didn't make my heart sing, so to speak, but I was proud of it, and it paid the bills while letting me still be there for the kids.

I looked at my watch and toward the darkened back door, waiting for Lainey. Steve followed my glance from the door, then toward Lucas, who was quietly snoring in a pillow nest on the sofa. He lightly rustled our son's flaxen hair. The two were like twins, born thirty-odd years apart. The evening had gone late, past Lucas's bedtime, and he didn't stir. "I'll tell you what. Why don't I take Lainey now, and I'll get Lucas in the morning."

"Really? You sure?"

"Yeah. He's wiped out. Let him sleep. I'll carry him up before I go. Just let him know I'll be here for him after breakfast. Sound good?"

"Okay, if you don't mind. I'd hate to wake him. He was up a couple of times last night, couldn't sleep." Fighting a yawn, I looked up again at the antique clock that hung above the mantel, inherited from Steve's grandmother. I supposed he'd want to take it eventually, but we hadn't yet started the process of sorting to that degree.

"Looks like he wasn't the only one. Not sleeping again?"

I shrugged. "I'm fine." In truth, it was just after eight o'clock and I was already dreaming of my bed. I collected a few half-dressed Barbies from a side chair, content that the room was sufficiently neat, and plopped down to wait for Lainey.

Then I heard it.

At the sound of his name on the television, a familiar jolt ran through me. His face lit up the screen, bringing with it an ache that I'd long ago learned to manage. It was always like that. I'd be walking through my normal life, doing my normal everyday things in my normal everyday world, when there it would be. Like walking into a glass wall. I suppose I'd grown somewhat used to it over the years, though; their music was everywhere, after all. I tried to look away, but my eyes stayed fixed to the screen. He was wearing a slim-cut tuxedo and dark sunglasses as he walked down a red carpet with a stunning brunette draped on his arm. *My god, you look so handsome in that tux,* I thought as a wistful smile crossed my lips, my breath momentarily stolen. All black. No bow tie, of course. Obviously. But still, a tux. I blinked back a prick at the corners of my eyes, a product more of affectionate pride than anything else.

"Is Carter Wills finally settling down?" the newswoman quipped. I swallowed, leaning forward just barely. "In this month's issue of *Rolling Stone*, Wills talks about his tempestuous rise as the front man of one of the world's biggest bands. In the rare interview, the singer comes clean about his life with girlfriend and actress Iliana Billings. Sources close to the couple say that an engagement is happening and wedding bells are in the future. So, ladies—"

I swallowed hard and closed my eyes with a deep breath.

And just like that, the ache returned right to the center of my sternum, where it settled in for the night. He was getting married.

"Hey, there's my girl." Steve stood, tossing the remote to the side just as Lainey walked in, eagerly chattering about the new turtle. The TV switched off. "Okay, Lainey Bear, just you and me tonight, kiddo. This little guy didn't make it." Steve nodded toward Lucas as he scooped Lainey into his hip. "We'll eat lots of candy and popcorn and stay up late watching scary movies that are too grown-up for you. How's that sound, Mom?" He nudged Lainey conspiratorially and winked, trying to get a laugh out of me when we both knew that he was the stricter of the two of us when it came to such things.

"Mommm-yyyy." Lainey waved her hand in front of my eyes, which had remained distracted somewhere in the middle distance.

"What? Uh, yeah. That sounds good, guys. Here, I'll help you." Steve gave me a curious look but let it go. We passed through the foyer where a small lamp was lit, and I opened the front door wide, letting the crisp night air in to clear my head of the newscaster's words. I helped gather Lainey's things while Steve carried Lucas up to bed. There was a blur of goodbyes and hugs. "Be good for your dad." "Love you." "See you Sunday." When the door closed, I leaned against it, the sudden quiet only serving to magnify the thoughts in my head.

A half hour later, the house closed up for the night, I lay in bed, staring at the ceiling. In the dark of the room, I heard the newscaster's words echo again. Wedding bells. Engagement. For a brief moment, I smiled as I imagined myself beside him. He'd smile at me, and I'd catch a glimpse of his eyes from behind dark lenses. A warm kiss on the cheek.

A car passed outside, and the headlights danced through the room. Images flashed before me. The secrets I'd kept. The mistakes I'd made.

It was a long time ago. Had it really been ten years? *Ten.* The time I'd spent with them all had become a part of my life that was so far away, it was hard to believe it had ever existed. It was nearly impossible to believe that woman and I had been the same person. As if on cue, I heard a small knock at the door and the uneven steps of a child in footed pajamas padding across the deep-pile carpet.

Lucas rubbed his bleary eyes. "Mommy, there's something scary in my room." His tiny voice quivered with distress. I smoothed his wispy hair and asked about his dream as I walked him to his room.

"There was a big orange lizard in my bed, and it was trying to get me."

"Well, let's go see that lizard and tell it to get out of your nice room." I snuggled him back under his covers and made a dramatic show of looking around, checking the closet and peering under the bed. "Hmm. I don't see any lizards here. I think they're all gone now." I sat on his bed in the dim room, a LEGO night-light in the corner casting a soft yellow glow on the walls. My shoulders felt heavy, and I wore a faded T-shirt and cotton pajama pants that probably had once been cute but had faded into old favorites. It was one of those nights when I felt older than I was. I thought of her in a barely there dress, his hands warmly on her waist. She was exquisite, while I sat with my hair piled on top of my head at the end of a long day.

It's so young, of course, midthirties. I know that now. But in the thick of it, when each day felt a lot like the last, it didn't seem that way. I was just an average and unmemorable mom in a quiet suburb. Nothing special. But still, just fine.

From a distant, contrasting land, an image of a man in his tuxedo and the lovely young brunette on his arm passed through my mind. I shook my head clear of it, looking around the room—at the steady world I'd created—to plant myself on firmer ground. I placed Lucas's small, delicate hand in mine, enjoying the fleeting smallness of it.

The sleepless hours ticked on. I often thought I was a fool, perhaps, with my eyes sometimes glancing toward the past like it was a place that actually existed rather than an empty space of what once was. Nonetheless, I'd always felt drawn to the comforts that lay there. I still do. The idea of forgetting frightened me, and after years of trying, I'd paid the price. Details had nearly slipped away. Like the exact texture of his hair between my fingertips or the green-and-gold flecks in his eyes that appeared in a certain light. The specific way he once laced his fingers through mine. The sound of him whispering in my ear as we lay beneath warm sheets. The sense of belonging I'd had with them. The filmmaking career that I'd been on the verge of. The thrill I'd begun to feel as we planned to travel the world. I'd tried to let them go, and mostly I had. But my memories were my own to enjoy without guilt, I supposed. I'd trained myself not to think of those things most of the time and had made a totally different kind of happy life.

But no matter how wonderful and wondrous the memories of those earlier years are, if I could time travel and pick just one night to go back to, it would be a night like that one at the end of summer, playing in the backyard. A regular, average day. A mom playing with her two young children and our dog in the backyard and picking up toys. I know the story I'm telling you might make you believe I'd choose a different time, but I promise, it's true.

45

EVIE

"Come on, guys, breakfast!"

When I close my eyes, I can still hear the sound of my voice calling up the stairs on school mornings. Two pairs of small feet pounding down the steps and passing by in a blur before jumping onto their chairs at the kitchen table. Pancakes in the center of the table, along with a pitcher of orange juice. A layer of shimmery dew on the grass and the brown wooden swing set. Checking backpacks for homework and lunches and straightening out clothes. "Hey, kiddo, you've only got one sock on under those shoes." Tickling Lucas's ankle with a wink. He insisted on doing everything for himself those days, which could be both frustrating and endearing at the same time.

"Ugh! I knew I forgot something!" he replied in a silly voice. A wink that made him smile.

I'd sweep my hair into a ponytail and toss on jeans, a light sweater, and a pair of canvas slip-ons, walk the kids down the block to the bus stop with Roxy trotting behind, tail wagging, then take my time walking back down the suburban street, admiring the perfectly manicured lawns and newly potted mums that were already dotting my neighbors' porches. Yard work had never been my thing, and after Steve left,

I hadn't kept up on it quite the same. But still, our two-story brick Colonial with its white shutters always looked as pretty as a picture. Just like all the others.

A few days after I'd seen the report about Carter's engagement, I went to pick up Lainey from school and joined Kate on a nearby bench. She and I had picked up our friendship without missing a beat in those early days when I'd returned to Pennsylvania. It had been easy; our husbands were best friends, our kids went to the same schools, and she had become the closest thing I'd ever have to a sister. She'd been trying to get me to date and begging me to let her set me up with a guy from her gym.

"Look, you have to have more than kids and your house and work in your life. You're going to end up with ten cats. A crazy lady at the end of the street."

"Too late," I joked. I had been to the shelter a week earlier and was considering a calico with a missing ear, named, somewhat inaccurately, Picasso.

"Just think about it?"

"There's nothing to think about! I'm not going." She sighed in exasperation, and I continued. "Look, someday, I'm sure I'll date again. But not now. For the first time in a long time, it feels good to be on my own, building my business, taking care of the kids, no one to answer to. It's good."

"Oh god, now that you mention it, that sounds pretty great."

"See?"

"Fine."

"Thank you. And thank you for caring." I nudged her shoulder. At that, I checked my phone and realized I was earlier than I'd thought. I tossed it in my bag and leaned back against the bench. A moment later, I realized Kate was watching me stare off into the distance.

"Everything all right?" she asked.

"Yeah, I'm fine. Why?"

"I don't know. You seem a little off."

"I'm fine." *Except oh, by the way, did you see that Carter Wills is getting married to Iliana Billings? It's no big deal. What's this have to do with me, you ask? Nothing. Nothing at all, actually. Silly, really. I'm fantastic. Couldn't be better.* "I didn't get much sleep last night. I think I'm just tired."

She gave me a suspicious look. "Okay, if you say so."

At that point in our lives, Kate still didn't know anything about Carter. No one did, really. And I was comfortable leaving it that way.

We chatted for a few minutes before the kids came out in a burst of shouts and disorganized running. In contrast to the others, Lainey walked slowly, always deep in thought, before sidling up to my hip. She wore a short-sleeve floral dress and black striped leggings over pink Converse sneakers. Her dark hair was pulled into a long, tidy ponytail. She had recently taken to choosing her own eclectic clothes in the mornings, and somehow, she pulled it off quite fashionably.

I leaned down and hugged her. "Hey, sweetie! Did you have a good day at school?"

She nodded pleasantly. "Uh-huh. Guess what?" Her voice was quiet and eager. "We got to finish our dinosaurs today." She held up a detailed papier-mâché sculpture of a T. rex with surprisingly realistic fat green splotches of damp Tempera paint, varying shades of scales, two beady eyes, and a surly expression.

"Ooh! Look at this! I love it!" I kissed her head, and she smiled proudly.

"What's your favorite dinosaur, Mom?"

I picked up the project, wiping a smear of excess glue on my pants. "This one, of course! The T. rex!"

"That one's too easy. Pick another one."

"Um, I'll have to think about this. Let me see . . . I think I like the one that starts with a B. What's it called . . . the big one that eats trees."

"Brachiosaurus. That's an herbivore."

"Right you are!" I winked at her.

"Where's Lucas?" she asked.

"With Daddy. One of his clients canceled at the last minute, and Lucas has been begging him to take him shopping for soccer gear, so he picked him up from school earlier. He'll bring him back for dinner."

Kate chortled behind me.

I turned. "What?"

The kids were busy talking dinosaurs. "So how's that whole 'schedule and routine' thing going for ya?" she asked. "You two are the most married separated couple I've ever heard of."

She wasn't wrong. "I don't know. He's a good dad. I guess that's what counts, right?"

She leaned over and spoke in a low tone. "Hey, Steve's Dad of the Year. We all know that. That's never been the issue. It's Husband of the Year where we had some serious problems." In all fairness, I wasn't exactly Wife of the Year either.

"Hey, Lainey," I called, changing the subject. "I talked to Mrs. Billeski today. You're all set for fall lessons."

"Awesome! Can I do the recital this year?"

"If you want. It's a lot of work, though. She wants you to play Rachmaninoff this year with the older kids. Are you sure?" I thought it funny that as someone who'd been obsessed with rock 'n' roll in my youth, I ended up with a kid who liked classical. Go figure.

"Definitely! Cool!"

Kate looked at us both, eyeing Lainey with incredulity, while her son, Jack, bounced around her, a walking tornado. "I don't know what you and Steve are putting in that girl's water, but you need to bottle it and bring some over to my house."

I laughed as we walked over to my black Jeep Cherokee and waved goodbye.

"Hey, don't forget," Kate called from across the parking lot, "next weekend's the barbecue."

"Wouldn't miss it. Want me to bring dessert?"

"Can you bring that butter cake with the lemon frosting thing that you make?" These were the kinds of conversations I was used to. Conversations about butter cake.

My life was so different from his.

On the way home, we stopped at the market to pick up some things for dinner. The store was crowded with after-school shoppers, and the line was long. Lainey stood alongside me, lost in a book that she'd brought along to pass the time. In front of us, a mother struggled with her screaming toddler, who threw a tantrum on the floor while refusing to relinquish a box of cereal. Eventually, the battle was lost, and a mixture of puffy corn shapes and marshmallows exploded everywhere. I offered a sympathetic smile and bent down to help her pick up the mess.

Out of nowhere, Carter's face on the cover of *Rolling Stone* ambushed me from the magazine rack next to the candy bars. I crouched in front of it, frozen. A dramatic, close-up photo of him staring straight ahead, his eyes dark and stormy, as if challenging the camera. He was shirtless from the waist up. The caption to the right read:

INSIDE THE MIND OF CARTER WILLS:

TALES FROM THE DARK SIDE AND A LOOK BACK AT
THE RISE OF ROCK'S MOST MYSTERIOUS GOD

It wasn't like it was the first magazine I'd seen him on over the years, and I'd managed to resist before. Every single time.

Turn off the music when the song came on.

Look the other way when his picture showed up.

It was better that way.

But something about that one was just . . . different. For one thing, he was half-naked. *Dear god.* His hip bones peeked up over the waistline of his pants. Instinctively, my fingers curled into the natural position, as if they were hooked inside his jeans. But it wasn't just that. To my knowledge, he never gave interviews. Ever. So it was unusual.

Over the years, the band had catapulted into massive success, and Carter's individual celebrity had exploded. The press was captivated by him, but he'd become the very definition of the enigmatic rock star, which had made things easier for me sometimes. But there he was, staring me in the face. It had been three days since I'd heard the news story about him getting engaged, and the hurt of it continued to simmer beneath the surface, no matter how hard I tried to ignore it. The last thing I needed was that magazine.

Obviously, considering it's sitting over there on the floor, twenty years later, you know I ended up buying it. Sometimes I wonder about that magazine and the impetus it had on the course of events that followed. Such a silly thing—a quick decision in the checkout line of a supermarket amid the chewing gum and candy.

46

EVIE

I played his music for you for the first time that day. For the first time in years, really. Intentionally, I mean. Any other time their music came on, I had turned it off.

I took the long way home, driving slowly on the back roads. The car was my place to think and to take a breath, and we were in no hurry.

"I like this song," Lainey said from the back seat. It was a song from their third album, *Astronium Nova*. Aside from the unusual choice of music, this was a ritual of ours over the years and one she enjoyed, the exploration of my iPod on car drives. I taught her to hear and think about the music the way I once had.

"Do you? I used to listen to this band a long time ago. A very good friend of mine used to play their songs for me." I was glad she couldn't see my face. The expression in my eyes.

"What's it called?"

"This song? 'The Air Beside You.'"

"He sounds sad," Lainey said. The trees above us formed a canopy as we drove through them on lazy bends that matched the rhythm of the song.

"You think he sounds sad?" I thought it sounded like a long walk in the park, slow kissing, and light nighttime rain.

"Yeah." Her little voice was soft. I looked into the mirror to see her staring thoughtfully out the window at the passing scenery.

"I don't think it sounds sad. I think it sounds . . ." I paused, memories playing in my mind to the sound of the voice in the song. "Wistful."

"What does wispful mean?"

"Wistful. With a *t*. It means . . ." The word sat grandly in my mind, perfect, and I tried to simplify it. "It means to remember something and wish very much to be there again. To miss something or someone or another time."

"So I was right. Sad."

"You know how sometimes you have a really great dream, and in the morning when you wake up, you're sort of half-awake and kind of want to go back to sleep so you can keep dreaming?"

"Yeah."

"That's sort of what wistful feels like."

"I like that."

"Me too."

"I still think he sounds sad, though."

I looked over and imagined him sitting next to me, his hand reaching out to take mine, as we drove down this road having this conversation that he would absolutely love. "Yeah, Laincy Bear. I guess he's maybe a little sad too."

The song continued to play, both of us quiet, before she spoke again.

"Hey, Mom?"

"Yeah, sweetie?"

"Can we listen to Katy Perry now? And can I eat my Goldfish?"

I laughed, the innocence you brought to my world.

In astrology, there's something called the Pluto Square. It tends to herald a reckoning of sorts. Drastic changes when old patterns can no longer be ignored and new action begins. That was that month for me, which I suppose is why I wanted to play the music for you, finally. Apparently, squares always shout the loudest when it comes to the planets.

He would get a kick out of me trying to explain this to you.

47

CARTER

I looked her up from time to time, wondering what her life might be like. I couldn't find much, which might have been a good thing. A couple of photos from a local event or some such, often showing her standing next to her husband, smiling, his hand wrapped around her waist. Her Facebook profile photo. I imagined her at dinner parties or playing with her kids. I learned she'd returned to her hometown, which had surprised me. I hoped she was having a good life. I didn't dare to wonder if she'd sometimes thought of me, as well.

Maybe it was best she wasn't there to see those early years. After she was gone, this unrelenting darkness descended over me until I went numb. I think the guys encouraged a kind of complete indulgence at first, hoping it might shake me out of it. But everyone I met felt invisible. I'd tried over and over to reach her in those first few weeks after she'd left. Leaving message after message. But I never heard back. She was just . . . gone. After that, I went off the rails. Alex didn't fare much better. Worse, actually. Nobody had realized it at the time, but she'd been this kind of stabilizing force that kept us all on solid ground, an unnamed fifth member of the group, and when she was gone, it went to hell.

I just wanted to drown in my own misery, and I nearly did. But then, after a while, those indulgences became the only thing that could make me forget for a little while. The world became huge. The audiences roared bigger and louder every single night and in every single city we went to. The decadence and availability of anyone and anything I wanted, right at my fingertips, became my drug of choice. I just stopped connecting. It was easier that way for a long time. Being numb.

Eventually, I guess I became the person people expected me to be. I'm the lead singer of a rock band, right? The awards kept coming, the crowds kept getting larger, and the distance to her kept getting wider until everything about that time of my life was eclipsed by a new reality.

Michael has been asking about the rumors that have circulated over the years, the women who came in and out of the tabloids alongside my photo.

"After a while, you become less connected with the real world," I tell him. "It's weird—you work so hard to become a success, but as the fame increases, the wall around you gets higher and higher until you can hardly see the real world anymore. We have to protect our privacy so carefully that eventually it becomes impossible to just meet a normal person outside of the business. One minute, you're onstage with thousands of people cheering for you, and an hour later, you can't find anyone to have a decent conversation with. It can feel incredibly isolating. Fame becomes this incestuous little pool of celebrities who live in a fortress of their own making. No one gets in and no one gets out, so we really just have each other most of the time. Even if you do meet someone . . . normal—someone who's not talking to you because you're famous or fit into their carefully curated publicity plan—there's this weird moment when a look crosses their face and you can see them comparing the real you to the public version."

Inevitably, you feel like a disappointment.

"I guess it's just easier to do the stereotypical Hollywood thing. Some of it's been true. Most of it hasn't."

48

Evie

Do you remember the Labor Day barbecue that Kate used to have every year? Her backyard patio would be set with tiki torches and a colorful assortment of flatware, plates, and cups in the colors of red and blue. That year was the last one we ever went to, and maybe that's why it sticks in my mind.

It was just before dark, and most of the guests had gone home, leaving a few of us stragglers scattered in patio chairs, drinks in hand. The local jazz station played through speakers from a nearby windowsill.

"Anyone want another?" Steve stood over a steel washbasin that had been filled with ice and fashioned into a cooler, Martha Stewart–style. Bottles of beer and wine coolers floated like bobbing apples.

I leaned toward Kate, who sat on the cushioned seat next to me, and I whispered, "I know we're trying the whole modern-divorce thing, but this feels weird." She followed my glance toward Steve. "I don't know if this was such a good idea. Maybe we should take turns hanging out with you guys or something."

"I know. I'm so sorry. But you're our best friends," she said. "It's not like we couldn't invite him. We love you both. Please don't do that thing where we lose our best friends because someone goes and gets divorced. At least you guys are getting along, right?"

"I guess. But I should be heading home, anyway. It's getting late."

"Oh, don't leave yet. Come on. What on earth do you have better to do at home? Will you please stay?" She had a point.

"What about you, Ev? Water?" Steve called over to where I sat.

I looked over to Kate and sighed, reluctantly giving in. "Sure. I'll take some more iced tea while you're up, thanks." When I spoke, Lucas burrowed farther into me. After a long day playing in the sun, he was tuckered out. He'd curled up in my lap a half hour earlier and was dozing. I brushed the hair off his forehead and lay a beach towel over his cool legs. The rest of the kids were all piled in Kate's game room watching a movie.

"I'll take another beer, buddy." Kate's husband, Jim, sat across from me, chatting with a friend who was admiring their newly redesigned landscaping. Jim and Kate had gotten married just a few months before Steve and I did. The two guys had stayed best friends since grad school, getting their MBAs together. The four of us had quickly become a comfortable four musketeers. There were a few other people and friends rounding out the crowd, including Kate's next-door neighbors, Brandi and Bob.

Steve handed me an iced tea in a blue plastic cup. "Heads up!" I chirped, looking past his shoulder. He spun around just in time to catch a football in his left hand. I grabbed the cup, barely avoiding spilling the contents on my black cotton sundress. He threw the ball back to Jim, who had taken his place in the grass, just off the patio. The two men, both dressed in khaki shorts and polos, tossed the ball back and forth with ease while sipping their beers. Steve ran a hand through his sandy-blond hair. One long afternoon out in the sun and he was already turning tan.

"So did you guys go to Myrtle Beach again this summer?" Brandi asked, turning to me. Brandi meant well, but when she asked a question like that, you got the sense that she might have been making sure she was appropriately keeping up with the Joneses.

"Brandi!" Kate hissed.

"Oh my god, I'm so sorry! I—I don't know what I was thinking . . . ," she stammered, looking horrified and glancing toward Steve and then back toward me. "Eek. I totally forgot. Too many margaritas." Her awkward high-pitched laugh cut through the night as her drink sloshed a little over the edge and onto her shirt. Her plump chest had grown red and splotchy in the sun, matching her hair.

"It's okay; don't worry about it," I said. "Steve's parents just bought a house at the shore. The kids spent some time there, but not much else."

"Well, that sounds nice!" she said, clearly trying to make amends but sounding mostly disingenuous. "We headed to the Hamptons this year." She sat up a little taller as she said this, and I got the sense she'd brought the subject up just so she could have this moment.

"Oh, nice! What part?" Kate asked.

"We rented a place in Montauk. Our kids don't need to go to college, anyway," she joked.

"Evie used to live in the Hamptons," Kate said, nodding in my direction, ever the good hostess.

Jim and Steve returned, evidently having tired of their brief game of catch. "You want me to take him inside?" Steve asked, looking down at Lucas. "Put him on the sofa?"

"Thanks," I said, gingerly shuffling the sleeping boy into his arms. I stretched, free of the extra weight.

"Really? When did you live in the Hamptons?" Brandi sipped her drink, clearly deflated.

"I didn't. I lived on Long Island. Not the Hamptons. Big difference."

"Why on earth did you ever come back here?" She scowled.

"She came back because she couldn't stay away from me, of course," Steve chimed in, closing the patio doors behind him. "Obviously."

I laughed, shaking my head. "Yeah, yeah, Casanova. I'm pretty sure that's not exactly how it happened."

"Sorry, ole boy," Jim chimed in. "I think you've got a few things backward. If I remember correctly, it was you who always did the chasing. Following poor Evie around like a puppy until she finally just gave in." He winked at me.

"Well, hey. How can you blame me? Look at her," Steve said kindly, a rare note of something quiet in his voice. Everyone paused, looking at us both as if unsure how to proceed. The divorcing couple messing up the flow of the night. Thankfully, Bob interjected, emerging from the house.

"What's this about the Hamptons?" His voice boomed, littered with the gravel of a Jersey accent. He opened another beer, which would make his personality a little more caustic than usual. He dropped into a chair with a heavy thump and put his feet up on the glass patio table, which let out a shrill creak in complaint but remained intact.

"We were just talking about how Evie used to live on Long Island," Brandi told her husband.

"Really? I didn't know that. You live there with your family?"

"No. In my twenties." I stood up to get a light sweater out of my bag. The evening had grown cool. "Speaking of moving, what's up with the FOR SALE sign next door? Are they moving?"

There was talk about the neighbors getting divorced. Something about someone having an affair with an office worker. The kind of suburban chatter and gossip that only serves the purpose of making everyone feel a little better about their own lives.

"Okay, people, this music is putting me to sleep." Kate jumped up and went to the stereo, adjusting the volume. A Dave Matthews song came on. "What is it about that guy's voice? Takes me back." Kate mused, bobbing her hips the way she did when she'd had one margarita too many. "If I could meet anyone famous, it'd be him."

"Seriously?" Jim asked, giving her a cockeyed look. "Really. Of everyone in the whole world. Dave Matthews? You're joking."

"What? Who doesn't like Dave Matthews?" She looked at him like he had two heads.

Steve raised his hand.

Kate shrugged. "Anyway, there's something . . . I don't know, kinda cute and quirky about him. I think he'd be fun to hang out with. Or . . . maybe if I could only meet one, hmm . . . maybe Bradley Cooper. Yes. That'd be cool too."

Jim joined in. "I'd meet—lemme think. Earl Warren."

"Who?" Kate and Brandi both asked in unison.

"Supreme Court Justice in the fifties and sixties. You know, Brown versus Board of Education. Miranda and all that."

"Steve Jobs," Steve said, walking up the steps and rejoining the discussion.

"Yeah, he'd be good too," Jim said, nodding.

"Oh my god, could you guys possibly be any more boring?" Kate groaned.

"Or Kate Beckinsale," Jim said. "She's kind of a badass. I dig it."

"Now we're talking." Bob and Jim clinked bottles in a toast.

"Robert Redford," Brandi added. "Definitely. Robert Redford."

"Aww, I love him," I said. "*The Way We Were*, ugh, gets me every time." I wiped a mock tear from my cheek.

"Oh god. Shoot me," Steve said.

"He secretly loves that movie," I whispered.

"Yeah. Right. Love it. Watch it every day. Sometimes twice." As usual, Steve had everyone chuckling again. Steve was the kind of guy who turned the game on when I'd tried to light candles and wear lingerie. Lovable but not huge on romance, that one.

"What about you, Evie? Who would you meet?" Brandi asked.

"Oh, don't ask her. She doesn't count," Kate added. "She's met everyone."

"That is not even a little bit true," I replied.

Bob looked between us, confused. "What? Why doesn't Evie count?"

"Because once upon a time, Miss Fancypants here used to meet famous people for a living."

"She's exaggerating," I said.

"I thought you did, like . . . some sort of part-time freelance thing from home? Writing for the local paper, right?" Brandi asked.

"Wait, you work?" Bob asked. "I thought you stayed home with the kids?"

"I started working again last year."

"And?" Brandi pushed.

"And back before that, I used to work in the music industry. I was a music journalist. And filmmaker. Sort of."

Bob narrowed his eyes, then waved his hand. "Nah, you're pulling our leg."

"No, seriously, she was kind of a big deal!" Kate exclaimed.

I shook my head. "No I wasn't. It was forever ago and only lasted a few years." Was that true? I supposed it was. But it felt like more.

"She even was supposed to go on some world tour with a band."

"Get outta here." Bob was now belly laughing. "What were you gonna do, be the official cupcake baker of the tour?"

"Uh-oh. Here we go again," I heard Steve mutter.

I bristled, annoyed but not surprised. "Ahem. Yes. Well, that's exactly right, Bob. How did you guess? I was going to bake cupcakes and make their beds. Put little daisies on their tables. And by the way, I'm pretty sure you told these same jokes last year. And the year before that."

Kate smirked at me sideways, and Bob rolled his eyes.

Jim deftly opened another beer, popping the cap on the side of the table. "I remember hearing about that when I was first dating Kate. You were leaving to go run around the world with a rock band. And Steve here was all pouty about you leaving for good. Still pining for his old high school flame."

I looked at Steve. "You were? I didn't know that! We weren't even together then."

Steve shrugged, looking uncharacteristically bashful for a moment. "What can I say? The man speaks the truth."

"Who was it? The band. Anyone we know?" Jim asked.

Mayluna had started playing stadiums. Everyone in the world knew them. I looked away, just above the horizon, and noticed the evening's first stars coming out above the silhouetted trees. "Nah, not really."

"Philly, man. It's in the blood. Brings you back every time," Bob said, popping a chip into his mouth from a leftover basket on the table.

Brandi leaned forward, excited. "How is it that I never knew this about you? I honestly, for the life of me, cannot picture this! So did you really meet, like, rock stars and stuff? Did you ever meet Steven Tyler?"

I had, actually, by the way. Met Steven Tyler. He had kissed me straight on the lips one night backstage. Though he did this with every woman he saw backstage. Endearing, I suppose. Or obnoxious. I guess it depended on the person. And the decade, obviously. Doubt that could happen now. Anyway, I didn't mention it.

"Aerosmith, that's a good band," Bob chimed in.

"It wasn't really a big deal. Mostly it was just, you know, work."

"You didn't like it?"

Bob slapped his knee. "I still think you're pulling our leg. I can just picture you walking around backstage: 'Would you like some lemonade, Mr. Tyler?'" Annoyingly, everyone else was chuckling along with him.

Yep, that was me. Suzy Homemaker.

"Miles Davis, now that's good music," Steve said. "Smooth like butter."

Never met him. Though that would have been very cool.

"Coldplay."

I'd met Chris Martin and the guys way at the beginning while I'd been in London with Carter, having seen them play a little show at Dingwalls and hearing buzz about them from others in the business. I'd sat at a pub with him while he sipped water and I sipped a beer. He had a combination of self-effacing charm and complete confidence, along with a buzzing, boyish energy that drew people to him, instantly charming. Two years later, people would be watching them headline Glastonbury.

I didn't tell this story either.

"Can never go wrong with the Beatles."

"Radiohead. Reminds me of college."

I could tell that story too. But I didn't.

"U2." Jim joined in the banter. "I saw them at the stadium. Amazing show."

Ditto.

"Mayluna," Kate added.

I looked away.

"Me, I like country, all the way," said Brandi.

"They're coming to town soon." Kate went to the margarita pitcher and, upon finding it empty, opted for a glass of chardonnay.

"Who, U2?" Jim asked. "Really? I'd go see them."

"No, Mayluna," Kate added. "Not like I could ever get this one to go with me." She elbowed her husband in the side. "He likes to be in bed by eleven at the latest."

"Hey, I never hear you complaining," he added, winking at her. She reached down and kissed his cheek. If there was a manual on how to do marriage well, Jim and Kate would have written it. They were perfect.

As the banter continued, I swallowed a long sip of tea. My mouth had gone dry at Kate's mention of the band. I looked into the backyard and saw Carter perfectly in my mind's eye. Leaning against the fence, fingers looped in his jeans. A knowing, mischievous grin on his face as he took in the scene, watching me, as if to say, *Are you kidding me right now? Let's get out of here.* I shook my head, biting my lip against the smile that formed there. While talk turned to baseball season and the upcoming game between the Red Sox and the Pirates, I nodded politely on occasion and threw in a line here and there as I tried to keep from jumping up and breaking loose of the role I played so well.

The previous year, I'd promised myself I wouldn't go to Kate's Labor Day picnic anymore.

"Who cares what Bob thinks? You barely like him, anyway." Steve had stood in the bathroom, wearing boxers and a T-shirt, talking with his toothbrush in his mouth. He spit the foam into the sink and wiped his mouth on the hand towel. "And Brandi's just . . . I don't know. Brandi. Who gives a crap what they think? They're obnoxious. Don't let it get to you." We'd just gotten home from Kate and Jim's, and we were both cranky and tired.

"I'm not going next year, I swear."

"You say that every year. And I'm sure—"

I groaned. "Can you please not do that? I hate when you do that."

"Do what?"

I pulled a long pink sleep shirt over my head. "That! Wipe your toothpaste mouth on the towel! It's gross! And then I dry my face with your gross toothpaste towel. Use a Kleenex," I barked as I snatched the towel and threw it into the hamper, retrieving a fresh one.

Steve followed me into the bedroom, crossed his arms, and stared at me.

"What?" I folded the covers down on the bed and fluffed the pillows a little too aggressively.

"Are you done?"

I looked up at him. Begrudgingly, I finally gave in, sagging. "I'm sorry." He raised his eyebrows. "No, really, I'm sorry. I didn't mean to bite at you. It's just frustrating. He's rude and condescending. 'Bake sales and PTA meetings'? What is it with him? I don't even like cupcakes! He acts like it's 1950 every time he sees me. And what's wrong with those things, anyway?"

"In all fairness, I think he just mentioned bake sales. And maybe aprons. But nothing about PTA meetings. I think he's just one of those guys who picks on the cute girls."

I broke a smile and sat on the bed. "Oh, I know. It's fine."

"Seriously, I don't know why you're making such a big deal over it. He's a jerk. Hell, half the time, I forget what you did before the kids. And I never knew what Kate did. Grants or something?"

"Are you being serious? She was in nonprofit management. And she was really good at it!"

"Right. Well, whatever."

"See, that's my point! You've known Kate since she was eleven, and even you couldn't remember what she did for a living. I guess it's just hard sometimes. I built up this whole career. And I was proud of it. I love that I can stay home with the kids. I do. I think it's one of the best things about my life. But it's like the moment you decide to leave your job, poof! Your entire identity pre-children goes up in smoke. Everyone looks at you like you sit around watching soap operas all day and baking. You don't know how frustrating that can be."

"Is that what this is about? Fine, then go back to work if you want to go back to work. I don't care."

"I don't see how I can! You're at the office till midnight half the time. And now even on the weekends."

He groaned. "Are we done now? I'm wiped out. And I have a meeting first thing."

I flipped off the light and lay back on the pillows. "Sure." Then quietly, I added, "It's not just about work. It's about—"

"Oh my god, would you stop? Remind me not to go to Kate's barbecue next year. Fine. You're right." He threw the covers off and grabbed his pillow. "I'm gonna sleep downstairs."

"Steve, wait, no. I didn't mean—"

"I have an early morning, anyway." He snatched his phone from the nightstand and closed the door.

But a year later, there we'd been again. Life on repeat. Albeit no longer together, a lot had changed since then, but not enough. Most of the time, I was happy and moving on, or maybe I wasn't. I'd been treading water with very little forward movement. But suddenly it seemed as if everything had started to unravel, time spinning backward instead of forward, making me question everything.

49

Evie

Sometimes, I thought it was all so romantic. Keeping the grand love of a lifetime a secret and all that. But other times, I thought the whole thing was nothing but madness. The night of that damn barbecue, representative of so many other nights like it when I wanted to scream out loud, was like a straw that broke the camel's back. The universe shouting at me until I could no longer ignore it.

I ended up plucking that magazine out of the trash that night, gingerly turning the pages, one by one, bracing myself for what I would find. Finally, I reached a full-page, full-body photo of him standing straight forward and looking directly at the camera. The first thing I noticed was the photo credit: Derek had taken the photos. And of course, the rest of it made me swallow. He appeared to be wearing absolutely nothing, covered only by the carefully placed font of the lettering. I imagined he and Derek had gotten a kick out of that.

I knew the writer, funny enough. A guy named Michael Fleming. We had both come up around the same time, making our way from fan to insider and telling the stories about the artists we'd covered. I'd always liked his writing style, and he was a good guy.

I traced the curve of Carter's mouth, the new illustrations that had been added to his body, the lines of his hips, remembering the exact way his skin had felt. Then, as my eyes drew downward to his hands, I gasped and pulled the magazine closer. Inscribed on his ring finger was a tattoo of the symbols for sigma and five. EV. And on the matching right finger—the mathematical symbol for infinity.

A little dazed from the discovery, I continued reading. From an interview that had taken place at a restaurant in Los Angeles, the story was a skipping timeline of sorts but was fairly sparse, with Carter evading most questions. He didn't seem to enjoy the attention, though maybe he'd grown used to it. I didn't really know him anymore. The article was also accompanied by a pictorial timeline, and my eyes went straight to a slightly blurred photo of him throwing a vicious punch in the midst of a crowd outside a hotel. I instantly recognized the scene from New York and cringed at the memory from our last days together.

It's no secret that Wills has had issues with paparazzi and crowds, not to mention the stories that came out from his school days. In 1999, charges were levied against him by a photographer over an altercation outside of a New York City hotel. Eventually, the suit was settled generously outside of court. Wills never commented on the incident, but after having followed him throughout his career, I can't help but wonder if he'd care to set the record straight. "People always made so much of that. Like I was some hot-tempered egomaniac. It's not who I am. It just happened, and that's it." But something made him do it. "Let's just say I was protecting someone I loved and leave it at that. It was a long time ago."

Someone I loved.
Past tense. A long time ago.

I took a breath and continued to read the discussion about the European tour that year.

> Bands come and go, but twelve years after the debut self-titled EP that quietly rocked the UK charts, Mayluna is bigger than ever, selling out venues all over the world. Well into rock-and-roll royalty, Wills seems unfazed by the level of their success. "We take it seriously and made a commitment not to screw it up. And we don't hate each other, which ostensibly, is key."

As I read more of the article, I barely recognized the Carter I'd known. He sounded like he had grown aloof and hardened. The boyish softness and optimism had been left behind. I suppose that happens to all of us at some point, though. I also read about Alex's struggles in the first few years, and my heart hurt.

The piece went into the music a bit and the creation of the albums, with *Sigma Five* being called out in particular because of what the writer called "iconic" with "darkly romantic musings." But little was revealed.

The interview came around to Carter's wide array of tattoos and the meanings behind them, landing on the one that I was most interested in. The part that had seemingly resulted in a bit of mystery and lore.

> *Sigma Five.* The album title. The tattoo. The general belief is that the tattoo is Wills paying homage to the album of the same title and that he's married to his music. But there have been hints of a deeper meaning. "The beauty of it lies in the mystery, doesn't it? It's one of the few things in life that's all mine to keep." Does the band know what it means? "Of course." When asked if anyone else knows what it truly means, the singer simply says, "Maybe."

Speaking of that ring finger, Wills has been linked with
his fair share of Hollywood women, including a recent
engagement to model/actress Iliana Billings, who Wills
calls "a wonderful human being." He claims rumors of
his philandering have been "highly exaggerated."

I nearly set the magazine down at that point, my shoulders curling
inward.

A few days earlier at a Mayluna show, teenagers were
screaming his name, right next to forty-something
women and men doing the same. It's not every day
that a dark-haired, tattooed rocker makes that kind of
impression.

I could so clearly imagine a younger Carter blushing and squirm-
ing awkwardly at the subject. At the same time, I, of course, knew the
answer better than anyone, though I could never put it into words.

"Poor judgment, perhaps?" Wills responds, when asked
if he knows the secret of his appeal. "But it's very flatter-
ing and kind. We're grateful that we've had the opportunity to be a part of people's lives."

Ah. There he was. I smiled.

The story was surprisingly brief, and as I read through it, I could
feel the holes being filled by the writer as best as possible while working
with Carter's natural and likely frustrating reticence. Funny that he was
so closed about answers but had no issue posing half-nude on the cover.
Then again, he was always more comfortable naked, always running
around like a bare-cheeked toddler, I thought with a laugh.

I sank back into my chair, resting my head against the back of the cushion, as I remembered that last day in New York. The look on his face before he drove away. I'd been so lost back then. I wanted to return to that girl, the younger version of myself, and say to her, *Wait. Take a breath. There's a better way.* Perhaps there was, but then again, perhaps not.

Despite my best efforts to leave the past where it belonged, Carter often entered my mind over the years. I'd wake up from a dream, desperate to return to it and the feeling of his kiss. His face would appear out of nowhere while I was making coffee, driving the kids to school, or having dinner with friends. Whenever I thought back on the way he and I had been together, sometimes it was hard to remember if it had all really happened to me or if it was just the product of my imagination. But of course, it had all been real, which made it both easier and harder to live with. But things have a way of working out for a reason.

When you were kids, I kept a box hidden at the back of the closet tied with a ribbon. It held a few mementos: the smooth plastic coating of the Mayluna All Access pass that had been my key to so many fun nights on the road. A small stack of photos. Tommy, Carter, and me, drinks in hand, looking a little worse for the wear, acting silly on New Year's Eve in London. A picture I took from the side of the stage of Carter performing. A note from Carter, ripped from a hotel notepad: *Gone for coffee. Back in a few. Sleep tight, pretty girl. xo—C.* I went through those things that night after reading the magazine, determined to face my past.

Beautiful, he would say. It wasn't a word that came to mind easily these days. I couldn't remember the last time I'd heard that word about myself. My mom's good genes had been kind to me and I looked mostly the same, I supposed. For that I was thankful. It was everything else that had changed. There was a glow that was absent. A light.

My mind flashed to a different time. A different place. A different me.

I remember hearts that pound
The taste of you, like summer found
Tangled in a sea of mist
for hours
Bourbon lips, the stolen kiss
I still can feel you with me love

I found myself humming the melody to the song. The lyrics were written in Carter's scratchy black handwriting on the back of a crumpled receipt that I'd spotted on the nightstand one morning and held on to. He'd written them during the night while I had been sleeping next to him.

"You like?" he'd asked, giving me a smoldering smile when he saw me holding the tattered paper.

"I love it."

He'd slipped under the tangled sheets, wrapping around me, warm from sleep. "What do you say we work on the rest of it? I could use some inspiration."

I thought of these things as the doorbell rang and the house exploded into noise in the way that happens with the unexpected confetti-cannon ringing of a doorbell in a family home. The kids shouting, "I'll get it!" in unison, pounding to the door in a race with the barking dog, all sliding on the hardwood to open the door for the neighbors.

It was often like that when Carter was mentioned, pulling myself out of another world while trying to maintain my grip on the real one.

I placed everything back in the box, and called Kate first thing the next morning. The band was on tour that year—the big stadium tour that everyone was talking about. Kate had been bugging me to go with her, and I'd made some excuse not to. But I changed my mind that night. Thank God I did.

"Hey, remember when you asked me if I'd go to that Mayluna show with you?"

"Yeah?" Kate said.

"I'll go."

In a sea of faceless fans, I'd be nobody—I wouldn't talk to him, obviously. But I could watch him. Be in the same geographical location with them. I could hear the music. I hoped it might be enough to put the past to sleep for good.

It's so easy to lie to ourselves when we really want to. Isn't it?

I suppose I was meant to see that magazine in the grocery store that day. Meant to see the news story on the television. Carter thought so, too, when I told him about it later, so I guess it must have been one of those signs that the universe places in front of us to wake us up and help shift our trajectory.

50

CARTER

"Like I said, I nearly lost my ass over that story," Michael says, echoing his earlier comment about the *Rolling Stone* piece we'd done a while back. "If you can even call it that."

"I never was much for interviews, as you of all people know," I admit.

"I figured you hated my guts that day. I was sweating the whole time." He scratches his head again. "Which still makes me wonder why, of all people, I'm the one here now serving as the interviewer for this film."

"Because," I say, "she said you'd be the right one. Said you were a good fit. In all fairness, if I'd known that when we did that last interview, I might have been a little more agreeable. But probably not."

"I don't understand. Have I met her?"

"The two of you used to work together a long time ago," I tell him, and his eyes widen.

"Cameron," he says, trying to place her. "Why has that name been sounding so familiar?" A moment later he locates the memory. His jaw drops a little. "Wait a minute, Cameron *Leigh*. That's her?"

I nod. "It wasn't her real name, but yes."

"I'll be damned. Wow, that's going back." He smiles slightly in the way people do when they're reminded of someone from their youth. "I remember her. We used to cover the same circuit. She was good. She was friends with Derek d'Orsay, I think, yeah?" I can see more memories of her rising to the surface. "She was going places. Striking, though, too, I remember," he says.

"I can't disagree with that."

"She was talented. But I never heard much about her after that. Left the business, right?"

It's hard to think of the talent that went unused, the dreams that were abandoned. She never blamed me, of course, but I blame myself. I wonder where her life might have taken her had she not met me. But she tells me she found happiness, and I'm sure in many ways that's very true.

51

EVIE

"Okay, what's up? You haven't said more than five words since you got in the car."

"I'm sorry," I said to Kate on the evening of the show. "I have a lot on my mind for work. But I'm glad I'm out with you!" I tried to relax and sound cheerful. "We'll have fun!" I gave her a broad grin, then looked away.

"Hey, I know you're not a fan, but I swear they're awesome live. Once you see them, you are going to love them."

"I'm sure I will," I replied, looking off to the horizon. Already the concert was proving to be a surreal experience.

The Infinitum tour had been going for nearly a year, starting internationally with multiple dates at Wembley Stadium, Stade de France, and the like before crossing over to the North American dates. They arrived in Philly with only a couple of shows left before heading to South America.

I remember taking my time that night getting ready—almost as if I were going on a date. Methodically taking a long, slow bath and allowing the warm water to soften my skin. I selected beautiful black lace from a drawer that was otherwise filled with cotton. With gentle care, I applied touches of makeup to a face that had earned its appearance from smiles and tears over the years. I let my hair flow long and loose down my back, and a light-gray sweater hung slightly off one shoulder, an homage to my youth. I felt pretty that night, I remember, looking at myself in the mirror. I wasn't dressing for a man. I wasn't dressing for Kate. I wasn't dressing for anyone else. I was honoring myself and the importance of the night. The healing that I hoped to achieve by allowing myself to face it.

I was quiet on the drive, gazing out the window while Kate chattered through the traffic. But she'd known something was off right away, of course, asking me more than once if everything was okay, while I'd smiled and assured her that, yes, of course I was excited about the show and our girls' night out. I'm sure she was hoping for better company, but she had no idea at the time what she was getting herself into.

The two of you were at your dad's for the weekend. Jim had been out of town that evening, and Kate had left her kids with a new babysitter and we'd gotten a late start. Between that and the traffic that plagued the expressway, we'd arrived to the thumping sounds of the opening act finishing their set, playing in the distance as we snaked through the seemingly endless stretch of parking lots. There were still a few stragglers tailgating, music blaring from overstressed speakers inside their SUVs.

More than once, I almost turned around. Said I wasn't feeling well or something, but I kept walking. Over and over, I told myself to breathe, as if my nervous system had forgotten how to perform the function on its own, while we made our way through the crowds. Sometimes when I'm in large crowds now, I'll look around at everyone's faces and think that you never know what's going on in someone's world while they walk through life as if everything is normal.

Kate had purchased the tickets late, so our seats had originally been in one of the top sections of the stadium. When she directed us to the gate for the floor entrance, I was confused.

"And hey, good news. We have awesome seats," she explained. "Sixth row!"

"What?" I exclaimed a little wildly, stopping short. "But I thought . . ." I thought we'd be far away from the stage.

"A friend of Jim's had great seats. He couldn't go at the last minute, so I bought them off him and sold the others. No way I was letting that opportunity go. Awesome, right?"

My feet were glued to the pavement. This was not part of the plan. Watching them from afar, where Carter would appear barely larger than the size of a postage stamp, was one thing. Watching from the sixth row would be a whole different story.

"C'mon!" she called, startling me to move. "I don't want to miss the first song!"

After weaving our way down to the floor, through the rows of chairs, squeezing past tightly huddled bodies, Kate tugged my hand toward our seats. I moved my unstable legs, staring up at the production that towered above us—a massive steel structure that supported a central video wall and side screens. A long runway jutted far out into the crowd to a second, smaller stage amid a sea of people. I would be twenty feet away from him, but he'd never know I was there, no different from the tens of thousands of other people just like me. One organism worshipping at the feet of the band they loved.

"These seats are amazing!" Kate exclaimed, then looked over at me and stopped abruptly. "Are you feeling okay tonight? You look a little pale."

"I'm great."

Kate checked her watch, jittery in the seat, and noted that the show was running later than she'd expected, while I watched dozens of tour crew in black shirts moving like the parts of the well-oiled machine I understood from a lifetime earlier.

"I hope they go on soon. The sitter has to leave by twelve, and it'll take forever to get out of here," she told me. "Thank God we're at least on the aisle."

We waited. Until finally the lights went down, the music swelled, and the crowd began to roar in a frenzy of anticipation. I remember closing my eyes, almost as though I was afraid to watch, and my heart pounding so hard in my chest that it was actually painful, while feeling Kate bobbing excitedly next to me. And then I opened my eyes, and there he was.

52

CARTER

Sometimes I'll wonder what the story is behind the people who have come to watch us play. Have they traveled far to get there? Taking money out of their paychecks to spend a few hours at a show with us. Traveling for hours, making arrangements for work, kids, whatever their life entails. It's humbling, and there's this huge responsibility in it.

People think that we can't see them from the stage, and usually we can't, of course, in a giant crowd. But we can always see the faces in the rows near the stage when the light catches them for a moment.

"It was definitely a weird vibe that night. Really big energy," Tommy says. "When you play enough shows for enough years, you can almost preternaturally sense when a show is going to be different. There's a different kind of energy to it. And that one was definitely different."

A lot of years had passed, and my life had carried me to someplace so far away that I barely recognized the world I'd once had in those early days on the road with her. She told me that she believed I'd cut her out of my life like she'd never happened. Like we had never happened. A type of numbing and avoidance she knew I was prone to. She wasn't wrong. I won't lie. I had intentionally shut her out of my day-to-day thoughts, if only because, if I'm being completely honest, my life had somewhat depended on it at one point.

But on that night, when we were huddled together beneath the stage, about to climb the steps, suddenly she crossed my mind in the oddest way. Just a flash, really, an echo of her, as I remembered the way it felt when she placed her hand in mine or kissed me just before I went on the stage. I dismissed it, of course, as I had learned to do from years of practice, giving my attention to the performance. I was onstage a moment later.

"I used to wonder if she'd ever come to see us play over the years, though I suspected very much not. I'd sort of imagine her out there in the crowd every once in a while, especially in those early years. But it was just my imagination," I told Michael. "If she'd actually ever been there, I thought I would have felt her presence. And I was right. Without realizing I was doing it, I think I started looking for her."

"We noticed the instant something was off. It was the end of the show," Alex says. "We didn't know what was going on at first, so we just kept playing. But then I looked over to where he'd been standing, to see if I could figure out what he'd been looking at, and that's when I saw her."

53

EVIE

It's a strange feeling to be near someone you've been intimate with, unbeknownst to others who stand alongside, unaware. To have an exact memory of the flashes of details and freckles and scars on their skin and the way they breathe and move and the way their eyes look in the quivering breaths of night. The map of their body and the way they smile when their head is on a pillow as the sun is rising. The two of you privy to a shared invisible memory that no one else can see. He had emerged onto the stage with a slow swagger while I'd drawn in the shallowest of breaths. He looked much the same. A tiny bit older, sure, but only in the way that some people get more attractive as they age. His stance was different. *Arrogant* was the word that came to mind. I wondered if he had become that way in truth or if it was a well-honed stage presence. He owned every single person in the audience, and he knew it, while simultaneously seeming grateful. He wore head-to-toe black, still favoring the plain T-shirt, pressed tightly against his body. Just as slim but more solid, like someone who clearly took care of himself. I watched his hips move with the music, remembering the way they'd felt under my hands. His hair was shorter but still in the same tousled style. My eyes followed the length of his left arm, noting multiple new tattoos, to where his hand gripped the microphone. From where I sat, I could just barely see it, only because I knew what it was, the *EV* inscribed on his left ring finger.

Kate nudged me, excited, muttering something about how it should be illegal to be that sexy, and ridiculously, I felt a flash of irritation and territorialism at her remark. Who was I to have any ownership? Up on that stage, he belonged to everyone and no one.

The elaborate screens displayed moving images of geometric flowers and diagrams captured from old astronomical texts alongside moodier elements and throbbing lights. I watched, hypnotized by it all, while we remained in the shadows. Whenever they played a song from their first album, I'd close my eyes, imagining I was on the side of the stage, as I had been so many times all those years ago. That I'd be in his arms by the end of the night. He talked to the audience occasionally, and I was happy to see that he still had some of the self-effacing charm I'd remembered, though it seemed to have developed a darker edge to it now. He ran the length of the stage, amid the outstretched arms of fans, having become the kind of performer who could command an audience of that size, a rare thing. A few acoustic moments were spent on a piano, and private smiles were exchanged between Tommy and him. I remembered the Post-it Notes that the guys would occasionally put in a hidden spot on each other's instruments—grade-school boy jokes and X-rated stick figures and words of encouragement. I wondered if they still hid such notes.

The show went on for nearly two hours. Too soon, he began rounding out the final songs of the show, and as the stage went dark and a familiar, low, haunting melody began, the crowd exploded in adoring euphoria. He sang the words that had once been intimately ours but had become the world's, the lyrics taking my breath away as much as they had back then, accompanied now by thousands of others, singing along. "We'll light a flame and let it burn. You and I." How many times had he sung it over the years? "And tell me this will never end. You and

I." *Did he think of me each time?* I wondered. *Or was it empty, the way a word loses its attached meaning when you repeat it over and over?* I closed my eyes, transported back in time, and for a moment, I could almost have been in that studio with him. I was abruptly shaken out of my thoughts by Kate pulling on my arm.

"We've gotta go!" she shouted into my ear, loud enough to make me wince. She pointed at her watch and grimaced, tugging my arm.

Had she not forced us to leave at that exact moment, while the audience was still and mesmerized by the song, had she not forced our way through to an empty space, an anomaly in the crowd, plummeting us into an empty pool of light, it might have never happened. But at the thought of it being the last time that I would ever see him in person, I turned around and looked up, and he wasn't more than fifteen feet away. He was bathed in the glow of magenta lights from the stage—as 65,000 people looked only at him—and his eyes, improbably, locked with mine.

Time stood frozen. Though the concert and the crowd continued to blare around us, unaware of the significance of what was happening, it was as if everything became completely silent in the bubble that had been formed. For a split second, I wasn't sure he recognized me, until I registered the expression on his face and saw the shock, realizing he'd stopped singing midphrase. Stopped moving. An instant jolt of panic swept through me for reasons I still don't quite understand, and oddly, once again, my instinct was to turn away. I caught up with Kate and kept moving. Away from my past. Away from the love that I'd lost.

"Geez, Ev. I'm not in that big of a hurry. Slow down," Kate said as I passed her.

The music continued behind us, but the sound of his voice remained noticeably absent from the stage. I glanced behind me to see him walk over to say something to a member of the crew perched on the side of the stage, while Tommy and Alex and Darren closely watched one another, and a few moments later, he picked up the last verse. The whole exchange had taken only seconds, barely noticeable to anyone watching. But it had felt like time moved in slow motion as I willed myself to leave.

Then I heard my name. Not from the stage but from much closer. Barely audible over the sound of the music. The voice was unmistakable, and not far behind me.

"Evie," Fred called out.

I froze.

Kate continued past me. She hadn't heard him. Turning around, I saw him red-faced, huffing, having evidently made his way from the giant enclave of the soundboard in the middle of the floor seats.

"Evie, what are you doing?" Kate shouted, turning back. "I didn't even think you liked them? Come on, groupie, we have to get to the car before we get stuck in traffic," she said, taking my hand.

I let out a breath. "I can't go yet."

"But—"

"There's something I have to do here. Someone I have to see. You can go on ahead. I'll get home on my own."

"You're joking, obviously." Her expression was one of confusion. "What? Who?"

"Just an old friend." Amid the roar, I could tell she barely heard. I turned and looked to where Fred stood watching.

"Ev, I'm not going to just leave you here. Where are you—?" She stopped talking as the large, surly man approached. Fred and I stood for a moment, facing one another. I tried to smile hello. I wanted to barrel into his arms and feel his hug, the combination of aftershave and diesel. But he was flat and cold as he motioned for me to follow him past the crowd, Kate tugging at me as Fred wove us past security guards standing sentry into the warrens of steel beneath the stage, covered from view in black curtains. Miles of thick cable snaked in every direction on the floor, and I heard the crowd roar as the show's finale began, then startled sharply at the sound of booming fireworks. I stopped, grabbing Fred's arm. He removed one side of the heavy black headphones covering his ears as I leaned into him.

"I don't think I can do this." I swallowed hard.

He looked toward me sharply before his face softened. I noticed the gray that had taken over his hair and the lines that had deepened into his weathered skin. "I think you already did, sweetie." He sighed heavily. "Don't you?"

Tears pricked my eyes. "I didn't think he would see me," I told him. And I certainly didn't think he would care.

"Well, he did."

"Evie, what is going on?" Kate asked nervously, leaning into me. My heart thumped heavily in my chest as I tried to process the unexpected turn of events and the way that gravity had, once again, begun pulling us toward one another, the force of something smaller being drawn toward something greater.

54

EVIE

It was Alex I saw first. Fitting, I suppose.

We'd reached the darkened dressing room hall as the show ended, and all that remained was the cacophonous white noise coming from the stadium of people making their slow exit into the night. Painted cinder-block walls enclosed the space, with fluorescent lights above us and the din of activity humming from nearby spaces. Kate stuck close to me, baffled, while adrenaline coursed through my veins, hot and electric. Then, out of nowhere, Alex rounded a corner and walked straight to me. I shuddered at the dark look he gave me.

"What the hell is she doing here?" he asked tightly. When Fred didn't offer an answer: "Fred! What. Is she doing here? This is no good. You've got to get her out of here."

My eyes welled as I realized how much had broken.

Fred held up his hands, trying to reason with him. "I can't do it, mate."

Alex turned to face me then. "He nearly blew the fucking encore thanks to you."

"I'm so sorry, Alex. I—I didn't mean . . . ," I stammered, my eyes welling with tears. I reached out to touch his arm, and he shrugged me away.

"Didn't mean what? You're standing here, aren't you? Evie, listen, if he ever meant anything to you, please would you just go?"

"She can't do that and you know it, Alex." Tommy appeared. He looked over at me, and I saw concern in his now-older face. I remembered the warm and jovial soul he had always been toward me. "Long time no see, stranger." He walked over to me and gave me a warm but reserved hug, kissing me on the top of my head. "Pretty as ever."

I smiled sadly through teary eyes.

Tommy nodded at Kate, as if to say hello, and she stood wide-eyed, awestruck.

Then I felt it. The surge in the air. And I knew Carter was there. I looked up to see him standing in the center of the dim hallway. No one said a word as the oxygen in the space seemed to disappear in a vacuum. I heard Kate gasp.

He stared at me with an expression I'd never seen—a face full of a thousand thoughts, fire and ice. I had imagined so many times what it would be like to see him again. But I had never conceived of anything like what happened that night. The mess of it. Neither one of us moved.

"Hey, Ev." His voice was quiet and carefully measured. I wanted to run to him. He didn't come any closer.

I swallowed the emotion rising in my throat and attempted a smile. "It's good to see you."

"Yeah." He paused. "You too." His face was taut. "Not quite the way I imagined it, I suppose. But hey, whatever." I blinked, unsure of how to reply. "Looked like you were headed out early." He nodded toward the exit at the end of the hall and pointed. "Weren't going to say hi, then, eh?"

"I wanted to." I felt everyone, as if they were holding their collective breath, watching it unfold. "I mean, I wasn't planning to, but . . ." I trailed off.

"I see. Of course not." He shrugged. "What's another decade or two, right?"

The sting went straight through me. I realized, unbelievably, that what I'd been seeing in his face was the unfamiliar look of pain. He didn't seem to know what else to say, but at the same time, he hadn't removed his eyes from me for a second.

Similarly, I wasn't sure what to do next, but then he spoke. "I guess I'll let you go, then." He looked at me for a few long moments, the years passing by in his eyes. He opened the door, paused as if about to say something else, but then thought better of it.

"Carter, wait," I called, taking a few steps. "Please."

But then he went through the door, halting me in my place. There, then gone.

Tommy walked over to where I stood trembling and spoke gently. "Look, Ev, I don't know what happened back then, but he's not the same guy. It's been a long time, and a lot's changed. I don't know what you're doing here. But I think whatever it is, you need to deal with it once and for all. You can't just leave again."

I searched his pale-blue eyes. "But you saw him. He doesn't want to see me."

"He does. If he didn't, he wouldn't have told Freddie to go and get you."

I looked quickly to Fred for confirmation, and he nodded.

"Oh."

"Listen, Ev, when you left, something inside of him broke. It took him a long time to put back the pieces. I'm not sure he ever really did. I think he needs to put it to rest. I think you owe him that."

"I know."

"Do you?" He pointed his chin toward the closed door. He looked at me closely, then kissed my cheek. "Anyway, it's good to see you." With that, he walked away, and I turned.

"Alex . . ."

But he walked away as well. Fred watched with arms crossed in resignation. I took a few steadying breaths; then I walked toward Carter's closed door. I looked then to Kate, who met me with wide eyes. "I'll explain, I promise," I told her. "I'm so sorry I haven't before. But right now, you need to get home." My voice was hoarse, full of gravel.

"Evie, I can't . . . I don't understand what . . ." Concern etched her face.

"I'm fine here," I assured her.

"You don't seem fine."

"I promise. I'll be all right. But you need to get home." I glanced at Fred, and he gestured to Kate to go with him. "I'm so sorry I made you late," I said. "Fred will get you out the back way. It'll be faster so you can get home on time. Okay?"

She hesitated, but then hugged me hard while whispering in my ear, "This is the craziest thing I have ever seen. And you have so much explaining to do. You're clearly not okay. But I'm going to go and let you do what you need to do. Whatever this is. Call me as soon as you're home. I'll be worried."

I nodded in gratitude at my dear friend as she walked away, leaving me standing there alone, taking a deep breath before opening the door.

55

EVIE

He stood at the opposite side of the dark dressing room, facing the wall, leaning heavily on it with one hand. I closed the door behind me and stepped backward toward it, as if for support. A tapestry hung loosely tacked on one wall. Candles sat lit on a tidy table with bottles of water and juices, a few innocuous bottles of beer, and one small, unopened bottle of bourbon alongside a basket of health-food snacks. Quite different from the way it had once looked. A leather love seat sat to the right, next to a large dressing mirror.

Outside in the hall, our brief exchange had been such an assault on my senses that I'd barely processed it. I'd imagined what it might be like to see him again so many times that I was having a hard time telling if it was real or yet another scene from my imagination. But there he was.

Eventually, he turned, wiping the sheen of the show's exertion from his face with a towel and tossing it aside.

"Hi," I said finally, alarmed at how timid my voice sounded. "I hope it's okay that I'm here. I didn't want to leave things like . . . like that."

He didn't reply at first, and for a moment, I thought he might tell me to leave. But then he smiled just a little. "I'm glad. I'm sorry I didn't . . ." He looked toward the hall. "I just wasn't expecting to see you."

"I'm sorry. Really. I didn't mean to cause a problem. I wasn't planning to try to come back here or anything."

He looked away. "Right."

"But I'm glad Fred came to get me. Really," I quickly added. "No pass these days." I laughed nervously, gesturing to the empty space where a laminated pass had once hung around my neck.

My legs wanted to move; I wanted to go to him, to wrap my arms around him and give him at least the barest hug of friendship, if nothing more. But instead, we both stayed where we were, unnaturally.

"So how are you?" he asked. He twisted the cap off a small bottle of coconut water, taking a long drink.

"I'm good." The word sounded ridiculously simple. Such a plain word for such a big question. "How are you?"

He watched me closely, then smiled, amused, and for a moment, I recognized the softer, younger version of him.

"What?" I asked.

"I don't think I've ever seen you nervous."

I smiled back, relaxing a bit at the surprising comment. "Really?"

"No. You were always so sure of yourself. Confident. It's different." Was that how he had seen me? I wondered. Confident? I didn't remember that girl anymore.

"I guess you could say I wasn't expecting to see you either." I ventured a step farther into the room. "Not like this, anyway."

"I can't believe you're here. That you're standing right here, right now." He cocked his head. "I'm not entirely sure this isn't my imagination."

"Trust me, I know what you mean."

He shrugged slightly, and I noticed where his damp shirt clung to him from the heat of the stage. "But I always think of you when I'm in this town. You live here now, right?"

"I do, yeah. For a while now." I wondered how he knew anything about where I'd been living.

"That's good. It's been a long time."

"Yes. It has," I said sadly.

"I didn't think I'd ever hear from you again. And now here you are. Out of nowhere." He watched me closely. "You're still beautiful," he said softly.

I wondered if he saw the warmth hit my cheeks as I smiled. *Beautiful. So are you,* I wanted to reply.

What I'd feared most, I realized—what I had expected—was indifference. That I'd been just a blip in the path of his life. That he'd barely remember or care about what we'd once been. I'd expected to feel foolish and profoundly forgotten. *Oh, hey, Evie Waters. I've gotta run, but, it was nice to see you. Take care.* As if we were kids who'd once had an inconsequential fling at a summer camp. But as I stood there, watching him look at me, I saw that this was something else altogether. There was a history of love and loss in his face that I recognized as if he were a mirror.

"Thank you. For saying that. You look pretty wonderful too," I told him. The years had been kind, serving only to improve upon what had already been perfect to me. But he'd changed. Was hard. Detached. Not like the man with the schoolboy hands-in-his-pockets stance I'd fallen for. I couldn't help but wonder what else he thought as he looked at me in return. It occurred to me that neither of us had moved barely a muscle as we'd been standing there, paralyzed by the shock of it all. As if reading my mind, he relaxed a little, leaning back onto the edge of a table and crossing his feet at the ankles.

"So why *are* you here?" His voice was quiet and restrained, but a dark undercurrent ran beneath it. "Now, I mean."

"Would it be okay if I said I didn't quite know?"

He nodded and smiled slightly. The lines around his mouth, the ones I'd loved to kiss so much, had enticingly deepened since I'd last seen him.

I looked away from him, toward the stage. "You were great out there."

"Thanks." He turned his head the same way. "You were leaving early?"

"Not by choice, I promise," I said with a smile. "My friend Kate had to get home to the babysitter." I realized how foreign and provincial that statement must have sounded to someone like him.

"Gotcha." And then he pointed to the hall, recognition dawning. "Wait, Kate? Your old friend from high school?"

"You remember that?"

"I remember everything."

My lips parted in surprise, but nothing came out. Several moments went by, the words hanging in the air. *I remember everything.*

The space between us crackled. I longed to fill it with words—something, anything—to relieve the pressure, but came up with nothing.

A loud noise from the hall startled us both as the crew had already begun disassembling the stage to move on to the next city. I was reminded of where I was and how fleeting and rare this opportunity might be. How long I'd waited for it. It was important to get it right, to find the words. Though I knew, I could never make all of it right. Some things are too big to fix.

"I've wanted to tell you . . . that I'm sorry," I said, surprising myself.

"For what?"

"I know it was a long time ago and you've gone on with your life and all of that." Once again, I felt foolish, presumptuously assuming that he needed to hear it, but I continued. "For everything. For the way I handled things back then."

"You're right. It was a long time ago. It's fine," he said kindly, but something in his voice told me he felt otherwise.

"I know I made a mistake, handling it the way I did. That day—in New York. I thought it was the right thing, but after a while, I knew it wasn't. I guess I waited too long. And I'm sorry."

"What do you mean, you 'waited too long'?"

"I mean I understood. Why you didn't want anything to do with me after that. I always have. I understand why you wanted to walk away."

"Why *I* walked away?" His eyes narrowed darkly. "Ev, you did the walking, not me."

"I know," I said, closing inward a little. "I just needed a little time to figure some things out." The words felt too simple. Not enough. Yet filled with regret.

His face softened again as he watched me. "A decade is a lot of time."

"It is."

"So did you?" he asked, smiling a bit.

"Did I what?"

"Figure it out."

I laughed slightly, able to breathe at last, and considered the honesty of the question. Carter had never been one to hold back from saying what was on his mind. "No. I suppose not," I answered finally with a small laugh. A true statement if ever there was one. Not much had changed—I still didn't know what was right.

"Ah." He shifted as he sat, looking away and then back. "Can I ask you something, Ev?"

Ev.

"Sure. Anything."

"What was it? Back then. What did I do that scared you so badly that you could just leave like that? Throw everything away between us." I heard something in his voice that hinted at whatever had been simmering. "I must've played those two days in New York over in my mind a million times, trying to figure it out. I knew that you were upset. I knew I'd been awful. But there had to be more to it. I thought we were happy." I was surprised at the intensity in his eyes. "It's been forever, so I suppose it doesn't matter. And you don't owe me an answer. But you're here, so I figure I might as well ask."

He was right, of course. There was far more to it than he knew.

"It wasn't you, Carter. You didn't do anything wrong."

"Well, I must have done something, right?" He said it a little harshly, then shook his head, looking away again. "You just left. Out of nowhere. And then I found out you quit the film, and I figured, well, hell, I guess that's it. I called you over and over for days, leaving messages. I kept hoping I'd hear from you but—nothing. I had no idea why, but you were just . . . gone."

"What do you mean, you kept hoping to hear from me? Carter, I tried to reach you for months."

"What are you talking about?"

Something wasn't adding up. "After I left New York, I regretted the way I'd handled things. I'm so sorry I ignored your calls." I could still remember the sound of his voice, pleading on my voice mail, leaving message after message in those first few weeks. I could barely listen to them. Until one day, they stopped. And then all I wanted was to hear his voice again. "I couldn't talk to you right away. But like I said, there were things going on, and a couple of months later—"

"What kind of things?" he persisted.

I swallowed. "I just needed a little time. But then when I tried to reach you a while later, you . . ." I stopped in surprise, caught off guard by the look of confusion on his face. "Carter, I tried to call you, but your number was out of service. Your email came back undeliverable." I shivered thinking about it. I'd sat by the phone nervously for hours the day I finally decided to call him. Rehearsing what I wanted to say. Stomach in knots. When I first heard the error tone on the line, it cut through me like a shard of glass. And then the email, the words on my computer screen: Undeliverable. Address not known. And the sickening feelings of regret and loss that followed.

By the time I tried, it was too late, and I couldn't reach him.

"We had to change all our contact info. We have to change it all the time," he said distractedly before looking at me again. "Why didn't you just try the label?"

"I did. Believe me. I left messages. With everyone I could. I waited," I said and then shrugged. "I figured you didn't want to hear from me. That's when I knew that I'd lost you for good." My eyes suddenly blurred with tears that I swallowed hard to stop.

He leaned forward. "What? Evie, why would you ever have thought that?"

"Because, Carter. I knew you. Knew how you operated. I'd been warned, after all. 'A clean break, and it's done.' Remember? 'Just forget her and move on, like it never happened.' That was your big philosophy on breakups for the guys. God, those words must've run through my head a thousand times. Over and over. I guess I'd hoped I was different. But when I didn't hear back from you, I knew that it had happened to me. And the worst thing was that it was my fault. All of it."

Like it had never happened. That was the hardest part over the years. The knowledge that he had the capacity to remove me from his thoughts in an instant and would never think of me again. Losing someone's love is heartbreaking, but to never exist again in their world is a pain like no other.

"Is that what you've thought all this time, Ev?" I turned and quickly swiped a tear before looking back at him. He shook his head and closed his eyes, then stood and came closer. "I don't know what happened. But I never knew you tried to reach me. And I'm telling you, the last I heard from you was that day in New York."

We stood just a few feet apart, the past swirling between us, then suddenly, it was as if a dark veil covered his face and he was a stranger again. He looked away, and I was reminded again of how much time had passed.

We would eventually learn what had happened. While Carter was lost in his own spiraling world in the months after we'd parted, my messages and a letter I'd written had all gone to Fred and Tommy and the others. After a long talk, they'd made the difficult decision to keep everything from Carter, thinking it was better to let him move on. An act of good intention that had forever altered our lives.

Carter went to the table and finished the water before opening the Knob Creek and pouring a scant amount in the glass—noticeably less than he would have poured years ago. His slender back was long and firm as he lifted his arm to take a drink. "Anyway, I suppose none of it really matters. I figured out what happened eventually."

"What do you mean?"

"I heard you got married not long after that." There was a little ice in the way he said it.

I startled a little, orbiting away from him to try to regain my composure. "You did?"

"Yeah." He rubbed his hand through his hair and turned back around to face me, looking weary in a way that comes from having old wounds revisited. "And that's when I figured out what must have happened. Your old high school boyfriend—Steve, right? That was his name?"

He took another sip and picked up a second glass, offering it to me as an afterthought. I shook my head. Something about the way he did it made me want to cry as I watched who he was now, compared to the warm and loving way he'd once been toward me. The coldness of the gesture as he held out the glass. Suddenly, I missed him more than I ever had before, though he was standing right there in front of me.

"Right. Steve," I said eventually, still reeling that he'd known about it at all.

He walked over to a black road case and sat down. "I was surprised at first. I didn't think you wanted all of that. You had so many plans." He shrugged a little. "But then again, I get it. I'm sure he offered you something . . . something I guess you probably needed, something much different than this whole circus." He looked a bit tired and gestured to the world around us. His world. "Something normal. I hope you guys have been happy. Really, I do. It's all I ever really wanted for you, Ev." He tried to smile when he said it, but I could tell that it took some effort.

"Thank you."

"It made sense; I don't blame you. I remember you mentioning him back then. Never forget your first love, I suppose? I remember you spent some time with him that Christmas when you went home. I understood. It was probably better." He took another slow drink, finishing the glass.

He had it all wrong.

"That wasn't quite how it happened, Carter. Not at all."

"No? So you didn't leave me in New York and then marry someone else less than a year later?"

"No. I mean . . ." I spoke softly. Too much had happened; I could see that now. It was too late to make him understand. "I was a little lost back then. After things ended between us. I didn't know what to do, where to go. I guess I was just trying to move on. To do what was best for—" I stopped short, tensing a little. "It seemed the right thing to do at the time."

He nodded, staying quiet. I could hear the bustle of trucks outside and noticed a clock on the wall. I was surprised to see how quickly time was passing. I smiled in spite of it all, looking around the room, the sights and sounds feeling like a time machine.

"There are a lot of memories—being back here with you, after a show," I said. "A bit bigger now, though, yeah?" He smiled a bit but didn't look up. "Is it always like this back here now? Seems awfully subdued compared to the way it used to be." He knew what I meant. Just a group of guys doing their jobs. Gone was the jovial party of it all.

"Yeah, not always. But most of the time. We're all pretty quiet these days. We grew up, I guess. Tommy and Darren have families. A lot changes. It's hard to believe it's been so long since we started all this. We don't have to hustle so much anymore. We do a show. Get on a plane. Get some sleep and do it all over again. Food's better, though," he joked. It occurred to me, with some importance, that this was the first time I'd thought about it this way. That life might have somehow grown quieter for him, too, in some ways, instead of louder and bigger, as I'd thought. I realized I'd imagined him all this time in the time capsule of our twenties, which wasn't fair.

I walked over and sat closer to him.

"Do you have a good life?" he asked.

I paused before answering. "I do." And then quietly, I added, "I'm a mom now. That makes me really happy." In spite of the weight of it, I smiled instinctively at the mention of them.

He smiled slightly, but it didn't reach his eyes. "That's nice, Ev. Good."

Tears pricked again, and I swallowed hard to force them back. "Two. A girl. And a boy."

He smiled again, looking away.

"And I hear you're engaged? Congratulations," I said, attempting to sound cheerful about it. The question seemed to amuse him for just a moment, and he opened his mouth as if to say something just as there was a heavy knock at the door. I watched him walk across the room, noticing the way he moved, lithe, tall, and strong. I felt like time was erased and I was back in my twenties. I looked away.

Fred glanced at us both. "Sorry to interrupt, but everyone's heading out."

"Okay, just give us a few minutes." He closed the door and leaned on it with a hip, placing his hands in his pockets. For just a second, I saw him again—the sweet, younger version of him, a little shy, looking down at his shoes on the day we first met, and I couldn't help but smile.

He cocked his head, curious as he seemed to notice the expression change on my face. "What?"

"Nothing," I said, smiling even wider. "You just reminded me for a second of someone I used to know."

Understanding my meaning, he laughed a little under his breath and shrugged, somewhat adorably.

"It looks like we're leaving," he said. "I've got to go."

I had so much yet to tell him. And so much I could not. But time had run out. The weight returned, settling in the way that regret can. "Where are you guys off to next?"

"Nowhere tonight, actually." He looked up at me as he said this. "We're staying here in town and heading out tomorrow."

"Oh." The word came out in a higher pitch as a flutter went through me. He took a step closer, and I began to feel the electric pull of him. I took in the sight of him standing there, committing every detail to memory. Then, as if both thinking the same thing, we closed the space between us, and he gave me a warm hug. We stayed that way for a while, melded together with my head on his chest as he held me, his hand on the nape of my neck. When eventually I pulled away just a little, I looked up at him and laughed nervously, wiping the tears from my eyes. He looked down at me and for a second, I could swear it looked as if he were about to kiss me. Though perhaps it had just been my imagination and the afterglow of times passed, because he took a step backward. The familiar scent of him remained on me, and I clenched my teeth against the hurt and longing that came with it. He reached his hand to his chin, watching me as neither of us spoke or moved to leave. "We're staying in a hotel downtown," he said. And then, catching me off guard, he added, "I know it's probably late for you. But I hate that I have to leave already. Would you want to come?"

"To the hotel?"

He laughed at the expression on my face. "I just mean we could take a walk or something. Maybe get a drink or coffee." For the first time, as I sifted through all that had been said tonight, I wondered if perhaps he had dreamed of me sometimes as well. If he remembered what our hands looked like together, fingers interlaced? Seeing him right then, it all came rushing back, and I knew that I wanted it all too much. And I knew also that I could not have it, which was as painful then as the day I'd lost him. More, maybe, because he was standing so close that I could touch him.

I knew that I couldn't survive losing him a second time. I had people depending on me now. I swallowed hard and looked away to bolster my strength before looking back. "I should probably get home."

I thought I saw a flash of disappointment in his face but wondered if I'd just imagined it. "I understand." And then a little lighter, "You have a family to get home to now. Husband, kids, and all." He moved away suddenly, collecting a few things from the room while preparing to leave.

I watched him move, wanting to close the space between us again. Drawn to him like oxygen after being submerged in water. "Well, no, not exactly," I said then.

"No?" He turned as he located his phone and dropped it into his back pocket.

"I mean, yes. But"—I paused—"they're with their dad tonight."

He raised an eyebrow, confused.

"We're not together anymore. Steve and I."

The energy shifted, and he paused. The news seemed to jar him, but he recovered quickly. "I'm sorry," he said sincerely. "Really."

"Thank you. I'm sorry I didn't clarify earlier. I don't know why I didn't."

"It's okay."

He finished collecting his things and walked over to me, the expression on his face a little warmer perhaps. "So why do you have to get home, then?" he asked as his eyes narrowed with a glimmer of mischief. I laughed, buoyed instantly by the hint of the man I used to know as he stood a little closer. I realized then that there wasn't an actual reason for why I had to leave, and I shrugged. "So," he said, cocking his head to one side with a slight grin that took me straight back in time, "are you sure you can't take that walk?"

56

EVIE

Knowing what you do, I imagine you're beginning to understand a bit better now why I changed so much that year. Why I cherish those times with you at the end of that summer, and those first months of fall, so much, the simple joys of our life before everything changed and fell apart. Especially you, Lainey, since you were a bit older. I'm sorry we didn't tell you the truth about what happened to me back then and in the months and years that followed. To all of us. But at least maybe it's starting to make better sense. I'm sure you used to wonder.

~

We'd driven together back to the hotel that night, Carter sitting beside me and the others mostly quiet as a light rain began to drizzle on the windows and we passed through the city. I watched the familiar sights go by as they had thousands of times, but it all looked different with Carter beside me. "Look at that, Ev. We finally made it to your hometown together," he whispered. He ran one finger over the back of my hand, then pulled away. The gesture took no more than a couple seconds but heightened every nerve.

The driver let us out at a rear entrance of the hotel, safely away from fans who might have discovered the band's location. Nonetheless, we were suddenly surrounded by a small mob. Tommy gave a polite wave, but in an instant, Carter had pulled me into him, shielding me as he maneuvered us to the elevators behind two members of their security staff. I looked up at him, and he was unfazed, though his lips were pursed in a tight line, and when the doors closed, he separated from me.

"Sorry about that. I should have warned you," he said.

"It's fine, really."

He looked a little sad, I thought. "Thanks."

He pressed a button. "Do you mind if we take a few minutes so I can shower quickly?" he asked. "I'd like to change. Might be better to give a little time for it to quiet down."

"No, it's fine." As we waited for the elevator to ascend the twenty-six floors to his room, he leaned against one side, his boots crossed at the ankle. Reaching the top floor, we stepped into his hotel suite, both of us avoiding coming too near to the other. I followed him into the dim living room and to a wall of windows overlooking the city and the river beyond. Two sofas flanked a large coffee table, along with a sleek side chair. The furnishings were sophisticated and stylish, contemporary but not overly so. An orange glow came from the city streets below and a lone, dim floor lamp illuminated the distant corner.

"No bus tonight, huh? You don't stay on Miss Penny Lane?" I asked, smiling as I indicated the posh surroundings.

"We retired the old girl a long time ago. No buses these days. We've got Lucy now. She flies."

"Wow, a lot *has* changed. And you didn't even like planes."

"Still don't." He smiled a little as he turned, dropping his things. "Can I get you something to drink before we head out?"

"Sure. Anything's fine."

"I don't know what you like anymore." Such a melancholy statement about such a trivial thing. "Glass of wine, maybe? Water?" he suggested.

"That would be nice, thanks."

"Which one?"

"Both."

He busied himself at the room's bar and handed me a glass of wine, setting the water beside it. My arm warmed from where our fingers brushed for just a scant instant.

"I'll only be a minute," he said. "Make yourself at home."

As he went to shower, I was left alone for the first time all night, suddenly awash in the acute awareness of all that had happened and the unexpected turn of the night. Hours earlier, I'd been dressing for the evening, checking my hair, turning this way and that in the mirror. I'd imagined being at home after the show, curled up in my bed in pajamas, crying no doubt. Instead, I listened to the distant sounds of the running shower as water poured over him. The thought of that woke me up in ways I thought I'd forgotten. No one had ever had the effect on me that he had. I steadied myself on the back of the sofa to keep from running to him. Or away from him. I wasn't sure which.

The back of my neck prickled, and I turned.

"I didn't hear you come out." I wondered how long he'd been watching me at the window. He'd pulled on a fresh pair of jeans and a T-shirt, his hair still wet from the shower. He leaned against a wall, arms crossed. He smiled a little as he bit at the side of his lip in a way that stirred the memory of long-ago times and made my breath a little uneven once again.

"We can go now if you'd like. Should be quieter downstairs by now."

"It's a nice night," I said, looking out the window again. "It's been a while since I've been in the city this late. I forget how pretty it can be."

"I wondered something earlier," he said. I turned to face him. "You said before that you hadn't planned to see me tonight. That you were just going to the show and then leaving." I nodded. "I was wondering—have you been to any others? It's so strange to think of you in the crowd and me having no idea."

"No. This was the first time."

He nodded and inhaled, letting the breath out slowly. "I used to look for you in the audience sometimes. A little ridiculous, I suppose, but I couldn't help it." He shrugged. "Why this one? Why tonight?" He seemed to be having as hard a time as I was believing that we were both there.

"After we were over, I had to figure out a way to go on without you, and the only way I could do it was to bottle it all up and put it in the past. I didn't listen to the music. I turned off the TV anytime you came on."

I walked over to the table where he'd set his glass of scotch a moment earlier. I picked it up, taking a sip, letting the alcohol's heat and the idea of sharing his glass slide down my throat.

He raised a brow. "You always did have a habit of nicking my drinks."

"Sorry." I laughed. "I think I need something a little stronger." He smiled at the intimacy of the gesture, and I swallowed again before continuing. "And I was different. My life was different. Everything about who I was back then disappeared." It occurred to me at that moment that I felt more myself tonight than I had in a very long time.

"What changed? What was different about tonight?"

"I know it sounds silly. It's been a long time, after all. I know that your life went amazing places. I'm so happy for you." He looked up, and I saw a glint in his eye that I couldn't quite place. "I just thought that maybe, if I came here tonight, if I could just see you, even from far away, I could finally make myself say goodbye."

He nodded. "Did it help?"

"What?"

"This." He motioned to the two of us. "Seeing me. Ready to say goodbye?" His mouth curved up a little at the corner, and he bit his cheek after he said it. The temperature in the room raised a degree.

"Mm, not quite."

A few long seconds passed; then he turned serious and distant once again. He walked slowly over to the other side of the room and took a seat on the edge of a long, modern dining table. He looked up into the distance, as if replaying a movie in his mind. "I knew I'd messed up during the weeks before the tour. Gotten too caught up in everything. It was crazy back then. We didn't know what the hell we were doing, and it was all happening so fast. I wanted to take you with me in it. To make you feel okay with it all, but I couldn't. I didn't know how."

"It wasn't that, Carter."

"I'd been worried about you. You'd been acting strangely. Everything was different after you left London. I couldn't get a minute to myself, being shuffled this way and that. And that last weekend, I knew something was wrong. I was just desperate to get out of New York. I kept telling myself it would get better once we had some time together. I shouldn't have gotten in that car. I should've stopped. I should've taken the time to talk to you and made you tell me what was wrong. Maybe things would've turned out differently. Maybe not. Who knows." He looked at me. "But no matter what, I'm still grateful for it all."

"I am too."

We both were swimming in the loss of what might have been. I realized then that the life I'd been living—the life I'd tried and failed to build in his absence—had been built on a foundation of quicksand. I thought I'd been doing what was best—for him, for all of us—but no matter my intention, it had never stood a chance against the love I'd had for him and the futile efforts I'd made to escape it all.

He walked toward me, each step erasing the years. He stood mere inches from me, electricity firing between us. "So you got married. Moved on, did you?" It wasn't a question. It wasn't a statement. It was a challenge. A declaration of what he knew wasn't true.

"I didn't move on nearly as easily as you think I did, Carter."

"No?" He took a step closer. Looked down at me.

"I've never loved anyone the way I loved you back then," I whispered. Hearing the words jarred me. They'd come out without warning, unbidden, as if from another person.

"I tried everything to let you go. I tried hating you—do you know that? I tried forgetting you," he said, and his gaze seared everything inside me. His eyes were liquid dark in a way that my body remembered, bidding me to come nearer. He took a step closer. "So tell me. What about now? How do you feel now, Evie?"

Again, another challenge. It felt like he'd opened my chest and was watching my beating heart. Then, a flicker. Something changed in his eyes, and he ran a finger across my cheek, down my neck. The next moment, his mouth was against mine. Everything about him fit perfectly, felt like a part of me.

"It's always been you, Ev," he whispered, holding me closer, kissing me. "Always."

57

EVIE

At this point, I'm sure you're probably wondering the same thing he was—did I ever truly love your dad? And I want you to know, I *need* you to know, that I absolutely did. He was a good man; you know that. He had bought me flowers on special occasions and my favorite perfume every Christmas. I had done all the same for him. We were good partners. We'd loved each other in the kind of way that two companions do.

There are different kinds of love in this world, and there is room for all of it.

But on that night, I wasn't thinking about any of that, and neither was Carter. All we felt was the wonderment of being near to each other again. Forgoing the walk we'd planned, we curled beside each other on the sofa and talked for hours, in a room lit only by the glow of the city lights below. We got to know each other again, providing general pictures of our lives. Our hands reunited in their familiar dance, our fingers tangling among one another as we basked in each other's company.

"I missed your hands," he said.

"You did?"

He traced each finger with his. "They're so delicate. Gentle. They were one of my favorite things about you." I warmed, smiling at the way he spoke to me, at the words he chose and the way he said them. He touched the silver bangle on my wrist, the one I'd worn when we were together.

He wanted me to tell him about my kids, and I loved that.

"Well, let's see . . . Lucas. He's my little bubbly one. Easy and pleasant. He bounces off the walls with happiness. It's sort of infectious."

He smiled at this. "And your daughter?"

"Lainey. She's beautiful. Striking really, but she hasn't figured it out yet. People stop us sometimes and tell us. She's sensitive and a little on the quiet side. Earnest. Focused. Sometimes I think she was born an old woman, wise already. When she was a baby, she had an unnerving way of looking at me like she knew far more than I did."

"Does she look like you?"

"A little. But she looks more like her father," I replied, taking in the sight of his face.

"And you made a nice life with him? Steve? Found your way back to each other, I guess."

"We did," I told him gently. "We'd grown up together. It was easy. Maybe too easy, I guess. He's a good man."

"And you loved him?"

"Very much," I said honestly, and he sighed. "But it wasn't like this," I added. "Not like it was with us."

He looked at me, almost as if amused. "Oh, I know that."

As if to say, *Of course not. Nothing could be like us.* So certain. I loved that about him.

"So anyway, what about you? Don't you have some fabulous model fiancée?" I asked, again trying to make it lighter than it was, feeling a pinch in my chest at the thought of the women who had been in his arms.

He shook his head.

"You're not together?" It came out a little jauntier than I'd have liked.

"No. We were, but it wasn't what everyone made it out to be. She's not my fiancée. Don't believe everything you hear. We're not even together anymore. We broke up a few weeks ago. But we'd ended a long time before that, I think. I'm not very good at relationships."

"I find that very hard to believe. I have experience with this, you know." I said it teasingly, but his face had grown serious. He leaned his back into the cushion and sighed, resting his arm on his closed eyes. It was a while before he spoke. "Evie, when you left, everything changed. I couldn't figure out how one minute, you loved me, and then you woke up one day and found everything we'd shared completely disposable. I never trusted anyone again after that. You just walked away. Everything went dark after that."

"It didn't feel that way. It seemed like you barely skipped a beat. You were back out on tour right away." Like it hadn't fazed him. That was when I stopped listening and turned it all off.

He let out a breath and shook his head. "Man, that tour. Sometimes I think it was better you weren't there."

"Oh," I said, smarting a bit from the comment.

"No, I just mean that it was crazy. Looking back, I have a hard time remembering a lot of it. It was nonstop. Nothing like that first one that you remember. We'd always said we'd keep it together, but honestly, sometimes I don't know how we survived that one."

"That good, huh?" I said, swallowing hard.

"That bad. Depending how you look at it, I guess. Or maybe who you ask."

I wondered where I'd been and what I'd been doing that first night he finally accepted the offer of some faceless woman. The thought made me shudder.

"And now? Are you still that way?" My fingers traced lazy circles on his leg as an attempt to distract myself. To tell myself that this was just an easy conversation, when in reality, it was excruciating.

He looked at me with a sad smile. "I guess I became the cliché, after all."

"I doubt that very much."

"Thanks."

"Did you love any of them?" I asked.

He let out a deep sigh. "Maybe. No. I don't know. It was hard to tell. Illa was special, I suppose. I'd started to think, *Finally, maybe this is it*, but it wasn't with anyone. They expected me to be someone I wasn't. Or maybe I expected them to be someone different." He turned toward me and drew a leg beneath him, resting his head on his hand. His eyes looked sleepy, and the stubble on his cheeks had grown darker. His hair was disheveled, but at the same time, he looked like he could be at a photo shoot or in a magazine. I reached up and twisted my fingers through his hair, just reminding myself that I could touch him, running my hand down to the warmth of his neck. He took my hand. "I compared everyone to you, Ev. To what we'd had, and everyone failed. I couldn't make myself settle for less."

I traced the letters of my name imprinted on his ring finger. He followed my gaze.

"I would've married you back then, you know," he said softly. I startled and looked up as he continued. "I knew that I wanted to spend the rest of my life with you. I'd been daydreaming about the idea of proposing to you. Getting married barefoot on some pretty little hillside or something. I'm sure you had something much nicer and more traditional."

I was so filled with emotion, I didn't know what to say. I traced the infinity symbol on his other finger, and he smiled. "Such a romantic," I said.

"More like a fool."

"No," I whispered. "You're not."

He leaned over and kissed me, sliding his hand down my side, around my waist. His breath grew unsteady, and I knew we were both feeling the same thing. I thought of everything I'd gone through over the years trying to let him go. I couldn't do it again.

I sat up slowly. "I should probably get going."

"Oh," he said, startled as he turned to look at the clock. "It's not that late, is it?"

"The sun's almost up."

I was already standing, fishing around the room for my shoes and my phone, trying to keep my eyes from lingering on how extraordinary he looked, sleepy on the sofa. "Lucas has a soccer game this morning that I have to get to and . . . Have you seen my purse? I can't find my purse."

"Evie, wait."

"And you have to leave soon to get to another show. Chicago, right? And I've got meetings to get ready for this week, and some research to do tonight, and the kids are back in school now, and—"

"Evie." He stood, walking toward me on bare feet.

"I can't believe how late it is. Time still flies with us." I tried to smile. "I can't find . . . Oh, wait, there it is."

I continued gathering my things until he grasped my shoulders. "Shhh." I reluctantly met his eyes. "Stop. Do not disappear again."

"I'm not disappearing, Carter. You're on tour and leaving. I have a life I need to get back to. It just is what it is."

"It doesn't have to be."

"I need to sort all of this out."

"I know."

"It's not just me. Just us. I have kids now. I have to think about them." I backed away again, not knowing what the future held, just knowing that I needed to get home. I was almost to the door when he spoke.

"All I want to do is take you with me right now," he told me. "But I can't. Not right this minute. But we can figure it out. At least talk about it." I turned to face him, and at that very moment, all I wanted was to be able to split myself in two. To leave with him and have a life together, while staying with Lainey and Lucas, secure in their world. He paused, watching me closely, before continuing. "The tour's almost over. And we have a break coming up for a couple of weeks. I'll be heading back to London. You could—"

"Carter."

"I understand that you need to get home right now. This has been a lot. If I could stay, I would. I promise. But after this week, we could spend some time together. I don't know . . . just see."

I shook my head. "This feels like déjà vu."

"Or a second chance."

"I can't just leave town. I wasn't expecting any of this. It's not like it used to be."

"I know that," he said.

"It's complicated, Carter."

"I know that too."

Except that he didn't. He didn't know at all.

"Evie, look at me." Slowly, I met his eyes. He reached down and kissed me, softly at first, then deeper as we clung to one another. The waves began to roll again, propelling us forward. "What are you doing here?" he whispered and kissed me again. "Tell me."

I tried to breathe but couldn't.

"Say it." He held me tightly. "Say it. I know it's true." The words roiled beneath the surface until I could no longer contain them.

"I still love you," I whispered finally. "I never stopped."

He took my face in his hands. "I know."

Once again, my legs grew weak beneath me. I'd been dreaming of this every day since we parted but thought it no more likely than a child's far-flung wish on a birthday candle. Suddenly, there it was, a second chance sitting right in front of me.

"Let me show you," he said then. I watched him choosing his words with care. "My life can be much quieter these days. It'll be years before we go on tour again, and I'm going back home to London. I know it's hard to see it, but we can have this. It can be okay. We don't have to decide anything—just come and stay for a little while. Don't let it end again here like this. Not tonight."

When I left that night, I already knew that I would go, of course. He was right. But it wasn't just about me. And sometimes decisions have to linger beneath the surface before we're willing to move.

58

EVIE

Can you imagine me at that soccer game a few hours later? You have to laugh—I mean, really. I must have looked half-insane, bleary-eyed from lack of sleep and no doubt in some sort of emotional shock. Living two lives, one inside my mind, with Carter occupying every free thought, as images of us swirled. And one on the outside, with the real world and my family. It was like trying to look in two directions at the same time. Then again, I probably just looked like the moms who smuggled wine in their massive coffee tumblers—glassy laughs and drifting sideways a bit. No offense, Lucas, I loved your soccer games, but that one took some serious maternal devotion, and I probably would have skipped it, but I remember there being something I was assigned to do that day—some parental responsibility on a sign-up sheet of dates. Snacks or something. Kate must have called me a hundred times through the night, and she'd shown up at our front door within minutes of me texting her that I was alive and indeed home.

We sat at my kitchen table as we had so many times before, as I told her the story I'd held in so tightly over the years, much like I'm doing right now. It spilled out of me in a cathartic wave as she sat in disbelief.

"Last night, I was so confused," she said. "But then it hit me. The musician. The guy you dated when you were in New York. I'd completely forgotten about that until last night. Evie, why didn't you ever tell me that's who he was? I always figured he was just some guy." She seemed a little hurt.

"I almost did a few times. But back then, you and I hardly saw each other, and we were busy with life. We barely talked. Then when it was over, I came back here. It was easier to let it stay in the past. And besides—" I gestured toward the walls of my kitchen. A refrigerator covered in school drawings and pizza coupons, granite countertops with a neat little basket of napkins, convection toaster oven, a row of cookbooks and a half-eaten banana that was more brown than yellow. Overflowing baskets of shoes sat by the garage door, with neat little labels written in pink and blue chalk. "Look at me; look at my life. I don't exactly look like the kind of person who spends time with someone like Carter Wills. Who would've ever believed me?"

"I would have," she said, and I knew she meant it. Though I'm not sure that even she would have truly believed the extent of it had she not seen the exchange between us. Until last night, Carter had been on a pedestal so high up in the stratosphere that he'd barely been a real, actual human being to her. Let alone one who could love her childhood-friend-turned-housewife. Then she rested her hand on mine, her eyes welling.

"Ev. You went through all of that alone."

I nodded, thinking back. "I wasn't alone exactly."

"It makes better sense now. You and Steve. Not that it didn't before, exactly. But still, it just fits better now."

"He's a good father. He's a good man."

"He certainly is," she said warmly, thinking of her old friend in a newer light. She peppered me with a few more questions before growing quiet. Then grinned mischievously.

"Okay, so aside from the fact that you had some crazy, heartbreaking secret life, and the whole mess you're in right now, let me get this straight. You've had sex—like real, naked-people sex—with Carter Wills."

I giggled and nodded.

"Many times?"

"A long time ago, but yes."

"And you just finished making out with him?"

I smiled. "We mostly talked." I thought of his hand resting on my leg and his fingers intertwined in mine. The bracelets of black cord, beads, and faint silver that adorned his tanned wrist. His thumb gently brushing over my skin. I felt the coarseness of his light beard in contrast with the softness of his mouth.

She squealed. "There are about a million questions I want to ask you right about now, including some really dirty ones. But the only two words that keep coming to mind are *Holy. Shit.* Seriously, Evie, I didn't know what the hell was going on last night. I thought some crazy guy you used to work with was dragging us backstage to yell at you for stealing his favorite stapler in 1999 or something. And then out of nowhere, Alex Winters shows up and starts yelling at you like he was sixteen years old and you'd just dented his new car or something. And then . . . *then*, when I thought it couldn't get even crazier, Carter Wills—Carter damn Wills—is standing there, looking like some kind of angry sex god, staring at you like you're the last human being on Earth. I swear to God, it was like we were in a movie or something. I nearly died!"

My giggle turned to the relief of raucous laughter as we carried on like two schoolgirls at the entire situation. Oh, how I loved her. Her presence was soothing. And talking to her lifted a weight from me.

"So how does it feel now?" she asked.

"I don't know yet. But after a while, it felt like it fit. Like I could breathe, Kate. His mere presence, just him near me, makes me feel safe. Like everything is just as it should be."

"Wow," she said softly.

"What?"

"You. Watching you talk about him. Your whole face changes—like a peaceful glow." She smiled. "It's just nice to see, that's all."

"All this time, I thought he'd forgotten, or hated, me. And now I find out . . ."

"He still loves you?"

I nodded.

"Wow." She shook her head, processing it. "Evie, what are you going to do? He loves you. And you clearly love him. You can't keep going on this way. You guys have to be together, obviously."

"It's not that easy. It's not like I can just pick up with him like nothing happened. It's all different. I can't turn everyone's life upside down."

"The kids are young; they could adapt."

"If he'll even still want me, you mean. After . . ." I trailed off.

"You have to find out. You have to face it. You know that, right?" We ruminated over the empty teacups before Kate finally spoke. "Look, I need to say something here as your oldest friend. I've seen the way you take care of your kids. You were always the perfect mom. The perfect wife. Had the perfect house. You've done a wonderful job. But something about you . . . I don't know, it was like you were trying to fill the role you thought you were supposed to. For you and for them. But it never quite seemed to suit you or make you happy. You were always a little different than the rest of us growing up. Like you were going someplace different. And then you ended up here, which is wonderful and great. But, I don't know, maybe it's not. I've never once seen you look at someone the way you and Carter looked at each other last night. And look at you," she said, taking my hand, "even in the midst of all of this, you're a different person. I feel like I'm seeing the real you for the first time in a really, really long time. Maybe this is the right thing, after all. Not just for you. But for him. For all of you. And he's right. You won't know until you know."

I sighed heavily and dropped my head on my hands. "It's all such a mess, Kate. All of it."

"You have to talk to Steve."

"I know."

"He'll understand, Ev."

"I can't hurt him again. He doesn't deserve it."

She looked at me sympathetically. "Who? Which one?"

"Both of them."

59

EVIE

Anytime I feel stuck, or like the rest of my life is a foregone conclusion and that no more mystery remains, just one day blending into the next, I think of that night—the night that Carter walked back into my life. The way I'd have never in a million years imagined it would go. The thought of me walking out the door that evening, as I so often did, with my keys in my hand, and then twelve hours later, arriving back home with Carter magically back in my world. And I remember that we never quite know what might happen and the delightful surprises the universe can give us if we're open to them.

Sometimes I sit outside and watch as the sun is setting across a coral sky, while the breeze picks up strands of my hair and birds have begun to quiet, and I find myself in awe. Not of the beauty but of the vastness of it all. There have been so many times when I found myself so low over these years that I thought I might never manage to get up again—curled into my constricted chest over a heart that is so closed, it couldn't possibly learn to open again, let alone receive love or give it. But then I see the way the last rays of the sun shoot off in every direction across the sky from a single point of light, and I realize something:

Each moment is like that. A sun. A star. A miraculous point from which unlimited bands of light shoot outward to places and paths much farther than we could ever see. So much of the time, the stories in my head have taken over—stories of loss and stories of hopelessness and the belief that every bright thing in my life was behind me and that nothing was left to dream of. But then I would see those rays of light as infinite possibilities.

If it's possible that tomorrow could be sad, then perhaps it's *equally* possible that it could be joyful. Equally possible that something wonderful could happen. Something that surprises me. Something that reminds me that the universe hasn't forgotten about me. Something that shows me that every day, there is . . . at least . . . the possibility that something miraculous, however large or small, will come from this single moment in time. *Probability* can be a little too hard to believe in sometimes. But *possibility* is enough.

And so I focus hard on that single point and don't look further. That way, all the possibilities remain, and I somehow stay in the light.

I sound like him talking right now, just so you know. I don't explain it as well as he would, but I hope you understand. Because just like I did that day, you woke up this morning thinking your life is a predictable series of days, and I know you're feeling stuck. But this is one of those unexpected moments when it's about to change in ways you never could have imagined.

When I think of you as a little girl, Lainey, I so often remember coming downstairs after tucking Lucas into bed in the evenings and finding you sitting at the piano. The room would be nearly dark except for the pale golden glow of the music lamp. Far beyond your years, you would be so focused on the pages in front of you that usually you wouldn't even notice me standing in the doorway watching you. Existing safely in the quiet of your life, in pale-purple ballerina pajamas and slippered feet that didn't yet reach the pedals. I'd watch the expression on your face, the intensity at just nine years old, the perfectionist's drive to get the sonatina just right. The angle of your chin and your long, dark hair. You are your father's daughter in every detail.

60

EVIE

The next evening, Carter and the others were off to another show in another city, and I thought of them there, far away once again, just as the car door slammed outside, startling me. I went to the porch to greet the kids just as they bounded in. They took turns calling out hello before running toward the backyard in a blur.

"Hey, guys! Did you have fun at the pizza—" But they were off. I looked up to see Steve standing on the sidewalk.

He shrugged. "Oh, to have their energy," he said, chuckling. He held a wilting handful of daisies with the dirt still clinging to them and a greasy box of pizza leftovers.

I eyed them curiously. "What do you have there?"

"Lainey picked them for you on the way to the car." As he handed them to me, particles of dirt dropped along with a few petals.

I smiled at the pitiful little bunch of stems, thinking that they were exactly what I needed at that moment. "I love them. Thank you. I'll just put them in some water." I took them from his hand, along with the slightly misshapen box, barely managing to meet Steve's eyes.

"Did you have fun at the show last night? How was it?" he asked.

"It was good." Visions of my night with Carter, his kiss, my fingers running through his hair flashed through my mind, and I looked away.

"Glad to hear it." He took the kids' bags from the car and set them on the porch. "All right, I'm off," he said, walking away. "Tell the kids I said bye."

"Wait. Steve . . ."

I told him then that I needed to talk to him and that it was important. I asked him to stay. I remember the concern on his face and my heart breaking at the thought of everything I was about to tell him. After making sure that the kids were likely to be occupied at the neighbors' house awhile, we sat on the sofa in the home that had once been ours together while he listened to what I had to tell him.

"Carter Wills." He raised his head from his hands and gave an acidic laugh, filled with disbelief. It was the second time he'd said the name, and I could tell it was hard for him to process. "Well, I sure as hell wouldn't have been able to compete with that."

"Steve."

"You should've told me that's who he was."

"You were clear. When you decided to raise her as your own, you told me you never wanted to know anything about him," I said defensively. "So I didn't think I should tell you."

"Are you kidding me? You didn't think it was important to mention that her father was Carter fucking Wills?"

"I thought about telling you a million times. But you didn't seem to want to know much about him, and I didn't think it mattered since he wasn't in her life." As soon as I said it, I realized at once that things had changed. "Or at least, it didn't seem to matter before," I added.

"It mattered, and you knew it. Otherwise, you would've said something."

I didn't respond. Perhaps he was right.

"I always knew that you were broken when we got together back then." I winced at the uncharacteristic cruelty in his words. "You only mentioned him briefly here and there—the mysterious ex-boyfriend who'd done a number on you in New York. I didn't push you, because I respected your decisions. I respected that there must have been some good reason that you left the way you did, pregnant. I knew he was some musician and figured it had been a fling that ended badly. You got pregnant, and he took off. I figured it was in the past and we were together. She would be our daughter. And here, all this time you were pining away over him—all these years." His words cut like shards of glass.

"Steve, we had a good life, and you've been an incredible father. What you did back then for me, for both of us, was something I'll always be grateful for. I've never for a day taken it for granted. I did love you. It's just that—"

"That you loved him more. I get it, Evie." There was nothing I could say to him that hadn't already been said in conversations leading up to the decision to end our marriage, so I stayed quiet. We both had hurt one another enough. But at least, the truth was out there. "So now what? I guess you guys are back together? Planning a happy little family reunion?"

"I don't know. We're just going to spend some time together."

Emotion filled his face, and he looked away, trying to stifle it. "She's *my* daughter." The words came out choked, defensive, and I ached for him.

"Steve . . ."

"From the first time I saw her, the first moment I held her, she was my little girl. *I'm* her father, dammit. Not him. It's my name on the birth certificate. I was the one with you the day she was born. I was the one up with you in the night when she had colic and the 104 fever. She's my daughter, Evie." A shudder went through his shoulders. My mind went back to the look on Steve's face the day that Lainey was born, his heart instantly belonging to her.

"You will always be her father, Steve. I'll always love you for that. When we decided to divorce, we agreed then that we'd keep the relationships with the kids as normal as possible. No matter what, you'll always be her father."

"So what's that make him, then?" He straightened and regained the look of pragmatic composure that I knew so well.

I swallowed. "He doesn't know. Not yet, anyway."

He looked up sharply, his eyes widening. "What?"

"I haven't told him."

"What do you mean, he doesn't know? Do you mean he never . . ."

"He . . . he never knew about her. About any of it. He never even knew I was pregnant. We broke up before I told him."

"But he knows you have kids now, obviously."

"He just assumed that you and I had the kids together. He never had any reason to think otherwise. But I was wrong. Steve, I was wrong not to tell him back then. I thought I was doing what was best for Lainey. And for him. For all of us. But I'm not so sure now. Seeing him again—it's making me question everything. They deserve to know each other."

He pleaded with me. "Don't tell him."

I shook my head. "I don't think I can keep it from him anymore."

"Evie. Listen to me." He stood suddenly. "There's no reason. Don't tell him."

"It's not right, Steve. And you know it."

"I'm not going to have her whole world turned upside down like this. And what about Lucas? Where's he in all this? He's our son, too, remember. *Our* son."

"We always said we'd explain it to her one day. To both of them."

"I don't think that's such a good idea anymore. Evie, so help me . . . don't tell him. Run off with him. Hell, screw him to your heart's content; I don't give a damn. But don't take her with you in all this."

Steve was panicking. I could see his head turning in all the directions that mine had over the years. But that was then. "He's a good man, Steve."

He threw his head back with a sardonic laugh. "Oh, sure, great."

"He's not what you think. Not at all."

"Oh yeah? Tell me. What's he like, then?"

"She's . . . she's a lot like him, Steve," I said. "I see him in her more and more every day."

A wave of fresh hurt dulled his blue eyes. "Ah. I see." He shook his head. "So? What's your grand plan?"

"I'm not sure, really."

"Just give it some time, will you? Don't rush into anything. Once it's out there, it's out there. Nothing will be the same."

"I know that."

"He might not even want anything to do with her. Have you even thought of that? Or he might decide later that it's too much. Have you thought of what that would do to her?"

"I have." More than he knew.

He sighed heavily, suddenly looking five years older. "If this is what you need to do, I guess there's not a whole lot I can say."

"Thank you."

He looked at me then, sadly resigned. "And what about you? How do you feel about all of this? Your big reunion after all these years?"

I didn't need to respond. Steve could see it all in my face. How deeply I loved Carter.

"I see. Well, I guess that's that, then." The room fell silent, the mantel clock ticking. Neither of us sure what to say next. He looked weary as he turned to leave but stopped. "You know, Ev, it makes more sense now, at least."

"What does?"

He shook his head. "I never could quite get it. What it was that was always off with us. I tried. I did. Evie, I have loved you every day since you were twelve years old. I know I wasn't perfect. I took you for granted. And I know you thought there was someone else at the office . . ."

"Steve, I didn't—"

"You didn't say it. But I know you did think that. And I don't blame you. Hell, I even let you think it. I figured maybe it would spark something in you to want to fight for me. But it didn't. You weren't happy, and I couldn't figure out why."

I went to him. Took his hand. "You have to know that I have loved you too. Truly. I have."

"I know you did. But you loved him more."

"It was just different."

"Right. Obviously." And then he walked out of the room and slammed the front door.

Your dad was so worried about you that day. He loved you so much, and he just wanted to hold on to you. So before I tell you more about Carter, you should know a little more about the man you've called Dad. And what a good man he was.

61

EVIE

I've always taken it as a bad sign when a person seems overly attached to their university days, and I found it intensely grating when middle-aged men, in particular, told college stories. Behaving as though the peak of life came at the sad age of twenty-two is as depressing as a comb-over, clinging to something that once was. I know it's judgy, but I also know I'm right. It's as if to say that anyone they've met later in life, any experiences they might have, will never compete with "that epic night out when James caught his scarf on fire outside Professor Floyd's house!"

We're meant to grow and meant to evolve, and it always seemed to me that people who kept that time of their lives on a pedestal, like a dusty award, never bothered to evolve. So yeah, sometimes your dad would get on my nerves. You know how much he loves those stories. I'd married my high school sweetheart, yes, but the moment he'd start in on this or that from college, I'd inwardly cringe and tune out.

Which was completely hypocritical, of course, considering that a) I'm telling you all about something that happened in my twenties, and b) our entire relationship was linked to our times together growing up in this town.

"Hey, Waters," he'd say (he always called me by my last name when we were kids), "catch!" A note would sail over the class from two rows away, folded like one of those little origami triangles. Inside would be some sort of joke in his familiar handwriting. Maybe a line that had made him laugh from his favorite TV show at the time. Sometimes a question that required me to circle "yes" or "no." Something like, "My house after school????? Nintendo death match." Or later, "Homecoming? Xoxo." He had this way of shaking his blond hair out of his eyes and a smile that was infectious to everyone around him. The first time he saw where I lived, unexpectedly showing up one afternoon on his bike in junior high, I remember standing by the broken doorframe with my cheeks flushed crimson. "Hey, Waters," he said quietly, peeking over my shoulder when he heard my dad calling gruffly from the smoky interior. "Wanna ride bikes?" I told him I didn't have one, and he told me it was okay, that he had an extra one at home I could use. He propped me up on the back, both of us all limbs and knees, and drove me away from that place.

After that, we were always at his parents' house—a big four-bedroom affair with a wreath on the door that changed with the seasons and a Yankee candle perpetually burning on the stove in scents like spiced pumpkin or clean cotton. His basement was half-finished with wood paneling and a remnant carpet, and as teenagers, we would all pile in on aging beanbag chairs and an ancient sofa after school, watching whatever was on HBO while the laundry spun in the dryer nearby. It was a perfect adolescent lair that became a home to ruthless games of Truth or Dare and movie marathons. His mom would order us pizza and send me home with the leftovers and a hug. I must have slept on that sofa a hundred times as we got older. When Steve and I were officially a couple, sometimes they'd invite me for Thanksgiving.

From the time I was little, whenever life felt like it was falling apart, or things got confusing, your dad was always there. Which I suppose explains so much about everything.

62

EVIE

Two weeks later, after having barely traveled much in years, I found myself back in London. I took a car from the airport, and when I pulled up to the driveway of his house, Carter was at my door, pulling me into his arms.

"You didn't run," he whispered.

"I didn't run," I replied.

"After we said goodbye, I wasn't sure what would happen. Thank you for coming. I know it wasn't easy on your end."

"You're still fairly irresistible," I whispered back.

He grinned and leaned his forehead against mine before searching my eyes. He kissed me gently, then took my hand. "C'mon. Let's get you settled in. I've only got you here for two weeks, and I'm not letting you out of my sight."

Just as I was about to step inside, I hesitated again, glancing behind me toward the set of wrought-iron gates that I'd passed through on the way in and the vintage Mercedes parked nearby. I raised an eyebrow at him.

"There's not going to be a supermodel or three relaxing on your couch, is there?" I asked with only half a laugh.

He smiled and placed a reassuring hand over mine. "Very funny. No. Just the dog."

"Mandy?" I asked hopefully.

"No, she died a few years ago, I'm afraid. But Marvin will love you too. C'mon." As he opened the door, we were greeted by a very friendly golden retriever bounding up to us. Instantly, my jaw dropped as I took in the scene of Carter's home—an enclave behind a hedgerow in leafy Hampstead Heath.

The walls were a deep charcoal gray and white, and a massive fireplace took up the far wall of a sitting room, flanked by two tall french doors that opened up to a tiered garden. An original Larry Rivers painting hung above the mantel. On a distant wall hung a Chagall, which I imagined was original, as well. "You used to have a couple of posters, I remember. Traded them in for the real thing, I see?" He seemed to enjoy that I'd remembered this detail and smiled with a mix of sheepish pride. A print of the Chagall—*Blue Lovers*—had once hung over his bed with tattered corners affixed with tape to the chalky white walls in their Camden Town flat when we were younger.

I walked over to a long wall of shelves, displaying an array of awards and photos of him alongside celebrities and heroes, casually intermixed with rows of books, many of which appeared to be rare first editions. I ran my finger over the rough cloth binding of one and drew back, almost afraid to touch it.

"I collect them now," he said, appearing behind me.

"They're lovely."

"So the bedrooms are that way and the main bathroom through there." He gestured from where he stood, watching me closely. I knew how incredibly surreal it must have been for him to see me there, as I knew it would feel the same if he had been in my home.

On one hand, I found myself enjoying the adult, sultry vibe of the space, but then, just as fast, imagined my children running through the extravagant surroundings. I saw fingerprints and heard the sound of the kids' shows blaring from the television. I wondered if he had yet realized how different our worlds were and suspected not.

"Are you going to say anything?" he asked after a few minutes had passed.

"It's stunning."

"But?" He could always read me in an instant.

"It's just different from my life. It's hard to adjust to, that's all. We've missed so much."

He nodded, understanding. "I'm a different person when you're not in my life. Evie, I always knew that. It was part of why I so desperately, so obsessively loved you and wanted you with me. Because I was afraid that without you, I would lose sight of myself and drown in all of this, and in many ways, that's exactly what happened."

His words resonated with me. Without him in my life, in many ways I'd lost sight of myself as well. We made each other feel at peace in our own skin.

He pulled me over to a sofa with ivory fabric and black pillows. I sat gingerly, feeling the expensive fabric beneath my fingertips. He leaned back and surveyed the room. "But—now that I look around, I think it could use a feminine touch. Bit of warmth? What do you think?" He gave me a slight, mischievous smile.

"What do I think?" As he'd been talking, a smile had begun spreading across my face. "Hmm . . . what I think is that it's finally just hitting me that I'm here. I'm in your house! You live here, and we're sitting on your sofa. I still feel like I'm dreaming."

He smiled broadly. "I'm going to keep you prisoner here, you know." His eyes sparkled, a momentary break in the sadness that seemed etched into his face. He took my hand and pulled me into him and kissed me.

"Huh. I see. Prisoner, you say?"

"Any complaints?"

"None whatsoever." The thought of the nearby bedroom and the time spread out before us settled into a low throb deep inside. When he ended the kiss and pulled away, his eyes were dark with heat, and I knew he was thinking the same thing.

"Hungry?" he teased.

"Famished."

That evening, after a small dinner we prepared together, we sat close on oversize burgundy floor pillows arranged on the floor in front of the marble fireplace. We spoke for hours, catching up on years lost. I lay with my head in his lap while drops of rain tapped the windows in a lullaby. I watched the flames dance in the fireplace and along the dark walls. I could feel the heat of him behind me, and I turned my head to see his eyes were closed while he ran his fingers through my hair. I watched him breathe, adoring everything about him. Sensing me watching him, he opened his eyes, returning my gaze. Our whole past was there. The love. The loss.

And then slowly, an unspoken shift.

I reached up and ran my hand along his chest, down his stomach, to remind myself that it was real. That he was here. I sat up, raising my face to kiss him. Lightly at first until he placed his hand behind my head and the kiss deepened into a pool of heat. He pulled me onto his lap and cradled me close. "Not a day has gone by when I haven't thought about you." His whisper was warm on my mouth. "What it felt like to touch you, to feel your skin. The way you tasted."

He was so much a part of me that I'd been lost without him for all this time. His face was lit from the side by the yellow glow of the fire, and the veil was dropped between us. No pretenses and no walls to hide behind. No fear of what the future held. It was so familiar in some ways, so like the way we'd been when we were younger. But there was a deeper intensity to it, as if we were trying to make up for years of lost time, every move deliberate and savored, until finally, he lifted me up and carried me to the bedroom while time and years faded away.

~

The sun had just begun to cast a glow into the room when I lay beside him, resting peacefully with my head in the soft spot of his chest as he cradled me beside him. The gray bed dominated the center of the room with a massive upholstered headboard and black nail-head trim. Another fireplace warmed a corner, lit by Carter during the night. Several expensive-looking guitars sat beside a large, dark linen chaise.

"I have dreams about you sometimes," I told him. "It's weird how real they are. Sometimes I close my eyes and feel you. Whisper that I love you when no one can hear me." I thought of how many mornings I'd woken with the feeling of such profound disappointment that the dreams I'd been having of him were over. "Sometimes I swear I can still hear you." I'd lay in bed, clamping my eyes closed as I tried to hold on to him. I trailed my finger down his stomach, around his hip bone.

"I have no doubt you can." He told me he loved it when he dreamed of me, too, waking up in the same state as I'd described, musing that perhaps we shared the same dreams on the same nights. "We've always been connected like that," he said.

"Clearly it feels like we never stopped." I smiled with a small laugh. "In dreams or in real life."

"Were you worried?" he asked, clearly amused.

I shrugged, feeling color warm my cheeks. "A little. It's been a very, very long time for me. Since I've been with anyone." I'd said it lightly, but his brows knitted together as if to say he was sorry to hear that. As if to say, *You deserve to be cherished. Every inch of you.* I could've cried at that look. He shook his head before kissing me deeply.

He whispered, "I plan to make up for lost time." I smiled, curling his arm closer into my chest. "We fit together, Evie. By the time these weeks are over, you'll never want to say goodbye again. And neither will I."

I pushed any conflicting thoughts to the back of my mind and felt a wash of comfort and peace. Over the years, sometimes, I would let myself remember what it had felt like to sleep next to him. The comfort and completeness that soothed my frayed nerves like a lullaby.

"I want to see what you look like at home. In your life. Shopping, hanging out in your living room. Watching TV and doing normal, everyday stuff with the kids. I want to see what that looks like," he told me.

"Well, it's not much to see. We lead a pretty quiet life."

He kept looking at me, wonder in his eyes, as he continued. "I want to see you at the end of the day when you're getting sleepy. Hair up and pajamas on. And I want to tell you that you're beautiful and make you believe me until you drift off in my arms. You deserve all of that."

I found myself wanting to take care of him in return. To make him feel loved.

"So when's the last time someone made breakfast for you?" he asked.

"It's been a while." I laughed.

"Why don't you go and get a good long bath, and I'll fix us breakfast. Don't think I didn't see you eyeing the tub last night." He winked.

He wasn't wrong. It was a classic cast-iron claw-foot bathtub, black with white interior and room for more than one, as we discovered. It was the centerpiece of the bathroom. Next to it sat a long glass table, set with several neatly stacked white towels and a candelabra with half-burned candles. The room featured white-and-gray marble on the floor and walls, with a floor-to-ceiling, glass-enclosed shower and half a dozen varying sprayers at multiple angles. When I took a bath at home, I often had to clear out the plastic bath toys and wipe it with cleanser first. I couldn't help but laugh.

"You still like to cook breakfast?" I asked.

"Don't look so surprised! Some things are still the same. The good things, of course."

"Is that so?"

"It is. Now, take your cute bottom out of here and let me work my magic."

"I could get used to this, you know," I said as I left the room.

"I'm counting on it," he called out.

Over the days that followed, we never left each other's side. Carter seemed to simultaneously need company and quiet, and I gave him both. We cooked, we brushed our teeth next to each other, our tooth-brushes intimately placed beside one another, such a simple joy. We curled up together with bowls of popcorn and watched movies. We spent the nights enjoying the simplicities of domestic life with one another as if it were a rare gift. It was so good that I was almost able to put the rest of it, and everything I'd come here to do, to the back of my mind. With each passing day, it weighed heavily. But I respected the promise I'd made to Steve—to give it time.

63

EVIE

One thing I'd learned by that point was that you never knew what the day was going to bring. For instance, there was the day I found myself inexplicably standing next to Iliana Billings while I wore no pants or makeup. This, I'll tell you, was not an easy thing.

I'd woken up late one day, just as Carter walked out of the closet wearing nothing but jeans. He came over and kissed my forehead, brushing my wayward hair from my face.

"You're up early," I said, cradling the pillow beneath me.

"I didn't want to wake you. You looked so peaceful." Marvin was sprawled out next to me, and he rustled the dog's ears, giving him a pat before he left the room.

A few minutes later, I grabbed one of his button-down shirts from a nearby chair and padded out to the kitchen, passing the gentle rain tapping at the glass and the garden beyond.

"Carter, where—" I called, rounding the corner, then stopped in my tracks as I took in the scene. Inside the open front door, he stood with a statuesque brunette who was reaching out to hug him as he returned her embrace stiffly. A look of anxiety crossed his face when he saw me. At the sound of my voice, the woman pulled away from him and shot a look like an arrow through me.

"Are you kidding me right now?" she growled as she pushed past him, glaring at me. I recognized her immediately, of course, and shuddered, remembering all too well the night when the reports of their imminent engagement had surfaced. I had brutally compared myself to her, falling short in every way possible, and now here she was, standing just feet away from me. Iliana Billings.

He clearly had a type; I'll give him that.

I don't know how I hadn't noticed it before, but I realized, somewhat oddly, as I watched her, that she and I looked alike. Okay, that's a big stretch, obviously. I just mean that if someone were to play me in a movie, it could be her. Though of course to say that out loud would be ridiculous—she, a world-renowned actress and model celebrated for her beauty, while I was plainly . . . me.

Still, I could see the similarities. Like the way I might look if my DNA had been arranged in just the slightest more favorable way. If I had been two inches taller, my cheekbones sitting just a tad bit higher, my nose in a delicate line with a tulip tip, my eyes sketched even a millimeter differently. If my skin were more effortlessly silken and flawless. Years later, there would be filters on phones that could make these adjustments, to give women a painful taste of what it would be like to be slightly improved. But now here it was in the flesh—the similarly long, delicate build—only with hers in proportions that made even the plain white V-neck T-shirt and baggy, oversize jeans she wore drape her body in perfect, sensual form. Her long hair was swept up into a high, messy bun. She didn't have a stitch of makeup on. But despite her plain appearance, she was anything but plain. She was easily the most beautiful woman I'd ever seen in person.

Evie 2.0. I wasn't sure if this was comforting or awful. And, of course, there was the hint of her lovely accent.

"Nice shirt," she said as she approached, tugging at Carter's shirt on me.

"Illa, please don't do this," he pleaded with her quietly. He seemed exasperated.

I watched hurt as it surfaced in her angry eyes.

Her stance softened, resigned as she turned to him.

"Carter, I don't get it. I know you said we were over. But this is low, even for you. First some asshole guy from the paparazzi asks me what I think about your new girlfriend in your house, and now I show up here to find out it's true. I haven't heard from you in weeks, and I've been worried about you. But I guess I was a fool. You could've waited at least five minutes before jumping into bed with someone else."

"Illa, you don't understand. It's not like that. Look, I'll explain sometime, but not right now."

Desperate to remove myself from her presence, I backed out of the foyer. "I'll give you guys . . . some . . . ," I muttered.

"No, Ev, wait." Carter was immediately at my side. "Illa, I'm so sorry. I don't know what else to say."

His behavior toward me clearly surprised her, and something told me she hadn't experienced the protective side of him. She opened her mouth to start a fresh torrent of wrath when a strange look appeared in her eyes and she snapped it shut again.

"Ev." She stated it in a way that sounded more like a place or a thing, and the puzzle pieces came together. Her gaze dropped to Carter's left hand and to the tattoo on his finger as her eyes pooled with tears. At her implicating stare, his thumb instinctively rubbed over the tattoo, much like one might fiddle with a wedding band.

"It wasn't *Sigma Five*. It was *EV*." She closed her eyes, shaking her head just slightly, and then smiled sadly. "She's the one who . . ."

Carter nodded. The defeated look on her face showed me how deeply she must have cared for him, and despite wanting to hate her, I felt for her. Sensing her pain, I nudged Carter toward her and gave them their privacy to say goodbye.

64

EVIE

Kate called repeatedly, as you might imagine. I finally answered one day, and it was comforting to hear her voice.

"This is craziness; you realize that, don't you? This life of yours! I'm still having a hard time wrapping my brain around it."

"You're telling me."

"I can't believe you saw her. What was she like? Was she perfect? It's the only way I can picture her. Remember that amazing dress she wore to—"

"You're not helping."

"I know; I'm sorry. How awful was it?"

"It was fine. Hard but fine. I felt for her."

"Ev. It's you he loves."

I smiled. "Thanks, Kate."

Just then, Carter walked up and then turned when he saw that I was on the phone. "Want to say hi?" I asked her.

"Uh. Yes. Yes I do."

I gestured to him, and he walked over to sit behind me, straddling his long legs on either side of my hips. I handed the phone over, grinning. "I think you might actually make her year."

He laughed, seizing the opportunity to finally talk to somebody from my world as he took the phone. "Hello?" The moment he said it, he pulled the phone away from his ear, wincing. I laughed. "It's lovely to finally meet you, even if it is just over the phone. I think we saw one another briefly last week, but I was a bit distracted, as you probably noticed. So I apologize." He listened as a smile played on his lips, but I could tell he was concentrating on something that she was saying. He mumbled a series of phrases, including, "Uh-huh. I know. Okay. I promise. Thank you. Yes. I look forward to it. Bye, Kate."

Curious, I retrieved the phone. "Uh, hello?"

"Uh, hello yourself. Are you trying to give me a heart attack?" Kate asked.

"He wanted to say hi."

"You haven't told him anything, have you, Ev," she said with concern.

"I'm . . . giving it time." From the corner of my eye, I watched Carter.

"For whom? You? For Lainey? For him? Evie . . ."

"For everyone."

"You have to talk to him."

"I know. I will."

We spoke for a few more minutes before I hung up the phone.

"What was that all about?" he asked.

"Nothing at all," I said. "So how'd you like Kate?"

"She screamed 'Holy shit.' Then I think she dropped the phone. Then she told me that if things didn't work out between the two of us, she would be happy to join me here anytime."

I cocked an eyebrow.

"Actually, she told me that she loved you. And that she wanted to see you happy. And begged me not to hurt you." Now that sounded much more like Kate.

Kate has been my ride-or-die in this for a long time now. The kind of friend everyone needs to have in their life. I hope you have that person. I just realized that I don't know much about the people in your world these days, now that you live so far away. But I hope you have a Kate.

65

EVIE

Sometimes we need a little perspective to get us out of our own head and pointed in the right direction. We ventured outside of the city a few times over those two weeks, including a visit to the house that Tommy shared with his wife, Haley. They had the most charming little three-year-old son, Wyatt, a spitting image of his father with long blond surfer hair who played in the sand. Seeing the little boy made me desperately miss you, Lucas. It had been the longest I'd ever been away from the two of you, and I'd grown homesick for you. But it was endearing to watch. I liked Haley instantly, and she had the same easy warmth as Tommy. A California girl, she wore a long, stylish, bohemian dress in black with ivory embroidery and a cinched waist that flattered her soft shape. Silver bracelets adorned her wrists, and strands of sun-bleached, pale-brown hair hung down her back in a loose braid. She and Tommy made such a perfect match. While she and I watched on, Carter, Tommy, and Wyatt chased one another on the beach, selecting smooth white rocks from the sand and tucking them into a jar. I had never seen Carter with children and found it fascinating to watch—the two of them inspecting each rock, nestled together and crouched low to the ground. It was like seeing an entirely different side of him as he followed Wyatt around the beach, tossing him into the air.

"He loves that little boy." Haley nodded toward the beach. "He's always been good with him. When the guys are on the road, I'm never quite sure who Wyatt misses more, his dad or Uncle Carter."

"It's fun seeing them this way. I'm not used to it." I suppose if I could pinpoint the moment I stopped being afraid of a future in which Carter was braided in with the love I had for my children, this was it. I began to imagine the life we might actually have together.

"Tommy tells me you have kids?" she asked.

I hadn't realized she'd known much about me. "He did? Yes, I do. Two."

She smiled at my surprise. "Evie, I've been hearing about you for years. Tommy used to talk about those early days a lot. I think they were all a little in love with you back then." She laughed lightly and smiled kindly again. "I can't tell you how glad I was to finally meet you. When you showed up back in Carter's life a few weeks ago, Tommy called me and filled me in." She nodded toward Carter. "It'll be good for him to have you around. I'm glad you've found your way back to each other."

"Oh, I don't know. It's . . ." I looked off again at him.

"Complicated?"

I smiled. "Yeah."

"It's probably easier than it seems right now. You'll figure it out. You made it back to each other, right? That's a good start."

66

EVIE

That evening, after we'd spent the day at Tommy's, I sat curled into Carter's sofa, talking on the phone to you kids. We'd told you that I was going away on a work trip. I can't remember where.

"Well, little bug, I'm not sure I can get all of that into my suitcase." I saw the corner of Carter's mouth turn upward as he walked into the room, overhearing the conversation. "Okay, I'll bring you something, I promise."

While Lucas talked, I looked toward Carter, sitting on the other end of the sofa. He wore a pair of jeans with a plain gray T-shirt and a faded Dodgers baseball cap, an homage to Los Angeles, the other city he sometimes called home. A five-o'clock shadow graced his chin. This wasn't the picture of a rock star, a celebrity. This was the picture of a man. Just a man. A husband. A father. Not someone defined by his career or his lifestyle. I saw the potential for lazy Sunday mornings, reading the paper side by side as we sipped coffee, my eyes buried into his shoulder while watching a scary movie. An afternoon holding hands while we decided what to have for dinner or how best to rearrange the living room furniture. *Move the couch here, no, wait, over there,* I'd say. He would look up at me, exasperated, then smile and oblige my request. Simple things. I saw what he might look like when he would begin to go just a little soft in the middle, with gray hair beginning to appear. Imagined him teaching the kids how to play the guitar, with quiet patience and a soft voice, or talking about his favorite books. He was just a man. And I wanted it all.

I wanted it for him. I wanted it for all of us.

Sometimes I think there's a place, in another life, another time, where this exists. It's nice to believe this.

"You did? Really? The whole way up the tree?" I said, replying to Lucas.

Suddenly, everything I'd worried about over the years faded away, and I saw in Carter what I'd failed to see all those years ago. I saw home. After ten years of running away and fighting the war within me, I finally stopped. The ache of loving someone you cannot have twists a person from the inside, seeping into every moment and every day, making colors less vibrant, smiles less felt. No matter how hard I tried to stop it, his face would always be the first thing I thought of in the morning and the last thing I thought of at night. That was no way to live.

"I collected some pretty stones—white ones. Maybe we can put them in a jar in your room. Sound good?" I asked. Carter stood and walked to the window, his back to me while Lainey took the phone and talked, with less animation than her brother but still telling her own tales.

I wanted something different for my life, and I wanted my children to see me happy and present in the moment. To spend the rest of my life making him feel loved, while giving him the daughter who should have always been his to love.

I wanted something different for your life, too, Lainey. I couldn't deprive you of knowing him, either, this extraordinary person who was part of you.

But what if it was too late?

I hung up the phone, setting it beside me. My heart pounded in my chest as I knew the time had come, and I urged the words forward, collecting the courage I would need to tell him what I'd come to say.

"It's nice hearing you talk to your kids." He turned.

"I've never been away from them this long."

"It must really be something, seeing you with them." There was a faraway sadness to his statement. "Do you think maybe—"

"Carter, we have to talk."

"I know." He walked toward me. "You're leaving Saturday. And I know you have a life and they need you more than I do. But I've been thinking, and Ev, I think we—"

"No, stop. You need to let me say this." I hesitated, taking a step closer to him, my pulse throbbing in my head. "I didn't come here just to spend time with you. There's something you need to know."

"Okay," he said slowly.

"Lainey." I paused, the word filling my throat. "Carter, Lainey is just a nickname. Her full name is . . ." I swallowed hard, my mouth going dry. "Her name is Elaina."

There was silence as the words hung there. It only took a moment before it registered on his face—his mother's name. "Evie, are you telling me what I think you're telling me?"

I nodded.

"She's yours. Named after your mother." I smiled a little, my eyes filling. He went perfectly still, and when he didn't say anything, I continued. "Do you remember, in New York, I'd been sick?"

His eyes flickered with flashing memories. "You had that bad flu."

I shook my head. "I was pregnant."

"I don't understand. Why didn't you say anything?" His voice was low, measured, with something simmering beneath it.

"I tried for a while. Over and over in the weeks after I got home from London. Remember? But you had everything with the Grammys. You were getting ready for the tour. We were barely talking."

"But we were together in New York," he demanded.

"Right."

"And you still didn't say anything."

344

"I'd planned to. But things—"

"You'd planned to?" His jaw clenched with anger.

"Carter, I—"

"No. No. This doesn't make any sense." He shook his head. "You and your husband, your kids."

"I was already pregnant with Lainey when we married. We had Lucas later." He walked to the other side of the room, resting one hand high against the wall with his back to me as he looked out the window into the backyard. The evening sky was darkening with clouds, and the remnants of the day's sun were just a hint of angry purple.

After a while, he turned, his face half in shadow and his eyes brimming with tears. "Why. Tell me. Why."

"I didn't intend for it all to work out this way. God, please believe me when I tell you that. But it just kept unfolding and unfolding, and eventually this was the path we were on, and I guess I felt like it was best for everyone to leave it be."

"Best for everyone? Who were you to decide what's best for everyone? You need to explain this to me, Evie. Why didn't you say anything? How could you have done this?"

He was right. I knew he was right.

"It just all happened so fast."

He shook his head, closing his eyes. "I knew something was wrong that weekend. I just thought if we could get back to London, it would be fine."

"I was hoping for that, too, at first!"

"Then why didn't you tell me? I'd have stayed, Evie! I never would have left you!"

"But don't you see?" I could hear the desperation creeping up in my voice, begging him to understand. "That's exactly why I couldn't tell you at first! I knew you'd be torn and that you would never have left me by myself with a difficult pregnancy. That you'd stay. That you would always want to stay. Everything was happening for you and the guys. Everything you'd worked so hard for."

"We could have figured it out."

"Maybe. But at the time, it wasn't any one thing. It was all of it. There was that awful scene outside the hotel, and I was worried about the baby. And then I showed up at the hotel room and it was a complete wreck and you guys looked like you hadn't slept for days. I could barely get five minutes with you, and I just panicked."

"I was calling you every day. You wouldn't answer. We should have talked!"

"I know, but I almost lost her," I said quietly. "And I got scared." Tears brimmed, and I looked away. I thought of my sweet little girl and how fragile she'd once been as a new life inside me.

"What do you mean?"

I explained how sick I was in those early months and that I knew I couldn't go with them on tour. I told him about the cramping and bleeding that had started the morning he left but continued for the next several days. My father had gotten me to the hospital, where they told me that the baby was in distress but okay. When the relief poured through me, I knew that I'd do anything from that point on to protect her.

"That's why I didn't call you back right away. I was in the hospital. And I decided to wait to tell you. Just until the end of the tour. But by then I couldn't reach you."

"You could've tried harder."

"I did! But I thought you'd moved on. And I wasn't going to go chasing you around, me and my baby!"

"You mean *our* baby." His voice was laced with such bitterness.

"And eventually, I thought maybe it was better for her to let things be. I wanted something more solid for her. I wanted her to feel secure. Not running around the world or having to fight for attention. And besides . . ." I hesitated, afraid to give voice to the phrase that had haunted me for years.

"What."

I exhaled and then shrugged. "You'd told me you never wanted to have children, Carter. What was I supposed to do with that? I felt like I was ruining your life. I felt like I was ruining everything you all worked for. And I didn't want her to be raised feeling like that. Feeling unwanted."

"I would've felt differently if I'd known you were pregnant, Evie! I would've wanted to have children with you. But you didn't even give me the chance," he interjected, his eyes filling again.

"I'm so sorry. I am. For everything. But think about it all. The way things were going at that time. I was just trying to do the right thing. Can you blame me?"

"For back then? No. I can't. But for the other nine years? You're damn right I do." He was seething.

I winced, closing my eyes, and then sighed, wilting. "I did the best I could. It's all I can say. I didn't think you wanted anything to do with me. And I wanted more than that for her."

He shook his head and exhaled a breath, running a hand over his head. "So what? Is this where you tell me that Steve thinks Lainey is his? Because that would be really fucking priceless."

"No," I said.

He raised his brow.

"He was just a good friend trying to help me at first. My father had shown up at the hotel the morning you were leaving."

Confusion crossed his face. "Your father? What does he have to do with any of this?"

The months that followed, and the way time carried on, played like a movie in my mind. I explained that I'd told my dad that Steve was Lainey's father, figuring it would get him off my back until I figured things out. It was just a spur-of-the-moment fix. But then after New York, I didn't have anywhere to go. I'd already moved out of my apartment, and so I went back home. Steve let me stay with him in

Philadelphia for a while so that I could get my feet back on the ground and figure out what was next. That's when I started trying to reach Carter. A little perspective and time made me wonder if things could work out, after all. But when I didn't hear back, I knew he was gone for good and I had to start over. Kate was dating Steve's best friend, and the four of us were all spending time together. It was a soft place to land, I guess.

Because of the timing of it—I'd seen Steve earlier that year at Christmas—everyone just assumed the baby was his, and he was willing to leave it that way. Eventually, life had taken over, and what was originally a temporary arrangement with a good friend grew into something real between us.

"Steve's a good father," I said after explaining all of this to him. "Carter, she's had a good life. We both have."

"A good father? As opposed to me. I see." He laughed bitterly.

"I didn't mean it that way."

"Sounds like you had it all worked out. Easy, huh?"

"No. It was never easy. Not a day went by when I didn't think about you. But I watched you from afar and celebrated everything along with you. The world had you, just like it was always meant to be." Everything was for the best. It wouldn't have been right to have kept him all to myself. These were the things I'd told myself in the long nights.

He didn't say anything but returned to his place in front of the window, arms crossed. "Right. Except for one thing that you conveniently seemed to leave out." He turned, looking at me with such harsh anger and pain in his eyes, I felt like I was looking at a different person. My shoulders pinched as I shrank beneath his searing glare. "She's my daughter! I've missed nine years of her life. And I've missed *you*, Evie. Both of you! She was my daughter!"

"I know. And I want you to know her," I said through thick tears.

"Do you?" His eyes went dark. "Why now? Why the sudden change?"

I shook my head. "I was wrong to keep it from you as long as I have. I wish it could've been different. But we're here now. She deserves to know you. And you deserve to know her."

"I see." He paused, and his voice turned low and quiet again. "All this time, I've been killing myself trying to get over you. To get past what happened with us. I've loved you, Evie. I loved you so much that it nearly killed me. And you were off living some half-life, quitting the job you loved, living in a suburban play."

"Half-life?" I was angry then. I may have made my mistakes, but I wasn't going to let him tear me down. "Is that what you think of me? Carter, I'm proud of the life I have. It's simple. It's by no means fancy. But I'm proud of the children I've raised. Just because I don't have an entire world falling at my feet or have my face on the cover of magazines doesn't mean that my life is less whole than yours. You can be angry if you want, but I won't let you make it sound like my life is a failure."

"Well then, good for you. I'm so glad you've been happy." He grabbed a few things and went to the front door.

I went after him. "Where are you going?"

"I need some time."

"Please don't leave like this." I reached out and took his arm, pleading, but he tugged it away. I quickly went to my bag and pulled out an envelope of photos, handing them to him. His eyes slowly turned to the image of his daughter, taken after her first recital, a proud grin and rosy cheeks, and the next, a baby picture. "She's really beautiful, Carter." He stared at the photo, and I extended it farther, inviting him to take it. But he didn't.

"Carter . . ." He looked up at me, eyes full of pain, and then walked out.

I always knew that I could lose him in all of this, and my heart was breaking. But I still had so much hope for you, Lainey. Hope that he could eventually come to know and love you, even if he couldn't forgive me.

67

EVIE

He didn't return that night, and by the next day, I started to think that I had quite likely lost him for good. Again. Maybe he wanted to be on his own. Maybe it was that he didn't want to be a father. Or maybe I had to take responsibility for the fact that I'd made too many wrong decisions. Though, in honesty, I didn't know if that was true. We only do the very best we can.

Even I was surprised when I found myself on Alex's doorstep the next afternoon.

"Oh god, not you again," he said, putting on a sneer for good measure. "Well, come on, then, don't just stand outside looking like a drowned rat."

I smiled. "Are you always still this cranky?"

"I am, actually." I leaned up and kissed his cheek, and he softened. "I see. Then I suppose I shouldn't take it personally."

"Come sit. Tell me what you're doing here," he said.

"Do you mean London or your living room?"

"Both."

Alex's place wasn't what you would imagine, given his reputation and public image. It was a treed-in, sunny little bungalow in a village of

North London, cozy and inviting in all its eclectic details. There were walls of books and framed vintage Hollywood posters, with deep, cozy sofas and plenty of windows. Chet Baker played quietly from a record player and distant speakers.

I smiled again. "I couldn't leave without seeing you. I needed a burst of cheer and sunshine."

He chuckled at this. "So how's it all going? It hasn't escaped my attention that you seem to be alone."

I looked down, thinking. "I'm worried about him. He's gone, Alex. He left last night, and I haven't seen him since. And I haven't heard from him."

He scratched at the whiskers on his chin. "Do you want to tell me what happened? What did you do this time?"

"A lot. It's complicated."

"Right."

As I talked, he disappeared and then brought me a cup of tea and one of his sweaters. "Here. Put this on. You look cold."

"I got lost trying to find your place, and it was raining," I said, pulling my arms into the long sleeves, wrapping up in the softened wool. "I only knew where to find you because Carter pointed toward it when we were passing by last week. I was only half sure you would answer. I like it."

He gave me a small smile, and I could tell this pleased him more than he let on. "Well, I do aim to impress. Thanks. It's home."

"All alone, eh?"

He shrugged. "Sometimes. Mostly."

"That surprises me."

"Does it?" He paused. "Really?"

I nodded. He had so much to give. So much more to offer someone than he realized.

"There've been a few people, I guess. But no one quite right. Not so far, anyway. We'll see," he told me.

I sipped the tea slowly while we sat in companionable silence. "I leave in a couple of days," I said eventually. "I don't even know where to find him."

"I do. Or at least I have a pretty good idea."

"Know where he is, you mean?" I asked.

"Yeah. He has a place he goes to up in Yorkshire when he wants to disappear for a while. People leave him alone there."

"Will you tell me where it is?"

"Will you promise to leave if I do?"

"Maybe," I said with a laugh.

"But I'd let him be. You know him. He needs to work things out in his own way."

I looked away, collecting my thoughts. "Do you ever wish you could go back in time, Alex?"

"Definitely not. Life's hard enough the first time around." He paused. "But maybe once or twice. There are a couple of things that would be nice to change." I leaned on his shoulder like I used to, both of us finding comfort in the familiarity. Funny how things turn out with people, isn't it? Those we think would be the least likely, sometimes end up meaning the most. "So what's next for you?" he asked, lacing his arm in mine.

"I'm not sure, I guess. Home. Kids. I have to get my life together. Make some changes. For so long, I've been living with the ghost of my past with Carter, trying to make my life look a certain way. I think I'm done with all that. I think it's time to move on and get a fresh start."

"With him or without?"

"I don't think it's up to me anymore. If there's something I've learned from my mistakes, it's that I can't make decisions for people. I love him. I'll always love him. And I know I want a life with him. That's the best I can do. Maybe it'll be enough. But it might not be this time." He nodded. "Do you think he'll come back?" I asked quietly.

"I don't know. Could you blame him if he didn't?"

I looked away. "No. I suppose not."

"Ev, you didn't just leave him. You left all of us. It's going to take some time."

"I know."

"And you left me."

I nodded sadly. "I know. I'm sorry. I've missed you, so much."

He sighed heavily. "Yeah. Me too."

We sat for a while that afternoon, Alex and I, catching up on life while he brewed another cup of tea and flipped to more jazz. When I left that day, I leaned up and kissed his cheek. I was almost to the door when he spoke.

"Maybe you two will work it out, Ev. Maybe you won't this time. But whatever happens, know this . . . he was always a lucky man to have you. You both were. And he'd be a fucking idiot to let you go this time. Okay?"

My eyes filled with tears, and I swallowed against them. "Okay."

He nodded, watching me closely. "Don't be a stranger, Ev. Promise?"

I did promise him. And when I left that day, he hugged me good-bye. Kissed the side of my head.

Just as I was walking out, he called after me one more time. "Hey, Ev."

"Yeah?"

"I saw you first." He gave me the smallest smile. "Don't forget."

I nodded, smiling in return at the old joke between us. "Yes, you did. And I won't."

68

CARTER

After she walked out of Alex's place that day, I turned the corner into the sitting room. I know some might find it hard to believe, but Alex is the wise one of the bunch. Anytime I need to figure something out, it's his place I usually end up, and I'd been in the back bedroom when she arrived. He hadn't told her I was there, which was a good thing. He knew me well. Knew I needed time on my own.

"So what are you going to do?" he asked me.

I told him I wasn't sure.

"You want my opinion? I'd say to hell with her. You don't need some kid running around. And your life is better without the both of them."

I couldn't help but laugh. "You're such an asshole," I told him.

"I've heard this. But I think it's my most charming quality."

He reminded me then how lucky we are. How he would give anything for what we had. We had found our way back, by some miracle. It didn't matter how long it'd been. Time's not real anyway, right? Just a man-made tool.

"I swear those two have been a pain in my ass for years now," Alex says to Michael, and I smile. I didn't realize he was still awake. We'd been talking for a couple of hours, and if there's anything that will put Alex to sleep, it's the sound of me droning on and on.

"They finally get back together and they're still causing trouble." He shakes his head, Michael watching him closely. "Are you done yet, for fuck's sake?" he asks me. "Please tell me you two will finally just sit down and shut up and be happy now. Or are you going to keep belly-aching for another couple of decades?"

"I think we're pretty good now," I assure him.

"Thank god. Now will you finally shut up and let us sleep?" He closes his eyes and dims the light, and I do the same.

The night after I left his place and returned home, I'd found her asleep in my bed, knees curled up, wearing one of my shirts. We talked for hours, and I fell asleep holding her. And then, a few days later, when we had to say goodbye again—we did it with smiles. Because for once, it was temporary. Finally.

I know it may be hard for some to understand this and they would criticize her for the choices she made. But she wasn't wrong for what she did, as much as I hate to admit it. I look around at everything we've created, and none of it would have happened for us if she hadn't made the choices she did back then. She was right. She knew that I hadn't wanted children, not because I didn't want to be a father but because I didn't want to be an *absent* father. And I know people will look around and point to all the examples of all the people who have done it well. Tommy is one of them, of course. He's an incredible father. But his son is young, and by the time he arrived just a few years ago, we were already set and stable, calling our own shots. But back then, it was different. If it had been just a couple of years later, it would have been fine. But it wasn't. We were just getting started. We were puppets on the strings of a dream, our schedules and plans and every moment dictated by the machine to which we had sold our lives.

And if I had known she was pregnant, I would have seen nothing but her and that child in my vision. I would have left the band. Mayluna as we know it would have never existed. The world would have never known the songs that we've written. Which, for me, may have been an acceptable, perhaps even preferable, trade-off. I would have been home with my family, teaching mathematics somewhere, maybe playing music on the side. But what about the others? Their whole lives would have changed as well, their dreams derailed. Because of me. Because of us. And if I had managed somehow to attempt to split myself into two, then what? Who would that have made me? What would that have made her? Our child?

No. She wasn't wrong. She made a choice out of love—one that altered the fates of many—and I understand her, just as she always understood me.

I'm a believer in the ability to cast our own lot and to bring to life our deepest wishes and fears, if only we feel them deeply enough in our bones to will them into existence. I've had more success than most in this world could ever dream of, and when I'm gone, my name will be remembered while other far more deserving people will fade into history, forgotten. It doesn't seem right, does it? Which is why I see now that again, she was right to do what she did. No one man deserves to have everything, certainly not me. And I've had a lot.

But now? I tend to wonder. Because here we are at this new precipice, and as I sit here watching the clouds float by beneath a million stars, while the same moon shines down on her and our daughter, asleep in their beds, I wonder if maybe I can still have more.

And maybe I still have some dreams left, after all.

"So what's next for you all?" Michaels asks.

Over his shoulder, the windows have gone dark as nighttime descends. We'll be landing in not too long, and I'm looking forward to playing these last few shows and then returning home to a new life. I like the way it feels. I'm preoccupied but return my attention to the question.

"I think it's safe to say we'll be enjoying some time off for a while."

"Time to settle down?"

I nod, agreeing.

"Well, I'll give it to you: as band stories go, this was all pretty damn romantic," Michael says. I can tell he's happy with the story he's gotten, and I feel like it's in good hands. Still, it's odd to know that when the plane lands and he's reconnected, it'll all be out there. "But certainly not perfect."

"Nothing ever is."

"When this gets out, her life will change. How are you feeling about that?"

Thunder rolls outside the window, followed by the distant glow of lightning a few moments later.

"More storms up ahead."

"Is that an answer to my question or a comment on the weather?" he asks.

I have to smile at that. It's been a long day, and I close my eyes, imagining what our future might hold, her on the side of the darkened stage, lit up by the purple lights and hazy glow. Beside her, I imagine a daughter leaning into her hip, dwarfed by giant headphones protecting her young ears from the roaring crowd beyond. It's a good fantasy. Even better now that it's actually possible.

Michael doesn't know all of that, though. It's the band and the album he wanted to know about. I've still kept some things, including the more recent time I've spent with Evie, to myself. When we first got the call to do the interview to celebrate the anniversary of the *Sigma Five* album, we of course declined at first. A knee-jerk reaction. But when Evie heard me mention the name of the journalist, she said good things. And it occurred to me, to all of us really, that maybe we didn't need to have so many secrets anymore. It's pretty hard to pull off the whole "mystique" thing when you're playing for stadiums, so really, we needed to just get over ourselves. It felt good to tell the story, surprisingly.

"So what happened?" he asks a beat later, as if reading my mind. "To the great love story."

"What happened is that she saved me."

357

"Forgive me for saying, but with your history, you seem more like a guy who may not have been saved."

"Yeah. I suppose you're right. But we don't always understand at the time. What's really going on in life. What the universe has in store for us—the endless possibilities available to us. We think we know what's coming next. But we don't."

"If you could go back and tell yourself one thing, what would it be?"

I think about this for a time before answering.

"From the moment I first met her, all I wanted was to protect her. But it turned out she was the one protecting me. That's what I would tell myself."

"So," he says, removing his glasses and stretching. It's just small talk now, and I want to get some sleep. "Last thing, I guess. The next album, *Universalis*, you're calling it, right? What's that title all about, dare I ask?" He gives me a look, and we have a laugh.

"It's an homage to Pythagoras."

"Pythagoras? You're serious?"

I nod. "I am. Pythagoras and Kepler." I explain then. "The *musica universalis*. It's the philosophical concept that regards mathematical proportions in the movements of celestial bodies—the sun, moon, and planets—as a form of music that is not audible to our ears but could nevertheless be heard by the soul."

Regardless of space, time, and distance, it'll be like that for us. She'll always hear me, and I'll hear her.

"Only you could make mathematics sound, dare I say, romantic," he jokes as he cleans his glasses and leans back into his seat. We switch off the lights, the cabin going dark, and I lie back, closing my eyes and drifting off toward sleep. "By the way," he says, posing his last question, "I just realized you never told me her real name."

"Her name." The words repeat, and I breathe in. To finally say it out loud to the world, the spell that is her name.

"Her name is Evie."

69

EVIE

After a long flight from London, I arrived home just after midnight. As I opened the front door of our house, a soft light welcomed me from the small lamp we kept lit on the kitchen counter, and I remember how comforting it felt, good to be home and back in familiar surroundings. You kids were at your dad's that night, and I couldn't wait to see you the next morning. I was nervous, knowing that everything in our lives was about to change. But I was elated at the thought that Carter and I were finally going to have everything we'd wanted together. For once, I didn't mind saying goodbye to him. "I'll see you soon!" he'd called out when he dropped me off at Heathrow. He had the purest smile on his face that day. I was asleep in minutes.

70

CARTER

The front door of a house opens, and there before me, I see a little girl with long brown hair, looking up at me with hazel eyes that are mirrors of my own. Behind her, Evie beams as I look down into the face of my daughter.

"Hello," she says simply.

"Hello there," I say.

I'm standing in place, barely breathing as I watch her, in awe, utterly charmed.

"Are you here for my mom?" she asks. "We're just about to go on a picnic."

I smile wider at the sound of her delicate voice as tears fill both my eyes and Evie's. "A picnic," I reply. "Well, that sounds very nice. I used to go for picnics with my mum, as well. We used to go at night sometimes so we could see the stars."

"I like that. That sounds fun." I look up again at Evie, at the surreal sight of the two of them, standing side by side in front of me.

"I'm Lainey."

I lean down and extend a hand. In turn, she places her small hand in mine. "So lovely to meet you, Lainey. My name is Carter."

The scene changes, and I'm onstage at a show. The crowd has been singing along with the lyrics of a song that I once scratched on a napkin or a piece of scrap paper. They've just done this now, and it still amazes me every time it happens. I've finished the verse while Alex does his thing, playing the interlude. I take the opportunity to run to the side of the stage, where Evie and my daughter have been standing and watching, cloaked in shadowy purple light. "How are my girls?" I ask when I reach them.

"Happy to be here," Evie replies, and I can't help but smile as she reaches up to kiss me. Lainey smiles widely, dangling her legs from where she sits, perched on a road case.

Behind me, the music begins to change, telling me our quick moment is up.

I brush Evie's lips with a kiss and then lean down and kiss the top of our daughter's head.

I turn around and glance at the stage, watching the lights change, flashing, and know it's time to go.

The music swells, I kiss her once more, and a moment later, I'm gone.

71

EVIE

On the day they fell from the sky, I was startled awake from the most beautiful dream, the sun already high. I heard the sound of the kids and Steve downstairs and would've been annoyed that he'd let himself in again, but I was in a hazy state, longing to return to the dream, pulling the covers over my head, willing the details back. Images of Carter meeting Lainey. A shy handshake between a wide-eyed music man and the curious little girl who looked just like him. Of the future we were imagining together, Lainey and me watching from the side of the stage in a haze of purple light. The music that brought us together. And the feel of his kiss. I like thinking that maybe he had been dreaming the same thing that night—we used to do that a lot.

It felt glorious, waking up that day, thinking of Carter back in our world, knowing that we had so much to look forward to. I was on the verge of starting a brand-new life, and despite the complicated waters that lay ahead, I glowed with the possibility of my future with him.

When I turned on my phone, there was a voice mail from him.

Hey, love. So we're off to Rio soon; hopefully you're sleeping peacefully and you'll probably get this in the morning. We'll be there for two nights, then Costa Rica, and then I'm home for good. Ev . . . I feel like the luckiest man in the world right now. I've got you back in my life, and now this whole new person exists in my world. A part of us. You and me. And I cannot wait to meet her. I know we've missed out on a lot of time. But hey, time isn't real, anyway, right? I love you more than anything, Ev. Sweet dreams. I'll see you soon.

I leaned back into my pillow, groggy and jet-lagged and still smiling. I splashed some water on my face and made my way downstairs, excited to see the kids. The coffeepot was already full, and Steve was in the living room, holding the TV remote.

"Sorry," he said quickly. "I hope you don't mind I let myself in. We just got here. I rang the doorbell, but—"

"I know. It's still broken. It's okay."

"I still have the key. We knocked, but—"

"Really, it's okay, Steve." At the sight of the concerned expression on his face, I added, "I promise. It's not a big deal. Thank you for bringing them over early."

He turned around and looked back into the living room nervously. "Evie . . ." The kids came bounding up, tackling me, and I greeted them with warm hugs.

"Ahh, my beautiful babies! I missed you!" I squealed, drinking in the sight of them. I could swear they'd grown up a teeny bit more since I'd last seen them.

"Mom, look at my leaves! Grandma took us for walks through the woods to collect them!" Lainey proudly presented a bag of her treasures, then looked more carefully at them. "Well, they looked a lot prettier before. But aren't they pretty!"

"Look, I got a boo-boo." Lucas pointed to a minuscule mosquito bite on his knee, proudly accented with a half-removed Spider-Man Band-Aid.

They both were clamoring for my attention, making my heart swell.

"Ooh, I love them, sweetie! I think this is my favorite." I pointed to one of Lainey's treasures.

"Really? That one's my favorite too!"

"And let me see this." I kissed Lucas's knee and replaced the Band-Aid. "All better now. I missed you guys!"

"Evie, I think you should—" Steve tried to interject.

"Missed you, too, Mom!" Lainey exclaimed.

"Hey, guys, do you mind going upstairs for a bit? I need to talk to your mom."

"Ugh," Lucas complained. "Fine." I watched them disappear around the corner and looked forward to catching up with them later. After putting a slice of bread into the toaster, I poured my coffee and noticed Steve standing halfway into the living room, strangely nervous as he glanced again toward the television.

"Your trip. Did it go well?" he asked through a shaky voice.

"It did. Thank you for asking. Really well, actually," I added gently. "We can talk about it later, though." He hesitated, fidgeting slightly. "Everything okay?" I asked. "You don't have to stay. I'm good," I said, mildly confused by his odd behavior.

He came toward me. Rested a hand on my arm. "I think you should sit down."

"What's going on? You're starting to worry me."

Just then, I heard something odd on the television. "What are you watching?" I asked. But it was as if my brain had already begun to register it, or maybe I had sensed it immediately when I'd awakened minutes earlier, and the hairs on the back of my neck raised.

The kids ran back into the kitchen, and Steve gathered them close. "Hey, guys, I need you to go outside and play for a few minutes." He scuttled them through the back door, glancing toward me. I took a few more steps toward the living room while he struggled to get Lucas's shoes unknotted and tied. "Ev, hang on. Wait."

My blood ran cold, and I stopped breathing.

Where it had been a low din from another room, my ears zeroed in on the voice coming from the television. ". . . the band." ". . . bad weather." ". . . over the Venezuelan border."

South America? My stomach lurched.

". . . the band was fresh off their North American tour and finishing up with several dates in . . ."

My mind was processing the information in parts, unwilling to acknowledge what it was beginning to receive, but as it did, a chill took over me, and my skin prickled. *Please.* I forced a deep, jagged breath as I concentrated on my desperate plea.

Please.

The carpet under my bare feet turned to razors as I continued walking closer toward the television with unsteady steps. Slowly, one inch at a time.

"Evie," Steve called.

As the screen came fully into view, I saw the remains of a small, crumpled white jet. And then photographs, one by one. Alex. Tommy. *No survivors.* I felt the bile rising in my throat and swallowed, my senses disorganized, each one in the wrong place. The photos continued. The pilot and the copilot. *Still searching. No survivors.*

"No," I whispered.

Steve was at my side.

"No," I said again to the universe.

And then, the final words from the screen:

". . . and Carter Wills."

"No."

I remember the coffee pouring from my mug as it fell to the floor that morning.

"Traveling with them, Michael Fleming, a journalist . . . interview to celebrate the anniversary of the release of the band's breakthrough album . . ."

Steve's voice sounded like it was in a distant tunnel as he called to me again, and the next thing I knew, I was on the sofa. The front door slammed. Kate was there. She was still wearing her pajamas as she came to my side. I strained to see the screen as Steve paced in front of it. Kate knelt in front of me.

I looked above her shoulder, and my eyes widened at the horror on the screen behind her. Red lines marked the plane's trajectory from Los Angeles to Venezuela. They kept showing images of the burned wreckage from various points of view, each one worse than the last. I was gasping again. Photos and videos of Carter performing were flashing across the screen, one after the other.

Kate glanced behind her and took my head in her hands, willing me to look at her. "Steve, turn off the TV," she ordered.

"No!" I yelled, gripping her arms. "I need to see it."

"No, you don't."

I pushed her away.

"Steve, get the kids and take them to your place. They shouldn't be here for this," she said, before adding, "and neither should you."

I looked at her, pleading, unwilling to believe what I was seeing. "Get me my phone. I need to call him. I need to talk to him."

Her eyes welled. "Shh. You're going to be okay. It's okay, sweetie. You're going to be okay." Kate held my hand, and a blanket was on me. I didn't cry. I didn't move. And everything went quiet.

72

EVIE

Over the days and weeks that followed, we learned more about what had happened. After flying from London, they'd been in Mexico City. That was where he'd been when he left the voice mail on my phone. They were traveling from there to Rio de Janeiro overnight. Somewhere along the way, air-traffic controllers received a distress call from the pilot. A combination of bad weather and mechanical failure. The rest of it was still under investigation, but they knew that the plane had gone down in a remote area shortly after passing over the Venezuelan border in the early-morning hours. The press had covered the crash nonstop for the first day, and then less so. Comparisons were made to other tragedies in music history—names like Buddy Holly, Ritchie Valens, Otis Redding, and Lynyrd Skynyrd—similar plane crashes, along with other early deaths, Kurt Cobain and Jim Morrison and other greats. Carter, of course, was the highlight of most of the stories. They called him a "legend in the making." It's sad, isn't it? The way people become legendary after they're gone. The pairing of Carter and Alex—Wills and Winters—was counted among iconic musical partnerships like Page and Plant, Bono and The Edge, Jagger and Richards.

There were services for each of them—small, private gatherings with close family and friends—where they were memorialized at a small church in Yorkshire near the town where they had all grown up. But that didn't stop the media, who staked out Carter's home in particular, with a fleet of press and fans. But behind closed doors, in contrast to the larger-than-life mark they'd left on music history, they were remembered quietly—attended by only a few, myself included. The cloying scent of funeral flowers and aging walls permeated the air over several days, and there were bittersweet comments about how Tommy would've been cracking jokes and making fun of it all. His wife, Haley, remained close by, moving in the methodical, slow-motion way that people do in the midst of tremendous grief; as if moving too quickly would bring on a fresh wave of pain. I was standing in a corner by myself at one point, looking off into the bleary distance, when a figure loomed next to me. I turned, and suddenly, all the strength I had left in me gave out, and I fell into his arms.

"Okay, honey, okay." Fred wrapped me into an awkward bear hug. He guided me over to a nearby chair in a quiet, private corner and sat next to me. I leaned on the man who had been witness to it all, from the explosive beginning to the tragic end.

Fred had flown to Rio a day earlier with the rest of the crew to advance the show, instead of traveling with the band on the private jet. The grief he felt over the loss of his "boys," as he called them, was etched into his face so deeply that it was like looking at the face of a father who had lost his sons. Although never one for words, he had a quiet that would then be born of loss more than predisposition. I curled into him as I would a father, and he held me as such. "Come on, honey, you're okay. We're okay." He handed me a handkerchief. I blotted my eyes and sat up. Just as I did, I became aware of Iliana eyeing me with interest from a distant corner. After a moment, we nodded at one another in grim understanding of a shared loss.

Fred noticed the exchange. "Hey. Look at me." He took my chin in his hand. I saw in his face a reflected sorrow in the red rims of his drooping, basset-hound eyes. "No matter what happened, no matter what you did or what he did, it was always the two of you. I've never seen anything like it, and I know I never will again."

I was surprised to eventually feel a sort of fondness for Iliana. She had genuinely cared for Carter and was the only woman in the world who could understand even a fraction of what I was going through. To the press and the rest of the world, it would be Iliana, of course, who would go on to be considered the great, final love of Carter Wills.

73

Evie

"I wrote a song for you," he'd said, once upon a time a long time ago, with a shy smile as the fire glistened off the golden flecks in his hazel eyes. He pulled out his guitar and started playing as I lay next to him, one lazy morning toward the end of that first tour years ago.

I'll sing you safe, my love
Though it's time to say goodbye
I know we'll make it anywhere
Sleep peaceful tonight
Darkness cannot touch, my love
My arms around you here
Just listen for my voice, my love
I'll be right beside you dear

When he finished the song, he'd whispered in my ear. "It's a lullaby. So you can always feel me with you when you sleep." On the night of his memorial, I curled up on his bed, wrapped in his covers, and felt the words he'd written to comfort me in the dark of night, recorded on an old cassette. From a quiet place inside came the comforting thought that somehow, I would be okay, though I knew it would take a long time. But I had been so intensely, and so exquisitely, loved by this one man that even in his loss, I could feel nothing but amazement and gratitude. On that warm afternoon, in the summer of 1998, my life had changed forever. Carter had seen me, and I had seen him—and I smiled at the certainty that in that extraordinary instant, the universe must have paused in song and held its collective breath, privy to the exact, precise moment of a lifetime of love being born. Just as I was drifting off, in the mysterious space that hovers between awake and asleep, I felt his arms around me and heard him sing quietly in my ear. *I'll be right beside you, dear.*

I stayed in his house for three days before finally returning home and realizing that nothing in my life felt like mine anymore. Bake sales and block parties had never suited me, anyway, and I was done trying to fit the mold. White picket fences were overrated. And then everything that had once been the light of my life was replaced by the darkness of a depression so deep that I thought it might never release its grip. Lucas, you were young enough that you didn't quite get what was happening, but Lainey, I know you felt the loss of the warm mother you once knew. The one who once played Peter Pan in the backyard. You grew up a lot then. For a while, the two of you lived with your dad most of the time. It was better that way.

There is a certain stillness that happens in the aftermath of great loss, when one is given a choice—to travel on in the path of darkness and pain, locked in a sight turned only to the past, or to emerge into the light and celebrate all that has been. It was a long time before I was able to find that light again. And when I finally did, it seemed like I never could quite get back that innocence of young motherhood that I'd once loved so much. It seemed like I'd missed so much with you both. Belly laughs and small toes, kitchen counters covered in chocolate batter and milk-mustached children—it felt like a distant past that belonged to someone else. But little by little, eventually, things started to get better.

You probably don't remember this, but I took you to see my father right around that time, encouraged by a therapist I'd begun seeing. He had become unwell. Developed Alzheimer's. He didn't recognize me but said I reminded him of his daughter. "I have a little girl. She lives with her mother, so I don't see her much. Cutest little thing you ever did see, though. Has these big, round eyes. And whip-smart, my Evie. She's a good kid. You'd like her." Sometimes we find forgiveness in the most unexpected ways.

Throughout it all, the currents of life went on, taking me with them, barely perceptible to the eye, yet powerful beneath the surface. As time moved forward, the raw wounds began to scar, and little by little, the chasm that existed between your dad and me began to close, bridged initially by the love of our children, but also by the strand of compatibility that had joined us in the first place.

One morning, just over two years from the day of Carter's death, I was unpacking the kids' bags when I found a letter tucked among their things. It was the only letter he had ever written me, aside from all those silly notes from grade school, and I knew how difficult it must have been for him to find the words.

> Dear Evie,
> For all those years, he had your heart. I know that now. But I also had something equally wonderful. I had your Christmas mornings and prom night. I had the births of our children, the worries over high fevers and the joys of first words. I had your first and only wedding dance. I had the home we created, your Sunday mornings and Friday-night movies. So while I know that he was the love of your life, please know that you have been the love of mine.
> Steve

It seemed that the path of my life had not only been destined to be intertwined with Carter but with Steve as well. In some strange way, one that I can't begin to comprehend, the cords of our three paths were tangled forever. Carter's presence never left our lives, but like one might acquiesce to the idea of sharing their home with a ghost, we learned to go on with acceptance of all that had transpired and the unusual path we'd taken.

"Love comes in many forms," I had told Steve on the night I'd received his letter. I had been gifted with the mating of souls with one man and a lifetime of loving companionship with another. A woman is blessed to receive either of these experiences in her life, yet I had been given both and was profoundly grateful. Along my journey, I had discovered a powerful truth—the one we love the most in life may not be the one we love the best. The realization brought with it renewed faith and provided the foundation to begin anew. Eventually, your dad and I formed a new bond that was based on honesty and respect as he got to know me once again. He moved back into the house, and we returned to being the family we had once been. In turn, I was able to give him all of what was left of my fractured heart. Unlike the exotic and explosive connection I shared with Carter, the relationship that your dad and I enjoyed was a quiet, steady one, suited for traveling the years with grace and contentment.

It was in those early days of the rebirth of our family that he asked that we never tell you the truth about everything that had transpired. Fearing the unnecessary pain it might cause you, I agreed.

We never spoke of it again, until just a few days ago, before he died. It was a quiet night in the hospital when he opened his eyes, likely knowing that this moment would come after he was gone. "Let her know that no matter what, she was always my daughter. And I was always her father." I took his hand and gave him the assurance that he needed. I'm so sorry if we made the wrong decision, but please know it was done with love.

74

EVIE

I started earlier by saying that sometimes I imagine my life divided into two sections, Before I Liked Autumn and After I Liked Autumn. You would think, given what happened, that I would've hated that time of year. But there's one more thing you should know.

Just before I left London, and before he left for that final leg of the tour, Carter woke me up early, telling me that he wanted to take me somewhere. That there was an old promise he'd once made to me and had yet to fulfill. Together, we drove for hours on an early October day, leaving London for the English countryside, the rolling hills of Yorkshire Dales, the place he loved most in this world.

Over a couple of days there together, we walked in the woods, listening to the crunch of leaves beneath our feet, dressed in woolens and boots. Just as he'd told me years earlier, the sunlight was a golden, magical hue picking up every detail, and we walked through trees that looked like slumbering princesses might be sleeping beneath them. The streams and waterfalls were made fuller and more spectacular by the temperamental weather and enduring rains from earlier in the week, and a misty haze hung over the hills beside stone walls like magic. He took me to the same field where he'd once stood with Jacob and his mother on the night we all, separately at the time, had looked up at the sky and seen the mysterious appearance of a star in the moon.

"Have I convinced you yet?" he asked me.

"To love autumn? Definitely."

He turned me toward him. "To believe in us. For good this time."

He had, of course. Though, honestly, I felt like it should have been the other way around. That I should have been the one convincing him. And I suppose we did have those moments, especially when I wasn't sure he would ever forgive me.

But he did. And I hope eventually you can too.

"No one leaves this time," I promised him. He'd reached out and picked a small length of grass, tying it around my ring finger.

"We just took a small detour, right?" he said with the warmest laugh.

"We've got this now."

"Think she'll like me?" he asked.

I nodded. "I think she'll love you."

We decided that day that we would make a life together, once and for all. And I know we would have. But most important is this: I want you to know that he wanted to be in your life. He loved you before he'd even met you, Lainey. This isn't my love story; it's yours. And he wanted to be here, right beside you.

75

Evie

As I talked that night in the den, Lucas had grown quiet, sitting nearby and allowing it all to unfold. In the end, he gave me a long hug before walking out of the room wordlessly. I've rarely seen my son at a loss for words, so I know it will take him some time to process things. But I also know he will come around.

All the while, my daughter sat, originally rapt with attention, circulating through a range of emotions, flush with anger one minute, then tearful at the next, around and around. She asked so many questions as I'd talked that the hours had gone into the early-morning sunrise on a cloudy day.

Finally, with nothing left to tell, Lainey sits in front of me, shaking and with eyes swollen with tears. I watch her breathing and silent, with all her questions answered and a million more she will have over time. I can barely take the pain I know she is feeling, and part of me wonders if I have made a huge mistake. Maybe she was better off never knowing. But no. I know better than that now. She deserved to know.

"Sweetie, I—"

"No." She recoils when I reach my hand out to her. My heart splinters.

"Okay. Just please know that—"

"You don't get to comfort me. Not right now." She shakes her head, barely looking at me. "You don't get to fix this. You can't fix this. What you've done. What you both did."

I let out a long breath, my eyes stinging. "I know. I'm so sorry."

She looks around at the images of the man she's learned was her father, the box of mementos that we'd opened throughout the night, scattered alongside.

Happy Valentine's Day, love. Today and always. Xo—C. A faded florist's note that once accompanied a dozen peonies. Backstage passes. Lyrics scratched on napkins. The dried piece of grass he'd once fashioned into a ring, carefully folded in tissue paper. Everything I kept hidden. She picks up the front page of a newspaper, the one that announced the details of the crash.

"You were just a shell of a person."

"What?" I ask.

"It's not just about him. About all of this. It's about you." She looks up at me pointedly. "You were a completely different person after that. I felt like the mom we'd had disappeared, and you just became this shell of a person, and I never knew why. You should've told me why." She chokes back tears.

"Lainey, I—"

"I was only nine years old, and I didn't understand. I thought I'd done something wrong. I have all these memories of this beautiful life we had, this incredible mom who played and cuddled and was there for me. And then you guys were separated, and then we were at Dad's all the time. I thought you didn't want any of us anymore. Lucas was young enough that he got through it better. But I missed you so much. Did you realize that?"

"Oh, Lainey." My eyes fill.

"Until finally"—she shrugs—"I guess I stopped."

"I did try, sweetie. Please know that. And we did manage to find our way back together, your dad and I. Our family. We had happy times, too, later. Right?" But by then she was a few years older. Into adolescence, which is such a delicate time even in the best of circumstances.

"It was never the same again, though. *You* were never the same again."

She's right, of course. After his death, I couldn't recover. It was like all the trauma of my whole life suddenly built up and crushed me with its weight, and it finally broke me. Eventually, I managed to find my way again, to feel some semblance of wholeness again. But just as she said, I was never the same.

"At least now I know why," she says.

I reach out again to touch her hand, but she takes it away.

"You never talked to us about your childhood. About this whole other life you had with these people, and a man who was my father. You just pretended you had this perfect, content little suburban life. Meanwhile . . . was any of it even real? You should've told me. About all of it. About him."

"So your heart could've been broken too?" I ask gently.

She looks at me then, fighting back tears laced with anger.

"So I could've at least understood."

We try so hard to be a good example for our kids. But maybe what they really need is to see us as human.

Eventually, she stands, looking once again at the photos of the man she never got to know scattered on the floor. As she walks to the door, she turns. "It would've been different if he was a bad person. Some awful guy who didn't want a part of either of us. But he was this extraordinary, loving person. And I never knew him." She pauses. "That plane didn't take him from me." Her eyes bore into mine. "You did."

She packs her bags that morning and is gone within the hour. And then I am left alone once again, while we both mourn the loss of not just one of the men who called himself her father but two.

378

In the time that follows, I pick up the phone what feels like a million times, desperate to make things right. But then I remind myself, she is like him—she needs time alone to process things. And it's the least I can give her.

It takes weeks before she eventually speaks to me, and there are times when I'm not sure if I will hear from her again.

But I do.

One day I pick up the phone, and there she is. My daughter. Ready to talk to me once again. Finally, she visits one day a few months later, showing up at the door with only a day's notice. And then our conversations about Carter begin to turn into conversations about life and, eventually, with all the secrets and shadows gone, we form a new kind of closeness that will endure the years. And the healing begins. For both of us.

"I'll never know him," she says to me one day, the two of us staying up all hours of the night talking. There's no anger left in her, just a wistful sort of longing that I recognize. "What am I supposed to do with that? How am I supposed to process the fact that I'll never know him? I won't know him any more than the rest of the world."

I'll never be able to heal the hole that will forever remain in her life. But there is something I can do to bring her a little closer to him.

The closet of the den is always packed, as such closets become in a family of four. But in a corner at the back, mostly unnoticed by the other members of the household, there is a small space beneath the attic, from which I pull a dusty box.

When I open it and she sees what it contains, her eyes go wide.

"In all, we filmed more than seventy-five hours of footage during the time we were together," I tell her, "of them on the road and in the studio. Not only the film planned for the documentary but some of it just for fun. Just us living our lives together. They're all here, plus the tapes from Tommy's collection, going back to Carter as a teenager. I promise you'll get to know him through this footage. You'll see who we were together. The love between us that created you. You'll meet the real version of him, not the fictional icon he became. I'm so sorry it's all I have to give you, but I hope it helps."

In the weeks after I left them in New York all those years ago, I knew I would never be able to continue work on the documentary. It was one of the hardest decisions I'd ever made, but I knew it needed to be in better, more impartial hands. Rather than send all the footage to the label, giving them control of it, I'd shipped it to Tommy. I imagined they would bring someone else in to do the final editing, but they never did, and Tommy had instead kept the footage in storage. With the success they'd found soon after, apparently the label never pushed the issue, and the project was shelved.

A few weeks after the crash, I received a box from Tommy's wife.

Evie—these belong to you, and it's time they find their way back home to where they should have been all along. He loved you. They all did. Be well.
—Haley.

Since that time, they've gone untouched.

Lainey and I source all the equipment we'll need to watch the old footage, and that night, with her by my side, I watch them walk back into my life on that screen.

"And in honor of our girl, we give you the man himself!" Tommy calls, dripping with salt water and tequila in a youthful mess of blond hair at the beach house as Neil Diamond's "America" begins to blare from the stereo system inside the house. They were so full of life. Carter and me laughing as he and Tommy serenade me.

"Get that thing out of my face," Alex grumbles at another point, pushing a hand at me. "Ev, seriously, I will steal you in your sleep and throw you off this bus if you don't move."

"What? This? This camera here?" I tease. In a scuffle, Alex wrestles me to the floor as the camera lies on its side, capturing him holding me down as I erupt into a fit of giggles. He snags the camera, turning it on me as I laugh with eyes so full of youth and happiness, I can hardly believe it's me, long hair pooled around me as I cover my face. "Ohh, see how it feels? You like this?" Alex teases back, and somewhere inside, I bloom, hearing his voice.

In another scene, Tommy sneaks up to us. "Aww, look how sweet." Carter and I are curled together like puppies and sleeping peacefully in a bunk on the bus, his head in the nape of my neck.

"We should draw on them. Someone get me a Sharpie." We wake disoriented just as Alex takes the camera and Tommy begins to draw.

"Look at that girl. You see her? I'm gonna marry that girl one day." Carter leans into the camera, pointing at me in the background.

I find myself laughing through the tears, and as the scenes play, I realize Lainey is watching me. "My god, Mom, you're a different person." She gestures to the screen. "You're . . . you're so beautiful. You're glowing."

I swallow, nodding. "We were very happy."

There are also quiet moments, just Carter and a guitar in silhouette.

"He's nothing like I imagined. He's . . . funny and silly and . . . he's remarkable," she says.

That he was.

"You remind me of him sometimes, you know," I tell her.

"People need to see this," she says. "The world should see this."

Which I suppose is how the idea first came about. And in that, a new project is born—one that was more than thirty years in the making.

76

EVIE

Two years later

"You ready?" Lainey asks.

I smile and nod. "Yes. I am." I take her arm.

We're holding hands as we walk into the theater in London's West End, taking our seats at the front, along with Lucas and Rick. From behind me, an aged, sandpaper-rough hand touches my shoulder, and I turn to see Fred, alongside Haley and Wyatt, all grown up. There are others I recognize from over the years, dotting the reserved seats among an exclusive crowd of three hundred that has been invited to the special screening.

A local member of the press takes to the stage, microphone in hand, introducing Derek. An interview takes place then, with Derek detailing the events and the two-year process that led to this night, starting from the day I had proposed the idea to him.

It began with a phone call I received one day after I'd been trying to reach him.

"Well, I'll be damned—this is a voice I never thought I'd hear again," Derek had said when I picked up. "When my assistant told me that someone named Cameron Leigh was trying to reach me, I about fell over."

I could hear the smile in his voice, and it lit me up in return.

"You're not an easy man to reach these days, mister," I said.

"Hey, what can I say? The public loves me."

I laughed. "As well they should."

"How've you been, my love? How's life been treating you?" The last time I'd seen or spoken to Derek had been at Carter's funeral, where he'd gently hugged me, offering only a few words and the teary-eyed shake of his head. Together, we caught up on two decades of life.

"So what's really got you on my phone?" he asked eventually.

"What do you think of working together again? I have something you might be very interested in."

"I'm intrigued," he said. "Tell me."

Two years later, here we sat, with him onstage, discussing the results of that conversation. Microphone in hand, he talked about the work and vision that had gone into the documentary and the origins of the footage. The story behind it. I knew Derek would be the only person I would ever trust to take the lead on it, handling the delicate material with grace, along with the artistic vision that he'd always shared with the band. We'd worked alongside one another in comfortable harmony, as we had when we were just kids getting started in the world.

As he speaks, Lainey and I continue to hold hands, gripping with nervous excitement and more emotion than one can possibly contain, knowing full well that our lives are about to change. Eventually, the room goes dark and the film begins—starting with black-and-white home-video footage of four teenage boys from Yorkshire becoming stars. Woven into the initial photographs and grainy scenes are audio voice-over clips from the recordings of the first day we met—the interview backstage at Jones Beach—our youthful voices comingled. Scenes of Carter, playing an old piano or sitting quietly in their Camden flat, skinny and boyish, then later writing songs for their first album, captured when he thought no one was watching, all contrasted with the older version of him and millions of people singing the songs in stadiums across the world.

"That's our band. And our future," his voice says. "To keep the dream alive and make a living at it and hope that somewhere along the way, someone will think that the music we made mattered."

I hold my breath as a song plays and words begin to appear.

MAYLUNA: RISING

A FILM BY DEREK D'ORSAY
EXECUTIVE PRODUCER—ELAINA WILLS ROWE
DIRECTED BY—DEREK D'ORSAY AND EVELYN WATERS HUTCHINSON

I think they would have liked what we did. The story we told. Their story and ours. A Grammy Award for Best Music Film sits on my desk now, as does a cat named Siggy, in the small beach house near Cupsogue where I live, not far from the house where it all began. After the film was released, life changed. The neighbors I'd once called friends looked at me as if I no longer quite belonged, with sidelong glances and awkward questions, and I'd sold the house in Pennsylvania. Lucas and his family visit often, populating the rooms overlooking the beach with the laughter of children. Lainey has found a new home in London—a city that made her come alive as if she'd always belonged. She's become good friends with Tommy's son, Wyatt, and a piano sits in her den. There's lots of travel in this new phase of life—very different from the quiet existence they once feared I would disappear into. Lainey and I often visit the Greenwich Observatory and the Queen's House when I'm in London. Together we'll sit at the bottom of the Tulip Stairs, looking upward at the spiral. "They say a spirit inhabits these stairs," I tell her, and I wonder, maybe, if it's true.

After the success of *Rising*, other films followed. Derek and I have started working on new projects together here and there when we feel moved to do so, breathing life into an old career and dreams I thought long gone. Carter would have liked that too. I often imagine him watching nearby, leaning against a wall with one foot crossed over the other as a smile plays on his lips.

Carter has been gone for many years. Steve now as well. And I'm on my own again. But what's remarkable about it is that I've realized I'm okay alone. I'm not scared of that anymore. Because I had what I needed all along; I had myself, and there is peace in that. Peace in the quiet that is left as I exhaled the last of my ghosts and secrets. It was the long shadows of my past that were keeping me lonely all along. And left behind, there has been a soothing calm and the new relationship I hoped to create with my daughter. My children. I always thought of their early-childhood days as the ones I'd cherished, constantly longing to go back. But now, this new phase of life, knowing them as adults, has grown in equal beauty.

On clear nights, I sleep with the windows open, and sometimes when I do, I can swear I still hear him, just as I always have. The music traveling on the salty breeze and with it, his voice. *I'll be right beside you, dear.* I stopped wondering where it came from a long time ago. It's best to just trust that there are things at work in this universe we can't begin to understand. He taught me that. And so, as I imagine grand geometric patterns spanning across the celestial sky in infinite beauty, the patterns of thirds and fifths and spirals and time dancing among the planets and stars, I stop and listen.

NOTE

On the seventh of March 1794, it was first reported that an event in the sky, which observers believed to be a luminous star, stationary in the dark portion of a crescent moon, had appeared for a period of time in such a way as to suggest that the moon itself were transparent. The event, having been witnessed from several locations in England, was reported to the Royal Society of Astronomy, Greenwich; thoroughly investigated; and published in several articles, the first of which was titled: *XXVI Account of an Appearance of Light, like a Star, seen lately in the Dark Part of the Moon, by Thomas Stretton, in St. John's Square, Clerkenwell, London, with remarks upon this observation by Mr. Wilkins and Astronomer Royal.*

Subsequent sightings have been reported over time. Though theories have been proposed, no explanation has been proven.

ACKNOWLEDGMENTS

You'll often hear writers say that they remember the exact moment when a story first appeared in their world, and I remember the day this one appeared in mine; Carter, the band, and Evie, all downloading in the span of a roughly three-and-a-half-minute song that was playing in the car at the time. Inspired by that song, and all the other music and memories that came rushing in with it, I ran to my computer the moment I arrived home, began writing, and haven't stopped since. Music does this, after all. Unlocks the soundtrack of our lives, both real and imagined. I was so sure this book would be the first one I sent out into the world, but just as in Carter and Evie's story, fate had other plans, and it would be over a decade before this novel would appear in the hands of readers. Time has a funny way of working these things out, just as they're meant to be.

Music has always had this hold on me, from as early as I can remember, transporting me to completely different places and times and inspiring dreams. "Music and writing, that's me," Evie says. And it's me too. I'm beyond grateful to have had the chance to weave my two loves together into this book in such a deeply personal way. And even more grateful to the people who have helped me make it happen.

First and foremost, this book would never have existed without the enthusiasm of my agent, Beth Miller—my ride-or-die on this story and perhaps the only person in the world who is celebrating as much as I am. Thank you for never giving up on it. TD forever.

I am deeply grateful to my editor, Alicia Clancy, for bringing this story to real-world pages and helping it shine. Thank you so much for helping me be a better writer and share my books.

I'm so lucky I get to work with such wonderful people in the publishing world. To the entire Lake Union team—I'm grateful for all you do. And to Olivia Fanaro at UTA, and the team at Writers House—thank you so much for championing my work.

To the Royal Observatory and Royal Society Publishing, thank you for keeping such an exquisite and inspiring record of history. Any inaccuracies are my own.

To the readers, librarians, and reviewers who embraced my first novel, *A Day Like This*, thank you for all of your support. It's because of you that I get to do what I love, and I never forget it.

My first career launched me into the backstage world of the music industry and the concert business. To those people who gave me that very first all-access pass, once upon a time, I'm grateful. And so glad for the memories.

To the musicians who played a role in all of this—I'm still listening, always. And I am eternally grateful for the magical place you've held in my world.

To my family, for all of your love and support—especially my mother—who played cassette tapes on the living room stereo of a little house I adored, bought me my first typewriter, gave me an appreciation for lost-love stories, and continues to be my biggest fan, always.

To my dearest friends, particularly Ariana, I'm so very grateful to have you in my life.

And most especially: "Everyone needs a Kate," Evie says. Me? I have a Christa.

The family members of writers put up with an awful lot. I imagine we're not especially fun to live with sometimes. We're often in our heads, on a deadline, talking to imaginary people, or in my case, dancing in the kitchen with headphones on while scratching notes on a notepad. Thank you for putting up with me and for listening to me go on and on. I love you. And, of course, this includes my furry little muses—a couple of cats and a funny dog with low self-esteem, my ever-present, trusted companions.

Much of this story was created while two little girls slept or played nearby. They still remember the songs I played on repeat in the car during the early stages of formulating the words in my head. To my now-older daughters, I'll say this: first, I hope you go on to make your own soundtrack in life and that it is absolutely amazing, and second, know always and forever, that whenever you need me, I'll be right here, right beside you.

Finally, to anyone reading this who still wonders if you're deserving of love or dreams or happiness, keep going. You never know what can happen. It's what Carter once told me. And it's what he would tell you.

ABOUT THE AUTHOR

Photo © Alyssa Kay

Kelley McNeil is the author of *A Day Like This* and *Mayluna*. Prior to writing fiction, she worked for over a decade in the entertainment industry. A native of Pittsburgh, she lives in South Florida most of the time but can often be found in London with a good pen, good music, and her two daughters nearby. Learn more at www.kelleymcneil.com.